Save The Last Dance

a novel

Save The Last Dance

a novel

Eric Joseph
Eva Ungar Grudin

Hargrove Press, LLC

This is a work of fiction. Names, characters, businesses, places,
events and incidents are either the products of the authors' imaginations
or used in a fictitious manner. Any resemblance to actual persons,
living or dead, is purely coincidental.

Hargrove Press, LLC
Williamstown, Massachusetts
www.hargrovepress.com

Book cover designers, Maureen Nicoll & David Moratto
Author photographer, Sarah Bowman
Interior book design, David Moratto

Library of Congress Control Number: 2016939432

ISBN: Hardcover 978-0-9975049-0-3
ISBN: Paperback 978-0-9975049-1-0
ISBN: Ebook 978-0-9975049-2-7

For Gary Arlen

*Such love may sound fantastical, sure to vaporize
in the light of day, but ... nothing could be further from the truth.
These are love relationships that never ended, not fantasies.*

—Pamela Weintraub,
"Lost Love: Guess Who's Back?", *Psychology Today* (July 1, 2006)

From: **Adam Wolf** <adam.wolf1402@gmail.com>
To: **Paul Bishop** <Paul.R.Bishop@dewey.com>
March 11, 2014 9:40 pm
Subject: The timeline

Paul,

I know a little about classical music, a little about film, a little about
baseball, hockey and I can recite the presidents, in order, in 15 seconds.
But I admit there are things I still don't understand. Death, for instance.
I would like to get your advice on it. Not Death so much as the State of
Being Dead. I'm not afraid of death, you know. I'm afraid of being dead.
Incidentally, Paul, I don't happen to believe in transubstantiation.
God forbid my parents are waiting for me on that Golden Shore:
"So I told you, son, you should have gone to med school. But a disc
jockey at a 12-watt station? I don't know. Why did I ever bother sending
you to college? Now, go get your rest and get cleaned up, son. We're
going to dinner with the Karl Marxes. I'm teaching them to speak
English. The only trouble around here—the goddamn Trotskyites."
I ask: "Leon Trotsky made it here? How the hell did that happen?"
Paul, I don't feel old. I don't think I look old. I'm not sick. But lately I
picture my marker on the far right of the timeline.
One day, when I was 28, alone on a Greyhound, late at night, I couldn't
stop thinking about what it really meant to be dead. I couldn't shake
the idea of being insensate, of not existing. I had a full-fledged panic
attack, Paul—heart racing, sweating. For whatever reason, my mind

reached out to Rick Marsulek, the resident juvenile delinquent from my high school days. My pal. Black leather jacket, complete with the wrench he always carried, in case anyone tried to mess with him. Duck's ass haircut. Angelic face that could darken instantly. In my panic I called out to him, "Rick, help me." He materialized and responded with little prompting.

"Fuck it, Adam, by the time you die, say when you're 70, you'll be okay with the idea. So stop sweating it." It calmed me. The panic dissipated. The advice has followed me all these years, and I learned to push the thoughts of death away. Until now.

Today the announcement for my 50th High School Reunion arrived. Dark thoughts seem to be gathering on the horizon again. But they're not just about being dead. They're about the sensation of being carried along on a conveyor belt. To Waldheim Cemetery. Feels as if life has become all predetermined ritual: the ten pills in the morning, the commute to the station, the commute back home, the same forced pleasantries in between, the six pills before bed. Lights out by 9:00.

I looked at the list of people on that reunion roster and one name jumped off the page. It conjured a time when death and ritual were far away. When we were free and invincible. When my pulse raced at even the mention of her name.

Here's my question, Paul—Do you think there's a way off of the conveyor belt or do you think I should just stay on it and go along en route to Waldheim?

—Adam

From: **Greg Dillon** <g.k.dillon30@comcast.com>
To: **Sarah Ross** <sarahross64@gmail.com>
May 22, 2014 1:17 pm
Subject: 50th REUNION—JUNE 22nd

Sarah, Sarah, Sarah—what's the matter with you that you won't let us see you in Cleveland? We have a blast planned. Party Friday, complete with Genelli's pizza. Dinner dance at the Beachwood Country Club on

Sat. night. A tour of Heights High that morning. Pastrami or corned beef lunch, your choice, at Corky and Lenny's. If only the Indians were playing on Sunday, we'd do that too. Everyone is asking for you. Sherrie, Madeline, Frank, Doug (who still looks good). And, above all, Adam. (Spoke to him last night. He wondered if he could have your email address. Here's his — adamwolf1402@gmail.com)

Everyone's coming. You're the only one letting us down.

xoxo

Greg

From: **Sarah Ross** <sarahross64@gmail.com>
To: **Gabriella Fratelli** <gabriella.fratelli@orange.it>
May 22, 2014 7:29 pm
Subject: darling, I am growing older

Cara Gabriella —

I think of you always, my bastion of sanity, and I always wish you were near again.

Gordon pursues me. After these years alone, flattering. Attention, companionship not to be minimized, I suppose. And I count myself lucky for it. But it's not like the days with you when my heart leapt with anticipation of our togetherness.

It's so odd. A lot of folks I see around me, my age, even younger, are ready to close up shop. Already have. I'm working hard to stay in life — my painting, the boutique, and a good time now and again. With nice people like Gordon, who don't need to be wound up in the morning — still fun. It's such a chore, though, to adjust to age. We become invisible — a shock when you lose your looks. You wouldn't know. You're forever young. But one day it happens. You look down and suddenly your dance card is empty. Guys look past, eyes locked on some chick behind you. Just as I was about to open a vein over this fate, the other day a not-bad-looking fellow, younger than I, lured me into one of those lingering eye-to-eye flirtations. Did me good. Remember when I could simply

bat the baby blues and charm my way out of a speeding ticket? Now?
Even tears don't work.

Tried botox. Only once. Maybe I told you already. Bruised my right
eye. Made the left one droop for weeks. When I first walked into the
shop with it, Nicole screamed, thought I'd had a stroke.

My 50th reunion is coming up. I suppose, if botox had agreed with
me, I might be going.

My love, my love to you,
Sarah

From: **Sarah Ross** <sarahross64@gmail.com>
To: **Adam Wolf** <adam.wolf1402@gmail.com>
May 23, 2014 10:13 am
Subject: hi

hi

From: **Adam Wolf** <adam.wolf1402@gmail.com>
To: **Sarah Ross** <sarahross64@gmail.com>
May 23, 2014 11:21 am
Subject:

Hi yourself—I'm sorry to hear that you won't be there next month.
I was looking forward to seeing you. How are you?

From: **Sarah Ross** <sarahross64@gmail.com>
To: **Adam Wolf** <adam.wolf1402@gmail.com>
May 23, 2014 12:46 am
Subject: why I'm not attending reunion

It's been a while hasn't it? Decades. When was it? 1966? I don't think
I would have had the courage to write to you, after all this time, if Greg

hadn't written me saying you'd like to get in touch. He's knocking himself out, isn't he, organizing all those get-togethers. Lucy and Mira too.

Forgive me for not attending the reunion. I wasn't aware you'd be there. But I decided that I couldn't stand just a glimpse of the people I long to know again. That's the fear that keeps me away. (That and the spectacle of Phyllis Mendelson using the occasion to hawk her latest book. What's this one called? "Beauty Tips for the Ugly Duckling"? Or something like that.)

I'm nudging Greg to arrange a meeting next year for just a few of us: you, Greg, Chris, Gail Krasner, and who else? Ah, me. New York City., Cleveland, Fargo — where doesn't matter.

Can I tentatively begin to ask about you?

Your parents? I remember them. Wolf's Drug, Saturday afternoons, chocolate phosphates, sitting on those ratty red naugahyde stools with rough tears. And your father — formal, wearing his drug-store face — good-natured, though. I remember you used to rail about how fake it was. We always giggled that the smiles were really intended for Ruby in her pink apron. And don't you miss jukeboxes? I remember the song we played over and over on the one jukebox at the drug store. Do you?

And of course your mother and her propensity to complain about your father. I found it poignant.

Are you okay? Your present family?

Me? Lots happened/happening. I've been living here in La Jolla for the last twelve years. My friend Nicole and I opened Naughty Niceties in 2010, a French lingerie shop in town. More amusing than lucrative. I'm a widow now. My husband Harold died 4 years ago. No kids. You know, I'm glad I didn't change my name. It felt wrong to disappear from the face of the earth, from people like you who knew me as Sarah Ross.

Adam, if I knew where the cockles of my heart resided, I would say they're warmed by your being on my radar screen again.

From: **Lola Wolf** <lola.wolf1402@gmail.com>
To: **Adam Wolf** <adam.wolf1402@gmail.com>
May 23, 2014 4:14 pm
Subject: Please answer

Adam—I've tried to call you 10 times already and you, for some reason, decided not to pick up. Please don't insult me by not answering. If Her Highness still has you tending court, just wrench yourself away for five minutes so you can get back to me. What if I had an emergency? Adam, could I count on you to answer? I suppose not.

Remember the party at the Dorman's. 8:00. I'll try to call later cause I know you're going to forget. Pick up this time.

Do you have anything decent to wear? Don't forget, no late stuff tonight at the station.

The way you just left this morning, without a look or a goodbye, or a sign of human recognition, made me sad and angry. Always the same story—that goddamn station. Your needs are first and the only thing that seems to matter to you. I know you're in your "turmoil" right now about the reunion. So anxious, insufferable. "Will I look ok? What will they think?? Blah blah." How about giving your wife the same consideration as those people you haven't talked to in 50 years?

Adam, I'm still an attractive woman at age 64, even if you don't think so. I got compliments at the grocery store this morning. "Mrs. Wolf, we think you're the most elegant woman who comes into the store." That's the woman at the check- out! I wore my old coat and hardly any makeup and she still thought I was elegant.

LOLA > ADAM   5/23/14 5:15 pm

They say dress casual, but doesn't mean faded jeans. I got some khaki slacks for you and put them on your bed. 36 x 32, right?

ADAM   5:19 pm

You didn't need to buy me pants. It's 34 x 32. I'm capable of figuring out for myself what to wear.

LOLA   5:24 pm

Everyone from the block will be there. Don't embarrass me dressing like you're still in college. Your pants are always too tight. I know you'd like to think you still have your girlish figure.

From: **Adam Wolf** *<adam.wolf1402@gmail.com>*
To: **Sarah Ross** *<sarahross64@gmail.com>*
May 23, 2014 5:57 pm
Subject: and back to you

I don't know why, but I feel strangely nervous writing to you.
Sarah, I knew a little about an opening of a watercolor show and of landscape courses you were giving, I've followed you on the internet, so you were in some way already on my "radar screen". Do you ever get back to Cleveland Heights?
My brother David retired from his real estate business, lives in the western suburbs. My mother died back in '97. My father, the World's Foremost Druggist, died in 2003 — managed to screw up his meds and had a stroke. I'm sorry, I don't know whether your parents are alive or not. What I vividly remember were your father's string quartet sessions on Sunday afternoons at your house — among a million other things. How's your sister? Is she still in Cleveland Heights? And you? It must have been difficult when your husband died.

I'm fine—live in Evanston, remarried since the last time we talked in 1979. I have a son 28, Michael, in IT, now in Houston. When he visits we still go to the batting cages. We swing and miss for half an hour and then pizza and sports talk.

I'm now Program Director at WCMQ—95.2 on your dial—boasting dozens of loyal classical music fans throughout Chicagoland. I still host "Your Classical Coffee Mate" (title's not mine). We'd have more listeners if only our signal could be picked up beyond the parking lot. The "on the air" gig is the only part of the job I still enjoy. For an hour every day I get to ad lib. I'm considering basing an entire show on composers whose last names begin with "X".

I've been here eons. No reason to stay, no reason to leave.

The song you challenged me to remember? *Save the Last Dance for Me*, of course.

Can we stay in touch and talk?

From: **Sarah Ross** <sarahross64@gmail.com>
To: **Adam Wolf** <adam.wolf1402@gmail.com>
May 23, 2014 6:35 pm
Subject: catching up

Let's see—what else? Not that long ago I entered into a relationship with a special man, a retired marine biologist. I think he may be a "keeper".

Esther and Herman still live in Cleveland. I don't think she's ever stepped a foot out of Cuyahoga County. She doesn't think she needs to. I love my sister, but I still can't stand to be near her. All that yakking about the bargains at Beachwood Place, the envelope licking for the Sisterhood.

I'm touched you remember the *Hausmusik*—so old world. Glad you witnessed it. My father and all his immigrant friends lived for those Sundays. He became remarkably civilized when he played his violin. Perhaps that's one reason I was attracted to you, Adam. I loved the way you devoted yourself to the piano. Do you still play?

My father died in 1987. My mother is 95, in a nursing home near Esther and not doing so well. I try to be back in Cleveland at least once a month to see her, but I'm no longer convinced she can distinguish me from her phlebotomist.

I'm touched you've been stalking me on the internet. And yes, I'd love to keep on writing, if that's what you mean by "talking". I need to fill in the gaps slowly. But no phoning. Okay? Can we just stay emailing for now? It's a miraculous way to communicate, isn't it? Easier than letters —instant gratification, not days between. And somehow I'm less shy, less inhibited just writing. Disembodied I feel emboldened, find it more intimate than the phone.

---

*From: **Adam Wolf** <adam.wolf1402@gmail.com>*
*To: **Sarah Ross** <sarahross64@gmail.com>*
May 23, 2014 7:03 pm
Subject: Re:catching up

Yes, let's write for now. You know, I've never really carried on a personal email correspondence. My friend Paul, we exchange chapter-length emails once in a while —fantasy film scripts, the escape from the everyday. But this "intimacy" is new. Like you, I'm already discovering the freedom to be myself. So forgive me if I'm awkward. I think I already messed up. My phrasing about following you on the internet was a little inartful, I admit. "Stalking" is too strong a word I think— more like "curiosity", then quiet admiration and interest.

You know, about 10 years ago I was in La Jolla several times. I went there with the station owner. We used to go to the West Coast on business. Unfortunately, or fortunately, we don't take those trips anymore. If I had known you were there, I would have tried to see you.

Tell me more about how you're doing now. Piano? I dropped Schubert, picked up Cole Porter, some Gershwin. It's my palliative, but I guess not so much other people's. So I keep it to myself.

Actually I have a thousand more things I want to tell you —if that's OK. I'll write again tomorrow if I can—

LOLA > ADAM   5/23/14 7:29 pm

What, are you going to make us late again? Is Her Majesty, Queen Amanda, commanding your presence? Can't she just let you do your work and have a life? Why don't you ever stand up to her? Oh, I think I know the answer to that already. I guess I'll go to the Dorman's myself. It's nothing new for me. I'll tell them I have no husband.

From: **Sarah Ross** *<sarahross64@gmail.com>*
To: **S.Gordon Wilson** *<S.Gordon.Wilson@csulb.edu>*
May 24, 2014 8:22 am
Subject: this weekend

Sorry I couldn't get back to you yesterday. Nicole and I didn't sit down all day. The new line of "amethyst" lace boy shorts and "anthracite" demi-bras brought in a flock of floosies. Do you believe these marketing people? I'd like the job—to invent the irresistible colors du jour. Almost as clever as "Häagen-Daz".

Yes, an afternoon on the new boat would be grand. Sounds relaxing. Believe me, I need that badly right now. How about I pack us a lunch? We can christen (or should I say baptize?) the boat with some Sauvignon Blanc.

From: **S.Gordon.Wilson** *<S.Gordon.Wilson@csulb.edu>*
To: **Jerome Mahoney** *<Jerry.Mahoney2028@verizon.net>*
May 24, 2014 10:05 am
Subject: THIS AND THATS

Hi there, Jerry —
Got the new boat! Going to christen her this weekend. Thinking Sarah
Ross might like to come along. I invited her and wish you and Mae could
come down here and help us celebrate. You and I would have a lot of
yucks. Anyway, there'll be a chance to get together this fall. There's a
conference up your way.

Heard a good one I think you'll appreciate:

Why don't blondes wear miniskirts in San Francisco?
Their balls show.

Here's another one I can tell you, but wouldn't tell Sarah:

What does a Jew with an erection get when he walks into a wall?
A broken nose.

Your chum,
Gordon

S. Gordon Wilson, PhD.
Founder and Editor of *The Ichthysaurus*
Fellow, American Academy of Underwater Sciences
Professor of Biology, Emeritus
California State University, Long Beach

From: **Sarah Ross** <sarahross64@gmail.com>
To: **Adam Wolf** <adam.wolf1402@gmail.com>
May 24, 2014 9:16 am
Subject:

Oh, the trouble with email is that it has no tone of voice. The "stalking" was a jest. Hyperbole R Us. "I'm touched by your curiosity" is a sappier way of saying it, I suppose. And a thousand and one things, by all means — a thing at a time, and back to you. I look forward to it.

After college? Your life trajectory?

From: **Adam Wolf** <adam.wolf1402@gmail.com>
To: **Sarah Ross** <sarahross64@gmail.com>
May 24, 2014 9:34 am
Subject: hmmm, my life

Trajectory? Mine is sort of like the Challenger spacecraft. Graduated from U of Chicago '68 and the Cleveland Heights Selective Service Board thrust me into a deferment as a VISTA volunteer. The remains of my Command Module came down in Bluefield, West Virginia. What did I do there? Same as anyone in any community action program — sat around contemplating how to connect with the poor. I sold the idea of a radio show to the public station there. Conducted interviews, sang some folk songs — short-lived — I guess too radical and too Jewish for W. Virginia. Careened back to Chicago in '69, stringing together occupational deferments — mainly working in psych hospitals. Auditioned unsuccessfully for radio jobs. First classical try-out I screwed up the German. Tripped on the *Einführung aus dem Serail.* Then '83, had success auditioning for this small classical station as the overnight announcer. The owner's wife, Amanda Schreiber, supervised the audition. Gave me the job and whispered afterward that I was too cute for radio. So here I am, parked in stationary orbit for the past 30 years.
Trajectory? Two marriages. One brief, fling-like. The current one, almost three decades. In neither case am I sure what prompted me to get married. Pretty boring, huh?

From: **Sarah Ross** *<sarahross64@gmail.com>*
To: **Adam Wolf** *<adam.wolf1402@gmail.com>*
May 24, 2014 1:29 pm
Subject: don't be hard on yourself

Boring? Never to me. Need to know who you are now. Sounds like an adventure — West Virginia, psych hospitals — can't wait for the stories. Radio celebrity to boot. Send an autograph. Make it personal and I can get more for it.

Do you think there are patterns to mistakes we make in relationships? I'm somehow attracted to men, and they to me, unfortunately, who dislike their mothers. That's one of the patterns that repeats. There are others.

From: **Adam Wolf** *<adam.wolf1402@gmail.com>*
To: **Sarah Ross** *<sarahross64@gmail.com>*
May 24, 2014 1:40 pm
Subject: Re: don't be hard on yourself

That's no pattern. Doesn't every man tell his girlfriend that he doesn't like his mother? What other patterns would you mean? Are they patterns that began with us? Was Sandy Chapman part of your pattern?

From: **Sarah Ross** *<sarahross64@gmail.com>*
To: **Adam Wolf** *<adam.wolf1402@gmail.com>*
May 24, 2014 1:43 pm
Subject: patterns

My other patterns? People who are hypersensitive. Like you were. Smart and funny. Like you were. Prone to jealousy. Like you were. Maybe so, maybe our relationship has always been my template. Yep.

Now your turn. I ask again — your patterns?

---

*From: **Adam Wolf** <adam.wolf1402@gmail.com>*
*To: **Sarah Ross** <sarahross64@gmail.com>*
May 24, 2014 1:46 pm
Subject: Re:patterns

My patterns? I can't think of any. Let me see. Maybe short skirts.

---

*From: **Sarah Ross** <sarahross64@gmail.com>*
*To: **Adam Wolf** <adam.wolf1402@gmail.com>*
May 24, 2014 1:56 pm
Subject: Re:Re:patterns

Really? Glad you're so forthcoming. Come on, Wolfie, fess up. Any patterns that have to do with us?

---

*From: **Adam Wolf** <adam.wolf1402@gmail.com>*
*To: **Sarah Ross** <sarahross64@gmail.com>*
May 24, 2014 2:03 pm
Subject: Who I've become

A pattern? Okay. I confess. Passivity maybe. But, Sarah, that's not a pattern that started with us, not what I remember. But me? For many years since us, it's been different. Pattern: letting myself be pulled into someone's orbit — then staying put — fearful to disrupt the daily sameness — afraid of being cast off into the cold if I opened my mouth. Could it really be that my last successful relationship was at 15?
Incidentally if I really was the template for all your relationships, how the hell did you wind up with Sandy Chapman after we broke up? (Hey, why did we break up anyway?)

From: **Sarah Ross** *<sarahross64@gmail.com>*
To: **Adam Wolf** *<adam.wolf1402@gmail.com>*
May 24, 2014 2:19 pm
Subject: breaking up

You mean, how could you ever have broken up with me? Let's see …

1. Your raging hormones
2. Darlene Cutler's short skirt

and

3. My desperate need to be with you every waking hour, which, I'm
    sure, would have gotten on anyone's nerves. I never again in my
    life have been that way. I've learned to keep a distance in my
    relationships. I've learned not to be dependent. Have suppressed
    the desire to be fused to anyone. But I recall I felt amputated
    without you by my side. Perhaps I became too independent after
    us. I hope it to be different with Gordon. I would like to be less
    autonomous, less mistrustful and submit to someone who I
    think would take care of me. Wish me luck.

From: **Adam Wolf** *<adam.wolf1402@gmail.com>*
To: **Sarah Ross** *<sarahross64@gmail.com>*
May 25, 2014 12:04 pm
Subject: Gordon

You used the word the word "keeper" describing your relationship with
Gordon. Sounds like partnership with a future.

From: **Sarah Ross** <sarahross64@gmail.com>
To: **Adam Wolf** <adam.wolf1402@gmail.com>
May 25, 2014 12:34 pm
Subject: Re: Gordon

    I met Gordon a year ago when we co-chaired the fundraiser for the La Jolla Center for the Arts. He's a strong, comforting presence. An old-fashioned gentleman. And he's taken me sailing a couple of times. Best of all, he can whip up some of the best bouillabaisse on this planet. So I made him one of my new best friends. People have begun to think of us as a couple. We're invited out together. I don't know how else to summarize my relationship with Gordon except to say we're comfortable with each other.

From: **Adam Wolf** <adam.wolf1402@gmail.com>
To: **Sarah Ross** <sarahross64@gmail.com>
May 25, 2014 12:48 pm
Subject: Fish Aversion

Bouillabaisse on the high seas. I've got to confess that's lost on me. My appetite for seafood is, as always, nil. He could have seasoned the bouillabaisse with Drano, for all I knew, and I would have been none the wiser. The only time in recent memory I had a taste for seafood was on Yom Kippur, late afternoon, when I started eyeing Lola's fish tank. Last week, you'll be thrilled to know, I ordered the tuna panini at Arby's. So, looks like you and Gordon are a good match. I'm happy for you. Incidentally, I would be jealous about the boat, except I get seasick just driving past Red Lobster.

From: **Sarah Ross** <sarahross64@gmail.com>
To: **Adam Wolf** <adam.wolf1402@gmail.com>
May 25, 2014 1:00 pm
Subject: Re:Fish Aversion

You inlanders, poor things, don't know what good fish looks like. Or for that matter, what it smells like. After those obligatory cruises in elementary school on the Cuyahoga River, with the dead fish floating on the scum, and the stench of rotten eggs wafting through the air, it took years before I'd go near anything fishy.

From: **Adam Wolf** <adam.wolf1402@gmail.com>
To: **Sarah Ross** <sarahross64@gmail.com>
May 25, 2014 1:11 pm
Subject: Re:Re: Fish Aversion

I'm glad you're so ichthyologically sophisticated now that you're with Gordon. Makes sense with a marine biologist. It's not everyone so lucky that they can eat their work at the end of the day. I'm happy for you. Gordon sounds perfect. Any flaws?

From: **Sarah Ross** <sarahross64@gmail.com>
To: **Adam Wolf** <adam.wolf1402@gmail.com>
May 25, 2014 1:34 pm
Subject: flaws

Any flaws? I wouldn't call them flaws exactly. Just annoyances. Okay, just between us, Adam, he doesn't make me laugh. If he has humor in his repertoire, I haven't discovered it yet. Odd, but when he tells jokes, I don't hear anyone laugh. I guess that's my most serious criticism. We don't laugh at the same things. In fact, he has an annoying habit of not laughing and, if there's something real funny, he'll just say, "That was very funny", and never laugh. You know what I mean. It's hard for him to open up. I don't want to complain, because for his age, you know,

73, he's remarkably active and engaged. I think it's the medication, and not the years, that sometimes make him distant and dispassionate. But he's a great human being. He says that he's so lucky to have found me and I tell him the same.

From: **Adam Wolf** *<adam.wolf1402@gmail.com>*
To: **Sarah Ross** *<sarahross64@gmail.com>*
May 25, 2014 1:55 pm
Subject: Re:flaws

It's difficult to imagine Sarah Ross with someone humorless. But then no one could make you laugh the way I could. That's one of the reasons I was crazy about you. Anyway, is there no Sandy Chapman in the wings if you decide to break up with Gordon?

From: **Sarah Ross** *<sarahross64@gmail.com>*
To: **Adam Wolf** *<adam.wolf1402@gmail.com>*
May 25, 2014 2:45 pm
Subject: Sandy Chapman?

Adam, I never even knew you noticed me with Sandy after the break up. Just happens that last time I was in Cleveland, just this winter, we ran into each other pumping gas at the Shell station on Fairmont. He recognized me. I didn't him, not at first — gray hair, not much of it. But for 70 doesn't look bad. He was telling me about his career in engineering (fluid engineer, whatever that is). Anyway I didn't really understand — something with hydro this or that.

From: **Adam Wolf** *<adam.wolf1402@gmail.com>*
To: **Sarah Ross** *<sarahross64@gmail.com>*
May 25, 2014 3:03 pm
Subject: Re:Sandy Chapman?

Sandy Chapman? Hydro? Probably something involving hydrocephalics. Sorry, just flashing those days I spotted you with him. In that gaudy red T-bird. Well, anyway, you seemed real happy. I heard you spent weekends with him in Columbus. The older guy. I wondered who's teaching her how.

From: **Sarah Ross** *<sarahross64@gmail.com>*
To: **Adam Wolf** *<adam.wolf1402@gmail.com>*
May 25, 2014 3:31 pm
Subject: Jealousy

Adam, cut it out or I'll invoke memories of that Cutler slut.

From: **Adam Wolf** *<adam.wolf1402@gmail.com>*
To: **Sarah Ross** *<sarahross64@gmail.com>*
May 25, 2014 4:16 pm
Subject: My son Michael

Just heard from Michael that he's coming in for the weekend — new girlfriend in tow. He had a bit of a wild time at Wisconsin as an undergrad — stayed on in Madison for a Masters in Environmental Science. Came back to Chicago and spent a season hunting down microbes in the Des Plaines River. Chased a girl to Houston. He stayed. Girl didn't. Now with Exxon. An I.T. job I never quite understood. Needless to say, his nascent crusade to Rescue the Environment from Capitalism is officially on hold.

From: **Sarah Ross** *<sarahross64@gmail.com>*
To: **Adam Wolf** *<adam.wolf1402@gmail.com>*
May 25, 2014 4:25 pm
Subject: Re:My son Michael

    If he rails against capitalism, I know he's your son and Manny Wolf's grandson. I looked for Michael on the internet. Think I found his Facebook picture — looks so much like you as a young man — beautiful, the curly blonde hair, the angular face, even the Adam's apple. Ah, to see you again in him! Makes me think of your broad shoulders and narrow hips. Sigh!

From: **Adam Wolf** *<adam.wolf1402@gmail.com>*
To: **Sarah Ross** *<sarahross64@gmail.com>*
May 25, 2014 4:40 pm
Subject: Re:Re:My son Michael

People do say he looks like me. I can't see it. Happy you can. I think the shape of his face is more like Lola's. Not much of a resemblance to me when it comes to classical music. Michael never showed much interest. Lola insisted for years my playing opera for the kid was a hazard to his auditory nerves. Maybe that's why. But you might like to know he's good at art. I should send you the link to drawings from his sketchbook. He posts that on Flickr. Just felt pen on scratchpads, the passing scene — likes to capture the world rushing by — some evocative images of workmen at the refineries — filthy, sweating in the sun.
Incidentally, what are you doing these days with your art? Or would you rather we talk more about your *liaison dangereuse* with Chapman?

From: **Sarah Ross** *<sarahross64@gmail.com>*
To: **Adam Wolf** *<adam.wolf1402@gmail.com>*
May 25, 2014 5:28 pm
Subject: flash of memory

Adam, enough Sandy crap!

I love it that Michael and I have art in common. I'm eager to see what he's doing. As for me, I'm teaching a bit, painting when I can. But you don't make a real living as an artist (or very few people do).

The shop keeps me busy. I'm in there 3x a week. Hate the accounting part, but rather like the income. Meager but it pays my Medicare supplement. Most of all, I love to go to Fashion Week in New York and discover the latest styles, colors. Long leggy models. Lovely to watch them glide unselfconsciously down the runway. Their thongs hugging the groove of their butts so compact that even I could grasp both cheeks with one hand.

One of them, when I saw her last fall, had hair so wavy and so wild, someone described it as "storm-tossed". And I have to admit, I thought of you. The 14 year-old you, your tossled hair and runway thin hips. And not just that image came through — but a passage from Homer, a day in 8th grade English class. Roosevelt Junior High, Cleveland Heights,18, Ohio. Old man Tubaugh's room. I quote this one, when I tell people one of the reasons I fell in love with my first boyfriend. Remember, Adam, we all had to memorize the same damn lines from the beginning of some translation of the Odyssey.

Then Tubaugh had us stand at our desks and one by one recite it. Boring. The same damn lines. (All that memorization back then sticks with us, doesn't it? That's the fun part.) "Tell of the storm-tossed man, oh Muse, who wandered long after he sacked the sacred citadel of Troy." Over and over.

And then it was your turn: "Tell of the storm-tossed man, oh Muse, who wandered long after he sacked the sacred citadel of Troy, and who, disguised as Clark Kent, mild-mannered reporter for a great metropolitan newspaper ..." and we were all on the floor.

From: **Adam Wolf** *<adam.wolf1402@gmail.com>*
To: **Sarah Ross** *<sarahross64@gmail.com>*
May 25, 2014 10:21pm
Subject: Goodnight, my Sarah

Pardon me, but I'm a bit preoccupied here — your hand on the model's rear? Gee, I hadn't remembered that story. I guess you were right to find me cute.

Yes, our days together have always been an anchor, a reference point for me too. Inevitably a phrase, a look, pulls me back to us. Programming Mozart's early operas, I think of how we inspired ourselves to finish homework by saying Mozart had written 13 symphonies by the time he was our age.

Or something as simple someone saying, "Meet my girlfriend", and I have always thought of you. "Girlfriend" has always meant only one thing to me. It meant Sarah. Isn't it strange?

Do you remember we could carry on entire conversations across a room? I knew what you meant — every wink, twitch and flutter. And I think I still would.

I've tried it with other people. Amanda (the station owner) and I might have had some moments of primitive non-verbal communication. During a meeting, say, but ultimately it didn't work. Usually ended up with her shrugging her shoulders, "I don't know what you meant". I doubt we'll ever master it.

From: **Sarah Ross** *<sarahross64@gmail.com>*
To: **Adam Wolf** *<adam.wolf1402@gmail.com>*
May 26, 2014 9:12 am
Subject: Good morning to you

Yes, I only wish other people were as sensitive to me as you were. Then I wouldn't have to be so blunt. "Blunt" is a good word to describe me, a flaw I'm not proud of. Some people are better than I at being circuitous. Criticism comes easily to me. I struggle, though, with how to couch it nicely. It doesn't come naturally. The students in my watercolor classes learn a lot, for instance, and I'm enormously patient with those who try. But the grousers, no matter how talented, set my teeth on edge, and I come close to growling at them. Klaus the Stubborn, in particular—retired, red-faced—probably a storm-trooper in his past life. Last week, down by the marina, at the little studio where I hold classes, I thought to mix things up and have the group work with the paper oriented vertically and not in the usual landscape format. Klaus resisted and resisted until I exploded and told him just to shut up and do it. Turned out to be his best work ever. A composition of lines and arcs—compelling—a sliver of the pier and its masts, as if glimpsed from the edge of a window. Praise for real talent does come easily to me, though. And it made Klaus feel good, I think, to hear me applaud him. The exercise inspired me too. I've gone out every day since to capture a slice of life in longitudinal section.

From: **Adam Wolf** <adam.wolf1402@gmail.com>
To: **Sarah Ross** <sarahross64@gmail.com>
May 26, 2014 11:45 am
Subject: Speaking out

Stealing a moment on break to be *avec toi*.
I always adored your bluntness and independence back in our day. I never learned to speak out. I remember that I secretly relied on you to speak my feelings when I was angry. In my house it was my role, wasn't it, to mediate conflicts all the time. Between my parents: "Tell him his supper is ready." "Tell her I'll get the window fixed on Saturday." (My parents once went a full year without talking to each other.)
Constant tensions between my father and brother also rode high. Once at the table when David got his first and only B+ on a report card, the usual belittlement got out of hand and before long my brother had my father in a strangle hold. (My mother ran out of the room, of course.) And it was my role to make peace. I stepped in between them, pushed them to their respective chairs. They sat seething. And I interjected myself into the silence by imitating the voice of the Gillette Friday Night Fight's ringside announcer: "No real damage inflicted in the first round.

They'll be coming back out soon for the second. The Champ seems a bit shaken. The Challenger has put together some brilliant combinations." Then they would eventually smile and laugh.

That was me then and me forever—conciliator, appeaser, mediator. It's who I am today. I turn away from conflict and equivocate whenever necessary to spare people pain. I needed you. You were the other part of me. Spoke out. Spoke up for me. Spoke my feelings because I couldn't and because you understood them. I have not had my "other half" since those days.

From: **Sarah Ross** <sarahross64@gmail.com>
To: **Adam Wolf** <adam.wolf1402@gmail.com>
May 26, 2014 12:09 pm
Subject: what you were for me

Don't underestimate the gift for making people laugh. It carried me through some rough times at home, in America. I was mistrustful of people ever since my parents lied to 5-year-old me about leaving Vienna. They told me we were just "going on vacation in the mountains via a big ship this time". In fact, I landed in an alien country, lost in translation. Eventually you were my verbal, educated, loving and oh so funny protector. AND a real American. I totally trusted you. Needed you.

I suspect masking your feelings creates problems. Leads to misunderstandings? I'm sorry about that, if it's true.

From: **Adam Wolf** <adam.wolf1402@gmail.com>
To: **Sarah Ross** <sarahross64@gmail.com>
May 26, 2014 3:28 pm
Subject: My troubles

I'm in trouble all the time. Right now I'm not ready to give you all the details of the trouble I've created for myself in my old age. Suffice it to say I feel like an outsider in my own life.

---

*From: **Sarah Ross** <sarahross64@gmail.com>*
*To: **Adam Wolf** <adam.wolf1402@gmail.com>*
May 26, 2014 3:50 pm
Subject: let's hear it for cyberspace

Details can wait. But I feel like I should be there to rescue you. Forgive me for staying away so long. You know, Adam, it's amazing to me how quickly we can confide in each other again. This magical forum —email. I doubt talking or phoning would have brought us together in such an intimate way. I keep marveling at that.

---

*From: **Sarah Ross** <sarahross64@gmail.com>*
*To: **Adam Wolf** <adam.wolf1402@gmail.com>*
May 26, 2014 5:28 pm
Subject: The Cleveland Indians

Do you remember how exciting it was to go down to Municipal Stadium together on a summer afternoon? Rocky Colavito? So cute. Tito Francona? You taught me how to fill out a scorecard, how to shout insults at the ump: "His seeing-eye dog could have called that one."

Hey, Adam Wolf, my parents subscribed to the *Plain Dealer*. But let's hear it for the old *Cleveland Press*!! Best reason to have grown up in Cleveland. Get straight A's, bring down your report card, and we'll hand you seven sets of tickets to the Tribe's games. I would have flunked out of school, I'm guessing, if I hadn't aimed for those tickets. Seven pair!! And two were box seats. Of course you remember. You got them every year. Me? Only in 9th grade—cause I cajoled Mr. Scott to change my B+ in Algebra to an A− because the Indians tickets were on the line. He was a great man.

From: **Adam Wolf** *<adam.wolf1402@gmail.com>*
To: **Sarah Ross** *<sarahross64@gmail.com>*
May 26, 2014 5:58 pm
Subject: THE TRIBE

Still at work.

Can you believe in those days we never thought twice about what an affront Chief Wahoo was? Even worse, he's still around.
But now here's a question. I'm sure you remember where you were when Kennedy was shot. Or on 9/11. But can you recall exactly where you were the moment you heard that Herb Score had been hit in the eye by a line drive?

From: **Sarah Ross** *<sarahross64@gmail.com>*
To: **Adam Wolf** *<adam.wolf1402@gmail.com>*
May 26, 2014 6:30 pm
Subject: Re: THE TRIBE

Ah, my dear Adam — you know me for the nerd I was — of course I remember. I was in bed. It was a night game. The Yankees. My radio was tuned to the game. Jimmy Dudley announcing. Herb Score pitching to Gil McDougal. And I recall hearing the crack of McDougal's bat and the screaming from the crowd. Herb Score. Poor Herb Score! Hit in his eye! Rookie of the Year the year before, right? Oh, I remember a lot of that moment. Early in the season. The *Plain Dealer* photos of him crumpled on the pitcher's mound. But did the game continue? Did the Yankees win?

From: **Adam Wolf** *<adam.wolf1402@gmail.com>*
To: **Sarah Ross** *<sarahross64@gmail.com>*
May 26, 2014 7:20 pm
Subject: Re:Re: THE TRIBE

Home at last.

May 7, 1957. Herb Score still played after that, but was never the same. Became an announcer for the Indians. Aren't you glad you we didn't see it on TV, in "living color"? A most gory sight, they said. McDougal was so distraught, said he'd quit baseball if Score lost his vision. Hey, Sarah, I love that you love baseball.

From: **Sarah Ross** *<sarahross64@gmail.com>*
To: **Adam Wolf** *<adam.wolf1402@gmail.com>*
May 26, 2014 9:44 pm
Subject: sleep tight

Just back from dinner. Tuckered out. Off to bed. Goodnight, Adam.
Gee, to be with you again, with our set of common experiences —comforting, extremely comforting.

From: **Adam Wolf** *<adam.wolf1402@gmail.com>*
To: **Sarah Ross** *<surahross64@gmail.com>*
May 26, 2014 10:04 pm
Subject: Re: sleep tight

Goodnight, my Sarah. I'll write to you in the morning—as soon as I am conscious.

---

*From: **Adam Wolf** <adam.wolf1402@gmail.com>*
*To: **Sarah Ross** <sarahross64@gmail.com>*
May 27, 2014 7:32 am
Subject: Familiarity

In all the years since us, I must confess, I have never again felt a sense of belonging, the "oneness" we had, Sarah. Strange, huh? As children we experience a kind of love that we then spend 50 years looking for and can never find again. But I shouldn't speak for you. I should say that "I" looked for and that "I" could never find again.

---

*From: **Sarah Ross** <sarahross64@gmail.com>*
*To: **Adam Wolf** <adam.wolf1402@gmail.com>*
May 27, 2014 9:15 am
Subject: Re: Familiarity

I'm touched Adam by your memory of us. It's been mine too, you know. All my life I've been looking for someone who loves me as much as you did.

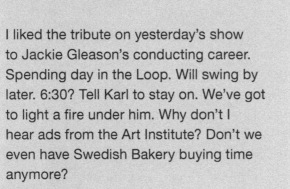

AMANDA > ADAM   5/27/14   10:18 am

I liked the tribute on yesterday's show to Jackie Gleason's conducting career. Spending day in the Loop. Will swing by later. 6:30? Tell Karl to stay on. We've got to light a fire under him. Why don't I hear ads from the Art Institute? Don't we even have Swedish Bakery buying time anymore?

ADAM   10:28 am

Sorry, can't tonight. Lola's drafted me for a wildlife fundraiser. How's about tomorrow? I'll make sure Karl is there if you promise to bring him a Big Mac.

AMANDA   10:39 am

OK. I could have guessed. We were overdue for a display of marital fealty. We'll make it tomorrow then.

From: **Adam Wolf** <adam.wolf1402@gmail.com>
To: **Paul Bishop** <Paul.R.Bishop@dewey.com>
May 27, 2014 11:36 am
Subject: Reunion Craziness

Paul,

I hope that crappy weather doesn't ruin the Baroque Festival for you. Playing outdoors in a driving thunderstorm with a priceless cello might get you some welcome notice. *The Asheville Times*: "From where I sat, I was unable to hear Mr. Bishop's interpretation of Telemann over the thunder claps and howling wind, but his fingering technique "wet" my appetite for more."

I need to catch you up on the latest madness with me — not just "50th Reunion Insanity Inc.", but something else. It involves Sarah, yes, THAT Sarah. I told you about her long ago — the "awakening of love". We're in touch again, all brought about by my old high school friend Greg, you know, the chess hustler who used to come to Chicago every summer (hate to remind you). He informed me that Sarah Ross wasn't coming to the reunion, and wanted to know how I was doing. So that started an email correspondence that's been clipping along for days and days. Paul, I'm nervous. At first it's pleasantries, then some innuendoes — although, Jesus Christ on a cracker! she owns a shop in San Diego that specializes in upscale panties. Not married — her husband died — so far, so good.

Each word to her I weigh a hundred times — so strange — so exciting. To keep Lola from knowing, I stay at the station til late, writing, waiting for replies. Every night now my heart pounding every second — reading into her language, so tentative. Paul, it's like on the ice, skating to the corner — you never see the hit coming — you don't feel it at first — you're flying, falling, submitting to the force.

I'll admit I'm insane. Incidentally, I'm going to call my urologist and suggest he return to medical school. He told me I was unlikely to achieve verticality without a pharmaceutical assist. All I have to do now is think of Sarah to prove him wrong.

From: **Sarah Ross** <sarahross64@gmail.com>
To: **Esther Lehman** <estherlehman88@yahoo.com>
May 27, 2014 11:36 am
Subject: Guess who's back?

Esther, do you believe it? I actually had a real talk with Mom today. She seemed to know who I was. Encouraging. Perhaps the exercise regime really does help.

Now for my news — at lunch today Nicole asked me why I looked so, how did she put it, radiant. And I smiled and shrugged and I didn't answer. But if you really want to know, it's because I've been in touch with Adam Wolf again. Yep, after all these years. He's remarried, so don't worry, it's all on the up and up. He seems to be interested in staying in touch, and that, I guess, is why the glow is there. Okay, okay, call me mushy. Why not "sappy" or "schmaltzy" while you're at it? Throw it at me. Tell me to concentrate on Gordon. I will, I will, but for right now I'm buzzing over this back-in-touchness with Adam. I've had so many pretend conversations with him over the years that real ones are heady. And when Harold betrayed me, my impulse was to find Adam again and have him reassure me that I was still loveable.

But I won't let him see me because I'm not 21 anymore. I wouldn't want him to run away in horror. What he'll get is the disembodied Sarah. We'll leave it at that, only email, no Skype, certainly no meeting, ever. Let him picture me as I looked then. Much better than the reality of 68. Maybe I can send him a picture of me at 36 and pretend that's the way I look now.

Anyway, hug Mom for me. And hugs to you and Herman too, of course.

From: **Adam Wolf** *<adam.wolf1402@gmail.com>*
To: **Sarah Ross** *<sarahross64@gmail.com>*
May 27, 2014 3:29 pm
Subject: Our ESP?

Sarah, this may sound loony, but in our day weren't we able to communicate, to talk to each other telepathically? I remember lying in bed at night hearing your voice and speaking to you. Did it really happen?

From: **Sarah Ross** *<sarahross64@gmail.com>*
To: **Adam Wolf** *<adam.wolf1402@gmail.com>*
May 27, 2014 4:00 pm
Subject: Re:Our ESP?

Gee, now I do recall attempts at telepathy. But don't remember its working, though. What do you remember my saying?

Will write again in a while. Off to teach a class.

From: **Adam Wolf** *<adam.wolf1402@gmail.com>*
To: **Sarah Ross** *<sarahross64@gmail.com>*
May 27, 2014 6:15 pm
Subject:

And I'm off to a charity auction. More later.

From: **Adam Wolf** *<adam.wolf1402@gmail.com>*
To: **Sarah Ross** *<sarahross64@gmail.com>*
May 27, 2014 9:21 pm
Subject: Telepathy

Scored a Wheaties box at the auction—with Sammy Sosa on it. I'll resell it and retire.
Hope your class went well and that Klaus suppressed his Hermann Goering imitation.
Up in my room. Can't bear another second of "Dancing with the Stars" blasting, rattling the mirrors.
You asked me before what you said to me telepathically. Oh, just something soothing, comforting, your soft voice, something like, "It's okay. I'm here." Or just, "Adam. It's me."

From: **Sarah Ross** *<sarahross64@gmail.com>*
To: **Adam Wolf** *<adam.wolf1402@gmail.com>*
May 27, 2014 9:41 pm
Subject: Re:Telepathy

   Class fine. We worked on still-life drawings. No Klaus.
   Adam, should we try this telepathy business again? I must confess, some years ago I did have an extraordinarily close friend who moved away to Italy and we seemed to be able to signal each other telepathically. I knew when she needed me. I haven't seen her in years, but we still correspond—a confidante.

From: **Adam Wolf** <adam.wolf1402@gmail.com>
To: **Sarah Ross** <sarahross64@gmail.com>
May 27, 2014 9:44 pm
Subject: Telepathy Tonight?

Sarah, how about 1:15 am your time? I'll send a message. See if you get it. I'll ask you tomorrow what it was.

From: **Sarah Ross** <sarahross64@gmail.com>
To: **Adam Wolf** <adam.wolf1402@gmail.com>
May 27, 2014 9:48 pm
Subject: Re:Telepathy Tonight?

Okay, let's try. I'll be asleep, deep asleep, but primed to receive you.

From: **Adam Wolf** <adam.wolf1402@gmail.com>
To: **Sarah Ross** <sarahross64@gmail.com>
May 27, 2014 9:55 pm
Subject: Re:Re:Telepathy Tonight?

How about a dry run right now? You think of something—a word, a place.
I'll tell you what I received.

From: **Sarah Ross** <sarahross64@gmail.com>
To: **Adam Wolf** <adam.wolf1402@gmail.com>
May 27, 2014 9:59 pm
Subject:

Okay. Sent.

---

*From: **Adam Wolf** <adam.wolf1402@gmail.com>*
*To: **Sarah Ross** <sarahross64@gmail.com>*
May 27, 2014 10:03 pm
Subject:

Wait. Wait. I think I got it. A hit. Is it something in Cleveland?

---

*From: **Sarah Ross** <sarahross64@gmail.com>*
*To: **Adam Wolf** <adam.wolf1402@gmail.com>*
May 27, 2014 10:07 pm
Subject:

Gosh, amazing. It is.

---

*From: **Adam Wolf** <adam.wolf1402@gmail.com>*
*To: **Sarah Ross** <sarahross64@gmail.com>*
May 27, 2014 10:16 pm
Subject:

Don't tell me, don't tell me. Ummm. It's about water. Dirty water. Cuyahoga River!

---

*From: **Sarah Ross** <sarahross64@gmail.com>*
*To: **Adam Wolf** <adam.wolf1402@gmail.com>*
May 27, 2014 10:20 pm
Subject:

Close. I sent "Corky and Lenny's Delicatessen". Their water wasn't dirty, though, was it?

From: **Adam Wolf** *<adam.wolf1402@gmail.com>*
To: **Sarah Ross** *<sarahross64@gmail.com>*
May 27, 2014 10:28 pm
Subject:

See. See! The place started with a "C". A little more concentration and we'll have it perfected. Tonight send some romantic thought. I bet that works.

From: **Sarah Ross** *<sarahross64@gmail.com>*
To: **Adam Wolf** *<adam.wolf1402@gmail.com>*
May 27, 2014 10:49 pm
Subject: sweet dreams

Goodnight, dear Adam. I'll do my best.

From: **Sarah Ross** *<sarahross64@gmail.com>*
To: **Adam Wolf** *<adam.wolf1402@gmail.com>*
May 28, 2014 5:47 am
Subject:

I didn't set the alarm, but somehow woke up at exactly 1:30. Did you receive my romantic thoughts?

From: **Adam Wolf** *<adam.wolf1402@gmail.com>*
To: **Sarah Ross** *<sarahross64@gmail.com>*
May 28, 2014 6:47 am
Subject:

That one's easy. The same as we used to sign our notes to each other, right?

From: **Sarah Ross** *<sarahross64@gmail.com>*
To: **Adam Wolf** *<adam.wolf1402@gmail.com>*
May 28, 2014 7:45 am
Subject: exercise

Right!

I'm getting ready to go to my NIA class. It's a non-impact aerobic dance/martial arts exercise. Jane, a great teacher. About a 45-min. drive, but worth it.

I also take a yoga class 3x a week. What do you do to keep your heart from attacking you?

From: **Adam Wolf** *<adam.wolf1402@gmail.com>*
To: **Sarah Ross** *<sarahross64@gmail.com>*
May 28, 11:33 am
Subject: Re:exercise

What I do for "exercise"? It's ice hockey. Taught myself to skate about 20 years ago when Michael played youth hockey. Now, about once a month, I play with some younger guys in their 50's. (Ah, to be 50 again!). Only one injury that needed stitches, only knocked unconscious once. Not as therapeutic as your NIA — only 2 hours of a grueling workout after 60 hours of butt shifting on the way to and from work. I'm likely to end my life stroking out on the ice.

From: **Sarah Ross** *<sarahross64@gmail.com>*
To: **Adam Wolf** *<adam.wolf1402@gmail.com>*
May 28, 2014 12:14 pm
Subject: hockey!

What a way to go! Dying when wearing sexy *tuchis* pads, no matter how sweaty? I'd take it. Fun to think of you moving quickly cross the ice — remembering how fast you moved around the track. But hockey? You mean you can stop on a dime and send ice chips flying? Be still my heart!

From: **Adam Wolf** <adam.wolf1402@gmail.com>
To: **Sarah Ross** <sarahross64@gmail.com>
May 28, 1:19 pm
Subject: Re:hockey!

Hockey, more humbling than romantic, certainly not sexy. I play with guys who started skating at the age of one and have played hockey every night of their lives since. They tolerate me, the lone Jew among the Catholic rink rats. Actually, by the time I get all my gear on, I'm too tired to play. Some nights I can't even make it to the first puck drop without begging for a substitute.

Even if I'm alone at the net with a wide-open shot, I miss most of the time. I hang around the net a lot, get to know the goalie very well. There ought to be rule that old Jewish players are awarded a point for amusing the opposing goalie. Let's call it a *schtick* shot.

But I'm a pretty good skater, can skate backwards as quickly as forwards.

From: **Sarah Ross** <sarahross64@gmail.com>
To: **Adam Wolf** <adam.wolf1402@gmail.com>
May 28, 2014 2:21 pm
Subject: Re:Re:hockey!

Now you've done it! Next I'll have to ask you what you're wearing.

From: **Adam Wolf** <adam.wolf1402@gmail.com>
To: **Sarah Ross** <sarahross64@gmail.com>
May 28, 2:45 pm
Subject: What I'm wearing

You can ask me what I'm wearing any time you like. Right now I have on my day uniform. It consists of a pale blue broadcloth dress shirt, with yellow stripes, a thin-waled tan corduroy jacket with leather patches at the elbow, a faded pair of straight-legged Levi's blue jeans, over pink satin thongs — floral pattern of tulips and peonies appliqued at the crotch, and naturally, a matching bra.

From: **Sarah Ross** <sarahross64@gmail.com>
To: **Adam Wolf** <adam.wolf1402@gmail.com>
May 28, 2014 3:02 pm
Subject: Re:What I'm wearing

Adam, don't you know? These days they don't have to match.

From: **Adam Wolf** <adam.wolf1402@gmail.com>
To: **Sarah Ross** <sarahross64@gmail.com>
May 28, 3:16 pm
Subject: Back to work

I'm on the air — covering for someone — playing the *Bruckner Fifth* — long enough for a quick hi. And bye.

From: **Sarah Ross** <sarahross64@gmail.com>
To: **Adam Wolf** <adam.wolf1402@gmail.com>
May 28, 2014 4:00 pm
Subject: classical music

You know, Adam, I can't imagine a person better at classical programming than you. Even when you were 15 you loved telling me about Vivaldi and Mozart. I trust you would be proud of me now that I've embraced Bruckner and Wagner. Gordon, who often indulges me, and does like classical music, declined my invitation to *Tristan and Isolde* when the San Francisco Opera came to town. He dismissed it as "noise". We had a fight. I said only people who've never bothered to listen to Wagner write him off that way.

From: **Adam Wolf** *<adam.wolf1402@gmail.com>*
To: **Sarah Ross** *<sarahross64@gmail.com>*
May 28, 5:01 pm
Subject: Re:classical music

Yes, I'm always taken aback by people's dumb-ass response to Wagner. You're right, Sarah, they've never listened. I'm excited you like it. Incidentally, lots of people could do a better job programming classical music than I — like a nine-year-old throwing a dart at the Grove Encyclopedia of Music.

From: **Adam Wolf** *<adam.wolf1402@gmail.com>*
To: **Sarah Ross** *<sarahross64@gmail.com>*
May 28, 8:33 pm
Subject: The seats for the blind

Long day. Demanding meeting. I was musing on the commute home, thinking about our times. About Cleveland. Do you remember when we went to see *Don Giovanni* at the Auditorium? My grandmother's Society for the Blind free tickets when the Met came to town. God forbid anyone should actually pay for tickets. God forbid anyone should ever have taken my grandmother herself. Even for the blind they were bad seats. We sat in that section upstairs against the wall where, when we were lucky, we spotted Leparello smoking a cigarette in the wings waiting for his cue. We never got to see Don Giovanni himself, no matter how much we strained. To this day, despite that, the end of *Don Giovanni* is still my favorite ending to an opera.

From: **Sarah Ross** *<sarahross64@gmail.com>*
To: **Adam Wolf** *<adam.wolf1402@gmail.com>*
May 28, 2014 8:51 pm
Subject: Re:The seats for the blind

You bet I remember that excursion. I went again with my mother to see *Tosca* when the Metropolitan Opera was in town (tickets, yet) from her cousin, the choral director at the Met, Kurt Adler. He must have seen us as his pitiful *mishpoche*. Wrangled complimentary tickets for us. ALSO IN THE BLIND SECTION! Almost got to see Renata Tebaldi. Actually did see her backstage. She looked exhausted after hurling herself off the parapet. An icepack on her ankle. She was furious. Apparently some stagehand fell asleep on the mattress that was supposed to catch her.

Hey, Chicago has a great opera house. Do you ever get there?

From: **Adam Wolf** <adam.wolf1402@gmail.com>
To: **Sarah Ross** <sarahross64@gmail.com>
May 28, 9:07 pm
Subject: The Lyric Opera

Actually, the station gets tickets, but I rarely go anymore.
For years, back in the 70s, I had a subscription to the Lyric. Went with a man I knew from the old Lincoln Park neighborhood. Let me describe the guy. Good-looking is too bland a word for it. Strikingly handsome. Think Jude Law with a Chicago accent. Wore Armani suits. Tall. Slender. When we walked into the lobby, everyone would turn to look. Of course both of us were completely heterosexual, but I liked being thought of as his date.

From: **Sarah Ross** <sarahross64@gmail.com>
To: **Adam Wolf** <adam.wolf1402@gmail.com>
May 28, 2014 9:10 pm
Subject: Re:The Lyric Opera

Completely heterosexual? Pity.

---

*From: **Adam Wolf** <adam.wolf1402@gmail.com>*
*To: **Sarah Ross** <sarahross64@gmail.com>*
May 28, 9:19 pm
Subject: Re:Re:The Lyric Opera

I guess you caught me there. If I were so completely heterosexual, I wouldn't have had to mention it.

---

*From: **Sarah Ross** <sarahross64@gmail.com>*
*To: **Adam Wolf** <adam.wolf1402@gmail.com>*
May 28, 2014 9:50 pm
Subject: nightie night

> Off to bed. Early morning meeting.
> Goodnight Adam. I'll compose more emails to you in my sleep.

---

*From: **Adam Wolf** <adam.wolf1402@gmail.com>*
*To: **Sarah Ross** <sarahross64@gmail.com>*
May 28, 2014 10:04 pm
Subject: Re:nightie night

Goodnight, my Sarah. I'll be with you again in my sleep.

---

*From: **Adam Wolf** <adam.wolf1402@gmail.com>*
*To: **Sarah Ross** <sarahross64@gmail.com>*
May 29, 9:10 am
Subject: My novel

Thought a lot about opera last night.
A few years ago, I wrote a short novel—25,000 words—and one scene involves a group of opera singers, including Renata Tebaldi, lost in space.

From: **Sarah Ross** *<sarahross64@gmail.com>*
To: **Adam Wolf** *<adam.wolf1402@gmail.com>*
May 29, 2014 9:25 am
Subject: Re:My novel

What became of your novel?

From: **Adam Wolf** *<adam.wolf1402@gmail.com>*
To: **Sarah Ross** *<sarahross64@gmail.com>*
May 29, 2014 11:23 am
Subject: Re:Re:My novel

Nothing came of it. I'll never show it to anyone, so don't ask. I now think it's dumb.

From: **Sarah Ross** *<sarahross64@gmail.com>*
To: **Adam Wolf** *<adam.wolf1402@gmail.com>*
May 29, 2014 11:56 am
Subject: Please send the book

Adam, I'm sure it's not dumb, and I really do wish to read it. Please. I remember a great novel you wrote when you were only 16. Thought you so brilliant. Trust you still are.

A memory flash—your backyard, a Scrabble game, you laid down a word on the triple-score squares—"queue"—a gazillion points in one simple move. I'll never get over learning the word right then and wondering how it ever got to be pronounced the way it was pronounced. And recall thinking back then how brilliant Adam Wolf was.

Just about a month ago, I was back in Cleveland going through the box of my mother's stuff—the one with my fading report cards and potato-print wrapping paper. And I came across a stash of letters written in study hall from you to me. Most went something like this: "Dear Sarah, I love you, I love you, I love you. The proof to Theorem #6 is …

ILU, Adam". And again I remembered thinking how brilliant Adam Wolf was and how lucky I was. (Though now I know why I didn't do so well in 10th grade geometry. You did all my homework for me.)

From: **Adam Wolf** <adam.wolf1402@gmail.com>
To: **Sarah Ross** <sarahross64@gmail.com>
May 29, 2014 1:37 pm
Subject: The ILU notes

Oh — the notes in study hall, notes after class, before class, during class. When I try thinking about those days it's like a dream — as though we were lost in the stars.

I saved your notes and photos too. I remember putting them in a box and hiding them in the crawlspace behind the rafters in the attic at the Silsby house. I wonder if they're still there where I left them. I never retrieved them, I'm sorry to say. The house was sold while I was away at college.

In the deluge of memories, a constant one for me through all time is a moment somewhere back in a classroom — don't know where or what day — when I looked at you and you looked back with your sweet quiet smile, touched your finger to your eye, made an "L" with your finger and pointed back at me — ILU — I think other people saw — but I remember that I didn't care. That was the start of our special sign.

I think they did see. At the reunion before the last one in 1994, I only went to the Fri. evening get-together. Early in the evening, someone (I don't remember who), a woman who I almost recognized (from English class, I think), very animated said to me, "We'll always be grateful to Sarah and you. You taught us about love. I just wanted you to know that." I don't remember if I responded. All I could think of at the moment was our signal: ILU — ILU2.

Sarah, talking to you could go on forever and I wouldn't miss sleep.

From: **Sarah Ross** <sarahross64@gmail.com>
To: **Adam Wolf** <adam.wolf1402@gmail.com>
May 29, 2014 4:51 pm
Subject: Re:The ILU notes

This time we will never stop. I won't take for granted that you're near again.

Yes, I remember the moment, the first ILU. It's why I looked forward to English class. I think about what we radiated. It was as if everyone else in the room was a pale shadow and only we were in living color. I'm off to teach my evening class. Then another night out. So I'll write tomorrow and the next day and the days after that.

From: **S.Gordon Wilson** <S.Gordon.Wilson@csulb.edu>
To: **Sarah Ross** <sarahross64@gmail.com>
June 2, 2014 2:22 pm
Subject: get well soon

Dear Sarah,

I hope you're feeling better. These summer colds can lay the best of us low.
I'm sure you'll be back in tip-top shape by Saturday. Would you give me the honor of dining with me at the Ocean Terrace that evening? Please call when you feel up to it.
Get better speedily!

Yours,
Gordon

S. Gordon Wilson, PhD.
Founder and Editor of *The Ichthysaurus*
Fellow, American Academy of Underwater Sciences
Professor of Biology, Emeritus
California State University, Long Beach

From: **Sarah Ross** *<sarahross64@gmail.com>*
To: **Adam Wolf** *<adam.wolf1402@gmail.com>*
June 3, 2014 4:51 pm
Subject: remarkable talent

Bravo!!!! A most wonderful novel. I'm so flattered that you entrusted me with it. I was drawn in from the start—absorbed by those characters, especially that piece-of-work Katya. The thought of being trapped in a small spacecraft with her for a year? Makes me want to open a vein.

You're still an astronomy buff, I see. Reading the book, I recalled how you were always oriented to the sky. How you tried to teach me about outer space. But the stars were too grand for my pea-brain to comprehend. Still are. We were standing by Boulevard School's playground. It was night. And you pointed to a star and told me how many millions of years it took for the light from it to reach us. You said the star we were looking at probably didn't even exist anymore. Long gone. Yikes! I didn't want you to go on. It felt as if I'd been socked in the stomach.

I wonder, though, if we got out in space far enough and had a telescope powerful enough, could we see Adam Wolf and Sarah Ross right there, in Cleveland Heights, July 28, 1960, standing by the playground, looking up? Time-travel. Would you want to go back there?

Anyway, a great accomplishment, this novel. I think you might wish to show it to an agent, no?

I'm delighted to know you're still so talented and clever.

From: **Adam Wolf** *<adam.wolf1402@gmail.com>*
To: **Sarah Ross** *<sarahross64@gmail.com>*
June 3, 2014 7:12 pm
Subject: Re:remarkable talent

Thanks for such a sweet response. I'm so glad you liked the book. But no, no agent. Let this be a secret between us.
Time-travel—back to you, to us, Sarah? I'd do it in a flash, but not if parents and curfews and homework came with the territory. Then even the lure of you wouldn't be enough to draw me there.

Well, and thanks for the compliment. I'm glad somebody still thinks I'm smart. But, in truth, I found out I'm not as brilliant as people once thought. Univ. of Chicago was a humbling time and since then I've had enough experiences that I've learned to accept my limitations. Anyway, I've had people around to remind me of them.

Just about daily Lola tells me I'm stupid: "What kind of idiot are you? You went to U of C and you can't separate recyclable from regular garbage?"

From: **Sarah Ross** <sarahross64@gmail.com>
To: **Adam Wolf** <adam.wolf1402@gmail.com>
June 3, 2014 7:23 pm
Subject: I'm sorry

In the name of domestic tranquility, I won't comment on Lola's remarks. But just to say, I hope she doesn't have a penchant for belittlement.

From: **Adam Wolf** <adam.wolf1402@gmail.com>
To: **Sarah Ross** <sarahross64@gmail.com>
June 3, 2014 7:35 pm
Subject: Re:I'm sorry

In the name of full disclosure, Lola actually goes beyond belittlement. More like mortification when she publically wants to put me in my place. She posted a video of the massive snowstorm we had last winter. The video featured me clearing the driveway, then falling flat on my face, and lying there in exhaustion. You could hear her laughing as the camera zoomed in.

From: **Sarah Ross** <sarahross64@gmail.com>
To: **Adam Wolf** <adam.wolf1402@gmail.com>
June 3, 2014 7:41 pm
Subject: Re:Re:I'm sorry

Geez!

From: **Adam Wolf** <adam.wolf1402@gmail.com>
To: **Sarah Ross** <sarahross64@gmail.com>
June 3, 2014 8:06 pm
Subject: Mo Spiegel

And then there's Maureen Spiegel. Remember her? She and her husband moved to Chicago and we saw each other a couple of times and then not at all. She had landed some big shot position as a vice president at Quaker Oats. The last time I saw them was five years ago at a barbeque at their McMansion in Glencoe. And that's also the last time I spoke to her. She let me know how limited I was. At the party she took me aside when the others were jabbering — wondered what had happened to me — that I'd been such a "golden boy" in high school — that everyone had great expectations of me. She looked at me pityingly. I saw it coming. "How is it", she wondered, "that you didn't amount to more".
When I tried to point out my few accomplishments at the radio station, she shrugged and walked away.

From: **Sarah Ross** <sarahross64@gmail.com>
To: **Adam Wolf** <adam.wolf1402@gmail.com>
June 3, 2014 8:27 pm
Subject: Mo the Ho

That sniveling little bitch Mo Spiegel. Lemme me at 'er! Your work makes people's lives fuller, gives them a way to transcend the tedium of the everyday. Is that not tremendously valuable? The arts are the oxygen of my life, many people's lives. What? Quaker's breakfast mush trumps Beethoven? I don't think so.

Your commie upbringing, I'm guessing, would lead you to avoid corporate America. Anyway, where were you supposed to get the money for grad school? Even if your father ever had a cent, he wouldn't have sent it your way.

Who the hell does little weasly Maureen Spiegel think she is? *Feh!* Sounds like she's still part of the Wiley-snob clique, the girls who took greater pleasure flaunting their cashmere sweaters than wearing them. In history class she always enjoyed knocking my books off my desk as she passed. Liked to see me scramble for them. A bully then. A bully now. Just ignore her. Leave it to me to be the one to tear her limb from limb. For old time's sake. Do you think you'll have to run into her at the reunion?

From: **Adam Wolf** <adam.wolf1402@gmail.com>
To: **Sarah Ross** <sarahross64@gmail.com>
June 3, 2014 9:23 pm
Subject: Re: Mo the Ho

The more I think about the last reunion, the more hesitant I am about the upcoming one. I debate with myself about it — I'm still a little un-decided whether to go. I went to the one 10 years ago and I did enjoy the repartee with Greg and Steve et al. Mostly though I recall people lodging grievances they had harbored for 40 yrs — slights I didn't intend or remember. It seemed like every 5 mins. someone who I barely re-membered would challenge me. Mike Newman asked me if it was true that my father was a Communist and did he raise us as Commies too? Greenblatt remembered how he caught me in the school parking lot, letting air out of the tires on his father's Caddie. And, oh, whether it was a political statement or something. I told him I didn't recall it. (I did and it was.)
And the strangest thing of all, Ellen Thomas, I think that's her name, asked me why, when she flirted with me in Chemistry, I never asked her out, etc., etc. When it was over I had a portrait of myself as an arrogant, insensitive asshole — and I guess people wanted me to know

that. So I dutifully apologized and they seemed satisfied that I wasn't the same person they knew.

More tomorrow. Goodnight, my Sarah.

From: **Sarah Ross** <sarahross64@gmail.com>
To: **Adam Wolf** <adam.wolf1402@gmail.com>
June 3, 2014 10:43 pm
Subject: spare me reunions

These tales of reunion are rather chilling. I can imagine the horror of a list of grievances. It makes me giddy to be not going. I still carry a satchel of grievances myself and would have the impulse to dump them on Janice Price. She always managed to make me feel unwanted in any group.

From: **Harold Weinstein** <Harold.W.Weinstein9933@gmail.com>
To: **Sarah Ross** <sarahross64@gmail.com>
June 4 2014 10:55 am
Subject: relocating

FYI. Leaving Ashland. Took 1 yr visiting post at St. Olaf's in Minnesota, beginning Sept.1. New email address to follow. H

From: **Adam Wolf** <adam.wolf1402@gmail.com>
To: **Sarah Ross** <sarahross64@gmail.com>
June 4, 2014 11:32 am
Subject:Our last telephone call

Sarah, this morning I thought about the last time you and I spoke — in 1979. I don't know if you remember — you called to tell me that Susan Cantor had died — and as we were speaking my wife (at the time) interrupted me, purposely, on some ruse — and we never finished the conversation. When we do talk to each other again, I promise no interruptions, at least not for the first 4 hours.

From: **Sarah Ross** <sarahross64@gmail.com>
To: **Adam Wolf** <adam.wolf1402@gmail.com>
June 4, 2014 1:51 pm
Subject: Re:Our last telephone call

Yes, I remember the call. Your mother gave me the number — groused about your father, maybe about you, and added that she always thought you and I should have gotten married. Mothers ...

I didn't just call you then to socialize. I was back in Cleveland that week and low — about getting older, about my parents deteriorating. Things were falling apart in my family. Esther was overwhelmed and screaming a lot. I needed comfort and I really needed to talk to someone, actually to you. My mother who, as you know, never recovered from what happened to her family in the War, had just been institutionalized. Went off the rails — listening to the radio, waiting for her name to be called, to be herded "to points East". She got better, eventually, somewhat, but that day I longed for a connection to someone who had known me as her child. And no one had known me as well as you.

And Susan Cantor dying on the operating table, so young, so unnecessarily. Too much. But I felt certain that your voice alone could comfort me. It did. But I do recall the painful and abrupt end to the conversation. I took it as a clear message, to stay away. Anyway, from that talk you knew I had dropped out of grad school, that I was married to a literature guy, that I was trying to get pregnant, but couldn't, that I was working with the Art dept. at San Diego, monotonous work, ordering supplies, making sure enough conté crayon was in stock, that sort of thing. Didn't last long. Anyway, you would have heard more if it hadn't been for that startling *interruptus* to the conversation.

There were things that I might have talked to you about had you stayed on the phone longer

1. That I had been held hostage by enemy aliens of the UFO sort, in their mother ship, for the better part of 1969 (or was that the LSD speaking?).

2. That after college I had tried going on with painting, on my own, but ripped up all the canvases deciding that I had no talent. Zero. That the only reason I thought I did was because Morris Nolinski at Bennington praised me to the sky, even named a painting (now in MOMA) after me, *Buena Sarah I* (there was never a *II*, cause I stopped the affair. Later, I discovered that *Amazing Grace I* and *II*, and *Katydid I, II and III* all lived in my dorm).

3. During grad school earned some chump change talking dirty on the dial-a-slut circuit.

---

*From: **Adam Wolf** <adam.wolf1402@gmail.com>*
*To: **Sarah Ross** <sarahross64@gmail.com>*
June 4, 2014 6:35 pm
Subject: Re:Re:Our last telephone call

Nothing so arousing here.
Thanks for jogging my memory about that call. Maybe I've repressed it. As a matter of fact, I do recall the scene, if not the talk—tethered to a wall phone, the cord one foot long. Brenda, who had answered the phone, so knew it was you, was literally in my face the whole time—challenging me to do anything—mocking every word I said. Needless to say Brenda was insecure. She knew how important you had been to me. All the intensity we felt. You may want to know that our aborted conversation back in '79 was a kind of turning point for Brenda and me. I was humiliated, enraged—and I snapped—for the first time in our marriage I wasn't Adam the Conciliator. Things changed after that and I guess I stopped being intimidated by Brenda. We split up six months later.
Tell me about Harold if you want. Sorry that you lost him.

From: **Sarah Ross** *<sarahross64@gmail.com>*
To: **Adam Wolf** *<adam.wolf1402@gmail.com>*
June 4, 2014 8:13 pm
Subject: Harold?

Adam, I had no idea about Brenda. Sorry I got you in trouble, or perhaps I'm not sorry, if it helped extricate you from such a one. Is rescuing Adam Wolf my life's actual calling?

Let's see, what can I tell you about life with Harold? The 70's, first his bucking for tenure, us needing to be pleasant to some boors in the senior ranks of the department. In particular, one who always greeted me by running his hand down my back and snapping my bra. Geezers. But I pretended to like that frat-boy vulgarity. Full Professors, whiskey-breathed by 9:00 am. For Harold's sake I had to giggle at their toilet jokes. I hated those years.

The only one of the senior faculty I could stand was Timothy Fielding, an evil sense of humor — once said if Harold got tenure he couldn't be let go, "even if he buggered a goat on the steps of the post office at high noon". Harold did get tenure. I don't believe he ever fucked a goat, but I wouldn't be surprised.

Well, you see, guess I'm not saying all that much about Sarah Ross in those years. (I still have a hard time talking about myself.) I didn't feel all that present in those days. It was all about Professor Harold Weinstein, PhD, the smiling, the entertaining. Once he got tenure I needed to get away from that. Quit my job in the Art dept., took fencing lessons, learned to deal blackjack at the Diamond Star Casino. Harold was embarrassed by all of it. He insisted I mention it to no one at the university. And I agreed to cease and desist. Me? I was transmogrified from the feisty Sarah you knew and loved, into the dutiful, robotic faculty wife.

Luckily some consciousness-raising group I joined jolted me back into myself. Began painting again and gave a fuck about dinner parties. Spent some time adventuring in Europe with my best pal. She stayed on in her family's home in Terni. And I almost did too. So you see, you're not the only one who's gotten themselves in trouble. Are you ready to talk more about your troubles?

From: **Adam Wolf** *<adam.wolf1402@gmail.com>*
To: **Sarah Ross** *<sarahross64@gmail.com>*
June 4, 2014 9:00 pm
Subject:

Wow! Forever the feisty Sarah, the adventurer. I want to hear more, much more, but can't right now. Duty calls. Lola's car broke down. I need to go see what's up. More tomorrow.
Promise.

From: **Sarah Ross** *<sarahross64@gmail.com>*
To: **Adam Wolf** *<adam.wolf1402@gmail.com>*
June 5, 2014 9:55 am
Subject:

Happy June 5th, Adam. It hasn't even been two weeks, but it feels to me as if we've never been apart. Odd, don't you think?

From: **Adam Wolf** *<adam.wolf1402@gmail.com>*
To: **Sarah Ross** *<sarahross64@gmail.com>*
June 5, 2014 11:33 am
Subject:

Happy June 5th to you too, my Sarah Ross. And it feels as if we've never been apart because we haven't been.

From: **Adam Wolf** *<adam.wolf1402@gmail.com>*
To: **Sarah Ross** *<sarahross64@gmail.com>*
June 5, 2014 4:51 pm
Subject:

I won't be able to write at any length until later in the evening. Command performance. Her Royal Highness, A. Schreiber, insists I redo next month's program schedule by tomorrow. Forgive me.

From: **Adam Wolf** *<adam.wolf1402@gmail.com>*
To: **Sarah Ross** *<sarahross64@gmail.com>*
June 5, 2014 9:41 pm
Subject: Possessed

Now, to get back to what I've really been wishing to do all day, schmooze
with you. Anyway, the short version of my troubles, as promised. After
Brenda, several years of frenzy, then a thirty year marriage of separate
lives, little intimate contact, appeasing and enabling my new wife's self-
destructive impulses. And then the day job — keeping the peace at all,
and I mean ALL costs. Accommodating that woman's professional and
personal expectations of me.

Whatever happened to you in those years, the Sarah I knew and loved
seems to have reemerged in full force. Sure hope Harold also tried
consciousness-raising. Still, it must have been difficult for you when he
passed away.

From: **Sarah Ross** *<sarahross64@gmail.com>*
To: **Adam Wolf** *<adam.wolf1402@gmail.com>*
June 5, 2014 10:21 pm
Subject: how I fell for you

"Difficult" is too thin a word for what I went through. I'd rather
not go there.

You know, Adam, I think my attraction to Harold in the first place
had a lot to do with you. Literature. You planted the passion for that in
me. Harold picked up where you left off— explaining Milton and Joyce,
to me, the way you had Tolstoy and Dostoyevsky. You liked Russian
literature, didn't you?

I need to tell you a story. You were a guru of sorts to me, the literate
American who could finally teach me what to read. I was 14. Before
you, I had no guide. We had no books in the house, at least no books in
English. Before you, I would go to the library and close my eyes and
run my hand along the shelf and take out any 5 books my hand landed

on. Very funny thinking about it. Roosevelt Jr. High. We had a book report due, one we had to deliver, orally, in Tubaugh's 8th grade Honors English class. I did my usual five book gambit. Three were geography or history books. The other two? One was Whitman's *Leaves of Grass* (which I couldn't make heads or tails of, of course. Still can't). The other book, a trifle. *See Here, Private Hargrove,* an amusing book about a bumbling private in WWII. So I ended up giving a report on it. Afterwards kids laughed at me for picking a stupid book. But what did I know? As I was returning to my desk one whispered, "Ever hear of Mark Twain?" Another, "You could have picked Dickens". When I tell the story of why I've been in love with my first boyfriend, I say he never made fun of me, the way the others did. But two days later gave me a copy of Steinbeck's *Grapes of Wrath* and I was so grateful. I joined a paperback book club, and you helped me select books. It's there I discovered Nabokov, whose writing still makes me melt. It is you who made me literary.

Goodnight, my Adam. Please, more tomorrow.

From: **Adam Wolf** <adam.wolf1402@gmail.com>
To: **Sarah Ross** <sarahross64@gmail.com>
June 5, 2014 10:25 pm
Subject: Re: how I fell for you

What a story! Of course more tomorrow. Goodnight, my dear Sarah. ILU

From: **Adam Wolf** <adam.wolf1402@gmail.com>
To: **Sarah Ross** <sarahross64@gmail.com>
June 6, 2014 7:10 am
Subject: Steinbeck

Up early to be with you and talk.

The Steinbeck—that was my father's. I took it from his shelf. A used book. I was with him when he "bought" it. One Saturday my father spent some rare time with me—not the ball game, no, not my father.

We went to the Saint Vincent de Paul thrift shop. He picked the book off the shelf and showed me that the price inside was 10 cents. He winked at me, took out a pencil, carefully erased the 10 cents and neatly wrote 5 cents in its place. And when we got back in the car, he gloated as if he had just pulled off a big Brinks heist.

Your memories are so vivid, funny how memory works. Now I remember when I gave you the book your look made my heart leap up. Your smile—hard to describe what happened to me, but it was a trance. The feeling—a profound warmth that surged through my body. Since we started writing I too have been awash in memories—and intense feelings—actually I've been unable to concentrate on anything else—nervously waiting for your replies.

From: **Adam Wolf** <adam.wolf1402@gmail.com>
To: **Sarah Ross** <sarahross64@gmail.com>
June 6, 2014 7:34 am
Subject: Another flash of the past

Sarah, as long as we're on the topic of memory, can you recall the one time before that 1979 call when we talked?

Maybe because today's the 6th, I do remember the date—June 7th 1968. I can picture exactly where I was standing in that old dumpy apartment of mine on 55th St., by the railroad tracks, staring out the window. And I know I was surprised that you called—and that you told me it was a predetermined day for us to reconnect. I can still feel the emotions. I was about to head off to West Virginia to become a Vista volunteer—kept me out of the draft—so I must have been anxious. And after the call, I had a sense of longing, maybe remorse, but I can't remember what we said. Can you?

From: **Sarah Ross** *<sarahross64@gmail.com>*
To: **Adam Wolf** *<adam.wolf1402@gmail.com>*
June 6, 2014 8:34 am
Subject: June 7th

Yes, I do recall phoning you June 7, 1968, missing you terribly. I was about to take off to Europe for the summer. First trip back there since childhood. Exciting!

1966. Do you remember, two years earlier, we spent one golden day together? A date. We hadn't seen each other since high school and we were about to go into our junior year in college. We were 20. It was the last time we ever saw each other.

So the call that day in '68? Before the phone call I had no idea we would stop communicating. After the phone call I chose to go into radio silence — at least for a decade.

It's odd what is coming back to me about that conversation. I now remember telling you I saved your love notes to me, and the childhood pictures you had given me. I felt very close to you that day. And you said you had put my pictures and letters to you in a hiding place in the attic of the Silsby house for safekeeping. (I didn't believe you, not until now.)

I supposed you didn't like my calling because when I tried to reminisce, you brought up Darlene Cutler and all that she had meant to you. And when I got off the phone I kept muttering to myself something like "Darlene Cutler? Darlene Cutler? That slut?" In the girls' locker room, we used to have a nickname for her, you know, "The Human Sperm Bank". I marvel that the call with me meant anything at all to you. I'm very touched to know now that you remember not just the call, but also the date.

*From: **Adam Wolf** <adam.wolf1402@gmail.com>*
*To: **Sarah Ross** <sarahross64@gmail.com>*
June 6, 2014 11:18 am
Subject: Re:June 7th

I guess I know now why I felt a sense of loss or remorse after that call. Forgive me if you can. What prompted me to push you away and talk about anyone else, I couldn't know.
Tell me what was so special, though, about June 7, 1968.

---

*From: **Sarah Ross** <sarahross64@gmail.com>*
*To: **Adam Wolf** <adam.wolf1402@gmail.com>*
June 6, 2014 11:29 am
Subject: Re:Re:June 7th

My diary records that you asked me to marry you on Feb. 15th 1961, when we had just turned 15. And we picked June 7, 1968 as our Wedding Day.

---

*From: **Adam Wolf** <adam.wolf1402@gmail.com>*
*To: **Sarah Ross** <sarahross64@gmail.com>*
June 6, 2014 12:25 pm
Subject: Golden day

I certainly remember holding you in the sunroom of your parent's apartment when I proposed to you and we set a date. I just forgot it was that day. Of course, June 7th was and maybe always will be our anniversary. And now too I thought all day about our last time together—that "golden day" all those years ago. I do recall a sweet time, but not many details. Are there more that will trigger my memory?

From: **Sarah Ross** *<sarahross64@gmail.com>*
To: **Adam Wolf** *<adam.wolf1402@gmail.com>*
June 6, 2014 1:18 pm
Subject: Re:Golden day

I do have other details, but I'll wait until I figure out how to for-
mulate them, if that's okay.

From: **Adam Wolf** *<adam.wolf1402@gmail.com>*
To: **Sarah Ross** *<sarahross64@gmail.com>*
June 6, 2014 11:18 pm
Subject: Re:Re:Golden day

Okay. I'll be patient. Long day—business dinner—this time with some
potential sponsors. It could have been a nice time, were it not for the
talk of politics—Tea Party line—ship immigrants back, they said—perhaps meant to include wetbacks like you, for all I know.
Goodnight. ILU

From: **Sarah Ross** *<sarahross64@gmail.com>*
To: **Adam Wolf** *<adam.wolf1402@gmail.com>*
June 7, 2014 4:56 am
Subject: Anniversary

Happy Anniversary, my Adam.

A sudden flash of that golden day, that last day we were ever
together, an experience that's so private and internal, it won't jog your
memory at all. We spent the day at the Cleveland Art Museum, their
50th anniversary show, 1966. Then we were in the car, at night—the
parking lot of our Roosevelt Junior High School. The street lamp the
only illumination. I was next to you, with you, intimately. Looking into
the side window, I saw my own reflection, but it wasn't my face I saw,
instead it was an amalgam of both our faces—I couldn't decipher the
parts, couldn't separate one from the other.

It's hard to put such a mystical moment into words. It cheapens it too much. But the vision had temperature, a warmth to it—beatific, glowing with some interior golden light. Most amazing. It felt so right.

I never dreamed I would have a chance to mention it to you.

From: **Adam Wolf** *<adam.wolf1402@gmail.com>*
To: **Sarah Ross** *<sarahross64@gmail.com>*
June 7, 2014 8:08 am
Subject: Golden day too

Happy Anniversary, Sweets!

In the silence here—I've read that message now a dozen times—that vision of us as one - I don't have words, only now a sensation (of longing I think) that I can't really describe. When your earlier note said you didn't know how to put the details of our "golden day" in words, I thought that something ominous had happened or I did or said something unredeemable. How the image stayed with you, Sarah—that image —is making me want to cry—a release of feeling—not sadness.
And then there are the years and years in between—all the June 7ths —which, if you wish, I could tell you about later.

From: **Sarah Ross** *<sarahross64@gmail.com>*
To: **Adam Wolf** *<adam.wolf1402@gmail.com>*
June 7, 2014 10:19 am
Subject: Re:Golden day too

Maybe I just need to hold the stillness a while longer. I'm a bit overwhelmed too by the memory—and for the occasion of being able to share it with you—and by my own reaction of tears—streaming tears —a weight off my heart too—and I know I could never have delivered this vision by phone—certainly not in person—so I'm glad we write—it will always stabilize the feelings now—always re-readable —I'm so glad you know now how deeply inside me you have lived.

More later, promise

From: **Sarah Ross** *<sarahross64@gmail.com>*
To: **Adam Wolf** *<adam.wolf1402@gmail.com>*
June 7, 2014 11:01 am
Subject:

You should know, Adam Wolf, the joy I feel when seeing your name in my inbox. No matter who else wants to get to me, I leap to you.

From: **Adam Wolf** *<adam.wolf1402@gmail.com>*
To: **Sarah Ross** *<sarahross64@gmail.com>*
June 7, 2014 12:54 pm
Subject:

I've spent the whole morning daydreaming of what I was going to say to you today and tomorrow. I think I would be in your inbox all the time, if I could.

From: **Sarah Ross** *<sarahross64@gmail.com>*
To: **Adam Wolf** *<adam.wolf1402@gmail.com>*
June 7, 2014 1:29 pm
Subject: Distracted

All along these many years I knew that no one could replace you. The idea of you. The fit. I see now how we fit. I feel the fit and marvel at it. I'm crazy and distracted. Nicole jabbers at me. I pretend to be listening, but I'm itching to get to your emails. I resent having to leave the screen for a customer. Don't they know I have better things to do with my time? Don't they know Adam Wolf might be there waiting for me? Fools.

From: **Adam Wolf** *<adam.wolf1402@gmail.com>*
To: **Sarah Ross** *<sarahross64@gmail.com>*
June 7, 2014 2:48 pm
Subject:

I'd like to be on the computer for a few hours with you too. But I have
to go on the air in a few minutes. Hold that thought. I'll do a little work
and touch your inbox in a while.

From: **Sarah Ross** *<sarahross64@gmail.com>*
To: **Adam Wolf** *<adam.wolf1402@gmail.com>*
June 7, 2014 5:17 pm
Subject:

Just wondering, Adam, is your email, our correspondence, secure
from prying eyes?
I won't be able to write much more today. Gordon's invited me out
to dinner and I better get ready.

From: **Adam Wolf** *<adam.wolf1402@gmail.com>*
To: **Sarah Ross** *<sarahross64@gmail.com>*
June 8, 2014 8:57 am
Subject: Trustworthy

To answer your question about our privacy. Sure. Absolutely. No one
here would snoop around. I trust them.
Does Gordon know we correspond?

From: **Sarah Ross** *<sarahross64@gmail.com>*
To: **Adam Wolf** *<adam.wolf1402@gmail.com>*
June 8, 2014 10:48 am
Subject: Re:Trustworthy

    Yep. I mentioned you and I were in contact. How about Lola? Does she know we're in touch?

From: **Adam Wolf** *<adam.wolf1402@gmail.com>*
To: **Sarah Ross***<sarahross64@gmail.com>*
June 8, 2014 10:53 am
Subject:Re:Re:Trustworthy

No, but she knows who you are.

From: **Sarah Ross** *<sarahross64@gmail.com>*
To: **Adam Wolf** *<adam.wolf1402@gmail.com>*
June 8, 2014 11:02 am
Subject: Amanda?

    Tell me about Amanda. She scares me. Does she know about us?

From: **Adam Wolf** *<adam.wolf1402@gmail.com>*
To: **Sarah Ross***<sarahross64@gmail.com>*
June 8, 2014 2:14 pm
Subject: Re:Amanda?

No, Amanda doesn't know about us, but she thinks I've been acting strange lately. Asks me a dozen times what's the matter. Keeps suggesting we meet over drinks to talk this over—that we don't spend enough time together anymore. Forget about it. Nothing to be scared of, Sarah. We just have a long relationship at the station. We've travelled together. We've worked on the program guide for years and years.

Lola has me doing hateful jobs around the house today. But most of my time has been spent chasing a chipmunk out. The cat likes to bring them in as souvenirs for us. You should see me with a wastebasket trying to swoop down on the scurrying, frightened thing. This isn't the first time. But just now the neighbor stopped over and mentioned that I could get it out by laying a trail of peanuts to the open door. And sure enough, it worked.

So I'm back with you, where I really need to be.

From: **Sarah Ross** <sarahross64@gmail.com>
To: **Adam Wolf** <adam.wolf1402@gmail.com>
June 8, 2014 4:23 pm
Subject: Re:Re:Amanda?

You do talk about Amanda a lot. "We" this and "we" that. What do you wish me to know about her? Are you trying to tell me something?

From: **Adam Wolf** <adam.wolf1402@gmail.com>
To: **Sarah Ross**<sarahross64@gmail.com>
June 8, 2014 5:28 pm
Subject:Re:Re:Re:Amanda?

Nothing to tell. Promise. I guess she's conditioned me to call it a "we".

From: **Sarah Ross** <sarahross64@gmail.com>
To: **Adam Wolf** <adam.wolf1402@gmail.com>
June 8, 2014 7:08 pm
Subject: Off for a week

Adam, I may have forgotten to tell you. I'm getting ready for a wonderful vacation, beginning tomorrow. I'm going up to Kennebunkport, Maine — an artist's retreat, with a teacher I had before. I do especially good work with him, learn a lot. Alas, dear friend, I kind of doubt they have internet there. I'm there until the 14th.

I'll write as soon as I return. Promise.

---

*From: **Adam Wolf** <adam.wolf1402@gmail.com>*
*To: **Sarah Ross**<sarahross64@gmail.com>*
June 8, 2014 8:05 pm
Subject: Re:Off for a week

Oh. How come you didn't tell me? How nice for you. Not so nice for me. How am I supposed to survive even a few days without you? Write if you can, but perhaps the whole point is to concentrate on your painting, uninterrupted.
I'll miss you. Hurry back. Are you going alone?
Goodnight dear Sarah. ILU

---

*From: **Sarah Ross** <sarahross64@gmail.com>*
*To: **Adam Wolf** <adam.wolf1402@gmail.com>*
June 9, 2014 9:17 am
Subject: Re:Re:Off for a week

Bye bye, Adam. It just slipped my mind. I'll miss you too! Remember me. Remind me there's good reason I'm leaving on this trip. I'll contact you if I can.
Yes, alone.

---

*From: **Adam Wolf** <adam.wolf1402@gmail.com>*
*To: **Sarah Ross**<sarahross64@gmail.com>*
June 9, 2014 9:28 am
Subject: Have fun!

You'll have a grand and rejuvenating time. Enjoy yourself. And no worries, I haven't forgotten you all these years. I'm not about to now. BYE, SARAH. Would you try to get the plane to touch down in Chicago, if only for an hour. I could meet you at O'Hare and we could hoist a few.

From: **Sarah Ross** <sarahross64@gmail.com>
To: **Adam Wolf** <adam.wolf1402@gmail.com>
June 14, 2014 5:44 pm
Subject: Back from Maine

I just walked into the house, Adam, grateful that I can finally be in touch again. Wonderful, productive time. I think it stretched me. I worked with watercolor, pen, pencil on the same page. Maybe I'll get up the courage to send you some pictures. Pleasant people on the trip. Their critique was gentle, but to the point and constructive. Great fun.

How have you been?

From: **Adam Wolf** <adam.wolf1402@gmail.com>
To: **Sarah Ross**<sarahross64@gmail.com>
June 14, 2014 7:58 pm
Subject: Re:Back from Maine

YOU'RE BACK!!! HURRAH. YOU DIDN'T FORGET ME!

The blackout was impossible.
So glad you had a great time. By all means let me see what you've produced!
Me? I've been okay this week. Same old drudge. My life is not as varied and exciting as yours. I wish I could change that. I spent most of the week longing for you.
The reunion's coming up soon. Text and emails come everyday — an on-going pep rally. People trying to convince me it's going to be transformative. I'm working myself up to it. Only a week til it's over with.

Welcome home,
Your Adam

From: **Sarah Ross** <sarahross64@gmail.com>
To: **Adam Wolf** <adam.wolf1402@gmail.com>
June 14, 2014 9:52 pm
Subject: Re:Re:Back from Maine

I just unpacked. I'm not one of those people who can put that off.

Wiped out. A long day. First getting to Boston, and then a 5-hour flight from Logan. I think we might have flown over your house. I should have waved.

Good night, dear Adam.

As far as I'm concerned, the reunion is already underway. And it IS transformative. And permanent. You and me.

From: **Adam Wolf** <adam.wolf1402@gmail.com>
To: **Sarah Ross** <sarahross64@gmail.com>
June 15, 2014 7:56 pm
Subject: Back from the future

Sarah, my love, picture this filmic episode:

We're 14 years old. It's 1960, a late spring afternoon. A path. Cain Park. I'm there waiting for you.

The dialogue begins:

Sarah: "Adam, where on earth have you been? I've been frantic. Your parents have been frantic."

Adam: "Been away, far away. Actually I've travelled to the future. Landed in 2014. Guess what? Everybody has air conditioning. Everyone has a phone you can keep in your pocket. Anybody can order movies and watch instantly on their portable televisions. And, guess what else, my love? Cleveland still hasn't won a World Series. But most important, you and I are together. What do you say to that?"

From: **Sarah Ross** <sarahross64@gmail.com>
To: **Adam Wolf** <adam.wolf1402@gmail.com>
June 15, 2014 8:04 pm
Subject: Re:Back from the future

I would have said, "You mean we're together six feet under, in adjoining plots?"

From: **Adam Wolf** <adam.wolf1402@gmail.com>
To: **Sarah Ross**<sarahross64@gmail.com>
June 15, 2014 8:17 pm
Subject: Re:Re:Back from the future

I'd tell you to hold on to your hat and not to be upset.
I'd say: "Except for one day and two phone calls, we haven't been together since high school — for most of our lives. Half a century later, though, we're back together again! Come to the future with me now, Sarah, and we'll skip the years in between. They're not worth it anyway."
Sarah, would you have come with me then, into the future? What would you have said?

From: **Sarah Ross** <sarahross64@gmail.com>
To: **Adam Wolf** <adam.wolf1402@gmail.com>
June 15, 2014 8:31 pm
Subject: Stop pulling my leg

No, I certainly would not have come with you. And I would have said, "Okay, Mr. Looney Tunes. *Adios. Aufwiedersehen.* You're crazier than I ever guessed. I'm not going with you anywhere, not now, not in the future. I'm going home."
I would have added, "Fess up and tell me the truth now. Where have you really been since Monday afternoon?" That's what I would have said,

And furthermore, I would have thrown in, "Oh, I get it, you're breaking up with me. Your voo-doo glimpse into the future, HA! Just a cover so you can wander off into the sunset with Claire Carlsen. Yeah, and when you turn old and your girlfriends don't want you anymore, then you'll expect me to push you around in your wheelchair, right? No deal." I would say, "See you, chum!"

From: **Adam Wolf** <adam.wolf1402@gmail.com>
To: **Sarah Ross**<sarahross64@gmail.com>
June 15, 2014 9:13 pm
Subject: Not pulling your leg

But I would insist I was telling the truth: "Au contraire, my Sarah. We may be in our late 60s, but not decrepit, not at all. A few ailments, but we avoid doctors, so we don't dwell on them. Besides you and I have Medicare". (And you would have asked me what Medicare was.)
 "Most amazing, Sarah," I would continue, "I never would have believed it either, if I hadn't seen it with my own eyes. Two septuagenarians rolling around the bed all night, a blowjob every morning."
What would you have said then, if I had promised you that?

From: **Sarah Ross** <sarahross64@gmail.com>
To: **Adam Wolf** <adam.wolf1402@gmail.com>
June 15, 2014 9:27 pm
Subject: Re:Not pulling your leg

1960? I would have asked, "Adam, what's a blowjob?"

From: **Sarah Ross** <sarahross64@gmail.com>
To: **Adam Wolf** <adam.wolf1402@gmail.com>
June 16, 2014 4:53 pm
Subject: picturing you

I just found some old photos — one of them from back when you were 14 and runner up in the Cuyahoga County Spelling Bee. (I bet you've never forgotten that "committee" has two "e's".) So thin, your body 6 inches deep, that charcoal suit with the slightly textured jacket. I knew it well. Put my head on it a lot. And that 50s hair cut, kind of adorable. I hope your ears still show. They're so cute — what a look — a kind of pompadour, short on the side, heavy on top and curled over, like James Dean. The hair such an amazing shade of sunshine.

Could you send me some recent pictures of you?

From: **Adam Wolf** <adam.wolf1402@gmail.com>
To: **Sarah Ross**<sarahross64@gmail.com>
June 16, 2014 4:53 pm
Subject: Re: picturing you

Ah, and that itchy wool suit, wore it to dances and it reminds me of my dance floor ineptitude — what a memory. I used to rehearse my "dance steps" in my closet, the only full-length mirror in my bedroom. It was hopeless. The quasi-pompadour is the handiwork of Bernie Fishman, long recognized as North America's worst barber. He led a fifty-year parade of unfortunate haircuts. As far as I could tell, the "parade" consisted only of my brother with his bi-weekly chop job—and me scalped every other month. You always knew he was a bad barber cause no one ever waited there—no one else was ever in there. Across the street—at Irv's barbershop—Sat. mornings, filled to the ceiling. Even on Saturdays there was never a wait at Bernie's. Did you know that Bernie would stand on the street and accost men passing by to tell them they looked like hell and needed a haircut? Fishman—a good name for him. Smelled like a three-day-old carp. His rotundity was accentuated by a filthy smock he wore, which started at his chin and descended at a 45-degree angle because of his girth.

In his barbershop none of that Vitalis or Brylcreem or any other good smellin' stuff. Not even disinfectant. Not one little bucket of combs at Barney's. And you were out of there in a matter of minutes. I remember bzzzzzzzzz and a couple of clips at the scissors. Eventually I stopped going to Bernie's cause my mother bought some miniature hair clippers. She announced we would never pay for haircuts again. Didn't know what she was doing. Cut too much, if you recall. I hated it. You were nice about it. You assured me it would grow back soon and that it didn't look all that bad. I think that's why I loved you.

I do remember some of the pictures you gave me—your pink prom dress with crinoline, pink high heels dyed to match—and standing in the kind of affected 1960 girl's pose—frozen in ballet 1st position, at an angle to the camera.

Sarah, I've scanned some pictures of myself for you and will send. Would you mind also letting me have some recent pictures of you? I've seen a couple of photos on the web. One at an event where you're standing in front of a group pointing to a picture. You looked radiant, and also, if I may say so, quite sexy in that saffron chiffon *schmatah*. Your hair was short—haphazard—I love the look. It was even a little gray, but I could recognize you easily. The broad features—high cheekbones, large eyes, sensuous lips, and there was that smile of yours, as ever, warm, too wide for your mouth. I could go on rhapsodizing. Those theatrically dark and heavy eyebrows. Still there. You've never been the tallest in a crowd, but you stand out. The people around you look mesmerized. More pictures, please.

*From: **Sarah Ross** <sarahross64@gmail.com>*
*To: **Adam Wolf** <adam.wolf1402@gmail.com>*
June 16, 2014 7:08 pm
Subject: Re:Re: picturing you

I know that picture. A gallery opening of my watercolors, 2007. That photograph is one of my favorites too, but I need to inform you that I don't look like that anymore. That opening was the last hurrah of "cute Sarah". The next day my face collapsed and my waistline expanded. I'll take a close look at your photos first, and then airbrush some of mine, if I end up sending any at all. (Oh, my hair is less gray now—an ash brown with some blonde highlights.)

---

*From: **Adam Wolf** <adam.wolf1402@gmail.com>*
*To: **Sarah Ross**<sarahross64@gmail.com>*
June 16, 2014 7:25 pm
Subject: Here's me

Oh, pish-posh. Don't you realize I would find you beautiful in any permutation?
I gathered some pictures. Be prepared. The old Jewish guy who appears in these is all that's left of me. Don't open the attachments before you read this:
Still a respectable helping of unkempt tresses, but visibly thinned, no more pompadour. The style is now called "be glad you have hair at all". Dishwater blonde mingling with gray. Meanness creases in my face. And just out of camera range, a slight paunch. Stooped shoulders but still 5'8½" +/-, and, incidentally, also hidden from the lens—white nose hairs and a quart of earwax.
So here are a few pictures– in front of the Evanston house and at the station.

From: **Sarah Ross** *<sarahross64@gmail.com>*
To: **Adam Wolf** *<adam.wolf1402@gmail.com>*
June 16, 2014 8:24 pm
Subject: the photographs

Oh gosh, the photo in front of your house is perfect, even the defiant pose, the sleeves rolled up. I like the way your arms are crossed. Anyway, my man, you look amazingly good — angular, and at your fighting weight. I'd forgotten what strong, square shoulders you had — manly now — hips still narrow, like a toreador. It's all coming back to me, even the deep blue eyes that like to squint, though now some impressively heavy blonde eyebrows, huh? You look goddamn 39 years old, 42 tops. Okay, now it's for sure. There is no way I'll send you a photo of me. I look my age. They'll haul me in for pedophilia. I'll star in the next episode of *To Catch a Predator*.

Hey, when was this station picture taken? You look dapper in the Windsor- knotted tie. And who's that dame in the peacock blue sheath standing close to you, glowering down? Looks like a tall, stony Nancy Reagan with a skunk on her head. What the hell is the band of silver on black hair all about? Amanda, I'm guessing. Tell me more about her. She looks scary.

From: **Adam Wolf** *<adam.wolf1402@gmail.com>*
To: **Sarah Ross***<sarahross64@gmail.com>*
June 17, 2014 12:36 pm
Subject: Your picture?

Glad you liked the photos, Sarah. Yes, that's Amanda. What else can I tell you? She's the owner now. Took it over after her husband died. Yes, Amanda can be stern, intimidating (though she also has a softer, more nurturing side). She has style. My tie is knotted well because Amanda insisted on tying it for me. You noticed she's more dressed up than the rest of us, spent two hours getting ready for the shoot — sometimes she's a bit insecure — kept adjusting her dress and asking me, at least 5 times, how it looked.

I have to confess the other picture, with arms crossed, is 8 years old. Just so you should know, my face has collapsed since then too.

Come on. Now it's your turn, my good woman, to send me a picture.

From: **Sarah Ross** <sarahross64@gmail.com>
To: **Adam Wolf** <adam.wolf1402@gmail.com>
June 17, 2014 4:56 pm
Subject: Re:Your picture?

So, now that I've seen that station photo, I have more reason not to reciprocate. I'm downright disheveled compared to Amanda. Nothing like her coiffed perfection. I bet she wears extensions. No one her age can have that full a head of hair. Maybe I should dye mine with a skunk streak too. Maybe I should grow it long too and consider extensions. Maybe I should lose 50 lbs. and grow 7 inches taller. Amanda looks noble, me hardly. I love the station picture of you. I guess there was no way to crop her out.

The other day in an elevator mirror I glimpsed a wrinkled old woman who turned out to be me. Forget about pictures, my friend.

From: **Adam Wolf** <adam.wolf1402@gmail.com>
To: **Sarah Ross**<sarahross64@gmail.com>
June 17, 2014 7:05 pm
Subject: Re:Re:Your picture?

I'm sure I will still love the way you look. I've always loved the way you looked—sweet, angelic. Just send the pictures, damn it. Look, Sarah, Amanda isn't as bad as you think. I know Amanda is expensively "coiffed", and can be imperious and flinty. But, again, in her defense, she's been loyal to me since she inherited the station, 25 years ago. Anyway, enough with your self-consciousness. Let me at least see a photo of you. Remember it's me. It's Adam, the boy who has always adored Sarah. Go shoot a selfie right now and send it over.

---

*From: **Sarah Ross** <sarahross64@gmail.com>*
*To: **Adam Wolf** <adam.wolf1402@gmail.com>*
June 17, 2014 7:29 pm
Subject: me

Oh Adam, okay. I trust you to be kind and not honest. Here are a couple of pictures. One on Gordon's boat, a few weeks ago. And, to lay my cards on the table, the other from a few years back when I had no hair after my chemotherapy.

---

*From: **Adam Wolf** <adam.wolf1402@gmail.com>*
*To: **Sarah Ross**<sarahross64@gmail.com>*
June 17, 2014 8:00 pm
Subject:

I'm so sorry. Can you talk about the chemo? I had no idea.

---

*From: **Sarah Ross** <sarahross64@gmail.com>*
*To: **Adam Wolf** <adam.wolf1402@gmail.com>*
June 17, 2014 8:24 pm
Subject: I'm okay now

Of course you couldn't have known. And I don't like to dwell on it much. Only my two closest friends Deborah and Carol knew and helped me through it. And of course Harold knew and tried to help, but had trouble accepting it. It was breast cancer. I underwent a double mastectomy, radiation, chemo. He didn't say it turned him off, but it turned him off. I couldn't deal with his revulsion when I had to concentrate on staying positive.

This was six years ago and I have a clean bill of health now (and my implants are a work of art, in progress). It used to be that before all my follow-up visits I kept busy by writing my last will and testament. I'm getting easier about this too as time passes. And I get on with life more or less optimistically because I don't like to allow adversity to define me.

From: **Adam Wolf** <adam.wolf1402@gmail.com>
To: **Sarah Ross**<sarahross64@gmail.com>
June 17, 2014 8:55 pm
Subject: Re: I'm okay now

I'm grateful you're okay. Excuse me for saying so, but am I right to assume your late husband could be a cold, unfeeling sort?

From: **Sarah Ross** <sarahross64@gmail.com>
To: **Adam Wolf** <adam.wolf1402@gmail.com>
June 17, 2014 9:33 pm
Subject:

Cold? Unfeeling? I suppose so. But he's gone, so what should it matter? Anyway, that's in the past. Let's focus on the "now" and the good part of the past.

Let's focus on tomorrow and the day after that and the day after that. So much to talk about.

Good night, Adam dear.

From: **Sarah Ross** <sarahross64@gmail.com>
To: **Adam Wolf** <adam.wolf1402@gmail.com>
June 19, 2014 8:12 am
Subject: Go Cleveland! "Best location in the nation"

Getting close! Tomorrow!! Are you excited about the reunion, about going home to Cleveland? You know, when I go back there to see my mother and Esther, I really don't "do" Cleveland anymore. I miss that. And I defend my city to all those fools who've never been there, and make fun of it. I tell them about what the Terminal Tower looked like, and how awed they would be by the grandeur of the Public Library, the old movie palaces—the RKO, the Alhambra (at 105th and Euclid?).

Do you remember how much fun it was to hang out at that glass-covered Arcade downtown? Magical. Or Euclid Beach? Bumper cars.

The Fun House where a blast of air puffed up my Aunt Edie's skirt. And I defy people who mock Cleveland to name five museums in America better than the Cleveland Art Museum. Or two symphony orchestras greater than the Cleveland Symphony under George Szell. Ignoramuses those people who knock Cleveland. Idiots. I loved discovering the city with you. I have such fond memories of it.

From: **Adam Wolf** *<adam.wolf1402@gmail.com>*
To: **Sarah Ross***<sarahross64@gmail.com>*
June 19, 2014 7:15 pm
Subject: Cleveland. "The mistake on the lake"

Brutal day at the office. Sorry to take so long to respond. Had to work through lunch hour so I could get everything done before taking off tomorrow morning, early. I'm mostly packed.

I need to confess the term "fond memories" of Cleveland doesn't work for me. Kind of an oxymoron. Sure, I cherish my moments with you in Cleveland—Cumberland Pool, sledding at Cain Park, riding downtown on the Rapid, chocolate phosphate at my Dad's drugstore, listening to the Indians' games, lying next to each other in your sunroom playing 50 kisses. These were all golden Cleveland moments.

I could shake off the world when we were together, for a few hours, but then the real life of home loomed. My father threatened any euphoria I could feel. "Where were you today?" And no matter the response, "Why don't you try doing something productive for a change?"

He dominates my memories of growing up in Cleveland. Racing off to spend sweaty afternoons in the airless storeroom at his drugstore. At home forced to stay mute while His Surliness held court at the dinner table. My mother in a perpetual state of anxiety, trying to mollify him. You want a memory of Cleveland? Late at night, hidden in the cramped little stairway to the basement, I would sit with the phone cord stretched to its limit, out of earshot, whispering love tones to you. Until, that is, Commandant Wolf emerged from the living room—like Hitler strutting out from the bunker—and proclaimed the call was over.

Want fond memories of Cleveland? For me they're all tainted by Emanuel Wolf and the oppression, malaise and despair that he spewed into the air of the city.

Downtown Cleveland? When you remember the beauty of the public library and the arcade in Public Square, I remember aging, rotting buildings covered in pigeon shit, my father cursing cause he could never find a parking space.

The Cleveland Art Museum? It shaped your love of art—to me the memory of it recalls Manny Wolf leading forced marches through the galleries on Sunday afternoon.

The Tribe? All I recall are rallies in the ninth, squelched with double plays—out of the pennant chase by June. My father leaping to his feet and applauding when the Indians lost. Cleveland. Bah. Humbug.

---

*From: **Sarah Ross** <sarahross64@gmail.com>*
*To: **Adam Wolf** <adam.wolf1402@gmail.com>*
June 19, 2014 8:20 pm
Subject: you forget the good parts

But there's always what we called "The Sanctuary" because we were hidden from everyone there. Out in the woods, over on Green Road, where we watched the streamliners shoot past. As far as I recall, you loved Cleveland there.

---

*From: **Adam Wolf** <adam.wolf1402@gmail.com>*
*To: **Sarah Ross** <sarahross64@gmail.com>*
June 19, 2014 8:29 pm
Subject: Re:you forget the good parts

I can only remember despair that we weren't aboard those trains.

---

*From: **Sarah Ross** <sarahross64@gmail.com>*
*To: **Adam Wolf** <adam.wolf1402@gmail.com>*
June 19, 2014 9:05 pm
Subject: I wanna tag along to the reunion

You hid those feelings from me. I'm so sorry. I think I hid a lot from you too. But I hope your time in Cleveland this weekend will be enjoyable. A request: would you consider me your long-distance date and take me with you to the reunion, you know — texts and photos and email — the whole 2014 arsenal of instant gratification?

---

*From: **Adam Wolf** <adam.wolf1402@gmail.com>*
*To: **Sarah Ross**<sarahross64@gmail.com>*
June 19, 2014 9:21 pm
Subject: Re: I wanna tag along to the reunion

You bet! I was planning to have you there with me, right in my pocket, all the time.

---

*From: **Adam Wolf** <adam.wolf1402@gmail.com>*
*To: **Paul Bishop** <Paul.R.Bishop@dewey.com>*
June 20, 2014 9:22 am
Subject: En route to reunion

Paul,

Greetings from the Booth Tarkington Service Oasis, Interstate 90. I'm heading back to Cleveland Heights for my 50th Reunion. Determined to no longer dither. When I get there I'm ready to confess to the troops that I have not lived up to the campaign promises that got me elected "Person Most Likely to Succeed" of the 1964 Class. FIFTY YEARS! Just imagine what my comrades will boast about in their allotted 250 words. Let's see — Jim Sherman, Star of Remedial Classes (and the Gridiron), now is " pleased to accept my second U.N. special humanitarian achievement award for tele-neurosurgery services to the African subcontinent".

Then of course, there's Morty Friedlander, once upon a time "The Little Nebbish Who Followed Me Around", casually revealing this: "After assuming occupancy of our 24-room cottage in Palm Beach, my bride and I caught our breaths by treating our four children and eight talented grandchildren to a nine-week cruise from San Francisco to the Pitcairn Island, where we reenacted the torching of the H.M.S. Bounty."

And then, Paul ... there's me: "Runner-up for New Chicago Radio Voice of the Year, 1982. One and a half spousal commitments. One expensively-educated, but underpaid son. The largest prostate in Northern Illinois and the smallest IRA on Morgan Stanley's books."

---

*From: **Adam Wolf** <adam.wolf1402@gmail.com>*
*To: **Sarah Ross**<sarahross64@gmail.com>*
June 20, 2014 3:18 pm
Subject: Arrived

Checked into the Hampton Inn in Beachwood and went out sightseeing. Drove through Cleveland Heights to see what it's like now. Seems joyless. No kids around. Air hangs heavy around Cedar and Taylor. Found Bernie Fishman's barbershop turned into a Tai Kwon Do studio. The buildings, though, their proportions are familiar, also the terrain—the dip down Cedar Hill. It's summer. Where is everyone? Seems lifeless. Maybe no one lives here and they use the whole joint as a movie set—a post-Apocalypse flick.

---

*From: **Sarah Ross** <sarahross64@gmail.com>*
*To: **Adam Wolf** <adam.wolf1402@gmail.com>*
June 20, 2014 3:51 pm
Subject: nostalgia?

Sometimes when I'm back there, I drive through the old streets and have strange associations. One corner near Heights High—a conversation with someone about Bob Hope and how he lived right there once. That his brother still lived on Meadowbrook, near your house. Peculiar feelings. Entered the high school parking lot, where I had a flash of the Driver Ed. coach pulling up in his dual-control Chevy. And then another of throwing a softball mightily from one end of the girls' gym field to the other. And at the same spot a flash of you teaching me some hobo song about jumping the freights "and he slammed the boxcar door". Memory is a jumble, isn't it? Each corner contains fragments of all the thoughts that went on there.

From: **Adam Wolf** <adam.wolf1402@gmail.com>
To: **Sarah Ross**<sarahross64@gmail.com>
June 20, 2014 4:00 pm
Subject:

Right now I'm focused on our sacred locations and am following the route from 3424 Silsby to your front steps at 1677 Colonial Drive.

From: **Sarah Ross** <sarahross64@gmail.com>
To: **Adam Wolf** <adam.wolf1402@gmail.com>
June 20, 2014 4:09 pm
Subject:

   Confession. Over the years, I've traced it too. Always struck by how nice I find these simple old houses now. And how embarrassed I used to be by them.

From: **Adam Wolf** <adam.wolf1402@gmail.com>
To: **Sarah Ross**<sarahross64@gmail.com>
June 20, 2014 4:23 pm
Subject:

I never looked at the houses. I just resented the distance between our two places. I look at the houses now — and don't see any charm, I'm afraid. I wonder if they always looked dilapidated and depressing. Sagging porches on Goodnor, not to be believed, propped up with scrap wood. They look used up, ready for demolition.

*From: **Adam Wolf** <adam.wolf1402@gmail.com>*
*To: **Sarah Ross**<sarahross64@gmail.com>*
June 20, 2014 7:08 pm
Subject: A little Raymond Chandler

Pizza Party at the Ressler Estate

It was one of those sullen stone chateaus off Fairmont — the type of joint you'd drive by as a kid and your mother would lean over to your father in the front seat and whisper so you and your brother could hear in the back, how the Mrs. ran off with the minister while the long-suffering husband was on business in Barcelona — how he came back — found a note on his pillow — took his Remington and sprayed his brains over the newly-finished marble floor in his wife's bathroom — the one she insisted she had to fix up — on his dime.

*From: **Sarah Ross** <sarahross64@gmail.com>*
*To: **Adam Wolf** <adam.wolf1402@gmail.com>*
June 20, 2014 7:11 pm
Subject: the party?

Hey, Raymond Chandler, what about the party?

*From: **Adam Wolf** <adam.wolf1402@gmail.com>*
*To: **Sarah Ross**<sarahross64@gmail.com>*
June 20, 2014 7:18 pm
Subject: A little Raymond Chandler, continued

And your brother and you would turn around and stare through the back window of your dad's jalopy, back down Fairmount Boulevard — back to the chateau a block away — and thrill that such wonderful things could happen so close to home.

From: **Sarah Ross** <sarahross64@gmail.com>
To: **Adam Wolf** <adam.wolf1402@gmail.com>
June 20, 2014 7:37 pm
Subject: Pizza party???

Hey Adam, seriously, let me in on what's really happening? I'm there with you, you know. Fairmont Blvd. Always intimidating. You and I would drive by when I got my license, to gawk. Never had friends there. One of those neighborhoods too good for the likes of me.

From: **Adam Wolf** <adam.wolf1402@gmail.com>
To: **Sarah Ross**<sarahross64@gmail.com>
June 20, 2014 7:40 pm
Subject: Pizza party

The *goyim* who once lived here moved way out to Chagrin Falls, I think, and raised Christian horses. Okay, Sarah — now I'm in the vehicle — out front — watching our once-upon-a-time playmates silently shuffling into Ressler's grand manse — from a distance I recognize none of them. Actually the house is like the ones my father used to rail about. He'd call them "monstrosities", "conspicuous consumption" — declared that one day they would be owned by the "workers" and turned into Museums of the Struggle.
I suppose I'm put into a Marxist frame of mind sitting here waiting for the valet to park my car. Yes, a valet to take my car. I haven't trusted valet parking since the Von Unruhs tossed the keys to their Lexus to some scam artist in front of the Udupi Palace, in broad daylight.

From: **Adam Wolf** <adam.wolf1402@gmail.com>
To: **Sarah Ross**<sarahross64@gmail.com>
June 20, 2014 7:56 pm
Subject: Dress code

Sarah, it looks like I'm woefully overdressed — in a tie and tweed sports jacket and a starched blue dress shirt. I see shorts, monochromatic short sleeves, chinos with the belts pulled too tight. Even some guys with t-shirts—makes sense, I guess, for 89 degrees. The women are all dressed the same. Is that possible? Grayish, yellowish floppy pants.

From: **Sarah Ross** *<sarahross64@gmail.com>*
To: **Adam Wolf** *<adam.wolf1402@gmail.com>*
June 20, 2014 8:00 pm
Subject: Re:Dress code

Oy!

ADAM > SARAH   6/20/14 8:02 pm

Enter the portico into the Great Room — lights ablaze — ceiling so high that the Cirque du Soleil could be swinging from the rafters and you might not notice.

ADAM   8:06 pm

What am I doing here on the geriatric ward? Aged humanoids spied at a distance, huddled in their groups.

ADAM   8:10 pm

The women seem buoyant and still full of sass. The men, not so much.
They're like the Yiddish Theater version of Invasion of the Body Snatchers.

ADAM   8:23 pm

I focus on the law firm of Krasner, Jensen, and O'Connor off in the corner — gesticulating with drooping pizza slices. Genelli's pizza. Crappy then. Still is. Looks like it was made in Home Ec. class. Bad Food Nostalgia.

ADAM   8:54 pm

The guys greet me with civility. But you'd be startled — Krasner's no longer ebullient. He and O'Connor speak in heavy five-word sentences. And Jensen needs to turn his whole body to carry on a conversation to the right or left.

AMANDA > ADAM   8:56 pm

Adam — I've been at the station since 8 am. That makes 12 hours, so far. 5x I tried calling. Please pick up. Is there a reason you're not inclined to answer? While you're away on your sentimental journey, I still have a station to run. We agreed you'd stay in touch. Let me know if it's too much to ask.

*From: **Adam Wolf** <adam.wolf1402@gmail.com>*
*To: **Sarah Ross**<sarahross64@gmail.com>*
June 20, 2014 9:01 pm
Subject: Self-reflection

I have retreated to the hallway mirror. I stare at myself, Sarah, am I in the right place? Am I time-worn too? Here is the overdressed Adam Wolf—some remnants of boyhood in the eyes—hair still unkempt —nose still proportional—same strong jaw line, wouldn't you say? But somehow 40 years have been added since I looked in the hotel mirror an hour ago. Now I notice the creases in my forehead, the stoop in my own shoulders, the folds of my neck. Only the secret knowledge of us checks the old man in me.

ADAM > SARAH   6/20/14 9:12 pm

Off with the tie and sports jacket — some tall elderly woman smelling of lavender smiles my way.

ADAM   9:20 pm

Now their faces start to focus. I recognize many of them through their age masks.

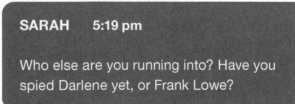

SARAH   5:19 pm

Who else are you running into? Have you spied Darlene yet, or Frank Lowe?

ADAM   9:28 pm

I thought Lowe died.

SARAH   9:32 pm

No. Far from it. His Facebook page is filled with class pictures from 6th, 7th and 9th grades. He'll be there, dead or alive.

ADAM   9:40 pm

No sign of Darlene. But Audrey Handler's here. Haven't spoken to her since U of C days. She just brushed by and whispered that I looked happy — at least that's what I think she said. My hearing's off, especially with the background din. Maybe she said I looked "hapless".

SARAH   9:48 pm

I love Audrey. She and I spent some days together a couple of years ago when she came to San Diego promoting that book — you know — the one on Gray Divorce. She's a fascinating human being, still looks fresh and boyish, doesn't she? Every now and again I tune into her TED lecture on YouTube, just to smile at the sound of her husky voice.

ADAM   9:57 pm

Death is, in fact, also a guest at this party.
I miss Danny Singer. He would have been
here. He should be here. Wrong that he isn't.

ADAM   10:32 pm

And now, semi-retired, but none-the-less insufferable
grain executive extraordinaire Maureen Spiegel — that
effusive grin — she leans in with all her 89 teeth
gleaming — seems elated — doesn't look too bad at
all — doesn't seem to remember the insults she
directed at me not so long ago — wants maybe to
make it up. The hug lasts too long. She wants to
know where Lola is. "Shit, I left her in the car," I say.
No smile.

ADAM   10:48 pm

I've mentioned your name as I make the rounds and
find myself talking loudly, wanting everyone to hear
we've been in touch. In a few moments I will slip your
name into another conversation.

"Sara Ross says hello — yes, we speak all the time —
yes still in La Jolla — couldn't make it — asked me to
be her surrogate — we're planning to see each other
soon —maybe pick up where we left off", I half joke.
They smile and nod.

> **SARAH**   10:53 pm
>
> "Saradam" was one word to them. Nice to know they still seem to like it.

> **SARAH**   11:15 pm
>
> Oh, do not stop telling me all your impressions. Vicariously — that's how I like this experience.

> **ADAM**   11:35 pm
>
> Let me fill you in later.

From: **Adam Wolf** <adam.wolf1402@gmail.com>
To: **Sarah Ross**<sarahross64@gmail.com>
June 21, 2014 1:16 am
Subject: Best Memory of the Pizza Party

Sarah, back at the hotel. Here's the highlight of the evening:

At about 11:30, at the center of the kitchen, close by the cold pizza slices, I found a weighty discussion already in progress. It was John Loeb, Phil Gerson, Davie Miller and Morty Epstein—about the urgency that comes from discovering you are 68 years old.

Davie declares that as of now there are only two more years left to enjoy our "youth". No one in the group of us laughs at the notion. My son Michael would. It goes on. John Loeb claims, "Whatever you haven't accomplished by 68 must be accomplished now. The drive to sustain security and gather riches must now give way to more soulful pursuits".

Phil Gerson believes that it's time to confront secret, long-suppressed desires—and finally embrace them or kill them off for good. So I ask him what his dreams for old age are. He shrugs and looks past me. "Travel, I guess."

John Loeb volunteers that he sold his electrical supply business 3 years ago, moved into Philadelphia from the suburbs, rented a studio and starting crafting metal sculptures. Now he's so successful he's hired three artists and never goes to the studio anymore.

Morty looks on, befuddled.

The urgency of being 68—the discussion touches me for a very specific reason. Sarah, *our* reunion has already started to reignite the buried longings. For love and adventure and expression I haven't sensed for years. I guess I'm not explaining this very coherently.

Anyway, John asks, "What about you, Adam? You still at that radio station in Chicago? Gonna stay there? Gonna retire? Any plans for the last few weeks of your youth?"

I have a proposal for them. "Let's ditch everything—go out and reenact *On the Road*, page by page."

The conversation stops. They look back at me stunned.

Loeb spontaneously blurts out that he's with me.

Davie pulls the edges of his lips up and narrows his eyes, as though contemplating an unorthodox, but nonetheless valid, solution to one of his math proofs. Then he nods two or three times in assent.

Morty Epstein continues his serial befuddlements. "You can probably get a copy of *On the Road* at Barnes and Noble. I have a coupon from last year that I haven't used."

Gerson's eyes glaze over. He peers deep into the mist. "OK, yeah. Me too. Let's go. *On the Road*. And Adam, you'll be our Dean Moriarty. Plan the trip, email the details and I'm with you. I'll go."

The conversation eventually returns to Earth: "Where you staying?", "Selling your house?", "Children all right?"

But, for a moment, I saw Adam (Dean Moriarty) Wolf, red bandana around his neck, brown bomber jacket, white tee shirt, 3 days growth of beard, rolled-up jeans, barely lit cigarette dangling from the lips, leading rowdy septuagenarians facing their end-of-life crisis—the accountant, the real estate broker, the math teacher, the radiologist—through a driving rain, down the embankment to the freight yards in Sioux City, Iowa, to snag the westbound, speed across the plains, then over the gray misty mountains to the shining Pacific and FRISCO, all of us taking turns singing something ribald about other carefree, irresponsible old men.

Jumping off the freight in Elko. To get a bite. At Denny's maybe. This time, of course, we'll use Phil Gerson's credit card. Eyeing nicely-aged women at a close-by table, Loeb and I sidle up to them. They're in Denny's for the Senior Special. They all live nearby at Freedom Village — husbands six feet under — wouldn't mind the company. Boys, the mountains and the coast will have to wait!!!

For twenty seconds we were sedentary, creature-comforted 68 year-old men seriously contemplating their escape to jazz, broads, and manic all-night car rides. And I, Adam, the ring leader. Sarah, it was a glorious moment

You want to know the funny part? After the conversation, Morty, never exactly a Jack Kerouac kind of guy, comes up to me, "What the hell was that all about?"

---

*From: **Sarah Ross**<sarahross64@gmail.com>*
*To: **Adam Wolf** <adam.wolf1402@gmail.com>*
June 21, 2014 8:40 am
Subject: On the Road again

Adam, wonderful to see you feeling so alive, sparking that in the others. But, geez. Kerouac again? Don't know about that. Thinking back on it, when you entered that Kerouac phase, I had to exit. To me Kerouac was a dangerous brew of testosterone poisoning for the guys your age. But, somehow, now I find this romantic impulse charming, the thought that life hasn't closed down just because time has passed. I'll tell you what. Ditch those gals at Denny's and dump those guys in Denver. I'll meet you at the Dee-Dee Diner in Gallup. Be there.

From: **Adam Wolf** *<adam.wolf1402@gmail.com>*
To: **Sarah Ross***<sarahross64@gmail.com>*
June 21, 2014 10:10 am
Subject: Mystery figure

Mulling over a mystery figure at Ressler's. Have you ever heard of George Wolfsohn? No one I talked to at the reunion had. A guy with that nametag was sniffing stray women all night. Never laid eyes on the guy before, and he would have sat behind me in classes, don't you think? He must sneak into reunions to hit on 70-year-old women—probably for money.
He's the only person who ran out of space, trumpeting himself in the reunion book. Most of it's about where he stuck his dick in the 70's. He would tell more about his phallic expeditions, he wrote, but he didn't want to make people jealous. Jealous?

From: **Sarah Ross***<sarahross64@gmail.com>*
To: **Adam Wolf** *<adam.wolf1402@gmail.com>*
June 21, 2014 10:15 am
Subject: Re:Mystery figure

George Wolfsohn, sure. Kinda cute once. Kept to himself. Shy. Carried my books home once. Spoke hardly a word. What's your problem with him?

From: **Adam Wolf** *<adam.wolf1402@gmail.com>*
To: **Sarah Ross***<sarahross64@gmail.com>*
June 21, 2014 10:21 am
Subject: Re:Re:Mystery figure

My problem? Am I like this guy? There was something depressing about it. I wondered if I was like him, an aging schlemiel living in the past. Sarah, are we living in the past?

From: **Sarah Ross**<sarahross64@gmail.com>
To: **Adam Wolf** <adam.wolf1402@gmail.com>
June 21, 2014 10:32 am
Subject: touching down on the past, not living there

Adam, I certainly don't live in the past. In fact, I'm relieved not to be there any longer. We have a common past that allows us to build a present. Our connection is immune to the passage of time. We travel back there as a way of talking about who we are now, don't you think?

From: **Adam Wolf** <adam.wolf1402@gmail.com>
To: **Sarah Ross**<sarahross64@gmail.com>
June 21, 2014 10:41 am
Subject: Re:touching down on the past, not living there

Right!
You know, Sarah, I think tonight I'll write you after I get back from the dinner dance at Crestwood Country Club, if that's all right. I just need to experience it.

From: **Sarah Ross**<sarahross64@gmail.com>
To: **Adam Wolf** <adam.wolf1402@gmail.com>
June 21, 2014 10:50 am
Subject:

Just as well. Gordon's invited me to a place near the shore I've never been and heard is great, a cute name, Whiskandladle. I'll report later too.

I hope you have a great time tonight. Think of me. Can't wait to hear. But, Adam, I feel funny asking this of you — an irrational request, but indulge me. If you dance with someone, don't tell me about it. And if you could keep from slow dancing ... oh, never mind.

From: **Adam Wolf** <adam.wolf1402@gmail.com>
To: **Sarah Ross**<sarahross64@gmail.com>
June 21, 2014 10:53 am
Subject:

Okay.

From: **Adam Wolf** <adam.wolf1402@gmail.com>
To: **Sarah Ross**<sarahross64@gmail.com>
June 21, 2014 11:57 pm
Subject: The Grand Ball

Before I left the hotel, I changed clothes 5 times, not because it was grazing 100, but because I wasn't sure what "casual dressy attire" meant. Is that a tie with blue jeans or is it trousers and a polo shirt? So I settled on black dress pants, a blue dress shirt and a tie. I planned my entrance so I could hedge my bet—quickly put on something or take it off—my jacket over my arm, my tie loose, my sleeves rolled up. Why, at 68, should I care what anyone thinks about how I'm dressed? But, for some reason, I do.

The Crestwood Country Club. Looked like the usual WASP antebellum mansion—white with a southern portico and quiet, whispering signs: Entrance, Members Only, Employee entry at rear. "This is your special retreat in the woods, your escape from the hoi poloi."

The oppressive heat followed me in. The air conditioner apparently has fizzled. I was fashionably on time, but the place was already jammed with our old people, used to Early Bird Specials. They were all in a state of animated suspension only millimeters from the trough of hors-d'oeuvres. At first no one talked. They only chowed down, getting their money's worth.

The entire evening was run like the first day of boot camp at Parris Island. You had to break rank in order to talk to someone. Summoned forward and forced marched to photo ops. "Mr. Lawson's sixth grade homeroom, front and center." "Mr. Day's Astronomy Club, right face, forward march."

Ten minutes finding your table. Then summoned and double-timed through the chow line. The grub: chicken tartar, and beef whatever. Stood in line behind Mo Spiegel. By the time she was through shoveling, her plate resembled Mount Kilamanjaro. It was like the woman just ended her hunger strike at Gulag 36.

I'll write more in the morning, love. I'm still a bit anesthetized. How was dinner at the Spinandmarty?

From: **Sarah Ross**<sarahross64@gmail.com>
To: **Adam Wolf** <adam.wolf1402@gmail.com>
June 22, 2014 12:14 am
Subject: Re:The Grand Ball

Oh, you're so sweet to write as much as you did under the circumstances.

I'm riveted, even by raw Chicken a la King. Luckily our dinner was a whole lot better than yours. *Whiskandladle*'s a top-notch restaurant.

Hope you're feeling well enough tomorrow morning to continue.

From: **Adam Wolf** <adam.wolf1402@gmail.com>
To: **Sarah Ross**<sarahross64@gmail.com>
June 22, 2014 9:51 am
Subject: Re:Re:The Grand Ball

I continue …

So, the *piece de resistance* of the evening's festivities — spousal declamations. Each spouse unconnected to the class was called up to the microphone. 30 or 40 of them. They all said the same thing — took more than forty-five minutes. "Hi everyone. I'm happy to be here. I'm Kurt Weintraub, Dotty's other half. She so looked forward to this. It's wonderful to be here. We're off to Manitoba after this where we hope to get in some fishing and see our son and four gorgeous, gifted and precocious grandchildren. They'll be with us for a lovely and precious week. My grandson Henry calls Dotty 'Pessy'. I'm not sure why. Now, I know that some of Pessy's old boyfriends are here. And I do mean 'old'. I will grant you each one dance with her, but no body contact, please. Just kidding. Hoping everyone has a grand time. See you all in 2024."

Before the spouses were done, there was mutiny in the air.

The rock and roll began. *That'll Be the Day, Love Potion Number Nine, Peggy Sue*. A straggling few were dancing to it. Ah, but then, at the first notes of *The Stroll*, a stampede toward the dance floor. Even I joined in on that one. Was having fun until pickle-faced Julie Hirsch sharply corrected me. "That's not how you do it!" "Who the hell cares," says I, continuing to strut my way.

From: **Sarah Ross**<*sarahross64@gmail.com*>
To: **Adam Wolf** <*adam.wolf1402@gmail.com*>
June 22, 2014 10:00 am
Subject:

I would have liked that — dancing *The Stroll* with you.

From: **Adam Wolf** <*adam.wolf1402@gmail.com*>
To: **Sarah Ross**<*sarahross64@gmail.com*>
June 22, 2014 11:12 am
Subject: Stormy Weather

Happy to report that I just arranged for a late checkout, so I don't have to rush.

One unplanned moment of the evening. A massive storm. Wind howling. Rain pounding. Thunder booming. There go the lights! Anyway, in the flashes of lightning, I think I saw Mo Spiegel tiptoeing her way back to the buffet line. Evelyn Nader whispered in my ear, "Let's go dance in the dark". You'll be glad to know I begged off. There wasn't even any music, but people were still slow dancing. And then, spontaneously, a group of people just started singing some of the old songs — *Bye Bye Love, Splish-Splash, Hound Dog, Bird Dog* — and from one corner a newly formed men's *a capella* choir performed Marsulek's famous version of *Blueberry Hill*—"I found my thrill on Susan Sable's hills."

From: **Sarah Ross**<sarahross64@gmail.com>
To: **Adam Wolf** <adam.wolf1402@gmail.com>
June 22, 2014 11:41 am
Subject:

Thank you for not dancing.

From: **Adam Wolf** <adam.wolf1402@gmail.com>
To: **Sarah Ross**<sarahross64@gmail.com>
June 22, 2014 11:45 am
Subject:

Larry Plotnick's wife overheard Evelyn's asking me to dance. Wondered if I came without Lola so I could hook up. I think the lovely Mrs. Lawrence Plotnick assumed that hooking up was the only reason anyone would come alone. I think she smelled sex in the air.

From: **Sarah Ross**<sarahross64@gmail.com>
To: **Adam Wolf** <adam.wolf1402@gmail.com>
June 22, 2014 12:16 pm
Subject: sex after 60

Adam, old people and sex. When we were in high school, the thought was revolting, wasn't it? To my 18 year-old know-nothing self, sex ended (or should have) by the time you hit 30 something. The thought of grown-ups having sex was kind of nauseating, as I recall, particularly if you thought about your own parents. Geez, I remember the first time I found out about how babies were really made, I wanted to run down the street with my fingers in my ear, screaming. My parents doing THAT? (Between us, even though we're much older now than

our parents were then, the thought of my father and mother "doing it"
is still unimaginable.)

---

*From: **Adam Wolf** <adam.wolf1402@gmail.com>*
*To: **Sarah Ross**<sarahross64@gmail.com>*
June 22, 2014 12:37 pm
Subject: Re:sex after 60

Do you realize that you used the phrase "doing it"? No one ever says
"my parents were having sex", or "screwing", or, god forbid, "fucking".
That's because they were just "doing it". They were certainly not
fucking.
That particularly goes for my mother. It's the Eighth Wonder of the
Ancient World
The Hanging Gardens of Babylon
The Colossus of Rhodes
Beatrice Wolf *in flagrante*

---

*From: **Adam Wolf** <adam.wolf1402@gmail.com>*
*To: **Sarah Ross**<sarahross64@gmail.com>*
June 22, 2014 1:03 pm
Subject: The last good-byes

After about 10 mins., the lights came back on. People started to mutter
about leaving. Some of us had drifted into a lounge area. Quiet. Comfortable. Peaceful murmuring. And all that anyone wanted from the
reunion seemed to be right there — a place where we could simply bask
in the familiarity of each other's presence. I helped Jason Noble to the
door. He's on crutches now. He hugged me. We hugged each other.
Frank Winters winked and sent a wave across the room to me. Then
when Audrey Handler said good-bye, she quietly repeated that I looked
especially relaxed and happy. Not just from tonight, I told her. And then
I mentioned that I'm in touch with you again. She stopped and smiled.
Nodded.

Sarah, it's as though you were here after all. How I wish you really were.

From: **Adam Wolf** <adam.wolf1402@gmail.com>
To: **Sarah Ross**<sarahross64@gmail.com>
June 22, 2014 1:36 pm
Subject:

I'll head back to Chicago now.

From: **Adam Wolf** <adam.wolf1402@gmail.com>
To: **Sarah Ross**<sarahross64@gmail.com>
June 22, 2014 10:33 pm
Subject: Home

Good night, my Sarah. The last two hours of driving are a blur.

From: **Sarah Ross**<sarahross64@gmail.com>
To: **Adam Wolf** <adam.wolf1402@gmail.com>
June 22, 2014 10:57 pm
Subject:

Good night, my Adam. What a swell time I had at the reunion with you. Thanks.

From: **Adam Wolf** <adam.wolf1402@gmail.com>
To: **Evelyn Nader** <evenader54@comcast.net>
June 23, 2014 1:33 pm
Subject: Nice to hear from you

Yes, Evelyn, it was also a pleasure for me to see you at the reunion. Still recovering from the weekend.
No, the information about me ain't accurate—I'm still with my wife Lola.

Sorry to hear your friend here in Chicago is doing poorly. Your visit will certainly cheer her along. Unfortunately, I won't be able to break away next week. However, if you're planning another trip in the future, let me know. It would be fun to have you out to the house, or maybe Lola and I could join you at a restaurant in town.

Best wishes,
Adam

---

*From: **Adam Wolf** <adam.wolf1402@gmail.com>*
*To: **Sarah Ross**<sarahross64@gmail.com>*
June 23, 2014 6:15 pm
Subject:

Thinking of the reunion and you constantly, even though Lola works overtime to puncture my exhilaration. Told her some stranger at the country club mistook me for the son of one of our classmates. "Don't kid yourself. You look your age. Why don't you stop wearing those jeans as if you were still in high school."

---

*From: **Adam Wolf** <adam.wolf1402@gmail.com>*
*To: **Darlene Cutler** <Darlene.Cutler@branch14.org>*
June 23, 2014 7:58 pm
Subject: Wonderful to see you too

Dear Darlene,

I agree—the weekend was way too short and I also wish that we had more time together. Yeah, just too difficult to communicate in any meaningful sense given all that manufactured din and hullabaloo. Oh, thanks for your compliment on my "dancing". It's I who should compliment you for tolerating my rusty lumbering. You, of course, were as graceful as ever. Forgive me if I confess that when they played "Misty" it brought me back to our senior dance half a century ago.

I enjoyed the walk with you. Yes, the garden was indeed so fragrant after the rain. And it was a relief to get away from the noise.

I'm sorry if it seemed like I "finked out". I promise I'll be more "with it" next time we meet.

Fondly,
Adam

From: **Audrey Handler** <ahhandler@whitmangold.com>
To: **Sarah Ross** <sarahross64@gmail.com>
June 26, 2014 5:19 pm
Subject: Reunion

Hey Sarah,

Gosh, we missed you last weekend. Your name came up and it propelled me back to our lovely visit not long ago. Tommy Breslin asked if I had seen you at all, sends his love. And Adam Wolf, looked more centered than I remember, bubbling with energy. He mentioned you and he were in touch. I'm so glad. You were so close once.

I'm pleased I went. I thought I would be going as a dispassionate observer, the social psychologist at work. But somehow the reunion struck a deep emotional chord. It's the realization that many of these people who were once at the center of my life still mean a lot to me. I needed to know they were healthy and doing well, and hoped that if they weren't, they would lie to me. A kid's perspective, I'll admit.

Sarah, I deeply missed the classmates who died too young, some of my closest friends like Maggie Brown, such a perky cheerleader, a great pal, like you. (You were with us, I think, when we got into that accident coming home from Cedar Point, because we were laughing too hard. Luckily no one was hurt, but I got grounded for weeks, not because of the accident, but because I couldn't describe it without bursting into laughter again. I'm sure Maggie would have remembered what we were laughing about.) Damn it, my boyfriend in 11th grade, Rich Jacobson, died last year of prostate cancer. I got melancholy about never seeing him again. I spent a bit too much time Friday night pining.

What perked me up at the reunion was the natural camaraderie and affection we showed each other. Greg kept his arm locked with old friends when they chatted. Eric needed his arm around Eva. Gerson and I kept stroking each others arms as we spoke. Adam held Darlene close on the dance floor, even after the music ended. If you squinted, you could imagine you were back at the senior prom. I guess we needed to let people know how much they meant to us.

I'm writing to let you know that about us too.

(I don't know, maybe somebody, not me, should write a book about 50th high school reunions.)

Love,
Audrey

From: **Adam Wolf** <adam.wolf1402@gmail.com>
To: **Sarah Ross**<sarahross64@gmail.com>
June 27, 2014 7:19 am
Subject: ??

No good night wish? No good morning greeting? My heart fell when I opened my email and there was nothing from you last night.

I'm used to at least one email every two hours. None at all last night has me concerned. My imagination is getting the better of me. Are you okay? Are we okay?

Please answer. ILU, as ever.

---

*From: **Sarah Ross**<sarahross64@gmail.com>*
*To: **Adam Wolf** <adam.wolf1402@gmail.com>*
June 27, 2014 3:22 pm
Subject: Re:??

I'm here. I've been helping out Gordon who's been laid low by back trouble. Still grateful for your report on the reunion. Also heard about it from Audrey — who gave me the low down — incisive observations. Characteristically sensitive and revealing.

---

*From: **Adam Wolf** <adam.wolf1402@gmail.com>*
*To: **Sarah Ross**<sarahross64@gmail.com>*
June 27, 2014 7:12 pm
Subject:

What did Audrey say?

---

*From: **Sarah Ross**<sarahross64@gmail.com>*
*To: **Adam Wolf** <adam.wolf1402@gmail.com>*
June 28, 2014 8:17 am
Subject:

Audrey focused on the affection, the tenderness, the clinging. You and Darlene, for example.

---

*From: **Adam Wolf** <adam.wolf1402@gmail.com>*
*To: **Sarah Ross**<sarahross64@gmail.com>*
June 28, 2014 11:26 am
Subject:

So, you're angry that I spent time talking to Darlene?

---

*From: **Sarah Ross**<sarahross64@gmail.com>*
*To: **Adam Wolf** <adam.wolf1402@gmail.com>*
June 28, 2014 3:22 pm
Subject

Talking? Just talking and ?

---

*From: **Adam Wolf** <adam.wolf1402@gmail.com>*
*To: **Sarah Ross**<sarahross64@gmail.com>*
June 28, 2014 3:38 pm
Subject:

We are 68, not 16. No cause for jealousy or whatever. If you had been there, I would have talked to no one else or danced with anyone but you. Anyway, aren't you with Gordon?

---

*From: **Sarah Ross**<sarahross64@gmail.com>*
*To: **Adam Wolf** <adam.wolf1402@gmail.com>*
June 28, 2014 3:41 pm
Subject

Okay. Yes. You're right. You can dance with whomever you want and hold whomever you want tightly in your arms all night, even Darlene Cutler. Have you been stalking her too?

---

*From: **Adam Wolf** <adam.wolf1402@gmail.com>*
*To: **Sarah Ross**<sarahross64@gmail.com>*
June 28, 2014 8:55 pm
Subject:

Sarah, I cannot believe we're having this conversation. This is the kind of stupid spat we used to have. Are you going to throw your ID bracelet at me again? Are we ever going to get past the subject of Darlene? Have

I earned no privileges for having survived 68 years? Will I ever be allowed to be free of adolescent jealousies leveled against me? Free of censorship and control? I'm not saying I should be able to do whatever I want at 68. But I should be able to reminisce with an old girlfriend without recrimination. I guess I'm overly sensitive because I've allowed myself, for too many years, to be passive and compliant. So forgive me for being so reactive and hypersensitive. Yes, Sarah, I admit, for 10 mins. I was delivered back to a time I was free. Yes, I admit, it was exciting to have Darlene back in my arms for those minutes. There, I said it. Now I want to tell you something else. If you can hear it, I have never cared for anyone in my life as much as you.

From: **Sarah Ross** <sarahross64@gmail.com>
To: **Gabriella Fratelli** <gabriella.fratelli@orange.it>
June 29, 2014 5:10 pm
Subject: Reality check

Cara Mia,

Who else but you would put up with my pathetic obsession with the Man Who's Reentered My Life? Thank you, my dear friend. I'm teetering right now and your support keeps me upright.

I'm beside myself and ashamed of it. Have backed off from Adam and stopped writing. Seems Adam's reunion hasn't been just with me. It turns out another past girlfriend surfaced too, Darlene Cutler. He paid her court at the reunion dance. Even admits it "excited" him. (I bet she's still pixie cute.)

I'm not sure I trust that Adam Wolf, if you want to know the truth. By the time he got to college, the guy had trouble keeping his fly zipped—that's what I dread. Infidelities, at any age. Now he invokes the specious argument that age has its privilege. I suppose by that he means he can diddle old girlfriends in order to be jump started. How do I manage to do it? First there's hubby Harold, the serial fornicator, and now the old Adam, at it again I fear.

Gabriella, you have GOT to shake me back to my senses. I've become a lunatic. Upset that Darlene Cutler will steal my Adam away? Do you hear me? Do you catch me? MY Adam, I called him? He's an old married man. MY Adam is long gone. I've been seduced into thinking I'm a teenager again and here I go acting like one. What the hell's wrong with me??

I have to keep reminding myself that Adam and Sarah are not really together. And, in fact, we will never really be together again, not physically. So what the hell's come over me? Remind me we're not going steady, for chrissake.

I need to come to my senses. I need you to hold me.

---

*From: **Sarah Ross** <sarahross64@gmail.com>*
*To: **Adam Wolf** <adam.wolf1402@gmail.com>*
June 30, 2014 5:10 pm
Subject: I'm sorry

You're right. You're right. I'm ashamed to be laying claims to your affection. I don't know what possessed me. We've never even met as adults and here I go pretending that you're mine, exclusively, again. Strange how connecting with you has made me regress. I apologize for being jealous. I was hurt by the image of her head on your shoulder. Perhaps it's because my head will never be there again.

---

*From: **Adam Wolf** <adam.wolf1402@gmail.com>*
*To: **Sarah Ross** <sarahross64@gmail.com>*
June 30, 2014 9:52 pm
Subject:

Sarah, I know it's not been part of our pact, but is there any chance we can talk to each other, hear each other, see each other?

3

From: **Amanda Schreiber** <Amanda.D.Schreiber@wcmq.com>
To: **Adam Wolf** <adam.wolf1402@gmail.com>
June 22, 2014 9:22 am.
Subject: missing in action?

Doesn't your phone work in Cleveland? Don't they have cell service there yet? Or are you back and trying to ignore me? Forgotten you have real world responsibilities? One of which includes taking my calls. Another responding to my texts, my emails. I have a business to run. You don't seem to care about me or the station anymore. Am I wrong?
I'm glad this adolescent nostalgia fest of yours is almost over and look forward to having my Adam Wolf back. Truth be told, it's not just the reunion itself that concerns me. For the past weeks you've seemed distracted, spacey, preoccupied. You're taking me to dinner this week, I trust. Weds. or Thursday. It's been a month.
By the way, who's Sarah Ross?

From: Adam Wolf <adam.wolf1402@gmail.com>
To: **Amanda Schreiber** <Amanda.D.Schreiber@wcmq.com>
June 22, 2014 11:11 pm
Subject: Breathing space?

I've never ignored my responsibilities at the station. I feel some resentment that you're questioning my commitment.

Yes, my phone worked in Cleveland. I decided to enjoy the reunion. I did, even more than I expected.

I'll be furious if I find out you've been violating my privacy by looking at my emails.

Dinner Thursday ok. MY Adam Wolf?

---

*From: **Sarah Ross** <sarahross64@gmail.com>*
*To: **Adam Wolf** <adam.wolf1402@gmail.com>*
June 24, 2014 4:56 pm
Subject: Your brother David

Thanks for forwarding the pictures Greg sent you from the reunion. There's one outside the Heights High auditorium where I think I see the track team photo with you and your brother. Cute outfits. Fill me in on how David and his wife are doing these days. You say they don't live far. I'm surprised you haven't mentioned him.

---

*From: **Adam Wolf** <adam.wolf1402@gmail.com>*
*To: **Sarah Ross** <sarahross64@gmail.com>*
June 24, 2014 6:39 pm
Subject: Re:Your brother David

I don't see my brother. I haven't for 10 years. Don't care to elaborate. Not in the mood to discuss it.

---

*From: **Sarah Ross** <sarahross64@gmail.com>*
*To: **Adam Wolf** <adam.wolf1402@gmail.com>*
June 24, 2014 8:10 pm
Subject: Re:Re: Your brother David

Okay. Sorry to hear that. If you ever want to tell me, I'm here.

From: **Michael Wolf** *<Michael.R.Wolf@brookstead.com>*
To: **Lola Wolf** *<lola.wolf1402@gmail.com>*
June 26, 2014 5:10 pm
Subject: Catching up

Hey Mom,

The usual frenzy at work, but I'm taking a break and trying to transcend.
Hot as blazes here, so Colleen and I decided to get away. We plan to take
a vacation to Vancouver, including a Canadian Pacific tour of the Rock-
ies, like you and dad once talked about. We can't wait to get the hell out
of here. Chicago winters are a sweet nostalgic memory for me these
days.
How's your garden doing? Tough, I bet, to keep it AND the garden blog
going at the same time. I'm guessing, as always, you'll be the highlight of
the Evanston Garden Club's tour again this year. Colleen said she couldn't
believe how exquisite your garden looks. "Hopping", she called it.
Anything else up with you? Dad must be back from the reunion now.
We texted. He sounded a little delusional, if you ask me. Weird. He used
words like "rejuvenating", "wondrous", "delivered". He came off as ridiculous when he spoke of "wresting free the last couple of years of
youth". That, I told him, slipped away 20 years ago. Have you been able
to bring him back to earth yet?
I've got to run. The boss is getting suspicious I'm slacking off. Imagine
that.

From: **Lola Wolf** *<lola.wolf1402@gmail.com>*
To: **Michael Wolf** *<Michael.R.Wolf@brookstead.com>*
June 27, 2014 8:13 pm
Subject: Re:Catching up

Mikey Mouse,

Good to get a smoke signal from you. You'll like Vancouver, I'm sure.
I'm glad you'll get a break. What's the doctor telling you about the itching
on your back?

My garden grows springtime nicely. The lilacs have come and gone. The tulips will return next year. But the impatiens are bedded down.

I think I told you I'm volunteering this summer over at the library. Three days a week. It's not exactly stressful. I'm having a good time with my Big Reader's Club. Seven, eight-year-olds. Volunteers take turns with story time. Here's something strange, though. One of the kids in the group hangs around the library from the time we open until late afternoon. They tell me the kid's dropped off with a sandwich every day and mostly sits on the steps or in a corner by the windows. I've tried to keep him company, but he turns away. This boy, Robbie, it turns out, is Gail Korschak's stepson. I saw her pick him up. I wanted to say something. No one has. They just grouse about it.

Your dad is back from his toot in Cleveland, more insufferable than ever. He hums and struts the stroll through the house. Combs his hair 20 times an hour. He behaves like a horse's ass. Tells Chas and Louise about how good some of the women at the reunion looked. I don't need to hear that. He's so full of himself, because some 68 year-old babes still found him cute. I wish the babes would give me a call, so I can set them straight. Adam looks like the same old man to me. Now he's attached a hideous picture someone emailed him to the refrigerator door. Your father—sweaty, one step away from a coronary, jitter buggering some dame on the dance floor. When was the last time he ever took me dancing? When? The year before you were born.

Love,
Mom

From: **Darlene Cutler** <Darlene.Cutler@branch14.org>
To: **Adam Wolf** <adam.wolf1402@gmail.com>
June 28, 2014 4:48 pm
Subject: coming your way

Glad you wrote. I hoped that last dance wouldn't be the end of it. I found an excuse to come to Chicago, if you think you'll be around in mid-September. It's a wedding I wouldn't attend otherwise. Elliot doesn't like to travel. Highland Park. Near you?

*From: **Adam Wolf** <adam.wolf1402@gmail.com>*
*To: **Darlene Cutler** <Darlene.Cutler@branch14.org>*
June 28, 2014 6:10 pm
Subject: Re: coming your way

Yes. I'll be here. Indeed. Spend an extra day and I promise to keep you clear of Highland Park.

---

*From: **Sarah Ross** <sarahross64@gmail.com>*
*To: **Adam Wolf** <adam.wolf1402@gmail.com>*
July 2, 2014 9:48 am
Subject: okay — let's do it

Adam, I've thought it over, and you have a point. I'm ready to talk on the phone. When?

---

*From: **Adam Wolf** <adam.wolf1402@gmail.com>*
*To: **Sarah Ross** <sarahross64@gmail.com>*
July 2, 2014 11:24 am
Subject: Re:okay — let's do it

Wow! I'm breathless. Let's make it this Sunday afternoon. Is that okay? Wow!!

---

*From: **Sarah Ross** <sarahross64@gmail.com>*
*To: **Adam Wolf** <adam.wolf1402@gmail.com>*
July 6, 2014 1:03 pm
Subject: sweet to hear you again

Adam, your voice surprised me. I braced myself for the stentorian boom of a classical radio announcer, instead your voice sounded so gentle and sweet. I'm still smiling from being with you this way too.

How did I sound to you? Wasn't it funny how long it took to even say anything? We must have been giggling for at least ten minutes straight, don't you think? Like a couple of schoolgirls.

And I loved the way we could jump from topic to topic — hop-scotching from DSLR cameras to German tourists in Navajo country to the Curiosity Rover on Mars. It's AMAZING to me that we have so much in common, so many eccentric interests. Even though we haven't been together for all these years, I think I actually have more in common with you than with anyone else I know. Could that be possible? Couples, as they age, have less and less in common, don't you think? How is it that we're so alike? Were we twins separated at birth?

It's fun to giggle and reminisce and, yes, let's do it again. But I need to keep up the email. I've been saying all along that when I talk on the phone, I can't be nearly as forthcoming and intimate. But it's still fun. Jumping from topic to topic with you was thrilling. Is thrilling. Will continue to be thrilling. But talking disappears into the ether. I can't even recall all we said a few minutes ago. Emails can be savored. I can read them over and over again. And I do.

From: **Adam Wolf** <adam.wolf1402@gmail.com>
To: **Sarah Ross** <sarahross64@gmail.com>
July 6, 2014 1:46 pm
Subject: Re:sweet to hear you again

Sarah,

Moi aussi. Astonished by all the things in common. Starting with the way our minds are wired. Like pinball machines, bouncing around randomly — from one association to another. I mean, Carl Maria von Weber? Recited in unison?? Yes, Sarah, it's destiny. Not separated at birth. Naw, maybe it's more. Think me insane, but is it possible we're the same person? Maybe it happened when we shared our first chocolate phosphate at Wolf's soda fountain. Wouldn't that make a great *Twilight Zone* episode?

Ah, your voice? Not exactly what I recalled or expected. Okay, the resonance of sweet sixteen Sarah somehow still there, but now cultured, measured, confident (except for the giggling fits). But you sound nowhere near 68. Actually, that's stupid. How are we supposed to sound at this age? Remember when 68 or 69 seemed ancient to us and we would imitate my grandmother with her croaky whine?

Let's set another telephone date. But you're right. Of course we write too. Of course. Of course. So much to say still. Yes, intimate. And trusting. There are some things I think I can tell you that I never confided to anyone else.

---

*From: **Lola Wolf** <lola.wolf1402@gmail.com>*
*To: **Michael Wolf** <Michael.R.Wolf@brookstead.com>*
July 8, 2014 5:00 pm
Subject: Gail Korschak's kid

A quick note. I wanted to tell you I finally did something about that kid who's dumped at the library all day. When Gail Korschak finally showed up, I did something unlike me, I took Robbie by the hand and walked him to the car. Gail asked if something was wrong. And I told her, "You bet something's wrong. Robbie seems upset most of the time. How would you have felt as a kid in his place? What makes you think it's alright just to leave him here all day? I know you're a better person than that".

We haven't seen Robbie since. I feel proud that I could do some good.

---

*From: **Michael Wolf** <Michael.R.Wolf@brookstead.com>*
*To: : **Lola Wolf** <lola.wolf1402@gmail.com>*
July 8, 2014 7:22 pm
Subject: Re:Gail Korschak's kid

Check the Wilmette library. She's probably dumping him there now.

---

*From: **Adam Wolf** <adam.wolf1402@gmail.com>*
*To: **Sarah Ross** <sarahross64@gmail.com>*
July 10, 2014 7:05 pm
Subject: Favorites

Shostakovich *Fifth*
Bruckner *Third* (with Haitink)
Verdi *Requiem*
Schubert *Quintet*
Mahler *Fifth* (Solti and the Chicago)

ilu

---

*From: **Sarah Ross** <sarahross64@gmail.com>*
*To: **Adam Wolf** <adam.wolf1402@gmail.com>*
July 10, 2014 9:26 am
Subject: Re:Favorites

Why no Mozart, Mr. Voice-of-Classical Music?

Mahler, *Fifth* (Barenboim and the Chicago)
Bach, *Cello Suites*
Schubert, *Schwannengesang*
Schoenberg, *Pelleas and Melisande*
Mozart, *Violin and Viola Duo, number 1*

ilu

---

*From: **Harold Weinstein** <Harold.W.Weinstein9933@gmail.com>*
*To **Sarah Ross** <sarahross64@gmail.com>*
July 11, 2014 8:45 am
Subject: My Robert Frost

Damn it, Sarah, please answer. Don't you think enough time has passed to be civil to each other? I repeat and repeat. I can't find that first edition of Robert Frost's *Versed in Country Things*. Signed, to boot. I need it. It must still be in the house. Would you please find it for me! It's a short thin book, bound in dark brown leather. —H

---

*From: **Adam Wolf** <adam.wolf1402@gmail.com>*
*To: **Sarah Ross** <sarahross64@gmail.com>*
July 13, 2014 2:23 pm
Subject:

Sarah, dear—

I know we just finished our phone conversation, but the oddest thing has happened. For the first time in over a decade, Lola has not only done my laundry, but also folded it and put it away.
Always cheers me to hear your voice.

---

*From: **Sarah Ross** <sarahross64@gmail.com>*
*To: **Adam Wolf** <adam.wolf1402@gmail.com>*
July 14, 2014 12:43 am
Subject:

Nice summer evening here—a party at Nicole's to celebrate that.
I love your voice too. I giggle at the Chicago accent.
Good night, my Adam. Sweet dreams.
Nice that Lola wants to make peace. Do you think she senses your heart is somewhere else? You've never really described Lola to me. What's she like?

From: **Adam Wolf** <adam.wolf1402@gmail.com>
To: **Sarah Ross** <sarahross64@gmail.com>
July 14, 2014 7:19 am
Subject: Lola

I'm not sure what to make of Lola's wifely impulse with the laundry. She's also been baking chocolate cupcakes and pecan pie and leaving them out for me when I get home. Odd. Maybe it's obvious I've become distracted. It is true. My life revolves around our communication — these emails — our phone calls. Maybe I should be a bit more attentive to Lola, but we've lived separate lives under the same roof for years and years. I wonder if I should tell her about us. I think maybe it's time. I have long dreaded retirement because I know I couldn't spend all day, every day in her presence.

What's she like? Well, she doesn't look like a "Lola". Never did. More like a Penelope. She's petite — small features, except her brown eyes are huge. They dart around incessantly, coming to rest on things that are "out of place" or need fixing. Her hair is now speckled gray, but the same pageboy she's worn since she was 20. She's never without her 12 bracelets, a shawl or a silk scarf — and purses by Louis Vuitton. And now that she's retired, she has the manicurist try out wild colors — sparkling purple this week.

She needs to be told she looks good. l suppose she does. I leave it to others to tell her.

She a nervous type, anxious, has trouble sitting still. Loves to garden, but can't enjoy just sitting on the deck. Keeps jumping up to pull this or that weed.

She has an outsized bellow. Used to barking out orders.

She has bizarre moments, as I've told you. Last summer she went out drinking with some of her girlfriends. She came home and boasted that she had demanded a show of hands from the entourage. "Raise your hand if you've had sex with your husband in the last five years." She smirked, told me she kept her hands folded along with most of the other women at the table. "So I guess that your impotence isn't that unusual after all."

*From: **Sarah Ross** <sarahross64@gmail.com>*
*To: **Adam Wolf** <adam.wolf1402@gmail.com>*
July 14, 2014 7:40 am
Subject: Re:Lola

    Words fail me.

LOLA > ADAM   7/18/14 3:22 pm

Grass needs mowing. Dryer still not working right. Vent? Garage needs organizing. Remember, I did your laundry.

ADAM   3:27 pm

Why don't you hire Kyle? This weekend is not good. I said thank you, but you don't need to do my laundry.

---

*From: **S.Gordon Wilson** <S.Gordon.Wilson@csulb.edu>*
*To: **Sarah Ross** <sarahross64@gmail.com>*
July 19, 2014 12:14 pm
Subject: an invite

Dear Sarah,

I know this is a ways off, but I've agreed to participate on a panel at the AAUS Conference in Seattle this fall. It's October 14-17. I'd be delighted if you could join me there for the weekend of the 17th–19th. Jerry Mahoney and his wife Mae have offered their houseboat, reserved for guests. Perhaps this will lure you. Seattle has superb seafood and, as you must know, a top-notch museum. Think it over.

Yours,
Gordon

S. Gordon Wilson, PhD.
Founder and Editor of *The Ichthysaurus*
Fellow, American Academy of Underwater Sciences
Professor of Biology, Emeritus
California State University, Long Beach

From: **Sarah Ross** <sarahross64@gmail.com>
To: **S.Gordon Wilson** <S.Gordon.Wilson@csulb.edu>
July 18, 2014 5:55 pm
Subject: Re:an invite

Hi Gordon,

So sweet of you to think of me, to want to include me in your Seattle plans. Could be fun. Can you let me think about it? A weekend away on the water might rejuvenate me. Let me see if I can shift around some plans I've already made with Nicole.
Let me know when you get back from Palo Alto. I owe you a dinner.

From**: Adam Wolf** <adam.wolf1402@gmail.com>
To: **Sarah Ross** <sarahross64@gmail.com>
July 22, 2014 11:16 am
Subject: Favorites, cont.

You'll be happy to know that I just programmed your Schoenberg *Pelleas* for the first time. Wow!

Okay:

Samuel Barber K*noxville, Summer of 1915*

Benjamin Britten *Peter Grimes*

Sound Track of *O Brother, Where Art Thou?*

ilu

From: **Sarah Ross** *<sarahross64@gmail.com>*

To: **Adam Wolf** *<adam.wolf1402@gmail.com>*

July 22, 2014 4:29 pm

Subject: Re:Favorites, cont.

Soundtrack of *Manhattan*

Soundtrack of *Vertigo*

Etta James, *At Last*

Annie Lennox, *Every Time We Say Goodbye*

ilu2

AMANDA > ADAM   7/23/14 10:14 am

I hope the dentist isn't causing you too much pain. A package came for you. From that Sarah. Isn't that the one who writes you emails all day, every day.

ADAM   11:19 am

I don't believe you feel you have the right to check up on me like that. Read my emails? Back off!

AMANDA   12:28 pm

Don't flatter yourself that I care. I give a damn about your emails. Had to look at your computer for email u sent Stan Metzger. Couldn't help noticing the name "Sarah Ross" comes up quite a bit. Doesn't it? Just don't be emailing on station time. I also know the name cause that package came. Opened it by mistake. A book about some amusement park in Clevld. A note attached. "Adam, Save the Last Dance for Me, your Sarah. ILU". Any schoolgirl knows what ILU means. Just wondering who your special friend might be, Adam.

ADAM   3:04 pm

Stay away from my computer and my mail. Maybe we should forget about dinner next week.

From: **Adam Wolf** <adam.wolf1402@gmail.com>
To: **Sarah Ross** <sarahross64@gmail.com>
July 25, 2014 4:29 pm
Subject: More favorites

Helen Forester *I'll Buy That Dream*
Vera Lynn *We'll Meet Again*
Doc Watson *Miss the Mississippi and You*
Bruce Springsteen *I Ain't Got No Home*
and then, of course,
Eddie Cochran *Summertime Blues*

ilu

From: **Sarah Ross** *<sarahross64@gmail.com>*
To: **Adam Wolf** *<adam.wolf1402@gmail.com>*
July 25, 2014 5:17pm
Subject: Re:More favorites

Oh, am I the only other person in the world who knows and loves all of these?

Doc Watson and Merle Watson, *Miss the Mississippi and You*

ilu2

From: **Adam Wolf** *<adam.wolf1402@gmail.com>*
To: **Sarah Ross** *<sarahross64@gmail.com>*
July 25, 2014 8:07pm
Subject: Still more favorites

Double Indemnity
Memento
Mad Max Beyond Thunderdome
8½
Panic in Needle Park
Jules et Jim
and, naturally, *Glengarry Glen Ross*

ilu

From: **Sarah Ross** *<sarahross64@gmail.com>*
To: **Adam Wolf** *<adam.wolf1402@gmail.com>*
July 25, 2014 8:44 pm
Subject: Re:Still more favorites

Double Indemnity
Memento
Vertigo

Shadow of a Doubt
Some Like it Hot
Scenes From a Marriage
and, naturally, *Jules et Jim*

ilu2

---

*From: **Amanda Schreiber** <Amanda.D.Schreiber@wcmq.com>*
*To **Frieda Reigel** <Frieda.M.Reigel@therapypartners.com>*
July 26, 2014 5:08 am
Subject: FODDER FOR THERAPY

NOTES FOR YOU. MAYBE I'LL EVEN HAVE THE GUTS TO
SEND THIS.

STUPID FOOL AM I. FOR YEARS YOU'VE TOLD ME THAT IN
ALMOST EVERY ONE OF YOUR OVERPRICED SESSIONS. HOW
MANY TIMES HAVE I HEARD THAT I MUSTN'T MAKE MR.
ADAM WOLF THE CENTER OF MY LIFE?

HOW MANY YEARS HAVE WE BEEN WORKING ON THIS?
AND HOW MANY YEARS ON MY FINDING A LIFE OUTSIDE
THE STATION? I'VE TRIED. MAYBE NOT HARD ENOUGH.
COULD HAVE STUCK IT OUT AT THE COUNCIL, I GUESS.
TOO MANY JERKS ON THE COMMITTEE. WASTE OF TIME.

NEED TO KEEP AWAY FROM STATION. TO ROGER IT WAS A
HOBBY. WHY SHOULD IT MATTER TO ME? WHY SHOULD A
SORRY EXCUSE FOR A HUMAN BEING LIKE ADAM MATTER
TO ME? I COULD SELL THE BANDWIDTH TOMORROW.
MAYBE I WILL. OK.

FOOL. THAT'S WHAT I AM.

SNAKE. THAT'S WHAT HE IS. DECEITFUL. MANIPULATIVE GIGOLO.

EVEN BEFORE ROGER DIED, ADAM AND I WERE INSEPARABLE. I TOLD YOU HOW HE TEXTED ME ALL DAY. HOW HE CALLED ME ON THE WAY TO WORK. ON THE WAY HOME. I COULD ALWAYS COUNT ON HIM PUTTING ME AND THE STATION FIRST. WHY HAS HE STOPPED DOING THAT? WHAT ABOUT THE PAJAMA PARTIES AT THE DRAKE? I MEAN HE ISN'T EVEN THAT COMPETENT IN ANYTHING ANYMORE.

FOOL. I FEEL LIKE A FOOL.

LOLA NEVER COUNTED. HE NEVER LOVED HER. HE DESERVES BETTER. HAVEN'T I TAKEN CARE OF HIM ALL THESE YEARS? WHERE WOULD HE BE WITHOUT ME?

WHEN WAS THE LAST TIME HE SAID HE LOVED ME, THOUGH? DIDN'T HE MASSAGE MY NECK THE OTHER DAY?

MAYBE HE'LL COME TO HIS SENSES SOON. HEAD IN THE CLOUDS FOR OVER A MONTH NOW. AND I SEE ALL THESE EMAILS LISTED THERE. CAN'T HELP IT. NOT TRYING TO LOOK. WELL MAYBE. THE ASSHOLE LEAVES HIS COMPUTER ON GMAIL. ADDLED. WHO COULD AVOID LOOKING? GLANCING?? I'M NOT A SNOOP. THAT ENDLESS STREAM OF EMAILS. ON STATION TIME, YET!!!!!!!!!!!!!

SARAH I THINK IS AN OLD OLD GIRL FRIEND. I KNOW I SHOULDN'T HAVE PEEKED. PROBABLY FROM THE REUNION. ONLY SAW THE BROAD FOR FEW HOURS AND AFTER 50 YEARS AND YET HE'S BILLING AND COOING WITH HER.

PREPOSTEROUS. INSANE. 50 YEARS! RIDICULOUS. ADOLESCENT. IT'S A DISEASE.

IS HE GOING TO THROW AWAY OUR 25 YEARS FOR THIS CRAZY FICTION OF HIS? IS SHE GOING TO REPLACE ME?

LISTEN TO THIS BULLSHIT. THEY'RE "JOINED AT THE HIP", THEY'RE "LOST IN THE STARS". THEY EVEN THINK THEY CAN COMMUNICATE TELEPATHICALLY, FOR CRYING OUT LOUD. BOTH DERANGED. BUT THEY'RE NOT TAKING ME AND THIS STATION DOWN WITH THEM. I WON'T LET THAT HAPPEN.

FOR HIS OWN GOOD HE NEEDS TO CEASE AND DESIST. HE'S GOT TO HAVE A SHRINK OF HIS OWN. HE WILL STOP. HE NEEDS TO KNOW HOW MUCH HE HAS HURT ME.

OK. OK. LET'S KEEP WORKING ON CONTROL-FREAK ISSUES. HELP ME GET OUT OF THIS FURY — NOT JUST AT HIM, AT MYSELF TOO. FOOL. FOOL. FOOLFOOLFOOLFOOLFOOL. I'VE HAD TO PUT UP ALL THESE YEARS WITH HIS LOLA, NOW THIS SARAH?

AREN'T HE AND I THE "WE"? GET THIS STRAIGHT, MISS SARAH. PEOPLE THINK OF ADAM AND AMANDA AS A COUPLE. THINK WE'RE MARRIED. TONY STOPPED IN AT THE STATION THE OTHER DAY. "ARE YOU TWO BICKERING AGAIN? TIME TO SEE A MARRIAGE COUNSELOR?"

WHO THE FUCK IS SARAH ROSS TO HIM?

I KNOW. I KNOW. I CAN'T CONTROL HIM. I CAN ONLY BE IN CHARGE OF MYSELF. TAKE CHARGE OF MY LIFE. WHO THE FUCK NEEDS HIM?

From: **Sarah Ross** *<sarahross64@gmail.com>*
To: **Adam Wolf** *<adam.wolf1402@gmail.com>*
July 27, 2014 1:29 pm
Subject: is something bothering you?

You once said we'd talk for at least 4 hours. Make that 5 ½. And we don't run out of topics.

But, you sounded a bit different today. Is it my imagination or might you be feeling blue?

Okay, Adam Wolf, let's have some fun. Give me some insight to who you really are now. Who would you want to play you in a movie?

From: **Adam Wolf** *<adam.wolf1402@gmail.com>*
To: **Sarah Ross** *<sarahross64@gmail.com>*
July 27, 2014 2:03 pm
Subject: Who should play me

Gabriel Byrne, of course. Who wouldn't want Gabriel Byrne to play them? And who should play you?

From: **Sarah Ross** *<sarahross64@gmail.com>*
To: **Adam Wolf** *<adam.wolf1402@gmail.com>*
July 27, 2014 2:05 pm
Subject: Re:Who should play me

Angelina Jolie.

From: **Adam Wolf** <adam.wolf1402@gmail.com>
To: **Sarah Ross** <sarahross64@gmail.com>
July 27, 2014 2:07 pm
Subject: Re:Re:Who should play me

No, really.

From: **Sarah Ross** <sarahross64@gmail.com>
To: **Adam Wolf** <adam.wolf1402@gmail.com>
July 27, 2014 2:29 pm
Subject: In Treatment

Well, I suppose, Diane Wiest. I love her face. How expressive it is, how capable of warmth. Her talent. Byrne's too. Wasn't *In Treatment* the best show ever? Especially the episodes with the two of them?

Gabriel Byrne. I especially loved him because someone I'm very close to is also named Gabriel. Or at least that was once her name.

Have you ever been "in treatment"?

Me? I've had several therapists over the years. One who slept through sessions, actually snored once, except when it came to the topic of sex. Then he was too wide awake, if you ask me. I tried to tell him about us. About the bad part, after you and I had our last golden meeting in '66. You promised to come to Cambridge to see me in a month, but you never showed up. I could never tell him. Too humiliating.

From: **Adam Wolf** <adam.wolf1402@gmail.com>
To: **Sarah Ross** <sarahross64@gmail.com>
July 27, 2014 2:32 pm
Subject: Re:In Treatment

I'm so sorry. What the hell was wrong with me?

---

*From: **Sarah Ross** <sarahross64@gmail.com>*
*To: **Adam Wolf** <adam.wolf1402@gmail.com>*
July 27, 2014 4:20 pm
Subject: shrinks

Another therapist, another guy, I finally talked it through with him. Made me feel okay about the disappointment, the profound feeling of rejection. He was quite good, got me through a lot. He got me to admit how much I hated my father. Then I transferred that hatred to the therapist, and just stopped going. I'm able to do that. Just cut myself off from people when my feelings are so much as nicked. Detach and feel nothing more for them.

Lisa, my third shrink, called it "dissociating". We worked a lot on "dissociation", on how it was a traumatized child's defense mechanism and counter-productive in adulthood. She encouraged me to stay in uncomfortable situations, work through rough spots in relationships. "Stay with the feelings. Observe what sparks them. As they happen record the feelings that make you want to run."

I was doing pretty well, dealing with tough moments, with friends, with Harold. Doing pretty well, I repeat. Until one day Lisa pissed me off and I stopped going. Just cut it. Never told her I wasn't coming back. Never said goodbye or talked about the "feelings". How do I tell her it still feels pretty good NOT to be going to sessions with her? It's therapeutic, actually.

---

*From: **Adam Wolf** <adam.wolf1402@gmail.com>*
*To: **Sarah Ross** <sarahross64@gmail.com>*
July 27, 2014 4:23 pm
Subject: Re:shrinks

What pissed you off?

---

*From: **Sarah Ross** <sarahross64@gmail.com>*
*To: **Adam Wolf** <adam.wolf1402@gmail.com>*
July 27, 2014 5:52 pm
Subject: unhappy

Harold and I were fighting a lot. I longed to be elsewhere. Anywhere but with him. My dearest friend, Gabriella, had moved back to
Italy, into a relationship that, even to this day, excludes me. I was depressed. Very. And I told my Lisa how I felt — that I had no friends,
nobody who liked me, let alone loved me. I was sobbing, told her that
when I died no one would come to my funeral. Now I ask you, Adam,
what would a supportive shrink have said to that??? How about, "You're
feeling sad. I see that. Let's talk about it."? Something like that. Instead,
Lisa said, and I still can't believe it, "I would come to your funeral". I
felt even worse coming out than going in. That's why I stopped going
to her. Cancelled the next appointment. Never phoned again.

---

*From: **Adam Wolf** <adam.wolf1402@gmail.com>*
*To: **Sarah Ross** <sarahross64@gmail.com>*
July 27, 2014 6:08 pm
Subject: My shrink

Therapeutic good riddance, good-bye. I would have left, even before
the 50 minutes was up had my therapist pulled that one.
Me? I've had several bouts with therapists. Most notable was during the
period I first began "courting" Lola. She was married. I wasn't. Craig,
my therapist, was a big shot at Loyola. He'd written the book on relationship therapy. For the most part, my sessions dealt with my "fornica-
tive" years. Often I was greeted with bemused silence while I described
my monthly declarations of undying love to the contents of yet another
tight pair of jeans.
As my relationship with Lola warmed up, he became more vocal, and
issued a stern warning, "If she does it to her husband, she'll do it to you
some day".

From: **Sarah Ross** *<sarahross64@gmail.com>*
To: **Adam Wolf** *<adam.wolf1402@gmail.com>*
July 27, 2014 6:19 pm
Subject: Re:My shrink

Do you mean to say that you had a shrink who tried to intervene and stop your pursuing Lola? Well, you've been together 30 years, after all. Guess he shouldn't have been so sure of himself, huh? Kinda cocky. Missed that one.

From: **Adam Wolf** *<adam.wolf1402@gmail.com>*
To: **Sarah Ross** *<sarahross64@gmail.com>*
July 27, 2014 6:38 pm
Subject: Sham

Camel cigarette butts in the ashtray in the bedroom. Once a receipt from room 383, Marriot Lincolnshire. I never said anything. We should have called it quits a long while ago, but for Michael. Lola would say, "Our marriage is a sham. It needs to end. I guess it's up to me to end it — another thing you force me to do without your help — to end it. You'd never have the guts."

From: **Sarah Ross** *<sarahross64@gmail.com>*
To: **Adam Wolf** *<adam.wolf1402@gmail.com>*
July 27, 2014 7:05 pm
Subject: Re:Sham

Were you seeing your therapist then?

From: **Adam Wolf** *<adam.wolf1402@gmail.com>*
To: **Sarah Ross** *<sarahross64@gmail.com>*
July 27, 2014 7:15 pm
Subject:

No. Craig ended therapy long before that. Told me I needed a woman therapist, one I couldn't seduce. Anyway, he never knew me fully enough. I guess I wasn't ready to divulge everything about myself to him. I wouldn't have for any other therapist either.

Over the past months, though, I've thought about what Craig would say about you and me.

From: **Sarah Ross** *<sarahross64@gmail.com>*
To: **Adam Wolf** *<adam.wolf1402@gmail.com>*
July 27, 2014 7:25 pm
Subject:

So you think you need to see a therapist about us?

From: **Adam Wolf** *<adam.wolf1402@gmail.com>*
To: **Sarah Ross** *<sarahross64@gmail.com>*
July 27, 2014 7:52 pm
Subject: Skeptical?

Maybe. I suspect Craig would have been skeptical about us. He would have wanted me to realize how potent a threat this kind of reunion could be to my marriage. Ironically, though, he once confessed to me during a session that he had planned to meet with his high school sweetheart on a trip to Denver, but stopped himself. Called it off. Pretty proud that he didn't let it happen.

From: **Sarah Ross** *<sarahross64@gmail.com>*
To: **Adam Wolf** *<adam.wolf1402@gmail.com>*
July 27, 2014 8:26 pm
Subject: Re:Skeptical?

Maybe it's a therapist's job to be skeptical, but your Craig seems a bit too directive for my taste.

You know, Adam, there were significant events in my life I also couldn't share with any of my therapists. I was afraid of their disapproval and feared they'd tell me to stop what I was doing.

I took a break early in my marriage to drive through Italy with Gabriel. He decided he'd move back there. He had decided to transition there to Gabriella. She's a sweet, sensitive person, petite. My height. Large chocolate-brown eyes, and wavy mahogany-colored hair. I thought of moving with her. Harold was too busy flattering his way to tenure to care.

Gabriella is still my confidante, like your Paul.

From: **Adam Wolf** *<adam.wolf1402@gmail.com>*
To: **Sarah Ross** *<sarahross64@gmail.com>*
July 27, 2014 8:34 pm
Subject:

Sounds like a script from one of those '60s Italian movies. You know, Antonioni.

Would you mind my asking, when you made this trip was it with Gabriel or Gabriella? Was your relationship also sexual?

From: **Sarah Ross** <sarahross64@gmail.com>
To: **Adam Wolf** <adam.wolf1402@gmail.com>
July 27, 2014 8:42 pm
Subject:

    Yes, sexual, intensely so. I fell in love with Gabriel, but was more comfortable with and attracted to Gabriella.

From: **Adam Wolf** <adam.wolf1402@gmail.com>
To: **Sarah Ross** <sarahross64@gmail.com>
July 27, 2014 9:11 pm
Subject: Man/woman

I suppose I can understand your preference. I always preferred to be around men who have a softer, feminine side. You know, when I went to the opera regularly, I found myself staring at the men who came in drag. At intermission some would sashay along the first landing to the balcony — like runway models. They were stunning. Every Tuesday night one breathtaking brunette appeared — statuesque, of course in heels. She often dressed in low-cut turquoise or creamy satins. Her shoulders always bare, except in winter, when she wore a white fur stole. Other than the narrow hips, it was a woman in there, delicate, chiseled features. She stared through everyone. The queen.
One final question, though, Sarah. Now that you and I are together again, do you still long to be with Gabriella?

From: **Sarah Ross** <sarahross64@gmail.com>
To: **Adam Wolf** <adam.wolf1402@gmail.com>
July 27, 2014 9:49 pm
Subject: Gabriella

    No, Adam, I haven't longed to be with her for decades. It's a moot point anyway.

Gabriella Fratelli lives in a posh villa atop a cliff on the island of Gavi, near Rome. I've only seen pictures of it—the jacuzzi, the pool, the view through soft gray rooms to vanilla-colored archways that frame the sea. Out of my league. Gabriella's too, once. I've never been invited there. Giancarlo, the rich, brutally ugly man, keeps her his bird in a gilded cage. But she and I correspond. And I deeply miss her company —can never understand how she could put up with such a situation —her comings and goings monitored. She was so full of life, fun—an olive-skinned beauty, her long black hair, perfectly kempt, and that sweet femininity. I'm sent pictures. It's been at least 30 years since I last saw her, but she has one of these eternally youthful faces that only Italian women can afford.

Now tell me about your friend Paul. Do you have at least one person in your life who will grant you the right to be with me?

From: **Adam Wolf** <adam.wolf1402@gmail.com>
To: **Sarah Ross** <sarahross64@gmail.com>
July 27, 2014 10:00 pm
Subject: Paul

Yes, Paul. Of course. Let me put my mind to how to describe him and answer you tomorrow evening.

From: **Adam Wolf** <adam.wolf1402@gmail.com>
To: **Sarah Ross** <sarahross64@gmail.com>
July 28, 2014 7:13 pm
Subject: Paul

How to describe Paul? Went to college with me. Freshman dorm. I heard his laugh from across the hall, and I followed the sound. It was brotherly love at first sight. I can describe him as someone who is soft—features are soft, still a schoolboy's face at 68. Voice is soft and gentle. He's soft to be around. I've never seen him lose his temper.

Eternally accepting. Anyway, I've shared many confidences with him over the years, but, funnily enough, they were never about relationships, or at least not until now. I write to him about you, and our phenomenon. He responds with quiet whimsy, in measured ways—like a biochemist fascinated by a charged reaction.

From: **Sarah Ross** <sarahross64@gmail.com>

To: **Adam Wolf** <adam.wolf1402@gmail.com>

July 28, 2014 7:43 pm

Subject: Re:Paul

I would really really like to meet such a human being. I hope he'd like me. I envy you such a friend. I have a few good friends here, but I don't really have any friends from college who I keep up with—not many are off drugs yet. Bennington, you know.

From: **Adam Wolf** <adam.wolf1402@gmail.com>

To: **Sarah Ross** <sarahross64@gmail.com>

July 28, 2014 8:09 pm

Subject: My radio show with Paul

You know I got into radio with Paul, on the University of Chicago station, WHPK. We revolutionized FM radio. Our half hour comedy show, *The Cultural Lag*, featured a couple of self-centered mopes ranting about right-wing business school pricks. The shows were dominated by marathon commercials for Paul and Adam's fledging businesses like the *Paul and Adam Bank*, fifty-six convenient locations at the most obscure intersections in the city. The bank prided itself on how well they could protect patrons during an endless series of bank robberies.

From: **S.Gordon Wilson** *<S.Gordon.Wilson@csulb.edu>*
To: **Jerry Mahoney** *<Jerry.Mahoney2028@verizon.net>*
July 29, 2014 6:12 pm
Subject: Coming your way

Dear Jerry,

I hope this finds you in good health. Infirmities seem to come by the dozen at our age. Don't get me going about my latest ticker check-up. I almost had another coronary when the nurse with the big tits leaned over me to hook up the EKG. But all tested well … for the moment. Incidentally, don't know if you heard that Pete Currier passed away last week. I talked to KJ. She's holding up, but I'm sure she'd like to hear from you.

Here's the email for my accountant, Sol Axelrod: solaxelrod@cheswick-andlowell.com. If anyone knows how to avoid Alternative Minimum Tax, it's this guy. He's Jewish, but not too Jewish, if you know what I mean.

I'm looking forward to seeing you before long. I just made reservations at the Hilton during the conference. Great of you to offer the houseboat for the weekend. I hope you'll get a chance to meet Sarah.

My best to your Mae,
Gordon

S. Gordon Wilson, PhD.
Founder and Editor of *The Ichthysaurus*
Fellow, American Academy of Underwater Sciences
Professor of Biology, emeritus
California State University, Long Beach

*From: **Sarah Ross** <sarahross64@gmail.com>*
*To: **Adam Wolf** <adam.wolf1402@gmail.com>*
July 29, 2014 4:32 pm
Subject: weekend in Seattle

Gordon's invited me to join him for a weekend in Seattle in October. I really hesitate going. I need to give him an answer soon.

---

*From: **Adam Wolf** <adam.wolf1402@gmail.com>*
*To: **Sarah Ross** <sarahross64@gmail.com>*
July 29, 2014 6:54 pm
Subject: Re:weekend in Seattle

Remember the decision is yours. Don't let yourself be pressured into anything. Why do you hesitate?

---

*From: **Sarah Ross** <sarahross64@gmail.com>*
*To: **Adam Wolf** <adam.wolf1402@gmail.com>*
July 29, 2014 7:11 pm
Subject: Re:Re:weekend in Seattle

I really need to think about this. You know, or maybe I haven't told you, Gordon and I have only been affectionate within limits, up until now. I know if I join him it's a commitment to be intimate, and I don't know if that's in my repertoire any more.

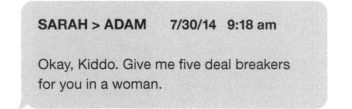

SARAH > ADAM   7/30/14   9:18 am

Okay, Kiddo. Give me five deal breakers for you in a woman.

ADAM 10:03 am

Do you mean a deal breaker for a long-term relationship or one night?
1) Republican
2) Doesn't have cable tv
3) Under the age of 65

SARAH 11:55 am

First of all, I got rid of cable tv. So long, Buster.

ADAM 12:03 pm

I knew it. Good riddance. THE END.

SARAH 12:15 pm

Only three deal breakers? You're easy to please. Aren't you going to ask me for my five deal breakers?

ADAM 12:29 pm

Yes, go ahead, but first I have one more deal breaker. Women who go off on romantic weekends with marine biologists, while at the same time reaffirming love for their high school boyfriends. OK. Your turn.

SARAH   1:00 pm

Whoa there, big boy, your jealousy is charming.
Let me ponder what my deal breakers might
be. Nicole and I are doing some inventory this
afternoon. I'll email later.
ocilu

From: **Sarah Ross** *<sarahross64@gmail.com>*
To: **Adam Wolf** *<adam.wolf1402@gmail.com>*
July 30, 2014 7:55 pm
Subject: my deal breakers

Rough day at work. I must be getting addled. Kept typing in the wrong figures, losing the Excel file, not hearing when Nicole spoke to me. Oy.

My five deal breakers? Let's start with number 1
1. "Unfunny", different from humorless, far worse. People who think they're funny, but they're not. I need genuinely funny.

From: **Adam Wolf** *<adam.wolf1402@gmail.com>*
To: **Sarah Ross** *<sarahross64@gmail.com>*
July 30, 2014 8:22 pm
Subject: Re:my deal breakers

Yeah, add that to my list too. Like my neighbor Bud, who believes he's a raconteur. Always announces he's about to tell a great joke. Five paragraphs later, when he arrives at the "punch line", he emits a loud guffaw to signal it's time for your forced laugh. They're always jokes about barnyards or priests or someone who went in their pants. They're always about something smelling bad.

I have to agree that "unfunny" is unacceptable. Go on.

From: **Sarah Ross** *<sarahross64@gmail.com>*
To: **Adam Wolf** *<adam.wolf1402@gmail.com>*
July 30, 2014 9:43 pm
Subject: Re:Re:my deal breakers

And the worst for me are all the unfunny misogynistic jokes out there. THE worst. Especially the old wife and the young thing, those geezers-will-be-geezers jokes.

okay four more:
2. Alcoholic. I couldn't live with a drunk (again). (Harold turned to booze, and bullying. Liquor breath alone nauseates me.)

3. Arrogance.

4. Small talk. Aaaaarrrgh!!!!!!!!!!! People who bore me. Some people seem to need it. I can't understand it, and they hate me for not playing the small talk game. But the other day, in a cab, the taxi driver started telling me that he was just shopping at the mall near Naughty Niceties. And I wanted to stimulate him into a small talk chat, just to see how far it would go. So I asked him whether he bought anything, and he was off. And, I must admit it was fascinating—no detail too small—an amazing gift. He told me that he bought the gray jeans by Wrangler, the only brand that fits him properly in the seat, sure Levis are fine, but Wrangler is what fits his bottom best, and they were on sale, the first day of the sale, so they were sure to have his size, and he didn't want any other color, but then the salesperson, extremely helpful, showed him some nice light brown cords, also on sale, so of course he had to get those, and back home he has a black denim pair for winter, and on and on. It was fascinating in its mind-numbing banality. I can't stand it.

5. Bad false teeth — too white, too straight, screams "Old Person on Deck".

From: **Adam Wolf** <adam.wolf1402@gmail.com>
To: **Sarah Ross** <sarahross64@gmail.com>
July 30, 2014 9:51 pm
Subject:

Very funny, love. I'm falling asleep dearest one. Come beside me and snuggle.

From: **Sarah Ross** <sarahross64@gmail.com>
To: **Adam Wolf** <adam.wolf1402@gmail.com>
July 30, 2014 9:57 pm
Subject:

Make room. Always there with you, my Adam Wolf.

From: **S.Gordon Wilson** <S.Gordon.Wilson@csulb.edu>
To: **Jerry Mahoney** <Jerry.Mahoney2028@verizon.net>
August 2, 2014 4:44 pm
Subject: Trip to Seattle and a yuck

Dear Jerry,

Thanks for getting back to me so quickly. If you can arrange to be there the week I'm in Seattle, I could skip out on the Wednesday sessions. There's still time to think about it, but let's aim for a round of golf that afternoon. Any recommendations?
Speaking of golf, just heard this one. I suspect you'll like it.

Two lesbians playing golf:

On the fifth hole, both of their drives go wide and end up on opposite sides of the fairway. They split up to look for their golf balls, and Alice finds hers in a patch of buttercups.

She takes a swing and her ball lands perfectly on the green, but the buttercups are ruined. As she turns around, she sees a strange, glowing woman with a crown of flowers. "I am Mother Nature," the woman says, "and you have destroyed my buttercups! I curse you! From this day forward, you shall never again enjoy the taste of butter!" With that, Mother Nature vanishes.

Alice is understandably confused, and decides to put the curse to the test. She gets a sandwich out of her bag, and indeed, the butter makes her choke and gag the moment it hits her tongue. Well, that's unfortunate, but I guess I can live without butter, she thinks, and she goes to find her girlfriend.

They meet back up in the middle of the fairway. "Oh, you wouldn't believe what just happened to me," says Beth. "I was looking for my ball, and found it in a patch of pussy willows ..."

Gordon

S. Gordon Wilson, PhD.
Founder and Editor of *The Ichthysaurus*
Fellow, American Academy of Underwater Sciences
Professor of Biology, emeritus
California State University, Long Beach

---

*From:***Harold Weinstein** *<Harold.W.Weinstein9933@gmail.com>*
To: **Sarah Ross** *<sarahross64@gmail.com>*
August 4, 2014 8:57 am
Subject: My book!

I need that book.

---

*From: **Adam Wolf** <adam.wolf1402@gmail.com>*
*To: **Sarah Ross** <sarahross64@gmail.com>*
August 16, 2014 10:13 am
Subject: More favorites

Loved a chance to talk last night. Your giggle is unchanged.
Here's some more old-time comedy that occurred to me. You can find
all of this on YouTube. Jack Benny. Charming, made me smile. Milton
Berle — we didn't watch him cause we didn't think he was funny.

---

*From: **Sarah Ross** <sarahross64@gmail.com>*
*To: **Adam Wolf** <adam.wolf1402@gmail.com>*
August 16, 2014 10:40 am
Subject: Re:More favorites

Milton Berle — creepy, you ask me. Not funny at all. Nor Red Buttons. Nor Phil Silvers. Lucy, now SHE was riotously funny. Mention the
Chocolate Factory and I giggle. Once, at a car wash, I goofed and re-
moved the hose from its sleeve and then started the machine. I got
soaked. Chased the hose as it smacked at my car and doused me in
water, and all the time thinking how great Lucille Ball would have been
in a fix like that one.

---

*From: **Adam Wolf** <adam.wolf1402@gmail.com>*
*To: **Sarah Ross** <sarahross64@gmail.com>*
August 16, 2014 11:12 am
Subject: Re:Re:More favorites

Lucy, the whole ensemble for that show brilliant! My mother loved her
too. My father found Red Buttons funny. Not me. Nor did I like Little
Rascals, but I watched them. My favorite — as most men will tell
you — The Three Stooges. Reels of them would run on the TV after
school and I couldn't live without them. Still can't.

From: **Sarah Ross** *<sarahross64@gmail.com>*
To: **Adam Wolf** *<adam.wolf1402@gmail.com>*
August 16, 2014 11:29 am
Subject: Three Stooges??

You know, Adam, I've never really found myself gender-bound to girlie stuff, often preferred the "Woodworking for Boys" kits to lanyard beading, but chromosomes run true when it comes to The Three Stooges. I, and all the other women I know, think The Three Stooges are stupid, gross and NOT AT ALL funny. You and I part ways over them.

But I remember you liked Groucho as much as I did. My top pick for your delectation. YouTube. Groucho singing "Lydia the Tattoo Lady" in *Duck Soup.* "For two bits she can do a mazurka in jazz, with a view of Niagara that nobody has, and on a clear day you can see Alcatraz. You can learn a lot from Lydia."

From: **Adam Wolf** *<adam.wolf1402@gmail.com>*
To: **Sarah Ross** *<sarahross64@gmail.com>*
August 16, 2014 11:40 am
Subject:

Let's pick this up tomorrow, Sarah. I need to drive up to Wisconsin with Lola for a rally. Lola is fiercely active in liberal politics and I admire that about her. She's been the catalyst to get me off the couch and on the street for causes that matter.

From: **Adam Wolf** *<adam.wolf1402@gmail.com>*
To: **Sarah Ross** *<sarahross64@gmail.com>*
August 17, 2014 9:49 am
Subject:

Tiring drive yesterday. Couldn't hear anything. Microphones didn't work.
Okay, back to business.

I would like you to watch Groucho in *Day at the Races* when the Administrator of the sanitarium calls the Florida Medical Board to investigate the license to practice of Dr. Hackenbush. If you like that, watch him give the medical exam to Margaret Dumont.

But you know who was funny, I mean really, routinely, roll-in-the-aisles funny? Sid Caesar. *Your Show of Shows.*

From: **Sarah Ross** <sarahross64@gmail.com>
To: **Adam Wolf** <adam.wolf1402@gmail.com>
August 17, 2014 10:13 am
Subject:

I'm sure everyone would agree with you. Sid Caesar and the whole ensemble of *Your Show of Shows.* Oh, thank goodness for YouTube!
What were your favorite routines?

From: **Adam Wolf** <adam.wolf1402@gmail.com>
To: **Sarah Ross** <sarahross64@gmail.com>
August 17, 2014 11:45 am
Subject: This is Your Story

The greatest *Show of Shows* routine ever done is the spoof of *This is Your Life.* Makes me laugh every time.

From: **Sarah Ross** <sarahross64@gmail.com>
To: **Adam Wolf** <adam.wolf1402@gmail.com>
August 17, 2014 11:49 am
Subject: This is Your Life

Hey, Adam, how would an episode of *This is Your Life, Adam Wolf* go?

---

*From: **Adam Wolf** <adam.wolf1402@gmail.com>*
*To: **Sarah Ross** <sarahross64@gmail.com>*
August 17, 2014 2:10 pm
Subject: Re:This is Your Life

Picture this. I'm on the sofa. Ralph Edwards looms over me and opens the big book:

Ralph Edwards:
Adam Wolf, when you were just a boy your father was rarely home. Often he was pretending to work at the drugstore, when actually he was at his communist cell meetings, passing A-bomb secrets. There was one man who would teach you to throw a curve ball. He became quite a father figure, even a friend. He took you to the movies, to the ball game and all he would ask in return, for each visit, was for you to touch his peepee.

Me:
Gee, that sounds like Uncle Pinchas.

Ralph Edwards:
When you were 12 years old — a teacher locked you in the cloakroom for an entire school day, as punishment for peeking up her skirt. At the end of the day, before she released you, she gave you words of advice that would stay with you the rest of your life:

The voice (a creaky, old, old lady voice):
Don't be a dirty boy. And if you have to be a dirty boy, don't get caught.

Ralph Edwards:
Then you met the person who would become the love of your life. Do you recognize the voice, Adam?

The voice:
Hello, Adam, don't you remember, every weekend you came over and let me rest my head on your lap while we watched The Twilight Zone?

Me:

I got it, I got it. Don't tell me. Give me a hint. It's either Sally Green, Genevieve Berkowitz, or Darlene Cutler

The voice:

No, Adam, this is Sarah Ross.

Me:

Oh, yeah, Sarah Ross, yeah. uh-huh.

From: **Sarah Ross** <sarahross64@gmail.com>
To: **Adam Wolf** <adam.wolf1402@gmail.com>
August 17, 2014 3:17 pm
Subject: Re:Re:This is Your Life

> I knew it, Darlene Cutler!
> Hard to say which is my favorite Sid Caesar episode.
> The German Doorman routine, I suppose.

From: **Adam Wolf** <adam.wolf1402@gmail.com>
To: **Sarah Ross** <sarahross64@gmail.com>
August 17, 2014 4:15 pm
Subject: Sid Caesar

Me too!! One of the top five for me. Sid Caesar could do gibberish better than anyone in the world.

I'm pretty good too at imitations, if you remember. They called me the man of a thousand voices, none of which were recognizable.

From: **Sarah Ross** *<sarahross64@gmail.com>*
To: **Adam Wolf** *<adam.wolf1402@gmail.com>*
August 17, 2014 4:34 pm
Subject: imitations

    I remember, of course. Marshall Dillon imitations, Chester of *Gunsmoke*. Remember your regaling the school over the P.A. system before homeroom some mornings.
    Do you ever get to do voices on the radio?

From: **Adam Wolf** *<adam.wolf1402@gmail.com>*
To: **Sarah Ross** *<sarahross64@gmail.com>*
August 17, 2014 5:40 pm
Subject: Re:imitations

Sure, every once in a while I sneak one in—an English accent, or German or Yiddish. I once interviewed a non-existent Uzbecki pianist for 5 mins. on Shubert—totally in gibberish. An Uzbecki listener complained.
I can imitate Vaughn Meader imitating Kennedy.

From: **Sarah Ross** *<sarahross64@gmail.com>*
To: **Adam Wolf** *<adam.wolf1402@gmail.com>*
August 17, 2014 5:59 pm
Subject:

    Ok. Now I'm really in love. You can do that AND skate backwards?

From: **Adam Wolf** *<adam.wolf1402@gmail.com>*
To: **Sarah Ross** *<sarahross64@gmail.com>*
August 17, 2014 6:16 pm
Subject:

I can do both at the same time.

From: **Sarah Ross** <sarahross64@gmail.com>
To: **Adam Wolf** <adam.wolf1402@gmail.com>
August 17, 2014 7:10 pm
Subject:

Golly, gee, Mr. Wizard.

From: **Harold.W.Weinstein9933**@gmail.com
To: **John.R.Nafkowitz**@ucsd.edu
August 21, 2014 11:14 am
Subject: Your "review"

Hello John,

Thank you for taking the time to read the manuscript. It was asking a lot, I realize. 491 pages. U. of Michigan Press said out of hand that it needed to be cut before they would even consider it. And I will take seriously some of your suggestions of what really needs to be excised. That being said, I was taken aback by some of your comments and wish you could go over the book once again to see that I did NOT, in fact, overlook Auden's debt to Pound, nor his scatological poems. What I selected is, I feel, most representative and illuminates my main point, the stanza patterns in Auden. I certainly take umbrage at your insinuation that I missed the critical challenge of the poetry.
And I dare say you are mistaken on another point. "Fornication" does not just apply to sex between unmarried persons. It also applies to a married person (usually a woman) having sex outside of marriage AND, the way I use it, is in its biblical form and has nothing to do with intercourse. Please see below: Eziekiel 16:29. There, as the author of this article in Yahweh Research articulates, it refers to idolatry. I'm surprised you didn't know this. Perhaps I would have been better off asking a first-year grad student to review the book.
Frankly, John, I can't help thinking that you prejudged the book because it was mine. I sense a bias against me in your comments. I know we haven't really been close colleagues for a while now and I

suppose that you, like too many others in the department, believed those absurd accusations against me and felt sympathy for Sarah. But I have a newsflash for all of you: Sarah Ross is no saint herself. I assume I need to thank you again for glancing at my manuscript.

Regards,
Harold

Citation: Retrieved from http://www.yrm.org/qna-fornication.htm

The word fornication comes from three separate words in the Bible, two from the Hebrew and one from the Greek. These words all share similar connotations. Each can mean literal fornication between two unmarried persons in a marriage contract; however, it can also signify adultery, whoredom, or an act of unfaithfulness on the part of Yahweh's people. The first place the word fornication is used in the Old Testament is found in II Chronicles 21:81. The word fornication found in this passage is from the Hebrew, No. 2181, Zanah, and is defined by **Strong's Exhaustive Concordance of the Bible** as follows: "to commit adultery (usually on the female, and less often of simple fornication, rarely of involuntary ravishment); fig. To commit idolatry (the Jewish people being regarded as the spouse of [Yahweh]) ..."
The Complete Word Study Old Testament suggests three possible meanings for the Hebrew word "zanah." The first being fornication (premarital, illicit sex), the second being adultery (marital, illicit sex), and the third being idolatry (worship of a person or thing besides Yahweh). The second word denoting fornication in the English is found only once in the Hebrew, in Ezekiel 16:29. The word fornication in this passage is from the Hebrew, No. 8457, taznuth, and simply means a type of idolatry. Being that this word is only used once, the quest for an exact definition should not be too exhausting.
The third word signifying fornication is found in the Greek and is first used in Matthew 5:32. This word derives from the Greek word, No. 4202, porneia and is defined in the **Strong's** as follows, "from 4203; harlotry (incl. Adultery and incest); fig. Idolatry: — fornication."

From: **Esther Lehman** *<estherlehman88@yahoo.com>*
To: **Harold Weinstein** *<Harold.W.Weinstein9933@gmail.com>*
August 24, 2014 3:43 pm
Subject: Sarah's book

Sarah asked me to tell you the book you insist on having does not belong to you! She says you must have forgotten President Bloustein presented it to her at her Bennington graduation, the dept. prize. She wants you to stop hounding her about it.

From: **Sarah Ross** *<sarahross64@gmail.com>*
To: **Adam Wolf** *<adam.wolf1402@gmail.com>*
August 28, 2014 8:08 am
Subject: frenzy

When you didn't phone to wish me good night, I confess I felt that stupid teenage sinking in my gut … "He stopped loving me." Embarrassing to admit. But, could I ask you to send me at least one text each night? Or is that unforgivably immature too?

You know, I love the calls, but do miss emailing. There's a lot I can say or take in, if it comes in writing.

Okay. Break it to me gently. What happened in the 70's, what you call those "frenzy" years? Sexual frenzy, I take it. ilu, in case you need reminding.

From: **Adam Wolf** *<adam.wolf1402@gmail.com>*
To: **Sarah Ross** *<sarahross64@gmail.com>*
August 28, 2014 11:20 am
Subject: Re:frenzy

Sorry about the call. Fell asleep with my clothes on. Exhausted. You know I like emailing too.

The Frenzy Years:

The 70's—not entirely sexual. I admit I spent a lot of time prowling the streets in search of compliant women, but that was only 10 hours a day. It tires me just to think about it.

After Vietnam was safely past, I left my position in the psycho wards, then the rest of the time was drift—half-assed jobs—H & R Block temp, bussing tables, working my way up to manager of a classical record store. Along the way, though, after I hooked up with Gerda Whatshername, I lost the girl, but kept the German.

Und du, meine Sarah?

How did your 1970s go? Sedate, I suspect.

From: **Sarah Ross** <sarahross64@gmail.com>
To: **Adam Wolf** <adam.wolf1402@gmail.com>
August 28, 2014 4:13 pm
Subject: warning: adult material ahead

1970's? *Nicht schlecht.*

Well, the 70s became too sedate after I married Harold, but if we want to talk wild frenzy, I can contribute. Do the late 60's count? I was kinda broke when I first got to San Diego. School kept me busy, but I had to earn money. I found time for the evening shift, as I once mentioned, as an adult phone entertainer. A Bennington pal started the business (subscriptions only in those days). No 900 numbers yet. It was called *Fantasy Flirt: "No taboos"*—paid more.

---

*From: **Adam Wolf** <adam.wolf1402@gmail.com>*
*To: **Sarah Ross** <sarahross64@gmail.com>*
August 28, 2014 8:04 pm
Subject: Re:warning: adult material ahead

Mein Gott!! My Sarah in the ersatz sex industry? Did your mother know? Where did you learn the trade? Did you have to take classes? I have a thousand questions to ask you. I've always had a fascination with phone sex operators. You're the first one I've ever talked to. So, may I ask? Did you ever get turned on yourself by the encounters?

---

*From: **Sarah Ross** <sarahross64@gmail.com>*
*To: **Adam Wolf** <adam.wolf1402@gmail.com>*
August 28, 2014 8:24 pm
Subject: phone sex

I'm sure your interest is strictly academic, Adam.

Of course I was sometimes turned on, but mostly my job was to hold people on the line talking dirty to them in slow motion, while I perfected my pasta primavera. I wasn't bad at it. I mean the phone sex. The pasta primavera sucked. I got a lot of compliments on my guided tours. The company liked me cause I had a gift for keeping guys aroused enough to stay on the line.

---

*From: **Adam Wolf** <adam.wolf1402@gmail.com>*
*To: **Sarah Ross** <sarahross64@gmail.com>*
August 28, 2014 8:29 pm
Subject: Re:phone sex

If I may continue the interview. Did anyone ever call to request something you never heard of before?

From: **Sarah Ross** *<sarahross64@gmail.com>*
To: **Adam Wolf** *<adam.wolf1402@gmail.com>*
August 28, 2014 8:32 pm
Subject: Re:Re:phone sex

Yes.

From: **Adam Wolf** *<adam.wolf1402@gmail.com>*
To: **Sarah Ross** *<sarahross64@gmail.com>*
August 28, 2014 8:36 pm
Subject: Re:Re:Re:phone sex

Details please.

From: **Sarah Ross** *<sarahross64@gmail.com>*
To: **Adam Wolf** *<adam.wolf1402@gmail.com>*
August 28, 2014 8:50 pm
Subject:

I won't go into details. Even though I went to Bennington, I was
still shockable. I couldn't show it, though, even when asked to be an
orangutan in heat, trapped with the client in a bathroom at the San
Diego Zoo, after hours.

From: **Adam Wolf** *<adam.wolf1402@gmail.com>*
To: **Sarah Ross** *<sarahross64@gmail.com>*
August 28, 2014 9:09 pm
Subject:

Serious, Sarah.

---

*From: **Sarah Ross** <sarahross64@gmail.com>*
*To: **Adam Wolf** <adam.wolf1402@gmail.com>*
August 28, 2014 9:19 pm
Subject:

OK. Some guys responded to aural oral stimulation. But mostly they were strange S & M requests — tying guys up, spanking them and nailing them to cars, for e.g. driving through town that way, naked. I don't mean to boast, but the Mistress Chiara in me is a legend in the industry even to this day.

---

*From: **Adam Wolf** <adam.wolf1402@gmail.com>*
*To: **Sarah Ross** <sarahross64@gmail.com>*
August 28, 2014 9:29 pm
Subject:

I take it that you don't look back to those days with misgivings. Tell me more. How did you provide oral gratification over a phone?

---

*From: **Sarah Ross** <sarahross64@gmail.com>*
*To: **Adam Wolf** <adam.wolf1402@gmail.com>*
August 28, 2014 9:41 pm
Subject:

Well, imagination, dear Adam, and a gift for gab. Plus, an ear for shallow breathing and what it called for. Can you believe that we're 68 years old, last saw each other as innocents, and are talking about this?

---

*From: **Adam Wolf** <adam.wolf1402@gmail.com>*
*To: **Sarah Ross** <sarahross64@gmail.com>*
August 28, 2014 9:55 pm
Subject: Phone me, why don't you

Perhaps we were once too young for this banter. But do you really think we're too old to be stimulated by it now? Let's find out. Would you be willing to give me a sample of your craft sometime?

---

*From: **Sarah Ross** <sarahross64@gmail.com>*
*To: **Adam Wolf** <adam.wolf1402@gmail.com>*
August 28, 2014 10:18 pm
Subject: Re:Phone me, why don't you

I think we would spend too much time giggling. On the phone, back then, I could be anyone they needed me to be—anonymously. I didn't know them from Adam. Ooops.

---

*From: **Adam Wolf** <adam.wolf1402@gmail.com>*
*To: **Sarah Ross** <sarahross64@gmail.com>*
August 28, 2014 10:23 pm
Subject:

Did you ever have women call you?

---

*From: **Sarah Ross** <sarahross64@gmail.com>*
*To: **Adam Wolf** <adam.wolf1402@gmail.com>*
August 28, 2014 10:28 pm
Subject:

Yes. Once.

From: **Adam Wolf** <adam.wolf1402@gmail.com>
To: **Sarah Ross** <sarahross64@gmail.com>
August 28, 2014 10:36 pm
Subject:

Did you enjoy that?

From: **Sarah Ross** <sarahross64@gmail.com>
To: **Adam Wolf** <adam.wolf1402@gmail.com>
August 28, 2014 10:49 pm
Subject:

    You know, Adam, it was a business. Enjoying wasn't part of it, or rarely was part of it. But, okay, once. I admit I did get rather aroused that time. She was good at it. I always thought she must have been another phone sex operator.

From: **Adam Wolf** <adam.wolf1402@gmail.com>
To: **Sarah Ross** <sarahross64@gmail.com>
August 28, 2014 10:58 pm
Subject:

Did you ever get calls from men fantasizing about wearing women's clothes?

From: **Sarah Ross** <sarahross64@gmail.com>
To: **Adam Wolf** <adam.wolf1402@gmail.com>
August 28, 2014 11:14 pm
Subject:

    Of course. All the time. I always enjoyed dressing up men. Some were turned on by red-plaid, pleated schoolgirl outfits. Others got hot talking about short latex skirts and what shade lipstick and nail polish went best with their slutty fuck-me heels.

Actually, Adam, we have a number of male clients at Naughty Nice-ties and I like that.

From: **Adam Wolf** <adam.wolf1402@gmail.com>
To: **Sarah Ross** <sarahross64@gmail.com>
August 28, 2014 11:22 pm
Subject:

I'll tell you what, Sarah. Why don't you send me something from the store's collection?

From: **Sarah Ross** <sarahross64@gmail.com>
To: **Adam Wolf** <adam.wolf1402@gmail.com>
August 28, 2014 11:30 pm
Subject:

Oh?

From: **Adam Wolf** <adam.wolf1402@gmail.com>
To: **Sarah Ross** <sarahross64@gmail.com>
August 28, 2014 11:34 pm
Subject:

"Oh" what?—I love you.

From: **Sarah Ross** <sarahross64@gmail.com>
To: **Adam Wolf** <adam.wolf1402@gmail.com>
August 28, 2014 11:37 pm
Subject:

Well, I just might.

From: **S.Gordon Wilson** <S.Gordon.Wilson@csulb.edu>
To: **Jerry Mahoney** <Jerry.Mahoney2028@verizon.net>
August 30, 2014 11:46 am
Subject: Sarah agreed to come!

Dear Jerry,

I wish you and Mae could stick around for the weekend of the conference. Sarah agreed to join me and I know you two will like her. She doesn't get away from La Jolla often, so I want to make it a special occasion for us. And it'll be healthy for her to cut the cord to her computer. Get this, she tells me that some prick from her high school days is pursuing her long distance. Now they have some kind of regular email going back and forth. It's a puerile waste of time, if you ask me. I hope the trip to Seattle will snap her out of it.

Gordon

S. Gordon Wilson, PhD.
Founder of *The Ichthysaurus*
Fellow, American Academy of Underwater Sciences
Professor of Biology, emeritus
California State University, Long Beach

From: **Amanda Schreiber** <Amanda.D.Schreiber@wcmq.com>
To: **Lola Wolf** <lola.wolf1402@gmail.com>
September 2, 2014 9:47 am
Subject: Concerned

Hey there Lola,

It's been a while, hasn't it? Probably the station picnic last year. Congratulations on your recent retirement. Morgan Stanley must regret losing you.

Let me jump to the reason I'm writing today. I debated with myself whether or not I should burden you with this. You may know what I'm talking about. I just feel obliged to share my observations. I'm concerned about Adam. He means a lot to us at the station. We all worry about him. For the past couple of months or so, he's strangely distracted, preoccupied. Barely speaks. He spends a lot of time on his computer emailing people from his reunion, especially one individual named Sarah Ross. Maybe you know who she is?

Have you noticed anything? Is it something I need to be concerned about? To tell the truth, I'm rather worried that his preoccupations are affecting his work.

Amanda

---

*From: **Lola Wolf** <lola.wolf1402@gmail.com>*
*To: **Amanda Schreiber** <Amanda.D.Schreiber@wcmq.com>*
September 4, 2014 3:04 pm
Subject: Re:Concerned

Frankly, Amanda, I'm not sure any of this is your concern. Adam would never allow personal things to interfere with his work.

Here's my take. It's all about the reunion. He temporarily lost his mind over the whole damn thing. Before he went, he weighed himself 40 times a day. He perseverated over which jacket to wear. Came back full of himself. Women "who still looked good" paying lots of attention to him. Don't worry, he'll snap out of it. So it's Sarah Ross. I see. His high school girlfriend. Michael and I trust he'll come to his senses soon. I've heard guys his age often go through some kind of retrogression like this. Dave, a neighbor down the street, ran off for a weekend to see some college flame. He came back with his tail between his legs. Sherry laughed it off.

Maybe that's what we ought to do.

Lola

From: **Lola Wolf** <lola.wolf1402@gmail.com>

To: **Adam Wolf** <adam.wolf1402@gmail.com>

September 6, 2014 3:16 pm

Subject: Please answer

Adam, I'm sending you email because you refuse to sit down and carry on a civil conversation. You don't bother taking my calls. But you need to know I found out. Words fail me. Sarah Ross? THE Sarah Ross? Did you see her at your reunion? Are you planning to escape with her back to your childhood?

From: **Adam Wolf** <adam.wolf1402@gmail.com>

To: **Lola Wolf** <lola.wolf1402@gmail.com>

September 6, 2014 4:54 pm

Subject: Re:Please answer

Congratulations, Fearless Fosdick. Another successful domestic surveillance job. Incidentally, as your investigation surely uncovered, I'm corresponding with many people after the reunion, including Sarah Ross.

From: **Lola Wolf** <lola.wolf1402@gmail.com>

To: **Adam Wolf** <adam.wolf1402@gmail.com>

September 6, 2014 5:12 pm

Subject: Re:Re:Please answer

Yeah, sure. Doesn't matter to me, but I'm concerned because it bothers Amanda. Apparently it looks to her like you're spending hours a day tending to Sarah, instead of to business. We need to sit down and talk about this. When will you be home?

---

*From: **Adam Wolf** <adam.wolf1402@gmail.com>*
*To: **Lola Wolf** <lola.wolf1402@gmail.com>*
September 6, 2014 5:46 pm
Subject

I don't need to explain anything to you, but if you must know, Sarah and I have a lot of history to recollect. We were just having fun reminiscing about notes we would pass in study hall. But do you really think a 68 year-old man would be deluded enough to try to reignite a romance with someone he hasn't seen in 50 years?

---

*From: **Lola Wolf** <lola.wolf1402@gmail.com>*
*To: **Adam Wolf** <adam.wolf1402@gmail.com>*
September 6, 2014 6:04 pm
Subject:

I believe you would want to see how far you could get, because you're that immature.

---

*From: **Adam Wolf** <adam.wolf1402@gmail.com>*
*To: **Sarah Ross** <sarahross64@gmail.com>*
September 10, 2014 11:22 am
Subject: Re:Your birthday!

Thanks for the birthday salutations — 69 years down — 69 years to go. Festivities are unfolding for the occasion here in the Windy City. I am naturally humbled by all the care that has gone into planning my "special day".
Lola left me a shirt on my bed — turquoise dress shirt — wrong neck (too small) — wrong sleeve (too long) — a Walgreen greeting card with a joke about old people pissing — and a handwritten note "Happy B day. Chinese for dinner later?"

Ok, but Amanda certainly outperformed her. When I got to the station, an email awaited me from the Duchess Herself. "Your birthday, right? Almost forgot. Let's do Lawry's Thursday. Stay late. We'll figure something out. Enjoy your day."

No one at the station knew it was "B" day, so there you go. Well, you should know, Sarah, I never really liked parties anyway, except for the one you threw for me at Manner's Big Boy when I turned 16. Who needs recognition, awards, testimonials? For high school graduation, my parents took me out for a cheeseburger. On graduation from college, it was deli for corned beef.

From: **Sarah Ross** <sarahross64@gmail.com>
To: **Adam Wolf** <adam.wolf1402@gmail.com>
September 10, 2014 11:27 am
Subject: Re:Re: Your birthday!

What's it feel like to be 69? I still have a few weeks to go before I find out.

From: **Adam Wolf** <adam.wolf1402@gmail.com>
To: **Sarah Ross** <sarahross64@gmail.com>
September 10, 2014 12:18 pm
Subject: Life, the condensed version

The more I reflect, the more I discover that there is no detectable fabric to my life. My memory conjures no great themes of learning, accomplishment, or even regret, just a series of sensations and brief images of the moments felt. And from these decades, there are only a few hundred brief scenes. No long story of any consequence.

Played end to end, the sensations and the images of my life last maybe 45 minutes. The prevailing sensations that accompany most of these images are depression and anxiety, lifted only by panic and humiliation. And, yes, there are sensations of triumph, of ecstasy. But those fade after a second or two.

The other powerful sensation—nausea! I am not surprised that I have spent more of my life nauseated than happy. Beyond those 45 minutes, until now, the rest of the 68 years, 11 months 30 days 11 hours 15 minutes—just endless days of numb repetition that I can't remember. Sarah, let's you and I start our own 45 min. highlight reel.

4

---

*From: **Darlene Cutler** <Darlene.Cutler@branch14.org>*
*To: **Adam Wolf** <adam.wolf1402@gmail.com>*
September 10, 2014 8:18 pm
Subject: rendezvous

Hey, Adam, thinking about the trip to Chicago and getting excited about this weekend. Can we fit in some sightseeing? Never have been there.

---

*From: **Adam Wolf** <adam.wolf1402@gmail.com>*
*To: **Darlene Cutler** <Darlene.Cutler@branch14.org>*
September 10, 2014 8:41 pm
Subject: Re:rendezvous

Absolutely! — Art Institute, Michigan Ave., Al Capone's grave, the site of the St. Valentine's Day massacre, and of course the Biograph Theater where Dillinger was shot. Fine Chicago attractions. And I'll even take you to a deli I think you'll love. Obama's favorite. Like Corky and Lenny's.

From: **Darlene Cutler** <Darlene.Cutler@branch14.org>
To: **Adam Wolf** <adam.wolf1402@gmail.com>
September 10, 2014 9:25 pm
Subject: Re:Re:rendezvous

You got it! Lunch on you. Dinner's on me, if you can free yourself up. I'm staying at the Marriott Suites O'Hare. A good restaurant downstairs, they say. So put on your dancing shoes. I'm almost there.

From: **Adam Wolf** <adam.wolf1402@gmail.com>
To: **Sarah Ross** <sarahross64@gmail.com>
September 11, 2014 8:55 pm
Subject: Sunday?

Can't wait for a chance to talk to you at length. How's Sunday afternoon about 2:00? Sat. no good this week. Cousin Janet's son is a frosh at Iowa. Homesick, I agreed to drive her over there. Next time we talk, would you like me to sing you some arias from the opera I've begun, *Il Strage San Valentino?* I'm especially proud of the leitmotif for Bugs Moran.
Last night I had a peculiar dream. You and I were together—in a peaceful hotel room somewhere—maybe in Europe, maybe Rome. I remember the grand balcony we were on, like Julius Caesar's, and the red tile roofs below. Then a plane started to land in the parking lot. "I think we need to run," I said. "We're in the wrong room, someone else's." You refuse to leave. "Nothing's wrong," you tell me. And I bolt. Down some long narrow stone stairway set at a terrifying angle. I clutch the rails and still I start to fall. In the distance I hear you call, "Do you still love me?" And awake now, I can assure that YES. OCISLU.

---

*From: **Sarah Ross** <sarahross64@gmail.com>*
*To: **Adam Wolf** <adam.wolf1402@gmail.com>*
September 11, 2014 9:30 pm
Subject: Re:Sunday?

    Being in Europe with you? Dreamy. You abruptly running away? *Deja vu* all over again. Nightmarish to me too. Yikes!
    Sunday? A long talk on the phone would be grand. But can we make it earlier in the day, say 8 am my time?

---

*From: **Adam Wolf** <adam.wolf1402@gmail.com>*
*To: **Sarah Ross** <sarahross64@gmail.com>*
September 11, 2014 9:36 pm
Subject: Re:Re:Sunday?

If we were ever together again, Sarah, I can assure you, I would never leave you.
Okay. Sunday morning it is. Why so early? Plans for a BBQ at the Captain's Table?
I'll tell you what. I'll forgive your dalliance with the captain, if you grant me five minutes of your Mistress Chiara patter one of these days.

---

*From: **Sarah Ross** <sarahross64@gmail.com>*
*To: **Adam Wolf** <adam.wolf1402@gmail.com>*
September 11, 2014 9:49 pm
Subject:

    OK. Will you be using Mastercard or Visa?

---

*From: **Amanda Schreiber** <Amanda.D.Schreiber@wcmq.com>*
*To: **Frieda Reigel** <Frieda.M.Reigel@therapypartners.com>*
September 14, 2014 2:52 am
Subject: Therapy this week

Frieda (dock me some time on Thursday, but, like I told you last week, I can't sleep. I have to vent and I have no one else to talk to about this.) Yes, I confess I have been monitoring their emails now. I tried to tell his wife about what was going on. She shrugged it off. But who cares? I have more to lose than she does.

Before you judge me, Frieda, before you indict me for snooping, consider this: I feel no particle of remorse about it.

Adam has let this Ross woman cast a spell over him. He's fallen into a trance. Betrays me every step of the way. He goddamn allows her, day-by-day, to take my place. Frieda, I have a right to defend myself. And, yes, to try to rescue Adam, to know the truth.

Every day he grows more pixilated with this biddy he hasn't even laid eyes on for 50 years. It's not just their nausea-inducing adolescent nostalgia — "moon eyes" across the study hall — lifting, shifting skirts in the park — pettings on the back porch and at the movies. Oh God, Frieda, I guess I could stomach that. But noooo, now I read how they were always "destined to resume" their lives together — maybe "**always married**". Can you believe this drivel??? How much they love the same things. How they are "**totally alike**".

For Christ's sake! All day long they exchange their moronic lists of artistic likes and dislikes: Shostakovich (really?), film noir, Seurat's Grande Jatte. (Adam Wolf hasn't been to the Art Institute in 25 years.) It makes me so sad, so furious, because I remember how Adam would romance me when he first came to the station, and we would exchange our "top ten" lists of operas, conductors, cowboy movies. But all that's gone. Our years together gone, forgotten, obliterated by his senile fixation on the Ross woman.

And they even list the pills they take, their blood pressure readings, his PSA, her yeast infections, the schedule of their goddamn dental appointments. (I wonder if she still has her own teeth.)

Annoying bullshit? I haven't even started. Have I mentioned the Jewish thing? I don't think Adam has seen the inside of a synagogue since 1989. He always told me he never thinks about being Jewish. In fact, he told me he loves to go to McDonald's and have a Big Mac on Yom Kippur. Yeah, that Adam — the no-religion Adam, the ham-and-cheese-sandwich-every-day Adam — the one I have to remind to wish our listeners Happy Passover.

But now that he's back with Sarah, he has become Adam, the torah-wielding Jew, swapping Yiddish phrases, yapping about kosher delis. What's next? The Yeshiva on Foster Avenue? See what I mean?

This week, though, their "soul sharing" plummeted to a disgusting new low. You'll never guess — their **favorite porn sites!!** Real perverted. Frieda, you tell me, because I'm dumbfounded. That's not the Adam Wolf I know. What the hell has she done to twist him so?

And Frieda, it surprised the hell out of me because Adam's told me a long time ago that sex is no longer important to him. I was always lead to believe that his lack of passion was just part of his quiet descent into old age. What a bullshitter! What a con artist!

So now do you blame me for monitoring those emails?

I need to do something before it is too late.

From: **Gabriella Fratelli** <gabriella.fratelli@orange.it>
To: **Sarah Ross** <sarahross64@gmail.com>
September 14, 2014 4:24 pm
Subject: Adam Wolf

My dearest friend,

I miss you too and wish there would be a way to break loose. I think you need my physical presence right now. Forgive me. But you asked my advice, and I am honored that you have, because I feel strongly on the subject of Adam Wolf.

Long ago, when you told me stories about him, I knew there was a great passion and deep love you expressed. But you also talked at length about how deeply he hurt you. I said to you then, and I remember this, "Good riddance!! If I met the man who would ever behave that way, especially to you, I would probably slip arsenic into his coffee, until it took". No one hurts my Sarah and lives to tell the tale.

AND I remind you … if your memory has slipped … you always repeated that as sweet as Adam had been as a young teenager, he became more and more wild. Untrustworthy. Went through women, you told me, to put notches on his bedpost. AND do you remember what you said??? You always, always ended these stories with the following lines: "There but for the grace of God go I. I would never, ever have tolerated such a cavalier cad in my life."

So I beg you, my friend, even though you sound head over heels about this man, be wary. He is capable of seducing women as a hobby. I can't stand the thought of your being hurt again. I do not trust Adam Wolf. Not at any age. Some men his age are defanged lions. Doesn't sound like him, though.

AND also, since you asked my opinion, think about what happens when reality takes over. Don't you think Adam Wolf will slink back to his "normal life" and decide to cut you again?

Multiple *baci* to you, my dearest Sarah.

Your Gabriella

From: **Adam Wolf** *<adam.wolf1402@gmail.com>*
To: **Paul Bishop** *<Paul.R.Bishop@dewey.com>*
September 14, 2014 12:03 pm
Subject: Got myself in trouble — again

Paul,

Chaos theory may well have predicted my latest screw up. I may have mentioned once another dame of the distant past, Darlene Cutler. At the reunion we close-danced in nostalgia. Took a little stroll through the garden. And the party's over. But Dame Darlene seizes on these seven minutes of attention as proof of life. So she connives to come to Chicago and despite all that's happening with Sarah, I acquiesce (chaos theory) and I squire her around town. Thence back to her hotel for dinner. Up to her room. Details omitted — in the end I told her I had a headache—I did. I told her I had weakness in my left arm—I didn't. She told me I sounded like her husband. Showed me a negligee she had brought along. Cried. It's all chaos, Paul. I fled. No contact since.

Paul, do you remember the name of the book Gregory Peck wrote in *Spellbound*? Sure you do. ***The Labyrinth of the Guilt Complex***. Here I am ensnared in the labyrinth of my own making. Engulfed by guilt for having lured and left Darlene in her hotel room. Encircled by guilt for misleading Amanda to her romantic illusions. Enshrouded in **guilt** for wishing Lola away. And while we're at it, encased in **guilt** for causing my mother discomfort when I was born. Paul, if you don't hear from me again, assume I have amnesia and have run off with Ingrid Bergman. Naw, not even Ingrid Bergman. The only person I want to run off with is Sarah. I should have eloped with her as soon as we came of age. Then maybe I would have been spared all these painful entanglements. Strange as it sounds, I now believe Sarah and I were always intended to be with each other—that all the other relationships were haphazard —were detours.

---

*From: **Adam Wolf** <adam.wolf1402@gmail.com>*
*To: **Sarah Ross** <sarahross64@gmail.com>*
September 16, 2014 3:20 pm
Subject: Amanda on warpath over "Lost Love"

Sarah,

Here's something strange. When I came in this morning, I found this article left on my desk. Called *"Lost Love: Guess Who's Back?"* Dates back several years. Amanda printed it out. Purple post-it attached with:

1. You need to read this article before it's too late. Sound familiar?
2. I know a good psychotherapist you should see.

Looks like you and I have become part of a trend. I'm thrilled that relationships like ours make the *New York Times* and *Psychology Today*. What are they calling us? "Rekindlers"? Oy!

Hey, we should be proud to be on the cutting edge like this. Maybe we'll even make the headlines of the *Cleveland Plain Dealer*.

Sarah, here's the part Amanda circled with red marker:

Psychology Today

"Lost Love: Guess Who's Back?"
Old flames still smolder, especially when they're early love affairs.
By Pamela Weintraub, published on July 01, 2006—last reviewed on November 19, 2012
Today, old lovers can type a name into Google. The act seems to be casual, whether it actually is or not. It's so easy to reconnect that many people look up old flames without appreciating what's at stake. Most of these romantic reunions, says California State University at Sacramento psychologist Nancy Kalish, are between first or early loves—those relationships that took place between one's teens and early 20s …
Yet for all the power and resilience of rekindled romance, Kalish has discovered a dark side. More of the encounters are now unpremeditated, and many of these people are swept away by feelings they didn't know they still had, placing marriages—even good marriages—at risk. In her latest sample, more than 60 percent of lost-love reunions involve affairs …
Her most compelling finding was the cataclysmic power of rekindled love. While most ordinary affairs don't break up marriages, reunions with first or early loves are much more risky. Some of the people she met during her research had been willing to forfeit everything—custody of their children, friendships, businesses and life savings—just to be together.

The Dark Side of Rekindled Love … Collateral Damage …
Most spouses don't realize the risk when a partner announces that first e-mail from an old high-school friend, says Kalish, but if the friend is of the opposite sex, alarm bells should go off. Likewise, she says, "if you're married, think long and hard before contacting that first love. Your life may be forever changed."

*From: **Sarah Ross** <sarahross64@gmail.com>*
*To: **Adam Wolf** <adam.wolf1402@gmail.com>*
September 16, 2014 7:19 pm
Subject: They're right. It's a force

    That they've given a name to the phenomenon we're living through is a surprise. I thought we were unique. I find the language in the article distasteful, but am awed by the similar intensity others like us have felt. That gravitational pull of first love. I read the whole article. I can see how Amanda might be appalled by the stories, convinced that you've contracted a fatal disease. Like that story of the woman who, after reconnecting with her high school sweetheart, "immediately" left her "happy marriage" and family to get her own place. So that she could talk to her old love, whenever she wanted. From the outside it sounds commitably insane. Maybe it is insane. So what? Doesn't a shared insanity equal a coherent reality?

    Anyway, I HATE the term "rekindled". It's not a "re" anything. Just picking up where we left off.

---

*From: **Adam Wolf** <adam.wolf1402@gmail.com>*
*To: **Sarah Ross** <sarahross64@gmail.com>*
September 19, 2014 8:09 pm
Subject:

You know, Sarah, I haven't been through a melodrama like this in decades. Endured a crying jag from Lola last night. Bitter words. "I'm your wife. I need the truth about you and Sarah Ross." Then vitriol about how I've neglected her all these years. A solo diva performance punctuated by the percussion section — slammed doors, frying pan smashed into the sink, chairs banged down. Then blaring TV, suddenly switched off. Aggressive silence. Then the second aria — harangues. "I'm your wife. I demand an explanation. When can I expect your craziness to end? You're not the Adam I knew. You've become mean, cynical, and deceptive. Is this payback for Marco?"

Withering — over an hour.

From: **Sarah Ross** <sarahross64@gmail.com>
To: **Adam Wolf** <adam.wolf1402@gmail.com>
September 19, 2014 10:16 pm
Subject: withering

    Why do you hang around for even five minutes of this? What's to tell? That you're in love with a woman you'll never see again?

From: **Adam Wolf** <adam.wolf1402@gmail.com>
To: **Sarah Ross** <sarahross64@gmail.com>
September 21, 2014 9:39 pm
Subject: It continues

Tonight Lola upped the ante. She collected the love letters I sent her when we were courting. Ceremoniously planted them in front of my plate when I was having dinner. "Maybe these will give you some ideas when you're writing to your old girlfriend."
I asked her to stop battering me. She informed me that it was she who was being battered. I informed her that at my age I didn't need permission from anyone to email anyone I wanted to, whenever I wanted to. Or permission to try to be happy.
That didn't go well. That added another half hour of recriminations. I asked her to admit that neither one of us had been happy in the other's presence for a very long time. She admitted that.
Her aim was to humiliate me. Like a kid caught with his hand where it shouldn't be. The longer she went on, the more she seemed to enjoy it. Therapeutic somehow. She even went on gleefully when the neighbors walked in. "He thinks he can do whatever he wants cause he's 70."

From: **Sarah Ross** *<sarahross64@gmail.com>*
To: **Adam Wolf** *<adam.wolf1402@gmail.com>*
September 21, 2014 9:47 pm
Subject: Re:It continues

Again I ask, why did you let it go on?

From: **Adam Wolf** *<adam.wolf1402@gmail.com>*
To: **Sarah Ross** *<sarahross64@gmail.com>*
September 21, 2014 9:52 pm
Subject: Re:Re:It continues

I wish I knew.

Amanda Schreiber
211 E. Garfield Street
Hinsdale, Illinois 60521

September 23, 2015

Mom,

You sounded well on the phone. I'm sorry it was so hard to hear me. I understand your hesitation to get a hearing aid. The old-fashioned kind scream "old person" here. You need to know, though, they now make new-fangled ones. Invisible. Effective. Never mind the cost. I've instructed Andrew to take you to a good audiologist and get you fitted for a pair. I hope you'll agree to it. My gift to you.
Father McGuire stopped by the station to see me the other day and to find out how you're doing. I took him to lunch. It was so nice to see him. He sends warm regards and wishes you were still here. He's leaning hard on me to come back to the church. You know, I might just take him up on it. It may be the very thing to get me through a nerve-wracking time in my life.

*Hug Andrew and Marjorie for me. I miss you all. You're my only family.
It's not fair that you're much too far away.*

*Love,
Mandy*

From: **Adam Wolf** <adam.wolf1402@gmail.com>
To: **Sarah Ross** <sarahross64@gmail.com>
September 24, 2014 8:13 pm
Subject: More assaults

More histrionics today. This time from Amanda. During coffee break,
she strides into the lounge, and in front of everybody launches a tirade.
"Some people here are more worried about lost loves than about lost
subscribers."
I try to shrug it off. At least I'm better at shrugging things off than I
used to be. There was a time I would have been devastated by public
humiliation. I'd spend every second for the next few days reliving the
encounter. Time, I tried to convince myself, would eventually make the
shame go away. I would wish just to be an old man—sure that by then
the pain would have stopped.
For the most part, I was right. One of the perks of old age is the ability
to wall yourself off from painful experiences like today's. Now I can
scoff that I once lost sleep because someone punched me on the
street—and I didn't swing back. I can now be amused that, in front of
her friends, some girl told me to fuck off when I asked her out.

From: **Sarah Ross** <sarahross64@gmail.com>
To: **Adam Wolf** <adam.wolf1402@gmail.com>
September 24, 2014 8:55 pm
Subject: Re:More assaults

You've always been sensitive and I always have loathed people who
would take advantage of that. Your father comes to mind. I liked him,
until I saw how he could behave toward you.

*From: **Adam Wolf** <adam.wolf1402@gmail.com>*
*To: **Sarah Ross** <sarahross64@gmail.com>*
September 24, 2014 9:18 pm
Subject: What a guy!

Yes, there are a few 3-D memories that still torment. And, yes, especially my father, the Humiliator-in-Chief, at the center of them.
You were there to witness some minor version of them. I rage to this day when I think of it. You and I were kissing on the Lee Road Library steps. Suddenly my father appeared, grabbed me by the coat lapel, dragged me down the steps to his car, shoved me in and drove away. We left you there.
But the worst was the summer after we broke up.

*From: **Sarah Ross** <sarahross64@gmail.com>*
*To: **Adam Wolf** <adam.wolf1402@gmail.com>*
September 24, 2014 9:25 pm
Subject: Re:What a guy!

Adam, what happened? Please tell me.

*From: **Adam Wolf** <adam.wolf1402@gmail.com>*
*To: **Sarah Ross** <sarahross64@gmail.com>*
September 24, 2014 11:54 pm
Subject: Humiliator-in-Chief

I've never been able to tell anyone about this, but I'll try.
The zenith of Manny Wolf's career in humiliation came during that summer after you and I broke up. I was 16.
What happened, what he did, sickens me with rage even now, fifty years later.
Reminding myself that he is long dead doesn't mitigate my fury one bit.
That summer I fell into romantic orbit around Emma Jean Mason. I don't think you knew her. Emma Jean was in the class ahead of us — a

slight, quiet blond girl, mischievous grin, a way of shaking her head when she spoke. Brilliant writer.

I fell for Emma Jean before we ever said a word to each other—memorizing poems of hers they published in the *Crest*—dreamlike visions of wandering and adventure. "Hear the steel rail rumble of the far off freight singing come be a rider of the rails … we'll go flying by those dim prairie towns, our lanterns swinging circles in the dark." I spent many nights fantasizing about Emma Jean and me on that train.

She came into the drugstore a few times. Once when we were face to face, I recited a stanza of hers and, well, we started up.

We never "dated". No movies or Manners Big Boy or dances—just hours walking, imagining our future escapades. Oh, and then of course, there was our time with Thomas Wolfe. We would lie on the grass in that park over by the Center-Mayfield, Emma Jean staring into the sky while I read passages from *Look Homeward Angel*. We reveled in the ecstatic prose, planning our own escape from Cleveland Heights.

One evening she and I walked down to the New York Central tracks by Euclid and Green. She wanted to see the *20ᵗʰ Century Limited* tear by. When it appeared out of the West and roared past, its wheels glowing red, Emma Jean let me put my arms around her. After it passed, we raced onto the tracks to catch a glimpse of the fluorescent blue logo on the observation car. Then she suddenly guided my head down and kissed me. She whispered something musical—"I like you Adam, I think."

It never went much further physically. I once began an exploration under her pleated skirt. Got not far above the knees before my hand was gently turned back. I was drunk in love with her. I was her Eugene Gant. So I wrote love poems to prove it. I don't really remember what they sounded like. I can just imagine.

Incidentally, Emma Jean never wrote a poem for me.

Her parents, as it turns out, were not Thomas Wolfe sympathizers, and certainly not Adam Wolf fans. They were severe Second-Baptist Churchers. Mrs. Mason always wore smileless, demonic, wrinkled, pale expressions.

One afternoon I was walking home from the drugstore—a car horn —and there she was—Emma Jean's mother. She summoned me over to her car with her crooked finger. She didn't look at me, but read from an index card. "You are a menace. Evil incarnate."

Mrs. Mason had come across my poems in Emma Jean's dresser. She came to the conclusion, from what she read, that we had committed "sins of the flesh". Proclaimed that I had placed her daughter's soul in peril. And, if I tried to see or contact Emma Jean again, then she would be compelled to "call the authorities".

Before she finished her presentation, I snapped. I shouted out that she was mentally ill and needed help. I think I even wagged my finger in her face. As I walked away, she issued a loud pronouncement, "You'll see what's in store for you, Mister!" I tried calling Emma Jean Mason —but she never answered.

Several days later, my father and mother were waiting on the couch for me when I came home. Arms crossed, my mother announced ceremoniously that they had something "serious" to talk to me about. I was ushered to their room.

They had spoken with Mrs. Mason. Gertrude had asked them over, claiming an emergency. I had put their daughter in danger, thus spake Mrs. Mason. She was considering the police unless ...

When I proclaimed my innocence, my father pranced to the dresser and triumphantly pulled a stack of papers from the drawer. Waved them in my face. "Innocent? Done nothing to bring shame? What about these?" And yes, the bastard started to read from my precious, purloined Emma Jean love poems. The humiliation my father inflicted was masterful. He was in his glory. Before each phrase, he pointed to the notepaper theatrically and asked, "What does this mean?" Then he proceeded to recite pre-selected stanzas in a boisterous, mocking tone: (My mother stood silent—silent through it, feigning concern.)

— *"We lie entwined, flesh to flesh, along the bank, gazing toward those distant lights"*

— *"Your eyes turn back to mine—you softly smile –slide your hands across my back and press your thighs inward "*

— *"My blood boils at your touch"*

A feeling of pure hate welled up. I tore the poems from my father's hands and pushed him away. He squared to hit me. He didn't. I wish he had. I would have strangled him with my bare hands then and there. I shredded the papers into bits. Threw them across the room. I screamed. I began to sob. Frustration, I suppose. Neither of them moved toward me. No one showed the slightest sign of concern. My father didn't try to block my way, though, when I went for the door. "Let him go," I remember him saying. "He's crying because he's remorseful for what he's done."

I fled from the house and ran down Taylor Road toward Emma Jean's, bent on mayhem, I suppose. But stopped soon and went home. For the next few days, I did a stakeout down the street from Emma Jean Mason's house. Never saw her. Found out she had gone to her cousin's farm in Iowa for the rest of the summer. I didn't see her again until that Christmas. Ran into her at Drexler's. She was cold, indifferent—now a college girl with college girl notions.

As for my father and mother—neither they nor I ever mentioned the episode again.

Once, many years later, when I was visiting Cleveland, I thought again of that day. Confronted my father with the story. He didn't remember it, but added casually, "Yes Adam, mistakes were made."

You know, Sarah, actually the more I think about those poems, the more I think that maybe Mrs. Mason was right to be concerned.

---

*From: **Sarah Ross** <sarahross64@gmail.com>*
*To: **Adam Wolf** <adam.wolf1402@gmail.com>*
September 25, 2014 12:35 am
Subject: unforgivable

Oh, oh, oh my darling. You were such a good boy. Only 16, for crying out loud! Working so hard at the drugstore—the dirty work of lifting supply boxes. Every afternoon, many weekends. You didn't deserve to be treated that way by an ungrateful father. I'm so, so sorry and wish I could take such an episode away.

What kind of savage human being takes pleasure in humiliating a kid? I love that you were interested in poetry, in literature, in writing, AND wanted to impress a talented girl. You did nothing wrong. How brutally unfair! I had no idea your father was so evil. I used to like his sweetness to me, his jokes. No more. Crazy, crazy Manny Wolf. Crazy Mrs. Mason. Of course kids can be florid at that age, imitative in their writing — that is, smart kids like you, with imagination and the wish to impress an older girl. I love you and would have rescued you, even if it meant getting you back with Emma Jean Mason.

---

*From: **Adam Wolf** <adam.wolf1402@gmail.com>*
*To: **Sarah Ross** <sarahross64@gmail.com>*
September 25, 2014 12:56 am
Subject: Re:unforgivable

Sarah, if he had swung at me that day, he would have died then and there. You know, I talk that way casually, in everyday anger, but that's bluster. Only impotent rage. In this case I mean it.

I would have killed him. You would have read about it in the *Press* the next day, and I would have been proud. A smile on my face. And as they dragged me away, I would have signed autographs.

My father never hit me. Tried once. Here's another confession I've never shared with anyone. Once when I was 17, I was going out on a date, to a show, and he blocked my way at the top of the stairs. Forbid me to go. We had words. He undid his belt. Swung to hit me with it. And I caught the belt mid-air. Wrenched it out of his hands. He tripped and fell backwards, and I swung repeatedly with the business end of that belt. After about 3 swings, hard, I threw the belt down on him. I ran out of the house, crying that I had to do that.

From: **Sarah Ross** *<sarahross64@gmail.com>*
To: **Adam Wolf** *<adam.wolf1402@gmail.com>*
September 25, 2014 2:08 am
Subject: deserved it

    Adam, I think it's so healthy to air these dark secrets. A therapist you trust could help, but I'm grateful you confided in me. IT WAS SELF-DEFENSE and thank goodness you were old enough, strong enough, enraged enough to stand your ground. To give him what he had deserved for years — a triumph I wish I could have had too. I had no idea. And I'm so sorry. Ah, the secrets we keep about abusive parents, when we should have screamed to the world what monsters they were.

    My father started hitting me when I was seven. You couldn't have known. I told no one. "Beating me" is more the truth. I think he was so frustrated in this country, starting over as a Displaced Person at age 40, his whole family swallowed up in the War. He had trouble making himself understood in America. I was the only one of us that spoke English intelligibly in the beginning. I had to make phone calls to bill collectors at that age — seven, eight-years old– I had to clear up all my father's fuck-ups. He once got a threat from Sun Finance. The 25% loan for the old car, the one Mr. Walter Ross had purchased (without credit or funds, mind you) was long overdue. I thought I understood from the letter that my parents would go to jail, if they didn't pay up immediately. Maybe it was the alarm in my voice, I don't know. But after I translated the letter, the beatings started. Like your father, he had trained as a boxer. Hard slaps, some punches. And he would make these horrible sounds as he beat me — like a third-grader pretending to shoot an automatic weapon.

    I hated him too. Begged my mother to divorce him. But I bore the shame, the idea that "I had asked for it, somehow." "Your father is sorry," my mother would say, "but you should be 'the big one' and apologize." I wouldn't. I used to wave to cops out the back window and smile so they wouldn't arrest my father for hitting me. Once when I was arguing with my cousin Mickey, Walter Ross strode over and banged our heads together. The pain is still palpable. It stopped the fight, and that sicko paraded around, chest popped out like a rooster, proud of his elegant parenting skills.

He hit me, most often when he was frustrated about something. I was the object of his fury. Esther was spared. She knew how to flee. I stayed to fight.

And finally my small triumph. One day, when I was 21 years old, he smacked me across the face and bloodied my lip. It swelled grotesquely. But this time, instead of lying when people asked me how it happened, I simply said, "My old man hit me." I told my father I was telling people. He grew sheepish—a surprise. And that ended the abuse. And, yes, on several occasions over those years I wanted to murder him too.

But children are conditioned to love their parents no matter what. Harold and I once had a sweet German shepherd. Such a sweetie. A bit of a pest, though, begging too much for attention. One day Harold kicked him away, in the poor dog's belly. I hit the roof, threatening to leave, with the dog, if that ever happened again. Threatened I would kick Harold the same way. The dog yowled. I kept thinking the poor thing doesn't know he can rip Harold apart. I wish he had. But something happens with the relationship between children and parents that makes us, I don't know, their humble servants.

I understand the shame you felt after hitting your father, but it wasn't a shameful act. You realized you didn't have to take the abuse, that you were a good boy, a proud human being. The moment you snatched away the belt and smacked him, I feel, was a triumph for all of us who were kicked in the underbelly as kids. I wish I could have found a way, like that, of standing up for myself and getting back at my father. Thank you! That's my reaction. That's what I say. Thank you.

ADAM > SARAH   9/25/14   8:20 pm

Oblig. dinner w. Amanda. Break in the action. She'll be back in sec. I'm ready to bolt. Vitriol. Full frontal assault. And I'm exhausted from little sleep.

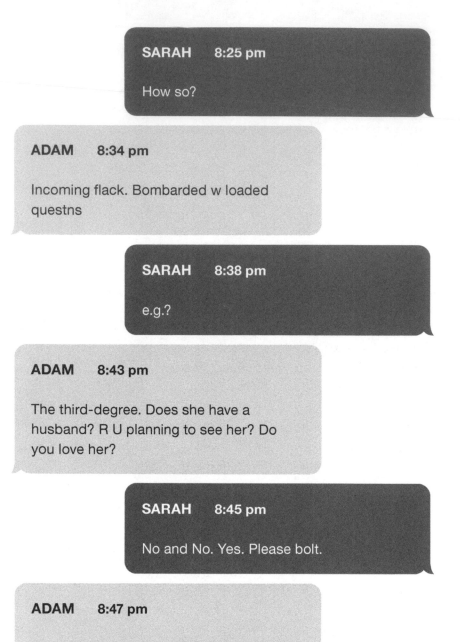

SARAH   8:25 pm

How so?

ADAM   8:34 pm

Incoming flack. Bombarded w loaded questns

SARAH   8:38 pm

e.g.?

ADAM   8:43 pm

The third-degree. Does she have a husband? R U planning to see her? Do you love her?

SARAH   8:45 pm

No and No. Yes. Please bolt.

ADAM   8:47 pm

Soon it'll be waterboarding. Are you ready to get help? How can you do this to me?

SARAH   8:48 pm

so sorry

ADAM   8:50 pm

Gotta go. ilu

SARAH   8:53 pm

U poor thing. Crazy bully. What keeps you
pinned down when you have legs?
Please call later. I'll try to make you feel
better. ilu2.

---

*From: **Adam Wolf** <adam.wolf1402@gmail.com>*
*To: **Sarah Ross** <sarahross64@gmail.com>*
September 25, 2014 9:57 pm
Subject: Weary

It was comforting to hear your voice. Sorry I was groggy. Gotta get
some sleep.
You keep asking why I put up with these castigations. I guess when
Amanda or Lola launch one of their withering assaults, I become para-
lyzed. True. I don't stand up for myself then. Wish I could. I'm afraid I
instinctively assume guilt when shamed. You know, Sarah, these are
no scenes for an old man. I'm weary. I wouldn't have had the energy to
respond.

From: **Sarah Ross** *<sarahross64@gmail.com>*
To: **Adam Wolf** *<adam.wolf1402@gmail.com>*
September 25, 2014 10:20 pm
Subject: Re:Weary

This kind of stress undoes us at any age, but it's especially difficult now. We're less resilient. I'm sorry. Wish I could help. All this for being in touch with me?

Try to find the strength to stand up for yourself. This is not the Adam I knew. You were feisty back then. What happened in my absence? I hope you're able to retrieve him.

From: **Sarah Ross** *<sarahross64@gmail.com>*
To: **Adam Wolf** *<adam.wolf1402@gmail.com>*
September 25, 2014 11:44 pm
Subject:

No call? I guess you must have fallen asleep.

I'm concerned and a bit worried about the attacks you have to endure. I guess I'm lucky that Gordon takes you and me in stride. He sees how happy I am to be in touch with you again. Calls it "cute".

From: **S.Gordon Wilson** *<S.Gordon.Wilson@csulb.edu>*
To: **Sarah Ross** *<sarahross64@gmail.com>*
September 27, 2014 9:34 pm
Subject: Free tomorrow?

Hi Sarah,

Thinking about our upcoming adventure in Seattle. I am very much looking forward to it. Surely Jerry and Mae will have some excellent suggestions for excursions and restaurants.

I thought to call you earlier. The *Court Jester* was showing on Turner Classics. Great fun. Then I remembered your book club met this evening. *Hare with the Amber Eyes,* was it?

Might you be free for lunch tomorrow? I could pick you up at the shop. Would 12:30 work for you?

Gordon

S. Gordon Wilson, PhD.
Founder and Editor of *The Ichthysaurus*
Fellow, American Academy of Underwater Sciences
Professor of Biology, Emeritus
California State University, Long Beach

---

*From: **Adam Wolf** <adam.wolf1402@gmail.com>*
*To: **Sarah Ross** <sarahross64@gmail.com>*
October 2, 2014 11:55 pm
Subject: I'm up

Trouble sleeping. Something from long ago keeping me up. A story I should have revealed in therapy, but never could divulge it. I think you would understand, but I'm reluctant to tell you.

---

*From: **Sarah Ross** <sarahross64@gmail.com>*
*To: **Adam Wolf** <adam.wolf1402@gmail.com>*
October 3, 2014 12:11 am
Subject: Re:I'm up

Still up. Do you want to talk? Whatever it is, I'm here. May I just ask, why you felt a long-ago event to be so pressing now?

---

*From: **Adam Wolf** <adam.wolf1402@gmail.com>*
*To: **Sarah Ross** <sarahross64@gmail.com>*
October 3, 2014 12:28 am
Subject: Trust

Let's just write, if that's okay. I suppose more of Amanda's theatrics yesterday prompted my associations to this event. I'm better now. A lot coming down on my head. Needed you. Finally, there's someone who might understand. I'll try to muster the courage to tell you.

---

*From: **Sarah Ross** <sarahross64@gmail.com>*
*To: **Adam Wolf** <adam.wolf1402@gmail.com>*
October 3, 2014 12:55 am
Subject: Re:Trust

You know, Adam, I've always thought it easier to tell secrets to a stranger than to someone you know. But this odd, long-distance intimacy we share is a safety zone I've never imagined. You know more truths about me in a few months than anyone has ever known. Sure, there are still compartments I'll probably never be able to open. I trust, though, that if I were to reveal them, you'd be accepting.

---

*From: **Adam Wolf** <adam.wolf1402@gmail.com>*
*To: **Sarah Ross** <sarahross64@gmail.com>*
October 3, 2014 3:14 am
Subject: Re:Re:Trust

3 a.m. Well, here goes.

For about a year, back in the 70's, I lived with a girl named Barbara Feinman. Pretty, a junior high English teacher, long black hair, green eyes, always dramatic facial expressions for every mood and conversation. Barbara always dressed to kill, even when she went to mail a letter.

The girl possessed an endless wardrobe of silky blouses, pastel sun-dresses, skirts—diaphanous shades of red—all hemlines as short as the law would allow. Do you believe it, the wardrobe covered two and half walk-in closets? Did I mention three drawers of underwear and stock-ings? You get the picture—like living in Neiman Marcus.

That June she took off for the summer—to Europe. We had sort of agreed to part ways when she returned. So she left me alone in the apartment with her two and a half closets, some good books, and an especially nice chess set (one of her Austrian relatives was a wood carver).

On Sunday afternoons. Keith, the bio-chem grad student next door, would come over to beat me at chess. While he waited to make a move, he'd wander around the apartment. One Sunday I went to get him. It was his move. I found him. In the dim light of Barbara's bedroom. Sitting with legs crossed, in the brown armchair across from a mirror. Admiring himself. Dressed in Barbara's blue-green paisley dress. Pink panties visible underneath.

Took me aback, though I must admit he didn't look half bad. He seemed unabashed. I retreated to the chessboard. After a while it became Keith's weekly ritual. Midway through the match he'd return to Barbara's closet. I said nothing. We never talked about it.

Gee, Sarah, I'm too tired to go on right now. I'll save the mortifying part of the story for later.

From: **Sarah Ross** *<sarahross64@gmail.com>*
To: **Adam Wolf** *<adam.wolf1402@gmail.com>*
October 3, 2014 8:00 am
Subject:

Did you ever participate in these dress-ups yourself?

---

*From: **Adam Wolf** <adam.wolf1402@gmail.com>*
*To: **Sarah Ross** <sarahross64@gmail.com>*
October 3, 2014 8:17 am
Subject:

Yeah, once or twice. Incidentally, I didn't look half bad either.

---

*From: **Sarah Ross** <sarahross64@gmail.com>*
*To: **Adam Wolf** <adam.wolf1402@gmail.com>*
October 3, 2014 8:49 am
Subject:

I can't say I mind the image of you as woman. In fact, I think of us way back when, and how I preferred your gentleness to the macho antics of so many of the other teenage boys.

---

*From: **Adam Wolf** <adam.wolf1402@gmail.com>*
*To: **Sarah Ross** <sarahross64@gmail.com>*
October 3, 2014 7:19 pm
Subject: Guilty, I suppose

Then the night Barbara Feinman returned. Back in town. Came, she said, to collect some of her clothes — new boyfriend in tow — husky, athletic, polo-shirted kinda guy. He spent the whole time standing cross-armed and confident in the front door threshold. Looked around and periodically stared at me without speaking, with a so-this-is-the-jerk-you-used-to-go-with disdain. I sat small in the corner armchair, while Barbara silently rustled through her closets.
Then she reappeared, stern-faced, brandishing Keith's paisley blue/green dress high in the air. Glowering at me.
With a school-marm stamping of her right foot: "Who's been wearing this? It's wrinkled -stained — who?" I shrugged my shoulders. "Don't know. Why?", I ventured, feigning no interest.
Brad (I'll call him) shifted his feet and stared triumphantly.

Barbara lifted the corner of that wrinkled and stained garment, like the DA on Perry Mason gesturing to the jury. She wouldn't let it drop. "Did you let someone wear my skirt, my clothes? I mean, did you lend my skirt to some girl? Let her wear it and put it back without getting it cleaned?" Her voice grew shrill.

Again I said, "Nope".

"Well," she continued, "someone did!"

Silence in the courtroom.

Then … she raised her eyebrow. "Did *you* put on my skirt? You did, didn't you? Christ! That's disgusting!"

Brad stared and smirked.

I was silent. Slumped in the armchair. Barbara gathered her clothes and she and Brad left — not another word.

---

*From: **Sarah Ross** <sarahross64@gmail.com>*
*To: **Adam Wolf** <adam.wolf1402@gmail.com>*
October 3, 2014 10:17 pm
Subject: Re:Guilty, I suppose

Oh, poor Adam, it seems you have a life-long collection of humiliations to deal with. I'm so sorry. And now these Amanda tirades …

I'm touched that you can confide in me.

---

*From: **Adam Wolf** <adam.wolf1402@ymall.com>*
*To: **Sarah Ross** <sarahross64@gmail.com>*
October 3, 2014 10:43 pm
Subject:

One last confession to make. This time it doesn't involve the murky past. Several weeks ago, Darlene Cutler came to town for a family wedding. I agreed to meet her, show her some sights and go to dinner. I guess she had romantic intentions. They were not fulfilled. At the end of the day I left. Nothing more happened.

---

*From: **Sarah Ross** <sarahross64@gmail.com>*
*To: **Adam Wolf** <adam.wolf1402@gmail.com>*
October 3, 2014 11:01 pm
Subject:

Adam, suddenly it's more difficult for me to be supportive. I'm glad you told me. Sorry to hear it. It must not have been a pleasant occasion for either one of you. Did you encourage her to come? Correspond with her?

---

*From: **Adam Wolf** <adam.wolf1402@gmail.com>*
*To: **Sarah Ross** <sarahross64@gmail.com>*
October 3, 2014 11:12 pm
Subject:

Yes. I'm sorry.

---

*From: **Sarah Ross** <sarahross64@gmail.com>*
*To: **Adam Wolf** <adam.wolf1402@gmail.com>*
October 3, 2014 11:21 pm
Subject:

So am I.

---

*From: **Lola Wolf** <lola.wolf1402@gmail.com>*
*To: **Michael Wolf** <Michael.R.Wolf@brookstead.com>*
October 4, 2014 7:19 pm
Subject: your father

Dear Mikey,

I haven't heard from you in a while. Is everything okay? Did the trip go well?

Here in Evanston: I'm closing the garden, visiting the farmer's market, romping with Schatzie at the dog beach. These are my only pleasures. Your father skulks out of the house with barely a word. He's in and out in the evening, and when he's home, he's always at his computer. That's strange behavior, even for your weird father.

I guess I shouldn't have called him on it, but I did. I asked him what's was going on. Is it the reunion with her? He admits to me that he needs to be with her, to telephone her now. I don't know where all of this will end. He says he's bonded to her. They have no intention to meet, he says. I say to him, it doesn't matter. You're with her and not with me. It saddens me that for 30 years he ignores me and is probably pouring his heart out to that old woman.

I'm sorry to burden you with this, but I need your help in talking your father back to his senses. Frankly, I fear for all of us what will happen next.

Love,
Mom

From: **Adam Wolf** *<adam.wolf1402@gmail.com>*
To: **Sarah Ross** *<sarahross64@gmail.com>*
October 4, 2014 7:19 pm
Subject: Weird

Sarah, this afternoon around 2 or so, I received another one of my "Old Age Notices". Never unexpected. Always unwelcomed. Working on the program guide, the words begin to line dance on the page. I'm dizzy. I look around. The room rotates. I feel confused. I stare at the stapler, unfathomable, unknowable. Maybe 3 mins., then the spell is over. Amanda waltzes in and I tell her about the episode. The British Journal of Medicine speaks: "Sounds a lot like a TIA. Told you to make an appointment months ago". Then, of course: "You're distracted. Your head's crammed with your adolescent fantasies. No wonder." Sarah, I guess she's right about that.

From: **Sarah Ross** *<sarahross64@gmail.com>*
To: Adam Wolf <adam.wolf1402@gmail.com>
October 4, 2014 7:36 pm
Subject: Re:Weird

Too much stress. I'm concerned for you. Yes, please, please, please see a doctor. When was the last time?

I've been thinking maybe we ought to cool it, take the pressure off of you. It's because I love you, I don't want you to go through this anymore. Should we stop communicating, at least for a while? It'll be hard for me, but it's becoming painful to watch the unceasing fury leveled at you. Can we do it? Should we do it?

From: Adam Wolf <adam.wolf1402@gmail.com>
To: Sarah Ross <sarahross64@gmail.com>
October 4, 2014 8:06 pm
Subject: Need to see you soon

Sarah, on the contrary. I want to be with you more than ever. Couldn't stand a day without word from you. In fact, I have an idea. I'll be off to Cleveland on Friday the 10th. Do you remember my cousin, Marty? (Funny that I remember this. Don't know why we were going downtown together, even though it was after we'd broken up, but Marty was with me. We rode the 32B down to University Circle and you sat with him and flirted. I have to admit I was jealous, just as I was with Sandy. I stared straight ahead when we got on the Rapid. And you asked if I was pouting. I told you, "of course not", but I'm here now to confess that it was an Academy-Award pout.)

Anyway, his daughter Felicia, age 33, is finally getting married. The bridegroom is something like 24. I heard she proposed to him after he pitched his team out of a bases- loaded jam in the last game of the Forest Hills Little League World Series. So I'm due in Beachwood on Saturday aft., the 11th. Driving there Friday morning. Lola-less. How about a Skype date, love, that evening?

From: **Sarah Ross** *<sarahross64@gmail.com>*
To: **Adam Wolf** *<adam.wolf1402@gmail.com>*
October 4, 2014 10:09 pm
Subject: Let's do it

Oh my, I've fantasized about skyping. I thought that either I should absent myself from your life, or, gulp, take the next step. To get closer. Am I a fool to agree? But, yes, a Skype date. I will be brave. I miss you. I love you.

But Friday nights Gordon and I generally go out. Is Saturday night a possibility?

From: **Adam Wolf** *<adam.wolf1402@gmail.com>*
To: **Sarah Ross** *<sarahross64@gmail.com>*
October 4, 2014 10:19 pm
Subject: Re:Let's do it

Wow! Now I really do feel like a teenager. Excited that I'll be seeing you again soon! Holy Shit! But no, Saturday night's out. If I know Marty, the celebration's likely to go past midnight. Okay, why don't you call me when you get home from your outing on Friday? And I'll do my best to look pretty for you.

From: **Sarah Ross** *<sarahross64@gmail.com>*
To: **Adam Wolf** *<adam.wolf1402@gmail.com>*
October 4, 2014 10:30 pm
Subject: Re:Re:Let's do it

Don't know what time I'll get back. This is getting complicated. Can we decide tomorrow?

---

*From: **Adam Wolf** <adam.wolf1402@gmail.com>*
*To: **Sarah Ross** <sarahross64@gmail.com>*
October 4, 2014 10:44 pm
Subject:

Let me uncomplicate things for you, Sarah. Forget about Skyping. Or, better yet, why can't you forego Commodore Gordon for the evening?

---

*From: **Sarah Ross** <sarahross64@gmail.com>*
*To: **Adam Wolf** <adam.wolf1402@gmail.com>*
October 4, 2014 10:50 pm
Subject:

Is this another Academy-Award winning pout, Adam? I love you even more when you're jealous.

---

*From: **Sarah Ross** <sarahross64@gmail.com>*
*To: **Adam Wolf** <adam.wolf1402@gmail.com>*
October 5, 2014 9:47 am
Subject: all set

You're right. Our skyping should take precedence over everything. What time will you call? Can we make it before 10:00 your time, so I don't fade?

And, sure, I remember Marty and the reputation he had—finding its way back to Cleveland from Columbus—a different woman every night, rumor had it. Does he still look like Warren Beatty?

*From: **Adam Wolf** <adam.wolf1402@gmail.com>*
*To: **Sarah Ross** <sarahross64@gmail.com>*
October 5, 2014 10:09 am
Subject: EXCITED!!

I'm shaking with excitement. Don't know about you, but I'm nervous. Yeah. I knew you had a thing for Marty. I knew it. I knew it. No, I'm sorry to disappoint. Now he doesn't look quite as much like Warren Beatty as he does, let's say, Don Rickles. Felicia is very cute though. So 9:00 pm my time on Friday we Skype! You can squint and pretend I'm Warren Beatty.

SARAH > ADAM   10/5/14   11:00 am

I'm really excited about seeing you again and I love you even if you're not Warren Beatty. And I also want you to squint and pretend I'm Natalie Wood.

ADAM   11:06 pm

I love you particularly because you're not Natalie Wood.

ADAM > SARAH   10/8/14   8:13 am

Two days before the trip and already packing. Friday can't be here soon enough.

SARAH 12:36 pm

Me too. Can't wait!

ADAM 1:09 pm

Why don't we just Skype for 48 hours and I'll skip the wedding? How did Gordo take your bowing out of Friday?

SARAH 1:18 pm

Please, Adam. His name is Gordon. And don't ask. He's pouting.

ADAM > SARAH 10/10/14 10:15 am

En route

SARAH 10:28 am

Cold feet

ADAM 11:14 am

I'll warm them.

> **SARAH**   11:33 am
>
> Adam, please no driving and texting. I'm scared. Before we go ahead with this, and when you have a safe chance, please read the email I sent this morning.

> **ADAM**   11:39 am
>
> OK. ILU

From: **Sarah Ross** *<sarahross64@gmail.com>*
To: **Adam Wolf** *<adam.wolf1402@gmail.com>*
October 10, 2014 5:11 am
Subject: Skyping today

Adam, my mind's racing. I need to prepare you for seeing me. So, here goes. Knowing you and the women who've been in your orbit, I suspect your wife must be attractive. I imagine her never without make-up in public. Her hair coiffed, short, streaked blonde, straight as a *schiksa's*, and perkily asymmetrical. Accessorized. A number of necklaces. Even the jeans will be accompanied by sapphire-studded earrings. She, I'm guessing, resembles an older version of Jennifer Aniston. Am I close? Didn't you once describe her as "elegant"? I bet she must be fetching. Please don't get your hopes up, my friend. "Elegant" is never a term sent in my direction. My mascara runs. Every new blouse has a stain on it by lunchtime. With me, you'll be trading down.

I've been cut and pasted and recombined with one botch after the other. I mean it. I know men your age often flock to women 10 or 20 years younger than they are. I'm the reason they do that. Remember what your father always said when he saw a mismatched couple. A handsome man with a horse-faced *meeskite*. He would say, "Jesus Christ!

It's amazing what love can overcome." I'm glad he's not around to see you with me, even on Skype.

---

*From: **Adam Wolf** <adam.wolf1402@gmail.com>*
*To: **Sarah Ross** <sarahross64@gmail.com>*
October 10, 2014 2:22 pm
Subject: Re:Skyping today

Got off for lunch near Toledo. Just read your email from this morning.
Lola's no Jennifer Aniston, believe me. You got the scarves and necklaces right. She looks more like Camilla Parker Bowles. But let's not dwell on Lola.
Look, Sarah, it's Adam here. Remember. I'm someone who knows you're beautiful and doesn't care what age has tried to distort. It's of no consequence. I'm not just someone you met the day before yesterday. Excited! Can't think straight.

---

*From: **Adam Wolf** <adam.wolf1402@gmail.com>*
*To: **Paul Bishop** <Paul.R.Bishop@dewey.com>*
October 12, 2014 4:54 pm
Subject: Finally saw Sarah, virtually

Oh Paul— "L'avventura" continues. No pauses for breath or thought. Since the last email, this thing with Sarah has detonated. We are now writing each other all day, every day, sometimes at night, on the way to work, at work, lunch, at intersections, on the back porch. I spend my days longing for her messages and panic when an hour goes by without. No more tentative phrases and innuendo. No more stuff about vague ambiguous longing. It's full blown, Paul. Jesus H—it's sweet passion and sexy -particularly exciting because we never had the chance in our first go-round way back when.

The day came. We decided it was the right time to finally see each other—to Skype. I was in Cleveland, alone. Sarah picked a time when I would call. I brought three changes of clothes and tried each of them on before we Skyped—stood back from the mirror and rejected them all. I finally settled on a button-down light blue shirt with one of those newfangled small-ish collars, and a dark blue crew neck. (I remembered that Sarah doesn't like V-necks.) The pants, Izod chinos with the pleated front and room to grow. I was now prepared with my best Belmondo charm to woo Sarah into bed.

It wasn't like that, though. I don't know what it was, Paul. Maybe it was modesty, perhaps fear about what we must look like now to people who last saw us when we were young. The mask of age. Anyway, whatever it was, when the time came we both sat in the shadows in our respective rooms and just peered at the camera. First there was giggling over nothing. Eventually, I decided to thrust my face forward into the light, regardless of the consequences. Sarah leaned forward herself for a moment, her hand over her face, just briefly let her eyes show and stared at me nervously. Later she said she thought me so handsome still. I told her I would recognize those beautiful baby blues anywhere, if only she would let me see them clearly.

I couldn't really see her face. The light was arranged so only a silhouette was visible. For a while she resembled someone being interviewed in the witness protection program. I expected her voice to sound shrill and electronic. "I foist met Vinnie da Butcher Bugliosi in 1946 at a pizza parlor in Passaic. He showed me a good time. His last words to me were 'keep your mouth shut'."

As for the rest of her, I conjured up the worst—telling myself I will love her no matter what. I had visions of Sarah Ross now—cauliflower ears and 7 teeth, four of which dangled precipitously. I feared her neck would show signs of some old rope burns from 10 years ago, when she tried to hang herself in the mental ward.

When Sarah finally spoke, her voice was soft. Softer than I remembered, sweet, more confident, deeper. At first she spoke out of the darkness. She said, "It's you. It's really you." The conversation deteriorated from there. And I said, "It's you, really you," but I wasn't sure. Except for the voice it could have been Golda Meier there, for all I knew.

When she finally leaned into the light, I must have lost my breath. I saw her—and despite the few wrinkles, the face more set in place, she was immediately my girl, her smile now even sweeter. Her gestures were more refined and confident. She was dressed elegantly for me—a silky salmon top and a paisley shawl. The years dissolved, and the fears about age were gone. My Sarah and she beamed at me.

We talked softly, nothing sexually charged about it, just soft remembrance. We imagined that we were back in her sunroom, with the low red love seat—tamely making out—her hand caressing my belly button, just under the belt—how we slept together at 15, quite literally, in that hot room, napping together in the heat—or about her head on my lap when we watched *The Twilight Zone* Friday nights—or the path we took through Cain Park when I carried home her books after school—or the people we routinely met along my paper route.

At some point, Paul, we stopped talking and simultaneously touched our fingers to our lips and reached toward the screen.

---

*From: **Adam Wolf** <adam.wolf1402@gmail.com>*
*To: **Sarah Ross** <sarahross64@gmail.com>*
October 13, 2014 10:45 am
Subject: Still with you

The experience with you on Friday makes it very difficult to return to my "life". At the station. Everything seems cold and grim. Planning what recordings will be played, where spots will go, the sort of thing I've been doing for years. Seems absurd, completely. It's like walking through shadows. My life here now is like a black and white dream—the enthusiasm for it, the meaning drained. Only the times with you are vivid. I'd like to try to Skype again soon.

From: **Sarah Ross** <sarahross64@gmail.com>
To: **Adam Wolf** <adam.wolf1402@gmail.com>
October 13, 2014 12:28 pm
Subject: Re:Still with you

I have the same feeling of distance here at the shop. Nicole jabbers at me and I just see her lips move — don't hear her at all. This moment again with you. For me it felt as if no time had passed, or, rather, that the time that had passed didn't mean much. Somehow seeing the way you looked at me gave me a confidence I haven't felt for a long time. I was desired and I desired. I can't wait to have another Skype date with you again too.

From: **Adam Wolf** <adam.wolf1402@gmail.com>
To: **Sarah Ross** <sarahross64@gmail.com>
October 13, 2014 3:14 pm
Subject: Re:Re:Still with you

Okay, how about Saturday afternoon? I should be alone in the house that afternoon. No Lola, no Amanda, no nobody. Just you and me, Miss Ross, on Skype. Not as "intimate" a setting as the Hyatt, I admit, but a chance to see each other again. ilu

---

From: **Sarah Ross** <sarahross64@gmail.com>
To: **Adam Wolf** <adam.wolf1402@gmail.com>
October 13, 2014 4:56 pm
Subject: Sorry

Oh Adam, I'm sorry. This weekend may not be the best time. Seattle. Gordon. Remember? I told him I'd be there. Right now I guess I'm a little regretful. You've been so supportive. It's emboldened me. And I won't be shy about skyping with you again soon, my Adam. ILU

---

*From: **Adam Wolf** <adam.wolf1402@gmail.com>*
*To: **Sarah Ross** <sarahross64@gmail.com>*
October 13, 2014 6:17 pm
Subject: Re:Sorry

I'm flattered I could be of service. Pardon me for the pangs of adolescent jealousy again. I hope the weekend is a roaring success—maybe skyping wasn't such a good idea.

---

*From: **Sarah Ross** <sarahross64@gmail.com>*
*To: **Adam Wolf** <adam.wolf1402@gmail.com>*
October 13, 2014 6:39 pm
Subject: Re:Re:Sorry

Nonsense. Of course skyping was a good idea! How about the following weekend? It's unlikely I'll be able to email from Seattle. Don't miss me too much. Anyway, won't you have your Lola and Amanda to tend to?

---

*From: **Adam Wolf** <adam.wolf1402@gmail.com>*
*To: **Sarah Ross** <sarahross64@gmail.com>*
October 13, 2014 7:18 pm
Subject:

Uh-huh. Guess so.

From: **Sarah Ross** *<sarahross64@gmail.com>*
To: **Esther Lehman** *<estherlehman88@yahoo.com>*
October 15, 2014 7:22 pm
Subject: update and received an odd note

Dear E—

This morning I tried to call mother's new aide. Isn't her name Riza? I left a message and she hasn't called back. What do you know about their plans for physical therapy?

Now, Esther, to quell your skepticism. An amazing experience, this Skype with Adam. He didn't scream. A good start. And I wasn't self-conscious with him, not after the first minutes, not after I laid eyes on those eyes. The color hadn't been right on my screen, not light blue enough, but I suddenly remembered how wonderful it used to feel just seeing the way his eyes softened when he looked at me. I think I will always be in love with that look.

I know, I know, "Come on, Sarah", you're saying. Somehow I'm glad I'm not telling you all this in person, or on the phone. I can spare myself hearing one of your chortle-and-snort laughs. Well, I would do the same, I suppose, if you came at me with this kind of sappiness. Sorry. I should keep these feelings to myself, the way people who have "seen the light" shut up about it cause no one would understand anyway. Just a feeling, a disembodied feeling of being whole again. Don't worry. I'll get over it, I'm sure. And even if I don't get over it, I'll not sputter around trying to explain anymore. Promise.

It's good to know Adam is there again, someone I can confide in, lean on. He bucked me up the other day when I was getting cold feet about Gordon and Seattle.

One more Adam related note, that gives me pause. I am not amused. I received a rather menacing email from the owner of Adam's radio station. I know she's snooped into his email, complained about how much we write to each other. Amanda is her name, her fangs poised. I've been asking Adam to tell me about her. I suspected there had been something between them. Seems to be ongoing. What do you think?

Anyway, here's the note:

"I don't know who you are, only that you're imposing yourself on Adam's life a bit too much, wouldn't you say? He has trouble telling people who pester him to back off. So let me do it for him. Ask him one these days who got there first. Maybe he'll tell you the truth." Amanda Schreiber

I won't respond. I'll keep it to myself. Adam would overreact. I'm trying not to. But I guess this Amanda Schreiber is right about one thing. Eventually he'll have to tell me the truth.

I'll come visit soon. Love to you both.

And please let me know when Mom gets the nightgown I sent.

ADAM > SARAH   10/17/14   2:45 pm

Hoping you arrived safely. Where are you staying? Years ago I travelled to Seattle on business with Amanda. The sunset from a little teahouse on the harbor was magnificent. Are you and Gordon going to brave the Space Needle? I think you can see Okinawa from there. Write me. I'll miss you.

SARAH   4:56 pm

Arrived safely. Hope all's well with you. Dinner plans here. Seafood, of course. It's a spectacular city. Gordon's spoiling me.

ADAM > SARAH   10/18/14   8:19 am

Glad your weekend getaway is going so nicely. But you sound distant. Is everything okay?

ADAM   11:09 am

No word from you? Guess you must be having a passable time.

LOLA > ADAM   10/18/14   2:37 pm

Urgent. Tried calling 5x. At Mill Race Inn in Geneva. I finished with the luncheon a while ago. I can't find the key to the Sorrento. The whole garden club is looking. It simply disappeared. Please bring the spare set as soon as possible. It shouldn't take you more than an hour if you take the tollway.

ADAM   2:46 pm

Are you sure you looked everywhere? It must be the 6th time you've lost the keys this month — and you always found them. So much for my Saturday afternoon.

ADAM > SARAH   10/18/14   5:27 pm

I'm very blue. Where are u?

From: **Adam Wolf** <adam.wolf1402@gmail.com>
To: **Paul Bishop** <Paul.R.Bishop@dewey.com>
October 19, 2014 7:40 am
Subject: Jealousy at my age??

Paul,

You are such a refined and tolerant friend to endure my tales of retro-
gression with Sarah.
You must think it pathetic, perhaps amusing. Don't tell me if you do.
For Christ's sake — at age 69 — letting myself be driven by a 17-year-old
boy's emotions.
Perhaps the *American Journal of Gerontology* could publish a case study.
No, No. Better. How about they sponsor a week-long symposium? At
the Orlando Hilton Conference Center.

Session III: Adolescent and First Love Retrogression Derangement
Syndrome Among Aging Baby Boomers — Causes and Treatment

Presenters

Beatrice Frumpelhorst, PhD, SM, BM, BS, FACPP, ASCT offers new
protocols for recognizing and defeating the syndrome in the first week

Frank Brashkoff, MD, Johns Hopkins University will present the first
trial results of the new nostalgia-suppressant medication, Pashblock

Adam Wolf, BA, Program Manager of WCMQ in Chicago, chronicles his own losing battle with the disease

Here comes the worst, Paul. Get ready. This week brought the return of the crudest of our known teen-hood emotional maladies—*Murderous Jealousy*. It seems my Sarah has another significant other. A Man. Not just any Man. A retired marine biologist Man. A beachfront house with a view of the ocean Man.

Yes, Sarah has mentioned Gordon in passing—even referred to him as a "keeper" once, but I've heard little of him for weeks and assumed that he was passing away, so to speak, as our feelings ignited.

Nay, nay Paul. He's been there all the time—daily calls, dinners, whale sighting in the Pacific (his own fucking boat!). From what Sarah has told me, they have not slept together or been *deshabille*—just "courting".

But Gordon + Sarah has taken a grotesque turn and I'm berserk.

Gordon invited my Sarah for a long weekend in Seattle, where he's attending a conference—"Can Swordfish Be Taught to Fence?" or something.

Sarah mystifies me, Paul. She confided she had mixed emotions. But she was still determined to go spend a romantic weekend with Flesh Gordon.

Incidentally, I researched Gordon on the internet. I caught a glimpse of him lollygagging with some fat cats at some uppity dinner. Sarah had led me to believe he was Robert Mitchum's doppelganger. Unless the caption was wrong, I'll be damned if he doesn't more resemble Captain Kangaroo anticipating a colonoscopy. He may be what Sarah "needs", but to think of him leading Sarah to carnal knowledge …

Last week when we skyped, Sarah seemed so vulnerable. Her shyness, her trepidation about how she would seem to me. Paul—the intense affection—how that love flowed and coursed through me. Now what do I think? I think maybe I was just the practice run, the trial, the convenient test subject to embolden Sarah for her tryst with Boatman.

Jealousy makes you think strange things, huh? Here's the insane thought that it conjured for me last night. She planned our reunion for years! Knowing all along I would fall! And then she would walk. Revenge.

Let's storyboard it. Think Barbara Stanwyck, 1949.

> *Camera medium close. Her voice heard on the track as she enters the hotel suite in Seattle:*

> *"The moment Gordo and I slipped into our suite and the door closed behind us ...*
> *the moment I saw the fresh gardenias and roses on the table, next to the whispering glasses of champagne. (Close-up of her gazing at the table) ...*

> *the moment I strolled past the four-poster bed through the open balcony doors (Tracking shot from behind) and gazed out to the sailboats on Puget Sound ...*

> *the moment I felt Gordon embrace me so confidently with his sinewy weather-beaten arms (Close up of arms, from behind, around her waist) ...*

> *the moment his moustache tickled my neck and his lips gently pressed (Close-up of her neck) ...*

> *At that moment the notion of my returning to Adam Wolf floated into the breeze and vanished (Close-up of Sarah's face beaming)."*

ADAM > SARAH   10/19/14   7:37 am

I'm happy you're being spoiled. You deserve it. I imagine what fun it would be for us to travel together too. I think the farthest we got in our day was Sandusky. Do you remember Cedar Point?

*From: **Adam Wolf** <adam.wolf1402@gmail.com>*
*To: **Paul Bishop** <Paul.R.Bishop@dewey.com>*
October 19, 2014 1:11 pm
Subject: The Undead

Paul, these are baffling times.

I went online and looked for the dearly departed Harold Weinstein, Sarah's late husband. He died, she told me, four or five years ago. But amazingly, I located Professor Harold in a YouTube presentation from 2012. The man appears to have overcome advanced putrefaction in time to deliver a stirring lecture on Mandeville's *Fable of the Bees*.
Paul, I need your wisdom. Tell me why she would be deceptive about Harold. Why would a woman need to fabricate her husband's death? Why Sarah, of all people? And, Paul, should I tell her I know? Why would she say that, why?

---

*From: **Adam Wolf** <adam.wolf1402@gmail.com>*
*To: **Sarah Ross** <sarahross64@gmail.com>*
October 19, 2014 10:56 pm
Subject: Earth to Sarah, Earth to Sarah

Sarah Ross, Adam Wolf here. Trying one more time. Have I ruined your weekend by bringing up unpleasant memories of Cedar Point? My spilling the mustard? The dead fish in Lake Erie? My ogling other chicks? Is that when you stopped loving me? Please write me, Sarah.

---

*From: **Sarah Ross** <sarahross64@gmail.com>*
*To: **Adam Wolf** <adam.wolf1402@gmail.com>*
October 20, 2014 9:45 am
Subject: Here I am

Sorry I didn't have a chance to write from Seattle. Tired out. Just a brief note now, more tomorrow, promise. Gordon came through. His friends let us stay in their houseboat. What an experience! I didn't know what to expect. Yes, we had small quarters, but they were cozy. I actually found the rocking soothing. Busy days, relaxing martinis at night. Lots of laughing. A perfect setting to overcome my self-consciousness. I'm glad I went.

From: **Adam Wolf** *<adam.wolf1402@gmail.com>*
To: **Sarah Ross** *<sarahross64@gmail.com>*
October 20, 2014 9:49 am
Subject: Re:Here I am

I'm glad you went too. Seems like you had a fulfilling time. "More tomorrow"? Why don't you wait until next week? There's no hurry now. And when you write, please spare me the details.

From: **Sarah Ross** *<sarahross64@gmail.com>*
To: **Adam Wolf** *<adam.wolf1402@gmail.com>*
October 20, 2014 10:07 am
Subject: Re:Re:Here I am

I don't quite understand what you mean by "spare me details". I had no intention of giving you details. You sound irritated.

From: **Adam Wolf** *<adam.wolf1402@gmail.com>*
To: **Sarah Ross** *<sarahross64@gmail.com>*
October 20, 2014 11:34 am
Subject:

Sarah, I felt so close to you during the evening we skyped. Maybe this is unrealistic, but I thought together we could build on that. We had a chance to be together again with no one in our way. I hoped if you went this weekend, it wouldn't be to consummate your relationship with

Gordon. Perhaps my feelings are too raw right now. I guess this all sounds irrational to you.

From: **Sarah Ross** <sarahross64@gmail.com>
To: **Adam Wolf** <adam.wolf1402@gmail.com>
October 20, 2014 1:34 pm
Subject: not fair

You know there are times when I long for us to be together again, I mean really together. But I've been around the block once or twice in my 69 years, and recognize that virtual reality is not real. And I don't think it's even fair for you to begrudge my relationship with Gordon, when you're tethered to at least two other women. Gordon has been there for me, a source of support and comfort for several years. It's ironic that my relationship with him evolved just when you reappeared. And, as you know, I've been open with Gordon about you. I've told him about the emails, the affection, even the Skype. I was worried he would want me to stop communicating with you. But he said he's not concerned about it.

From: **Adam Wolf** <adam.wolf1402@gmail.com>
To: **Sarah Ross** <sarahross64@gmail.com>
October 20, 2014 6:15 pm
Subject: Re:not fair

Yes, virtual reality is not reality, but my feelings are real, and I was hoping that our relationship would "evolve". I suppose I should be grateful that you got Commodore Gordon's permission to proceed with our correspondence. Please thank him for me. Tell me, did you read our emails to him? Is that what all the laughing was about? Incidentally, Gordon, if you're reading this, I promise not to send Sarah any more selfies of my crotch.

---

*From: **Sarah Ross** <sarahross64@gmail.com>*
*To: **Adam Wolf** <adam.wolf1402@gmail.com>*
October 20, 2014 6:46 pm
Subject:

No, of course, I didn't show him your emails, and didn't go into any details with him either. I'm not like that. But you are in my life again. And I needed to be upfront about that. He reassured me he was okay with it. What more do you want?

Clearly Amanda Schreiber doesn't feel the same way. Here's something I haven't told you. And you need to know. Ms. Amanda Schreiber seems to have gotten hold of my email address and sent me a No-Uncertain-Terms Note. Let me know if you would ever like me to quote line and verse. The gist of it: I need to back off. You are spoken for. And she got there first.

---

*From: **Adam Wolf** <adam.wolf1402@gmail.com>*
*To: **Sarah Ross** <sarahross64@gmail.com>*
October 20, 2014 7:32 pm
Subject: Damn it!

I'm livid that she monitors my emails and furious that she sent that note to you. I can't imagine what she could have meant. She got there first?? Believe me, I'm going to deal with this. Amanda Schreiber's intrusions into my life are going to come to an end—*tout suite.*

---

*From: **Sarah Ross** <sarahross64@gmail.com>*
*To: **Adam Wolf** <adam.wolf1402@gmail.com>*
October 20, 2014 7:59 pm
Subject: Re:Damn it!

Adam, I'm grateful you'll call Amanda on these antics of hers. But might I ask you something? And don't get mad. What are the chances that you'll ever level with me completely? I suspect you have your hands

full, but just won't tell me how full. Perhaps our lives are too complicated to take our passion for each other so seriously.

From: **Adam Wolf** *<adam.wolf1402@gmail.com>*
To: **Sarah Ross** *<sarahross64@gmail.com>*
October 20, 2014 8:32 pm
Subject:

I'm happy that you're being so open and truthful with Gordon and want
me to level with you. How about if you level with me then, Sarah Ross?
Why did you say that Harold was dead? Or do I have it wrong? Might
your hands be full too?

From: **Sarah Ross** *<sarahross64@gmail.com>*
To: **Adam Wolf** *<adam.wolf1402@gmail.com>*
October 20, 2014 10:58 pm
Subject:

    You know, Adam, I think it might be a good idea, just about now,
that we retreat to whatever's left of our separate lives.

---

5

*From: **S. Gordon Wilson** <S.Gordon.Wilson@csulb.edu>*
*To: **Sarah Ross** <sarahross64@gmail.com>*
October 21, 2014 8:02 pm
Subject: Where are you?

I'm sitting at the club, by the bay window. Nostalgic. I keep thinking about our weekend and how special it was. I just spoke to Jerry. He and Mae say hello and look forward to a repeat soon. Me too.
I guess you're too busy to call back. When you have a chance, please do. I'd like to invite you here again.

Gordon

S. Gordon Wilson, PhD.
Founder and Editor of *The Ichthysaurus*
Fellow, American Academy of Underwater Sciences
Professor of Biology, Emeritus
California State University, Long Beach

---

*From: **Adam Wolf** <adam.wolf1402@gmail.com>*
*To: **Sarah Ross** <sarahross64@gmail.com>*
October 23, 2014 9:16 pm
Subject: Where are you?

Is it to be complete silence then? I'm sad beyond words that we would stop talking. If it's the question of Amanda that troubles you, then here's what

I need to say. Yes, Amanda may believe that she has staked some sort of claim. Perhaps I haven't done enough over the years to disabuse her.

Please come back.

From: **Gabriella Fratelli** <gabriella.fratelli@orange.it>
To: **Sarah Ross** <sarahross64@gmail.com>
October 26, 2014 3:25 pm
Subject: Re:Break with Adam

Carissima,

You sound serious. Is this a retreat from Adam rather than a break with him? It's at moments like this that I wish I were at your side again, to stroke your hair and kiss your forehead. Please do not be angry with me that I cannot be there.

From**: Sarah Ross** <sarahross64@gmail.com>
To: **Gabriella Fratelli** <gabriella.fratelli@orange.it>
October 26, 2014 5:16 pm
Subjext: Re:Re:Break with Adam

Cara Mia,

What am I going to do?
After Seattle I now have to live in the reality of just Gordon, don't I? Seattle was okay, but ... Gordon of the Leaden Touch. Kind Gordon. Sweet Gordon. Snoring Gordon. Goddamn BORING GORDON. Is this it? Sipping Tito martinis on deck? Coquilles St. Jacques at *The Captain's Table?* What to send the grandchildren for their birthdays? Where we'll go for the next meal, even while we're still consuming this one? Some days I don't want to go on one minute longer with him. Other days I like the attention, and he's comfortable to be around. Sort of the ideal man for the older woman. But I don't feel I fit that description yet.

But would I be so dismissive of Gordon, if Adam hadn't reappeared? Am I being fair? Who can compete with teenage passion that makes you feel so young when you're far from it? Perhaps my soul needs to be with Adam. But I myself live here. In the here and the now. Don't I need stability? Don't I need security, emotional security for these last few years? I've never had that. Don't I deserve it, at last?

AND aren't Adam and I both entangled in other relationships? Damn it, he's doubly spoken for. By a wife, supposedly in name only, and a boss who thinks of him as her possession. It's simply too complicated, especially for this stage of my life. Do I even really know who Adam Wolf is now, just because I knew him so well then?

Enough of love affairs in the ether!

I miss you so.

---

*From: **Adam Wolf** <adam.wolf1402@gmail.com>*
*To: **Sarah Ross** <sarahross64@gmail.com>*
October 29, 2014 6:21 pm
Subject: Please answer

I'm breaking my head trying to figure out how to set things straight with you. Not even any goodnight messages?
Please, Sarah, I apologize again for my reaction to your time with Gordon. I have no right to resent your attachment to him.
ISLUVM. And hope that you still feel the same.

---

*From: **Adam Wolf** <adam.wolf1402@gmail.com>*
*To: **Sarah Ross** <sarahross64@gmail.com>*
October 30, 2014 12:14 pm
Subject: Please answer

Nostalgic tonight remembering that party at Marilyn's. You went as Dale Evans to my Roy Rogers. Or was it the other way around? How cute were we?

From: **Adam Wolf** <adam.wolf1402@gmail.com>
To: **Paul Bishop** <Paul.R.Bishop@dewey.com>
October 31, 2014 8:46 pm
Subject: No word at all from Sarah

Paul,

I'm brimming with gratitude for your calm voice. No friendship in the
solar system can compare. You were so right to remind me, yet again,
of Principle Uno: *Women are mysteries never intended to be solved.*
Your wisdom carried me through Sarah's weekend dalliance with Captain Kangaroo. They stayed on a houseboat. They got comfy. They
romanced. Everything I predicted in my "film script" to you.
You are right to aver that jealousy had no place in this geriatric adventure of mine. I agree I should cherish Sarah for her honesty and willing-
ness to act on what she needs in her real life.
Paul, you're likely right too about Sarah's reanimated husband. Probably
means he is dead to her. I have to remember that.
Anyway, this is all moot. Sarah's refusing to communicate. Almost two
weeks of gloomy radio silence — still counting. So sad.
How peculiar — back in love at age 69, with a woman I last touched
nearly 50 years ago. But this vacuum. Airless. Suffocating.
How can this happen? Is there no cure? Am I insane? Does Medicare
cover this condition?
I'm afraid, Paul, that I lost her — again.
The hours tick. My melancholy twists and then morphs into something
darker. I start once again to script for you a tale of Sarah's Revenge
But now the film is in the hands of Brian DePalma

*Gordon pulls up in Sarah's driveway and parks. He gets out and reaches into
the back seat to retrieve a wrapped present — a large white box with a promi-
nent gold bow.*

*Sarah seen as a shadow, watching from the living room window as Gordon
closes the car and approaches the door.*

A close up of Sarah's face — a look of determination, strangely menacing.

She answers the door.

He enters. They kiss, but not passionately.
He offers the present.
She intones, "Pour moi? My darling, how thoughtful. What occasion, my Gordo?"

"It's our three-month anniversary since the houseboat, my dear," says Gordon.

Sarah smiles and looks up into his eyes.

"I turned on the sauna for you, sweetie. Why don't you go ahead and get situated in there and I'll join you in a moment?"

She follows Gordon down the basement stairs. He eagerly undresses. The camera catches a brief glimpse of his tuchis as he slowly pulls the sauna door open.

A reddish glow illuminates the sauna. Gordon catches his breath and tries to focus his eyes.

A shot back through the door into the light of the basement. It's Sarah, standing quietly, hands at her side.

Gordon flips the light switch. Close-up of Gordon's face — a shaking hand across his mouth, terrified eyes and a muffled scream.

The camera swings over his shoulder to reveal that someone, or something, is already in the sauna, slumped in a seat on the far wall. The camera focuses on a shrunken body resembling a mummy. Leathery. Agonized eyeballs protruding.

As Gordon stares in horror at the corpse, Sarah appears behind him, at the doorway to the sauna.

She whispers, "That's Harold. It's our anniversary today too."

Sarah slams the door of the sauna shut.

Gordon lunges for the door. It's locked. He begins to pound on it.

"Out, let me out. Sarah, Sarah, Sarah!" Close-up of his face at the window. Then the screams fade.

A hand is seen turning the sauna thermostat up to the clearly demarked red zone.

Sarah stands, hands at her side, a blank expression. She gazes at the closed sauna. Muffled screams are heard.

Who's next, Paul?

NICOLE > SARAH   10/31/14   1:54 pm

Where have u bn? Did u forget we had appt this am w Artie? Concerned. Not like u.

SARAH   2:30 pm

Geez, I'm terribly sorry. I forgot the appointment. Distracted these days. But I suppose a side of me resists getting fancy advice from the high-powered.
I think you and I need to sit down and discuss the whole marketing plan sans Artie.

GORDON > SARAH   10/31/14 8:43 pm

Sorry you've been so busy lately.
It would make me happy to lay eyes on
you. A chance?

ADAM > SARAH   10/31/14 9:31 pm

I just need you to tell me you're okay.

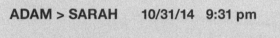

*From: **Adam Wolf** <adam.wolf1402@gmail.com>*
*To: **Sarah Ross** <sarahross64@gmail.com>*
November 1, 2014 12:36 pm
Subject: Lament

If indeed we are not to speak again, can I tell you this? Perhaps none of
this will make a difference. But I need to say it.

I've been thinking about how inevitable our reunion seems to have
been. But if it was inevitable, why did I miss the chance to make this
happen all those years ago? You know, Sarah, the time I saw you in the
summer, home from college, 1967. You weren't with Sandy anymore.
At the end of that wonderful day, I really remember I committed to visit
you in Cambridge. Yes, we set the date. I know, I know I never came. I even
remember now. It was August 25th. I don't know why I wasn't there.

That phone call, June 7th, 1968, the date we had picked as kids to get
married. I forgot the date. You reminded me. But on that day I was
overwhelmed with anxiety. The next day, as I told you, I was to be off
to Vista and Nowhere-in-the-World, West Virginia. The moment I hung
up, you've got to believe me, I felt an ill-defined regret and longing that

I still recall. Why did I feel the intensity in time, only after the call? Too late. Can you forgive that boy? The regret lingered. Three months later, I tried to find you and practiced what I would say if we connected. I would have said, "I don't know what will happen with us, but I need you now, I need to be with you, I'm scared and alone."

And the impulse to find you reoccurred to me over the years, a number of times. I actually knew you were in California and I looked for you. I asked Greg. He didn't know. In 1979, that time Brenda stood menacingly in my face while I spoke to you, I found myself unable to continue. I'm so sorry.

And then, ever since the internet, I started thinking about you. Not fixating, but following you, looking at your pictures, some poetry you had written. Sarah, I confess I've known your address in La Jolla for years. I can picture your street cause I found it on Google maps. I started to construct film scenarios of our reunion. With every passing year and month, the memories became more intense, the passion revived. Although I had fantasies of seeing you again, I couldn't bring myself to act on them. I imagined you might say, "You're a foolish old man. What makes you think after all these years I have any feelings for you?"

I also failed to contact you, I think, because I felt immobilized. Maybe I sensed what would happen if we communicated with each other. I had a premonition it would change my life. Part of it is I grew used to the idea of walking through life like a robot — convincing myself I was content. I dreamt about travelling to the stars, about writing books, about you.

I fantasized about happy endings too. We would meet the first time and figure out how you could get an hour free from Harold to spend with me. That it would only take the hour to win you back.

I would look at your picture and think you were looking at me, saying, "Adam, call".

Well, Sarah, I fell in love with you again in the 30 seconds it took to read your first email. Seeing you when we skyped confirmed it. Perhaps you can understand my sense of panic, then, that I lost you when you went off with Gordon.

From: **Sarah Ross** *<sarahross64@gmail.com>*
To: **Adam Wolf** *<adam.wolf1402@gmail.com>*
November 1, 2014 3:44 pm
Subject: Re:Lament

Why now, at age 69, and not then at 23 or 34 or whatever? I ask that too. What I do know is that we wouldn't have lasted, if we had married then. You had too many wild oats to sow and I wouldn't have been able to stick around for planting season.

And though I always loved you, your not showing up in Cambridge sliced into my heart and I was so traumatized and embarrassed by the rejection, I couldn't even tell my shrink for years. I was too angry and hurt to be with you comfortably for a long time. But now, from this sage vantage point of 69, I not only forgive the boy, I understand him. It all makes sense. I'm no longer judgmental or hurt or angry. I have enormous sympathy for that sweet lost kid. Sure it took a long time to get here, but that's the gift of the 40 plus years apart. I want to rescue him.

From: **Adam Wolf** *<adam.wolf1402@gmail.com>*
To: **Sarah Ross** *<sarahross64@gmail.com>*
November 1, 2014 3:55 pm
Subject: Re:Re:Lament

Yes, my love, please rescue the old man too. I need you in my life for keeps now. Don't ever drift away again. Is there a word for "beyond distraught"?

From: **Sarah Ross** *<sarahross64@gmail.com>*
To: **Adam Wolf** *<adam.wolf1402@gmail.com>*
November 1, 2014 4:12 pm
Subject: more than ever

I can't be away from you, my Adam. Too painful. That much I've discovered. I've been trying to make sense of what's happened to my life in these past months and realize it's not possible to think rationally. I do know this, though. I love you with an intensity not leveled by time.

---

*From: **Sarah Ross** <sarahross64@gmail.com>*
*To: **Adam Wolf** <adam.wolf1402@gmail.com>*
November 2, 2014 10:06 am
Subject: Billy Friedman

Just wanted you to know that Greg sent me a note that Billy Friedman died. Did you see him at the reunion? Greg said heart attack. I'm stunned really.

---

*From: **Adam Wolf** <adam.wolf1402@gmail.com>*
*To: **Sarah Ross** <sarahross64@gmail.com>*
November 2, 2014 12:33 pm
Subject: Re: Billy Friedman

I know about Billy. Greg told me too. I spoke briefly with Billy at the reunion. We reminisced about our constant Bob and Ray routines on the way to school.
Everything and everyone we passed became fodder for our imaginary radio show.

Adam: Say Billy, I don't mean to interrupt your erudite commentary but isn't that Cosmo Pecararo, the legendary bully, approaching us from the opposite direction.

Billy: Why yes, Adam, that would be one in the same. Perhaps we should again rehearse our bully confrontation scenario in case he elects to pick on you. You be him and I'll be you.

Adam (as Cosmo) in a loud gruff voice: "Hey, where do you think you kids are going?"

Billy (as me): "I'm going home. Is that okay with you?"

Adam (as Cosmo): "Hey punk, what did you say? I oughta bash your teeth down your throat, right now!"

Billy (as me): "Yeah? You and what army?"

Adam (as Cosmo): "Me! Well, anyway I would bash your teeth down your throat, but I don't have the time. It's my first major rumble of the semester in Cain Park and I'm running late. But watch out ladies, just consider yourself lucky this time!"

Billy (as me): "Ok Cosmo-- see you tomorrow"

Adam (as Cosmo): "You better hope not, punk!"

Billy (as himself again): "Well Adam, I think that rehearsal of ours went well. I believe we are fully prepared now for Mr. Pecararo. Incidentally, your portrayal there of young Cosmo was quite life-like and compelling. I think our listeners will agree."

Adam (as myself again): "Yes I certainly hope so, Bill. Needless to say, I'm glad for the opportunity to rehearse with you. Of course, I would like to take this opportunity to compliment you on your richly detailed and award-worthy depiction of me."

Funny, I don't remember much else about Billy, except that he was a marvelous kid.

From: **Sarah Ross** *<sarahross64@gmail.com>*
To: **Adam Wolf** *<adam.wolf1402@gmail.com>*
November 2, 2014 1:24 pm
Subject: Re:Re: Billy Friedman

I sat next to Billy in homeroom and couldn't wait for him to get going under his breath. And his thick glasses. And so sweet and droll. And I always got in trouble for laughing out loud. Adam, did you know that it was Billy in junior high, took me aside in the locker alcove and passed it by me that Adam Wolf wanted to ask me to go steady and if he did, would I? And I said, "You bet". Isn't it clever how at that age we insulate ourselves from rejection by using our friends as canaries in a coal mine?

And, Adam, another hit. How you walked me home from school shortly thereafter and sat me down on a bench and said you had something to ask me. Something serious. And then you asked me to go steady, or I thought you did, in French, knowing I spoke none, and showing off what you could do. And when you were done, you asked me if I would. And I said yes. And then you laughed and said that the romantic French you had just wooed me with was a nursery rhyme about a fox and a crow. Insulated all around.

From: **Adam Wolf** *<adam.wolf1402@gmail.com>*
To: **Sarah Ross** *<sarahross64@gmail.com>*
November 2, 2014 2:21 pm
Subject:

It's not so easy to insulate myself from my feelings these days, since we stopped writing for a couple of weeks. Strangely, I felt as lost now as I would have years ago if you had said "no" to going steady.

From: **Sarah Ross** *<sarahross64@gmail.com>*
To: **Adam Wolf** *<adam.wolf1402@gmail.com>*
November 2, 2014 2:37 pm
Subject:

It's inconceivable that I could ever have entertained the thought of saying "no". I loved you forever. There was no beginning to it. It just was. I've been thinking these past weeks whether I could ever have been in love with anyone as deeply as I was in love with you.

From: **Adam Wolf** *<adam.wolf1402@gmail.com>*
To: **Sarah Ross** *<sarahross64@gmail.com>*
November 3, 2014 7:18 am
Subject:

The long conversation last night did me good. You know, Sarah, despite our unresolved issues about our lives, will you go steady with me?

From: **Sarah Ross** *<sarahross64@gmail.com>*
To: **Adam Wolf** *<adam.wolf1402@gmail.com>*
November 3, 2014 10:39 am
Subject:

You're making yourself exquisitely vulnerable by not using a go-between this time round. But there's no question about it. I could forsake all others for you.

From: **Sarah Ross** *<sarahross64@gmail.com>*
To: **Adam Wolf** *<adam.wolf1402@gmail.com>*
November 4, 2014 1:35 pm
Subject:

Adam, I think I owe you an apology.

*From: **Adam Wolf** <adam.wolf1402@gmail.com>*
*To: **Sarah Ross** <sarahross64@gmail.com>*
November 4, 2014 1:56 pm
Subject: Apology?

No apology necessary. For what? On the contrary, I realize that it's not really any of my business what your personal life is like, your romantic life. I have no right to pry or be jealous. I barged into your life and it should just be enough that I watch from the sidelines. I do not want to lose you, no matter what that entails. I was lost when we weren't in touch.

---

*From: **Adam Wolf** <adam.wolf1402@gmail.com>*
*To: **Sarah Ross** <sarahross64@gmail.com>*
November 4, 2014 6:10 pm
Subject: My apology

I realize, Sarah, I stepped where I shouldn't have gone. Forgive me. Now back to going steady. What exactly would "going steady" mean at 69? Do you want my ID bracelet or would my Life-Alert bracelet do? This odd phenomenon of reconnecting with you, as though we were returning to reality after just a brief detour. Fifty years as though two hours. I guess that some people might say that I'm nuts, leaving reality, not returning to it. Are we nuts?

---

*From: **Sarah Ross** <sarahross64@gmail.com>*
*To: **Adam Wolf** <adam.wolf1402@gmail.com>*
November 5, 2014 3:17 pm
Subject: what is this force that attached us again?

Maybe we are nuts. Maybe reconnecting is just a cheap form of electroshock therapy. Or maybe an original bonding so intense it can't be severed. Whatever, I've discovered even more surely these last several days that life with you feels much better than without you.

---

*From: **Adam Wolf** <adam.wolf1402@gmail.com>*
*To: **Sarah Ross** <sarahross64@gmail.com>*
November 5, 2014 7:54 pm
Subject: That bond

Sarah, that bond. Why should anyone else understand it? That force is indescribable. Even to us. Overwhelming. Obsessive, the way our original love was. They're right to ask what hit us. I don't know. But the feelings are big and real. You make me happy. I want to grab that and hold it for whatever time we have left.
What would you think of skyping again soon? Can I call you now? I know you need to savor words. But I need to hear your voice remind me that you love me.

---

*From: **Sarah Ross** <sarahross64@gmail.com>*
*To: **Adam Wolf** <adam.wolf1402@gmail.com>*
November 6, 2014 1:20 pm
Subject: Harold

It has been fun to talk again, dear. I love your Chicago accent. Remarkable. Do people there think you have a Cleveland accent?
You must still wonder why your discovery about Harold upset me. It's hard to talk about. I get on with life by not looking back. Over the years Harold let me down in many ways. Perhaps I disappointed him too. But in the end, he outdid himself. It was Harold who killed me off first.

---

*From: **Adam Wolf** <adam.wolf1402@gmail.com>*
*To: **Sarah Ross** <sarahross64@gmail.com>*
November 6, 2014 2:53 pm
Subject: Re:Harold

I see you're brittle on the subject. I don't want to push you. But when you're ready, I really want to know.

From: **Sarah Ross** *<sarahross64@gmail.com>*
To: **Adam Wolf** *<adam.wolf1402@gmail.com>*
November 8, 2014 7:01 pm
Subject: What killed Harold for me

I've been mulling over how to explain my abhorrence of Harold to you. If you really wish to know, read these emails from a few years ago.

◇◇◇

Oct. 15, 2010

Hello Mrs. Ross,

I'm sorry to bother you with a question, but it's a simple one, and I think an important one. Are you the wife of Harold Weinstein, Prof. of English Literature at U.C. San Diego?

Regards,
Christie Ellen Walker
Publicist, College of Liberal Arts
University of Nevada, Las Vegas

◇◇◇

Oct. 15, 2010

Dear Ms. Walker,

Why, yes, I am. Why do you ask?

Sincerely,
Sarah Ross Weinstein

◇◇◇

Oct. 11, 2010

I ask because I've been dating Harold Weinstein for the last 3 years. We met after a lecture he gave at UNLV. We began seeing each other soon after that. You should know that he told me from the outset that he was a widower. Until a friend recently suggested that I check it out, I trusted him. I guess I was naive. I thought we had plans. Now my only plan is to never see him again.

Sincerely,

Christie Ellen Walker
Publicist, College of Liberal Arts
University of Nevada, Las Vegas

So there you have it, Adam

---

*From: **Adam Wolf** <adam.wolf1402@gmail.com>*
*To: **Sarah Ross** <sarahross64@gmail.com>*
November 8, 2014 8:47 pm
Subject: Now I see

Outrageous! I'm so sorry. Let me get this straight. Three years earlier —your cancer surgery, right? Betraying you—by counting you out —just after your mastectomy? That's unforgiveable! He doesn't deserve to be alive. I wish I were there to hold you right now.
Are you really divorced from him?

---

*From: **Sarah Ross** <sarahross64@gmail.com>*
*To: **Adam Wolf** <adam.wolf1402@gmail.com>*
November 8, 2014 8:55
Subject:

Yes.

---

*From: **Adam Wolf** <adam.wolf1402@gmail.com>*
*To: **Sarah Ross** <sarahross64@gmail.com>*
November 8, 2014 9:40 pm
Subject; Betrayal

You know, Sarah, I have my own story of betrayal. It involves a friend
of my brother's and Lola. About ten years ago. David knew about them.
Never told me.

---

*From: **Sarah Ross** <sarahross64@gmail.com>*
*To: **Adam Wolf** <adam.wolf1402@gmail.com>*
November 8, 2014 9:55
Subject: Re:Betrayal

I guess that helps explain why you don't see much of your brother
anymore. I'm sorry.

---

*From: **Sarah Ross** <sarahross64@gmail.com>*
*To: **S.Gordon Wilson** <S.Gordon.Wilson@csulb.edu>*
November 9, 2014 11:28 am
Subject: dinner soon?

Hi Gordon

Sorry I've been under the weather lately. I didn't mean to be uncom-
municative. Why don't you make time to come here for dinner Friday
or Saturday? Would that suit you?

---

*From: **Adam Wolf** <adam.wolf1402@gmail.com>*
*To: **Sarah Ross** <sarahross64@gmail.com>*
November 9, 2014 12.01 pm
Subject: Had it out with Amanda

Sarah, I think you'll be proud of me. I meant to tell you. During the days of our silence, I confronted Amanda about her offensive message to you.

Told her it's not just that she violated my privacy, she violated my trust when she communicated with you. I said, "You do not own me. What you did was destructive and unforgiveable. I need you to leave me alone." I left with her crying.

Then she cornered me down the hall. The usual harangue. "What am I to you now? Just a friend? Like Paul? You're not the Adam Wolf I knew. We have a history. Then along comes someone you haven't even spoken to since you were a kid."

I was starting to feel sorry for her. But then she went too far. "You were ready to let Sarah Ross take my place. You know, if I succeeded, if it's all over with her now, it's for the best. I'm actually proud of what I did. I rescued you."

Sarah, I told her you and I were far from over (even though I had my doubts that day).

---

*From: **Sarah Ross** <sarahross64@gmail.com>*
*To: **Adam Wolf** <adam.wolf1402@gmail.com>*
November 9, 2014 4:36 pm
Subject:

I appreciate your telling me this. You were courageous. It must have been difficult, especially given your personality and your dependency on the work. I'm proud of you. ilu.

How is she behaving now? Does she know we're together again?

*From: **Adam Wolf** <adam.wolf1402@gmail.com>*
*To: **Sarah Ross** <sarahross64@gmail.com>*
November 9, 2014 6:17 pm
Subject: Don't worry about it

I don't care if she knows or doesn't. It's just business between us now, and I prefer it that way.
Sarah, I want to touch you. I wake at night thinking of lying with you. Thinking uninhibited thoughts. When can we skype again? I need to see you.

---

*From: **Sarah Ross** <sarahross64@gmail.com>*
*To: **Adam Wolf** <adam.wolf1402@gmail.com>*
November 9, 2014 6:50 pm
Subject: all through the night

　　Yes, please. Skype. Soon!
　　Now, my love, don't think me silly. But I have a wish. Don't laugh. But I'd like to watch you sleep sometime. On Skype. We need not talk. Just set up the camera and leave on enough light for me to watch you. Is this too weird for words? I just have a deep urge to see you through the night.

---

*From: **Adam Wolf** <adam.wolf1402@gmail.com>*
*To: **Sarah Ross** <sarahross64@gmail.com>*
November 9, 2014 8:59 pm
Subject: Re:all through the night

Let's do it and I want to watch you as well. It's where we left off, isn't it, on those Sunday afternoons all those years ago, with your head on my shoulder. Our naps together.

From: **Lola Wolf** <lola.wolf1402@gmail.com>
To: **Michael Wolf** <Michael.R.Wolf@brookstead.com>
November 11, 2014 11:23 am
Subject: schmuck

It's gotten out of hand, Michael, and I'm beside myself. Your father is offensively distant now. I pretend I don't hear him come into the house. Sometimes he doesn't look up. Sometimes I don't either. There's not even a sign he's eaten anything. He disappears into his room. He's talking to her, no doubt. I hear noises. Worse still, I hear laughter, and that's the hardest to bear.

Why should I care? Maybe because it's so insulting. So humiliating. The other day the Knolls stopped in. I called to Adam and he didn't even come downstairs, just waved to them. What must they think? I'm lonelier than I would be all by myself.

He'll have to leave. I can't stand the sight of him. I long for a peaceful life at my age.

I should have left him years ago, when I was still viable. Now who would want me? And who would I want? Some creaky old man with his ears filled with hair?

But even if we don't have much in common anymore, we have our history and our traditions for what they're worth. Sunday walks with the dog. That's over too! What's happening? Thanksgiving's coming up and he already said he's not going to the Allen's. Do you believe it?

I don't mean to put you in the center of this mess, but I needed to unload. You know what? After the Ross spell wears off, I'll lay down money he'll return to normal. I don't want him back. Why couldn't he just have let the clock run out?

*From: **Michael Wolf** <Michael.R.Wolf@brookstead.com>*
*To: : **Lola Wolf** <lola.wolf1402@gmail.com>*
November 13, 2014 10:25 pm
Subject: Re:schmuck

Mom, Wish there was something I could say that might help. I hate to see you pathetic. You have more dignity than that.

You're right that I don't want to be caught in the middle. Is it time to have it out with him once and for all? Wouldn't a therapist be a good idea for you?

You do sound conflicted. I like it when you let yourself get pissed with Dad.

But, excuse me for saying this, what's all the fuss about? You two haven't gotten along as far back as I can remember. Are you sure you need this kind of crap?

I'll skype you on Sunday. Maybe things will be back to normal by then. You'll have had a chance to sit down and talk reasonably.

ADAM > AMANDA   11/14/14 9:25 am

I got your message this morning. No need to apologize. I've calmed down. But tickets to Symphony tomorrow? Your "peace offering"? I'll gladly accept that. Stravinsky's Four Studies for Orchestra. Do you know it? The final study was apparently based on things he'd written for the player piano! Great!

I guess I can't stay angry with you for long.

I hope you know I really appreciate how generous a friend you are!

ADAM > SARAH   11/14/14   12:49 pm

Amanda's being contrite. Got us tickets
to the Chicago Symphony for tomorrow.
Looking forward to it.

SARAH   1:28 pm

Are you used to dates with her? Happen
often?

ADAM   3:46 pm

No, to both your questions. But moot
now anyway. Amanda back on the
warpath — no symphony — discovered you
and I are still together. She can go to hell.

ADAM   3:58 pm

I changed my password on the computer,
but now I learn she checks cell phone
minutes on the bill.
White hot furious that she won't let up.

SARAH   4:56 pm

For chrissake, the woman is relentless, out
of control.
Took the afternoon off. Driving up coast on
this lovely aft. in sunny CA. Wish you were
here.

ADAM   5:16 pm

With Gordon? Same question. Date often?

SARAH   5:28 pm

Stop it. It's not the same. Gordon doesn't claim ownership of me. In fact, he asks about you.

ADAM   5:30 pm

asks what?

SARAH   6:32 pm

where u went to school? when graduated? do we write every day? do we ever talk on the phone?

ADAM   6:39 pm

ok. do you tell him?

SARAH   7:29 pm

not quite. why upset him?

ADAM 8:16 pm

Hope it won't upset him that we have a Skype date tomorrow. Or do you plan to invite him to chaperone?

SARAH 11:47 pm

Adam, please don't be jealous. It doesn't become you. You know very well how much I've been looking forward to Skype tomorrow night! 9:00 still okay?

From: **Adam Wolf** <adam.wolf1402@gmail.com>
To: **Paul Bishop** <Paul.R.Bishop@dewey.com>
November 14, 2014 10:04 pm
Subject: On trial — help

Paul,

My virtual love affair's reconstituted. But I now find myself on trial. I cower alone at the defense table. Get Dershowitz. Tell him to hurry.
Day in and day out my two self-appointed prosecutors haul me to the witness stand, argue their cases. The charges? DOMESTIC TREASON RESULTING IN PERSONAL INJURY.
Lola, who's lived independently of me for years, senses capitulation. She levels new indictments. Criminal denial of responsibilities. Dereliction of uxorial duties.
Amanda accuses me of first-degree betrayal. Also throws in "denial of responsibilities". Of impersonating a snake.
I'm "hurtful", "heartless", "cruel". They both pronounce that.
I could use a character witness. Are you available?

Paul, I want the trial to stop. I know all I have to do is admit my guilt, by reason of insanity, and it will. I'm tempted. Otherwise, I fear, they will verbally beat me into submission.

What's your advice, counselor?

ADAM > SARAH   11/15/14 8:47 am

Love, can we postpone this evening's Skype? I'm so sorry, but I forgot obligatory visit to neighbors — their anniversary — whine and cheese. Dread it, but promised to go. Forgive me. Can we be together tomorrow instead?

SARAH   10:23 am

Disappointed, but okay. I'll try, if it can be in the afternoon. How's 3:00?

ADAM   11:48 am

Perfect. That's even check-in time at the Hampton Inn in Skokie, near my favorite deli. We'll have virtual corned beef together. I can't wait!

SARAH > ADAM   11/16/14   8:12 pm

Wow! Still thinking about our Skype
session. Now THAT was worth waiting for!
Amazing! Who would have guessed?

ADAM   8:20 pm

Let's try that again soon! I feel so alive, alive

From: **Sarah Ross** *<sarahross64@gmail.com>*
To: **Adam Wolf** *<adam.wolf1402@gmail.com>*
November 17, 2014 7:00 am
Subject: still breathless

I always knew from my phone-sex internship that the mind is the
erogenous zone. Adam, I'm crazy about you. I didn't know I was still
so susceptible to your wooing and cooing and whispering.

From: **Adam Wolf** *<adum.wolf1402@gmail.com>*
To: **Sarah Ross** *<sarahross64@gmail.com>*
November 17, 2014 am
Subject: Re:Still breathless

Colder than hell. Gonna snow. I didn't even wear a jacket today. What
do I care? I've got my love to keep me warm. Still in a trance. I've been
replaying every second in my mind since we hung up. You know, I think
we've invented something new, not skyping. What should we call it?
How about if we just combine skyping and phucking. There you go:
skyphing"? Do you think someone has already published a book about

it? "Skyphing for Dummies", no doubt. For this old man it was as intense as any love-making has ever been. But I suspect it was because it was you and I love you.

From: **Sarah Ross** <sarahross64@gmail.com>
To: **Adam Wolf** <adam.wolf1402@gmail.com>
November 17, 2014 12:22 pm
Subject: Skyphing

Yes, I do think others have come up with the same concept, Adam. Don't they call it "cybersex"? There are probably dozens of words for it. But none, I'm sure, as cool as "skyphing".

It's made for 70 year olds. I didn't feel at all self-conscious about what age had done to my body. And that made it possible to be myself again. And ... geez, did this really happen???

From: **Adam Wolf** <adam.wolf1402@gmail.com>
To: **Sarah Ross** <sarahross64@gmail.com>
November 17. 2014 3:17 pm
Subject: Re:Skyphing

Now, Sarah, don't you think a Skyphing "app" would have commercial possibilities? We could conduct seminars at assisted-living facilities: "Golden-Ager-Remote-Access-Computer-Fornication". We'll get a grant from the World Health Organization. I love you so much. Can't live without you.

From: **S.Gordon Wilson** *<S.Gordon.Wilson@csulb.edu>*
To: **Sarah Ross** *<sarahross64@gmail.com>*
November 17, 2014 10:10 am
Subject: are you okay?

Dear Sarah,

Forgive my writing to you, but I've been unable to get through this morning. I'm concerned about you, about us. You seemed distracted yesterday at the club. It was hard to keep you in conversation. Dale Mason commented on that, and wondered if she had said something wrong. I assured her that was not the case, but I have to admit I felt insecure myself. What is most unlike you (I hope you're not offended), is the brittle, and, it seems to me, testy mood that emerged. I may have misspoken when I referred to your drawings as "feminine", but I felt hurt that you reacted so sharply (and publically). I merely meant it had a soft, womanly perspective.

Are you okay? Your health? Nicole? Adam Wolf?

Please reassure me. I feel on shaky ground.

Gordon

S. Gordon Wilson, PhD.
Founder and Editor of *The Ichthysaurus*
Fellow, American Academy of Underwater Sciences
Professor of Biology, Emeritus
California State University, Long Beach

From: **Adam Wolf** <adam.wolf1402@gmail.com>
To: **Paul Bishop** <Paul.R.Bishop@dewey.com>
November 17, 2014 10:26 pm
Subject: Modern intimacy

Paul,

Guess what? We spent a virtual night together, thanks to Skype. The miracle of modern intimacy. Brought to mind those old 50's newsreels. You know, the ones about how technology would alter our lives in the future.

Remember?

Patriotic music swells. The camera sweeps over a sun-splashed futuristic skyline. An official-sounding voice intones:

"The City of the Future. Here the American common man will be surrounded by wondrous conveniences — devices that would make the pharaohs of old sick with envy, would impel Alexander the Great to lead his armies to battle. The future will bring inventions not even conjured by the fevered imagination of Jules Verne.

Let's meet Leonard Farkish, family man of the 21st century. Today he's off on a business trip. He kisses the little woman goodbye."

"See you later, hon." (*He winks.*)

(*Gwendolyn runs her hands through her hair and shyly giggles.*) "OK, sweetie. See you on the UNIVAC tonight. I'll be ready. I'm glad we thought to replace that faulty vacuum tube last week."

"Leonard arrives at the Rocketport, calm, even though he has to meet his client 3000 miles away in only 45 minutes. No worry! Our Sales Executive of the Future has a ticket on *Missileair*. Just imagine,

**his business trip employs the same technology Adolph Hitler used
to successfully devastate London."**

*Later, in the evening, we find Leonard in his 21ˢᵗ-century hotel room as he steps
out of the bathroom in his silk pajamas, combing his hair—a salacious grin
smears his face.*

"Yes, the hotel suite comes equipped with a Univac Junior. Leonard
dims the light, sits at the console. An image appears on the small screen.
It's Gwedolyn!"
"Hi, Honeybun. Is it cold there in Iceland? How was your day?"
"Fine. Made the sale. Kids put down?"
"Yes (*coquettishly*), they are, sweetie. I'm wearing something special
tonight. Do you recognize it, darling? You gave it to me for Christmas."
(She steps back from the console and twirls to reveal her negligee.)
"Wow, that's certainly alluring, my dollface. It sure primes my pump,
you know. Remind me again, what color is it?"
"It's turquoise blue, my Univac beefcake."
"I have such good taste, don't I? Come closer, my little vixen."

**"Well, we best leave the Farkishes alone now. Our Man of the Future
has his hands full, even though his Missus is 3000 miles away. Yes,
it may be the future, but some things, well, let's just say, they won't
ever change."**

---

*From: **Sarah Ross** <sarahross64@gmail.com>*
*To: **S.Gordon Wilson** <S.Gordon.Wilson@csulb.edu>*
November 18, 2014 10:13 am
Subject: Re:are you okay?

Gordon,

Please forgive me. There's a lot on my mind, I guess. Nicole in part.
Doctor's visit and 162/99 blood pressure. Mother failing.

You're right to call me on being out of sorts. I promise to return to my sweet self by Friday evening. You deserve better.

From: **Adam Wolf** <adam.wolf1402@gmail.com>
To: **Sarah Ross** <sarahross64@gmail.com>
November 18, 2014 11:34 am
Subject: "How to" Books for Boomers

I'm still basking in our skyph encounter, Sarah. Don't you agree that we're qualified to write sex manuals for the geriatric set?
How's this: Volume One: "Fuck me When You Wake from Your Nap"
Or Volume Two: "Mazel Tov. Who Needs Viagra?"

From: **Sarah Ross** <sarahross64@gmail.com>
To: **Adam Wolf** <adam.wolf1402@gmail.com>
November 18, 2014 4:54 pm
Subject: Re:"How to" Books for Boomers

Yes, good idea. We can call the book *Fifty Shades of Graying*. Publishers will knock down the door.

Here, back in reality—trouble with Nicole again today. She keeps insisting Artie, her new beau, devise a marketing plan for us. We don't need him. Why is Nicole so susceptible to a man's attention, especially one like Artie's? The guy's I.Q. is below body temperature.

From: **Adam Wolf** <adam.wolf1402@gmail.com>
To: **Sarah Ross** <sarahross64@gmail.com>
November 19, 2014 9:53 pm
Subject: Fessing up

Sarah, I thought it was time I admit to Lola about the depth of my connection to you, that it's more than casual. Yes, when pressed, I said "romantic". It was a death-defying experience. I sat her down in the kitchen, taking advantage of the fact she seemed rational and receptive. I kept one eye on the door.

Her first response was no response.

She got up and clattered the dishes for a while. Then sat back across from me and glared. I characteristically averted my eyes. For three or four minutes the only sounds were the refrigerator motor and the cat, scratching and digging in the litter box.

"Sarah Ross. I KNEW there was more. Why would you do this to me? Don't come near me."

I told her you and I have never even been together. That fell flat.

"Why do you pretend that makes a difference?" Nothing I could have said would have helped.

She stalked upstairs to her room and crashed the door shut. For the rest of the evening I heard the television blaring. Loud, really loud. Maybe I heard her crying. I was tempted to console her, but thought better of it. Sarah, I'm low, very blue right now. Please remind me you love me.

From: **Sarah Ross** <sarahross64@gmail.com>
To: **Adam Wolf** <adam.wolf1402@gmail.com>
November 19, 2014 9:57 pm
Subject: Re:Fessing up

Oh dear. Of course, of course I love you, love you. Can you turn on Skype so I can watch you sleep tonight?

From: **Adam Wolf** <adam.wolf1402@gmail.com>
To: **Sarah Ross** <sarahross64@gmail.com>
November 19, 2014 10:00 pm
Subject:

Maybe not tonight

---

*From: **Adam Wolf** <adam.wolf1402@gmail.com>*
*To: **Sarah Ross** <sarahross64@gmail.com>*
November 21, 2014 8:19 pm
Subject: What did I do wrong? Never the right thing

You know, Sarah, Lola has always been a sort of a mystery to me. Always unpredictable. But now that you and I are known to her, she's become particularly erratic, or maybe I should say "volatile".

In any given ten minutes she can transit from sarcasm to resignation to recrimination to pathos without taking a breath.

There were even a few bizarre moments where you don't exist. When I got home tonight, she suggested we take a vacation to Italy next summer. (We haven't had a vacation together since we took Michael to Niagara Falls when he was nine-years old.) She wonders if we should sign up for the charter flight the Holdens next door recommended, and we need to make a decision cause they're filling up fast.

Yesterday she brought home strawberry ice cream. Plopped a dish of it down in front of me on the table. "I still bring you your favorites. Would Ross do that for you? I don't think so."

She asked, "What is the hold that Sarah Ross has?" (I can sense an ill wind about to stir.) "Tell me. Tell me. What's the hold she has?"

I searched for the answer that wouldn't trigger the whirlwind — volunteered that you and I were bonded for life in our early years. "The bond is strong. Anyway, I enjoy talking to her. It's not like we're carrying on. We haven't seen each other."

Then I realized as I said it, I'd made a mistake. Too late. Rather than holding the storm at bay, I hastened it. Now the deluge:

It began: "What difference does that make — you keep repeating it — but you're still cheating on me. You've still deceived me."

I pushed the dish of ice cream toward her, to the other side of the kitchen table. I watched as the storm unleashed its full fury. I watched her mouth move. I noticed the volume wasn't loud, but the tone was intense. Her face contorted. Her age now fully apparent. Her eyes narrowed and focused, as if beams emanating from her pupils would suddenly cure me of the Sarah cancer. First she gripped the edge of the table. Then with her right hand she began to sweep away the crumbs that weren't there. I comprehended only a few phrases:

"I don't know who you are."

"Who are you?"

"I don't recognize you."

"Who is this person I've married?"

"You're strange to me."

"Does Amanda know the full extent of this? She told me she suspects something. Your work probably suffers. She probably thinks you'll destroy the station over this. She won't put up with it."

"Am I such a shrew? Has your life been so miserable that you have to run to another woman for your happiness? I think I'm still a pretty woman, but you haven't told me that in years. Who is Sarah Ross? I've looked her up. She's nobody. She runs a lingerie shop. Is that what interests you? I can only imagine her at 68 in some baby doll negligee. I could understand if she were a young thing, but this Ross is an old woman."

As the downpour of recriminations subsided, the soft rain of pathos began.

"How could you do this to me at 65. To a woman in her hour of greatest vulnerability? What will become of me? You need to move out. I'm not putting up with this."

And I said, "You're right. I'll look for my own place."

The storm passed. I got up to leave. Lola's face brightened. She reached out with her right hand and shrugged. "Eat your ice cream. We can talk this through. There's no need for acrimony."

---

*From: **Sarah Ross** <sarahross64@gmail.com>*

*To: **Adam Wolf** <adam.wolf1402@gmail.com>*

November 21, 2014 8:59 pm

Subject:

I'm sorry Lola is so upset. This thing that happened to you, to us, happened so fast that I suppose all of us are reeling. But it's not your fault. You thought you did the right thing to level with Lola.

I'm just concerned that suffering through storms is your default setting. That you gravitate toward it? Because that's what's familiar to you? Since I've known you, since you were a kid, you took the blame for everything that went wrong. Adam, please protect yourself.

From: **Adam Wolf** <adam.wolf1402@gmail.com>
To: **Sarah Ross** <sarahross64@gmail.com>
November 21, 2014 9:08 pm
Subject:

Yes, I'm used to these storms—30 years of them.

From: **Sarah Ross** <sarahross64@gmail.com>
To: **Adam Wolf** <adam.wolf1402@gmail.com>
November 21, 2014 9:37 pm
Subject:

I'm so sorry. It shouldn't have come to this. So sorry for both of you.

From: **Adam Wolf** <adam.wolf1402@gmail.com>
To: **Sarah Ross** <sarahross64@gmail.com>
November 21, 2014 9:51 pm
Subject: I want to see you

Lola's right. I do want you. I do not want to be married to her anymore. I do need to leave. Sarah, maybe it's time for us to think beyond this virtual relationship of ours and get together for real.

---

*From: **Sarah Ross** <sarahross64@gmail.com>*
*To: **Adam Wolf** <adam.wolf1402@gmail.com>*
November 21, 2014 10:22 pm
Subject: Re:I want to see you

My dearest Adam, I feel the pull, the need to be with you too. Believe me. But I don't want this magic we have right now to disappear. We have too much to lose, if it doesn't work out between us. Then I would be devastated. And, if it did work out, I don't think I could bear to be apart from you again after that.

If you can assure me that I'm not the reason you're leaving your marriage, I might dare to get together. Maybe we can arrange something in the spring? Maybe.

---

*From: **Adam Wolf** <adam.wolf1402@gmail.com>*
*To: **Sarah Ross** <sarahross64@gmail.com>*
November 21, 2014 10:44 pm
Subject: Re:Re:I want to see you

Too many conditions, Sarah. You sound ambivalent. Scared.
Is Gordon part of the reason you're tentative? I guess you have your entanglements too. I'm also scared, but I guess we need to take the chance.
I have an idea. What if you came here for a few days in late December? Lola spends Christmas with her sister's family in Louisville. I generally have a light schedule at the station. Possible?

---

*From: **Sarah Ross** <sarahross64@gmail.com>*
*To: **Adam Wolf** <adam.wolf1402@gmail.com>*
November 21, 2014 11:04 pm
Subject:

   That soon?

   But, you're right, I would really need to extricate myself too. Gordon has his traditions — Xmas, the eggnog he's famous for — throws a party — grandkids gathering. I myself hate Christmas! Reason enough to escape. Don't know how I'd break it to him, though. Any ideas?

---

*From: **Adam Wolf** <adam.wolf1402@gmail.com>*
*To: **Sarah Ross** <sarahross64@gmail.com>*
November 21, 2014 11:16 pm
Subject: Please come!

Why don't you tell him you don't want to be with an asshole that time of year, but rather in the arms of the one person you ever really loved? I'm sure he can take it like a man.

---

*From: **Sarah Ross** <sarahross64@gmail.com>*
*To: **Adam Wolf** <adam.wolf1402@gmail.com>*
November 21, 2014 11:27 pm
Subject: Re:Please come!

   It's a thought. But I won't go quite that far. I think I'd rather invoke an emergency with my mother in Cleveland. And book my flight to you now. You choose the hotel. This is scary. (Or have I already said that?) Reality is frightening. I fear the end of our romance when we discover we're not compatible after all.

---

*From: **Adam Wolf** <adam.wolf1402@gmail.com>*
*To: **Sarah Ross** <sarahross64@gmail.com>*
November 21, 2014 11:43 pm
Subject: Re:Re:Please come!

Impossible that we wouldn't be a great fit. It'll finally be our chance to hold each other, touch each other, gaze at each other in bed, whispering.

---

*From: **Sarah Ross** <sarahross64@gmail.com>*
*To: **Adam Wolf** <adam.wolf1402@gmail.com>*
November 21, 2014 11:56 pm
Subject:

Now, I guess, I'm not as scared.

---

*From: **Adam Wolf** <adam.wolf1402@gmail.com>*
*To: **Michael Wolf** <Michael.R.Wolf@brookstead.com>*
November 23, 2014 7:38 pm
Subject: Sarah Ross

By now, Michael, your mother undoubtedly has saturated your ears with stories of how I've gone astray. In particular, I suppose you know now about Sarah Ross. I don't think I've ever mentioned her to you. Sarah Ross and I bonded for life when we were kids. What's wrong with my marriage and my commitment to end it has nothing to do with Sarah. In fact, years ago I declared the desire to live alone. You've been quick to tell me on any number of occasions that it hasn't been a happy togetherness, a good match. Lola and I have little in common, except for you.

I wish you and Colleen a happy Thanksgiving. I'll spend the day in bed.

---

*From: **Michael Wolf** <Michael.R.Wolf@brookstead.com>*
*To: **Adam Wolf** <adam.wolf1402@gmail.com>*
November 24, 2014 9:14 pm
Subject:

I don't judge you. I don't blame anyone for wanting to break free of suffocating patterns.

For years I watched you travelling between your two masters. At home. At the station. You haven't had much of a life outside that. But why do you need to break free now? Why not twenty years ago?

---

*From: **Adam Wolf** <adam.wolf1402@gmail.com>*
*To: **Michael Wolf** <Michael.R.Wolf@brookstead.com>*
November 24, 2014 10:09 pm
Subject: Why now?

Twenty years ago I wouldn't have left.

I know it's difficult for Lola to see me happy when she feels so unhappy. But in our more rational conversations she admits that she would prefer a more peaceful life, with someone more like her—someone who won't complain about the bugs when they walk through the forest preserves. Someone not afraid of horses. Someone who, like her, likes to cook and eat outdoors. I guess she deserves an outdoor type. You know what I mean, Michael.

The occasion of my 50th high school reunion cattle-prodded me out of my stupor. My bond with Sarah is difficult, almost impossible to explain. Despite all the years apart and three marriages between us, we are more alike, more simpatico than any two people are likely to be. The relationship wasn't planned. It just happened. As if it were inevitable. It has catapulted me back into life.

From: **Adam Wolf** *<adam.wolf1402@gmail.com>*
To: **Michael Wolf** *<Michael.R.Wolf@brookstead.com>*
November 24, 2014 10:40 pm
Subject: Just one more thing

Long ago I told Lola I wanted to go off by myself. Permanently. The split was inevitable, regardless of who entered my life. Sarah is only the catalyst.
I wouldn't have retired to Boca Raton or Tampa Bay or Flagstaff—or wherever the hell your mother's notions took her that week. Some retirement site where I'd be expected to join the organ recitals and wine-making classes. In fact, I'm surprised that Lola's surprised by my wish to move out.

MICHAEL > ADAM   11/25/14   11:12 am

I understand, Dad. Just concerned that Mom will be ok.

From: **Adam Wolf** *<adam.wolf1402@gmail.com>*
To: **Lola Wolf** *<lola.wolf1402@gmail.com>*
November 25, 2014 11:32 pm
Subject: Michael

Dear Lola,

I've been corresponding with Michael. I'm struck by what a decent and moral man he's become. He seems squared away (in a way I never was). I'm sure that's mainly because of you—the time and attention you paid him—how you were always responsive and affectionate. You were a great mother. You are a wonderful person—everyone you've ever come across, the many people you've *you* helped, all seem to agree on that.

Lola A. Wolf
1402 Madison St.
Evanston, IL 60202   *November 27, 2014*

Dear Sarah,

Forgive my writing under these circumstances. I suspect if the situation were different, you and I might enjoy each other's company. In years gone by, of course, Adam has mentioned you, the relationship you had when you were children. I'm aware of your accomplishments as an artist, and I do not doubt that Adam and you have a very strong bond. I respect that, and that he is happy you have reconnected.

But the circumstances are what they are. I am Adam's wife. We have a child. We have shared a life for thirty years, a house, a family, a bank account. And, yes, like any couple, our marriage has been visited by some sadness and misunderstandings. I guess, despite all the romantic illusions that float about in your imaginations, our marriage vows mean something. I'm sure you agree.

Adam's romance with you is perfect because you didn't have to raise a kid together, struggle to pay the endless bills together, keep the house from collapsing around your ears. No, of course not. No, your relationship is free of all that. You and Adam are 14 going on 70 with no history of struggle or angst.

I wonder if you and Adam ever have a sober moment in which you feel guilt for what you are destroying. But I don't suppose you have. And why would you? You and Adam seem to be in a flush with this illusion of romance, rescuing each other from old age and unfulfilled lives. But, Sarah, perhaps I should be the first to help you get past your illusions about Adam. I'm the one who's had to live with him day after day for the last 30 years. If you're contemplating taking my place, you ought to know what you're getting into. Consider this:

Maybe it's his cardiac meds, but the man lacks passion. He refuses to hold hands, or look you in the eye, doesn't like to touch at all. Cold. He's easily cowered, expends all his energy satisfying an overbearing boss. Nothing will be left for you—no time, no attention. Now, let's see, what else do you need to know? Well, he degenerates into schtick every time you want to talk about something serious. To boot, you can look forward to a panic attack every morning when he can't find his keys, and I mean full-blown tantrum, chairs overturned, papers thrown to the floor, dog cowering in the corner. Oh, and catch this one. You'll find out, if you haven't already, that Adam Wolf has no libido.

A lot of people, you know, tell me I'm fairly attractive and elegant and say Adam's a fool if he thinks he can do better. But please don't flatter yourself for one moment that I'm jealous. I'm beyond that with Adam. But Adam needs to recognize his responsibilities, and you do too.

One last thing, and I hope you forgive my frankness, but Adam surely won't tell you himself about the other dalliances he's had in the past. In the end, though, rest assured, he's always come back to the ranch.

I expect that you are going to respond to this.

Sincerely,
Lola Wolf

December 3, 2014

Dear Lola,

I'm so sorry you have had a rough go of it with Adam. It must have been so irritating all these years. Couldn't have been a happy time, especially over such a long haul. Didn't you ever think of parting ways before this? Should one stay in a marriage where every nanosecond you become more and more miserable? And why? Should dalliances be forgiven so easily, especially from a man who doesn't meet your needs?

It is not my place to advocate for or against Adam's staying in a marriage. That's between the two of you. Perhaps it merely hurts to the one left and not the one leaving. Should we stick out relationships, no matter what, because we've stuck them out so long? Should we expect someone to stay with us so we can feel good about ourselves and look intact to the neighbors? But not to worry. I'm sure, now that your child is 28, you and Adam can more easily figure out an equitable custody solution for Michael.

I'm sympathetic if your marriage hasn't worked out, but not at all responsible for that, or the least bit guilty about it. I wish better for Adam and for you. (I have no doubt that you are more attractive and elegant than I.)

Sarah Ross

6

From: **Sarah Ross** *<sarahross64@gmail.com>*
To: **Adam Wolf** *<adam.wolf1402@gmail.com>*
December 3, 2014 7:05 pm
Subject:

Adam, I have a question. If you and Lola lead these separate lives, don't you think it odd that she clings to the marriage? Might you be sending her cross signals?

From: **Adam Wolf** *<adam.wolf1402@gmail.com>*
To: **Sarah Ross** *<sarahross64@gmail.com>*
December 3, 2014 8:19 pm
Subject:

I'm not sure what you mean. I've told her about us. No cross signals. But, yes, I agree, it's odd that Lola suddenly wants to take a romantic vacation. It's bizarre that she bakes me chocolate chip cookies.
I guess change is difficult, no matter how unsatisfying a relationship has been. Especially at our age. Don't you agree?

*From: **Sarah Ross** <sarahross64@gmail.com>*
*To: **Adam Wolf** <adam.wolf1402@gmail.com>*
December 3, 2014 8:23 pm
Subject:

Do you ever feel guilty that you contemplate changing your life?

---

*From: **Adam Wolf** <adam.wolf1402@gmail.com>*
*To: **Sarah Ross** <sarahross64@gmail.com>*
December 3, 2014 8:43 pm
Subject: If you want me to be honest

I don't admit guilt to Lola when she confronts me with that question. But I know from guilt. I feel guilty if there's a traffic jam. I feel guilty if it rains on a picnic day. Now? Of course. But I'll learn to live with it. Except for a few formalities, my relationship with Lola is kaput.

---

*From: **Sarah Ross** <sarahross64@gmail.com>*
*To: **Adam Wolf** <adam.wolf1402@gmail.com>*
December 3, 2014 9:11 pm
Subject: Re:If you want me to be honest

Is this the first time Lola's experienced you backing away? Has she had to reel you in before?

---

*From: **Adam Wolf** <adam.wolf1402@gmail.com>*
*To: **Sarah Ross** <sarahross64@gmail.com>*
December 3, 2014 9:15 pm
Subject: Re:Re:If you want me to be honest

This is different.

---

*From: **Harold Weinstein** <Harold.W.Weinstein9933@gmail.com>*
*To: **Sarah Ross** <sarahross64@gmail.com>*
December 4, 2014 3:13 pm
Subject: Moving Back

Hi Sarah,

Wanted to let you know that I'm going into retirement and have decided to move back to San Diego. We're likely to run into each other. Don't you think it's time we admit mistakes were made, on both our parts? I'll be in town in a few weeks. How about we go have a drink together? I can even give you a copy of the paper I'm delivering at the MLA—the influence of Louisa May Alcott on Toni Morrison.

What do you say?

---

*From: **Sarah Ross** <sarahross64@gmail.com>*
*To: **Esther Lehman** <estherlehman88@yahoo.com>*
December 4, 2014 5:30 pm
Subject: rearing his ugly head

Esther dear, do you believe it? A ludicrous email from Harold today. Inviting me for a drink because he's moving back to these parts. I'm not answering. Frankly, I'd rather drink cyanide-laced Kool Aid than have a beer with Harold Weinstein, PhD.

---

*From: **Adam Wolf** <adam.wolf1402@gmail.com>*
*To: **Sarah Ross** <sarahross64@gmail.com>*
December 4, 2014 1:13 pm
Subject: It won't stop!

Amanda was oddly high-spirited today. She's apparently still monitoring my calls on the station cell phone and saw that my calls to California have stopped. She congratulated me, with full snark, on overcoming my obsession with you.

I roared back that you and I have our own phone now, that my private conversations with other people were none of her concern.

Amanda lashed out — called me/us absurd. Said she saw her old boyfriend back at her own reunion and felt nothing. Not even a twinge.

I thought of blurting out that there's a difference between just any old boyfriend and your original love.

---

*From: **Sarah Ross** <sarahross64@gmail.com>*

*To: **Adam Wolf** <adam.wolf1402@gmail.com>*

December 4, 2014 6:18 pm

Subject: Re:It won't stop!

IT DOESN'T STOP! Don't you think it might stop if you changed the way you interact with Amanda? Aren't you outraged at the intrusions into your life? I want her out of mine. She's butting into my private life too, not just yours.

You know, Adam, if the story of you and me and Amanda were a book, it would drag right about now, and readers would put it down.

---

*From: **Adam Wolf** <adam.wolf1402@gmail.com>*

*To: **Sarah Ross** <sarahross64@gmail.com>*

December 4, 2014 7:34 pm

Subject: Re:Re:It won't stop!

My work at this station has defined my life. It's what I've devoted myself to, and what I'll be remembered for. I'm reluctant to jeopardize that. Don't worry. I'll figure it out.

From: **Lola Wolf** *<lola.wolf1402@gmail.com>*
To: **Adam Wolf** *<adam.wolf1402@gmail.com>*
December 5, 2014 9:58 am
Subject: I'm your wife

Since we're not talking, maybe you'll still take the time to read this. Renting your own place? You can't be serious. Where's the money going to come from?

Do you really intend to precipitously end our marriage? After 30 years? That's incredibly cruel and malicious.

We need to sit and talk about this, free of Sarah Ross's intrusion. She is not your wife. I am. You owe it to me, as your wife and the mother to our son, to talk things through. I cannot believe that you would let this happen at this stage of our lives. It's just not done.

We need to go to a professional counselor and see if there's hope. I think there is. I do not deny that we have had our issues and that we've grown apart. I think this happens to many couples. I know they've often been able to reconnect with counseling. I think your obsession with this Ross is pathological. I'm sure a therapist would agree. In the end, I trust you will come to your senses and start to act more responsibly.

From: **Adam Wolf** *<adam.wolf1402@gmail.com>*
To: **Lola Wolf** *<lola.wolf1402@gmail.com>*
December 5, 2014 11:27 am
Subject:

I don't want therapy. I'm through with therapy. You've said many times, and for a long time, and rightly, that the best thing for us would be to eventually part. Now the time has come.

---

*From: **Lola Wolf** <lola.wolf1402@gmail.com>*
*To: **Adam Wolf** <adam.wolf1402@gmail.com>*
December 5, 2014 12:27 pm
Subject:

I don't remember ever saying that. If I did, I didn't really mean it. Don't pretend that kind of talk was anything more than the normal bickering all married couples go through.

---

*From: **Adam Wolf** <adam.wolf1402@gmail.com>*
*To: **Lola Wolf** <lola.wolf1402@gmail.com>*
December 5, 2014 1:17 pm
Subject:

The conflicts we've had were never mere bickering. We haven't gotten along since Michael was a child. We haven't really been intimate since then either. Neither one of us has been happy in this marriage for all that time.

---

*From: **Lola Wolf** <lola.wolf1402@gmail.com>*
*To: **Adam Wolf** <adam.wolf1402@gmail.com>*
December 5, 2014 2:10 pm
Subject: Stop kidding yourself

How disingenuous! Your saying that our marriage is hopeless seems a little bit too convenient. You know damn well, Adam, that if it wasn't for Sarah Ross, you would never have had the guts to do anything about your "unhappiness". I have been a good partner, tolerating your:

- indifference
- absence
- moodiness
- and, yes, dalliances

I would like to believe. I do believe this is your final dalliance and like all the others you will come home when you're done with it. We're both too old for anything else.

---

*From: **Adam Wolf** <adam.wolf1402@gmail.com>*
*To: **Lola Wolf** <lola.wolf1402@gmail.com>*
December 5, 2014 3:45pm
Subject:

I could also make a list. What good does it do now? I also endured.

---

*From: **S.Gordon Wilson** <S.Gordon.Wilson@csulb.edu>*
*To: **Jerry Mahoney** <Jerry.Mahoney2028@verizon.net>*
December 6, 2014 10:33 am
Subject: Glad you'll be here soon

Hey Jerry

Looking forward to you and Mae coming down next weekend. I'm already icing the Molson.
Thanks for asking about Sarah. I expect she'll join us, though I'm not sure. Between you and me, she's acting a bit standoffish, skittish lately. I can't figure out why. It's not like her. Late-onset PMS? Sarah's charming one minute, distant the next. She hasn't laughed at any of my jokes lately. Now she's come up with some lame excuse to be out of town at Christmas. I can't help but take it personally.

Hey, pal, I think you'll like this one, via Chuck, at the club last week:

A flat-chested young lady read an article in a magazine that stated Dr. Oprescu from Bucharest could enlarge your breasts without surgery. So she decided to go to Dr. Oprescu to see if he could help her. Dr. Oprescu advised her, "Every day after your shower, rub your chest

and say, *"Scooby doobie doobies, I want bigger boobies!"* She did this faith-
fully for several months, and to her utter amazement she grew a terrific
D-cup rack!

One morning she was running late, got on the bus, and in a panic realized she had forgotten her morning ritual. Frightened she might lose
her lovely boobs if she didn't recite the little rhyme, she stood right there
in the middle aisle of the bus, closed her eyes and said, *"Scooby doobie
doobies, I want bigger boobies."*

A guy sitting nearby looked at her and asked, "Are you a patient of
Dr. Oprescu's?"

"Yes I am. How did you know?"

He winked and whispered, *"Hickory dickory dock ..."*

See you on Friday!
Gordon

S. Gordon Wilson, PhD.
Founder and Editor of *The Ichthysaurus*
Fellow, American Academy of Underwater Sciences
Professor of Biology, Emeritus
California State University, Long Beach

From**: Adam Wolf** <adam.wolf1402@gmail.com>
To: **Sarah Ross** <sarahross64@gmail.com>
December 6, 2014 1:42 pm
Subject: Countdown to you

FOUR HUNDRED AND EIGHT HOURS UNTIL WE'RE TOGETHER
AGAIN!
I hope I can survive the excitement.

Here the pressure mounts. It doesn't let up. Catch this. Amanda ceremoniously announced that she's going to lunch with Lola on Thursday. Huh? They've never been able to stand each other. Lola always refuses to come to the station's Christmas parties, for fear of having to endure Amanda's pontifications. Amanda, for her part, likes to imitate Lola's voice whining about my long hours. I'm mystified. But sure it concerns *moi et toi.*

Amanda Schreiber
211 E. Garfield Street
Hinsdale, Illinois 60521

December 6, 2014

Dear Maria,

Please remember my mother goes into the hospital Monday. I'm terribly distressed that I can't be there. My brother Andrew will be close by, though. Call him if you need anything. Surgery is at 7:15 a.m. You should be there by 9:00, just to be sure, even though I know hip surgery takes a couple of hours. Another private nurse, Nina Marcus, will be relieving you around 5:00. I can't tell you often enough how grateful my family is to have your kind assistance. My mother speaks very highly of you, and appreciates your company. You like the same movies, I hear.

Mother knows I'll be coming out in early February. I'll check in with her, her doctors, you and Nina, every day.

With gratitude,
Amanda Schreiber

From: **Sarah Ross** <sarahross64@gmail.com>
To: **Adam Wolf** <adam.wolf1402@gmail.com>
December 6, 2014 5:17 pm
Subject:

Adam, I'd be amused by Amanda's new-found concern for Lola, were it not about plotting to demolish me. I'm counting on you to call her on it.

Whatever this is about, it's another form of Amanda's working you over, making you uncomfortable. I'm so sorry about this latest manipulation. You say you're mystified, but aren't you mad too?

From: **Adam Wolf** <adam.wolf1402@gmail.com>
To: **Sarah Ross** <sarahross64@gmail.com>
December 6, 2014 6:42 pm
Subject:

Maybe I should get angry. Amanda's antics just tire me out.
Incidentally, Amanda's got yet another ploy. Now she's talking about selling the bandwidth. I don't know if it's meant to frighten me into obedience. I actually don't care. I think this should be my last year with the station. I'm way too old for this shit.

ADAM > SARAH   12/7/14   10:58 pm

I'm in love with you, Sarah
Good night. Turn on skype. I need to watch you sleep.

SARAH > ADAM   12/8/14 9:29 am

I loved how we seemed to wake up at
the same time during the night, and the
way you smiled at me before falling back
asleep. I'm sorry that Skype cut out.
But it didn't matter. All morning I've felt
protected and protective. I adore you.

From: **S.Gordon Wilson** <S.Gordon.Wilson@csulb.edu>
To: **Sarah Ross** <sarahross64@gmail.com>
December 9, 2014 2:50 pm
Subject: Did I do something to offend?

My dear Sarah,

As you can surely see from your call log, I've tried phoning you six times
now, to no avail. Are you okay? If not, what might be the matter and
how can I help?
Perhaps there's something I said or did to put you off. Was it last Friday
night at Sonny's? I usually don't drink that much, you know. Anyway,
I apologize for whatever it may have been.
Meanwhile, I'm counting on you to help me host the Mahoneys this
weekend. Mae and Jerry really took a shine to you. 7:00 Friday still okay?

Always,
Gordon

S. Gordon Wilson, PhD.
Founder and Editor of *The Ichthysaurus*
Fellow, American Academy of Underwater Sciences
Professor of Biology, Emeritus
California State University, Long Beach

From: **Sarah Ross** <sarahross64@gmail.com>
To: **S.Gordon Wilson** <S.Gordon.Wilson@csulb.edu>
December 9, 2014 5:52 pm
Subject: Re:Did I do something to offend?

My phone must have been shut off. So sorry.

Sure, Gordon, of course we're still on for Friday. It'll be nice to see Mae and Jerry again. Should I meet you there or would you like to swing by the shop to fetch me?

I just finalized my plans to fly to Cleveland, Dec. 23rd. Nicole said she'll take me to the airport.

Looking forward to the four of us being together Friday. 7:00 is fine.

From: **Adam Wolf** <adam.wolf1402@gmail.com>
To: **Paul Bishop** <Paul.R.Bishop@dewey.com>
December 13, 2014 8:21 pm
Subject: Self-doubt

Paul,

Ten days and counting until the great reunion. But yesterday afternoon Self Doubt walks in and sits across the room from me, chewing on his cigar. He stares. Then starts. No amenity. He's a rat hockey player as it turns out—kind of figures, huh?

"Adam, Adam! Yeah, I'm talking to you. Where does an old man like you get off with this dross?"

"Hey, Mr. Prostate! Are you listening? Sarah Ross? Sarah Ross? You haven't laid eyes on that broad in five decades. Where do you come off with crap like that? You sick mother-fucker!! Feed that line of shit to everyone—to your wife? I shouldn't waste my breath."

"Email romance? Old feeling? Takes you back to the day? What is this, Romeo and Fucking Juliet? Fuck that shit! You know what you sound like? One of those stupid ass operas you make people listen to on the radio—always hated them things. Still hate 'em!"

"So emails don't do it no more? Chick flying in to shack up with you at the Hilton? Over fucking Christmas yet? While the wife's away? You cocksucker! And for a piece of ass as old as you? What are you? I know what you are, you're frickin' out of your fucking mind, you fuck."

"Try this, asshole—and listen good because I don't want to repeat myself over and over again. You have an obligation to your wife—yeah, an obligation! You want some fresh pussy? Go get some up on Sheridan Road, like I do. But don't make a big fucking deal about it. Keep it to yourself. There's hookers who like to deal with antiques like you, Adam—no danger, no threat. They even take Medicare, some of them."

"And Amanda—that bioche? I sat you down when you started with her. I told you. Remember, you asshole, what did I tell you? What did I tell you? Jack off, prick! It was going to come back and bite your ass. I told you—leave it alone. I said—walk away. You didn't listen. You don't listen to shit! I don't know what I'm going to do with you."

"Where do you get off with crap like this?"

Paul, where do I get off with crap like this?

---

*From: **Mae Mahoney** <Mae.Mahoney1348@verizon.net>*
*To: **Sarah Ross** <sarahross64@gmail.com>*
December 15, 2014 9:16 am
Subject: Lovely seeing you

Such fun! Jerry and I envy your balmy December weather. It didn't seem like Christmas season at all. It was hard to come back to gray Seattle. We had such a grand time with you both. The Marine Room! What a romantic spot Gordon picked to pop the question. Hope you weren't uncomfortable it was in front of us. You seemed surprised. Don't be embarrassed. I wouldn't have been able to answer under those circumstances either.

Jerry and I think you're a lovely couple. We know how lonely Gordon has been for many years. We also know how glowingly he speaks of you and with so much affection. I hope you'll consider that when you respond to him.

Our love to you,
Mae

---

*From: **Sarah Ross** <sarahross64@gmail.com>*
*To: **Gabriella Fratelli** <gabriella.fratelli@orange.it>*
December 15, 2014 4:56 pm
Subject: Gordon troubles

Dearest Gabriella,

My life is simply too complicated. How did I ever get into this fix? Blindsided. Angry to be put in such a position — publically yet. Gordon proposed. But I'm sure he didn't mean it. It was the Cutty Sark speaking. But it's all the more embarrassing because now his friends take it seriously and even write endorsements.

Perhaps, not so long ago, I might have felt flattered, and, if meant, might have even said "yes". But now? Impossible. The mistake, I think, was to take my friendship with Gordon further. We have little in common. He's begun to annoy me, frankly. And I'm not in love with him.

At this point in my life, though, shouldn't I think of my old age? Don't people right about now marry for assurance they'll be looked after, if it comes to that? Maybe I should think about that. Maybe I would, if I ever really felt old age knocking. I wonder if that's why Gordon pursues me? Has he been afraid of growing old alone? He has me as a friend, always. Shouldn't that be enough?

I'm not asking for advice, dear heart. Just venting. Just clarifying why living with Gordon is out the question — married or not. Plus, he voted for Bush, twice.

---

*From: **Lola Wolf** <lola.wolf1402@gmail.com>*
*To: **Joan Margolis** <jmargolis@carswell.net>*
December 16, 2014 9:09 pm
Subject: Re:You're with us for Christmas

Joanie, I'm not sure I'm up to the Xmas trip this year. I've been feeling poorly, a bit depressed under the circumstances. Would you cut me some slack and let me wait until the last minute to decide? I hope you're all thriving and wish you lived closer.

Love,
Lola

---

*From: **Adam Wolf** <adam.wolf1402@gmail.com>*
*To: **Sarah Ross** <sarahross64@gmail.com>*
December 17, 2014 7:16 am
Subject: Foiled again?

Oh Sarah, Lola just threw me a curve ball. Announced she may take a pass on Louisville this year. I don't know what to say. If she doesn't go, what do we do?

---

*From: **Sarah Ross** <sarahross64@gmail.com>*
*To: **Adam Wolf** <adam.wolf1402@gmail.com>*
December 17, 2014
Subject: Re:Foiled again?

Don't worry about it. We'll take it as it comes. I'm flying to Chicago anyway. I can stay at the Hilton and explore Chicago on my own. Come to me if you can. I'm not about to remain here in La Jolla.

---

*From: **Adam Wolf** <adam.wolf1402@gmail.com>*
*To: **Sarah Ross** <sarahross64@gmail.com>*
December 17, 2014 11:20 am
Subject: Re:Re:Foiled again?

Are you free to talk this evening? We can talk this through.
ILUSVM. Thanks for being so patient with me.

---

*From: **Sarah Ross** <sarahross64@gmail.com>*
*To: **Adam Wolf** <adam.wolf1402@gmail.com>*
December 21, 2014 3:39 am
Subject: Re: coast is clear now

Good news about Lola's trip! I guess it's really going to work for us,
isn't it. Can't sleep. Anticipation. Should I bring you a little something
from my shop?

---

*From: **Sarah Ross** <sarahross64@gmail.com>*
*To: **Adam Wolf** <adam.wolf1402@gmail.com>*
December 22, 2014 3:14 pm
Subject:

Adam, it's getting close. I'm tingling with excitement. But at the
same time I need you to know I'm on the verge of bowing out. Several
times, even today, I knew I should cancel the flight. It's so scary — the
thought of really being with you. I shudder to think our togetherness
will end in the light of day.

And yet I need to be with you, even if it's only for one more time.
If anything, we need closure for all those years ago. Or I do. I shouldn't
speak for you. Yes. I'll be there. We need to touch each other again. That
would, for all my fright, be worth the journey back to you.

My plane gets in, as you know, in the early afternoon. Please, please
don't pick me up. Seeing you again with the world looking on feels
wrong. I'll take the hotel shuttle. Wish to catch my breath from the long

flight and get ready for you. Could you come to the hotel in the late afternoon? ilusvvm

---

*From: **Adam Wolf** <adam.wolf1402@gmail.com>*
*To: **Sarah Ross** <sarahross64@gmail.com>*
December 22, 2014 1:25 pm
Subject: So close

Just dropped Lola off at Midway and hope she doesn't change her mind in the airport. She's a nervous flyer, and I'm a nervous wreck. If you don't hear from me, call Uber and get a lift to Evanston Northshore Hospital. I'll be in the cardiac care unit, third bay on the left. Then, at least, I can die in your arms.
Sure, Sarah, it's all right of course. I had planned in my mind to pick you up at O'Hare. Rehearsed the airport scene. You on the ramp — a spotlight illuminates the way. You see me and begin a slow-motion run — your arms stretched out towards me. But, never you mind, I can accept the change.
I'll sneak up to your hotel around 5 o'clock.
Seriously, Sarah, please no fretting. It will be sublime. Although I do have to confess, I fear that something, or someone, is going to try to disrupt. I've decided I won't let that happen.
Soon, my sweet one, soon! Remember there are no deal breakers.

---

*From: **Adam Wolf** <adam.wolf1402@gmail.com>*
*To: **Sarah Ross** <sarahross64@gmail.com>*
December 28, 2014 2:13 pm
Subject: Thinking back on our time together

Sarah, dear Sarah,

I'm at the piano and thought I'd write a song to commemorate our first days together in 47 years.
A ballad. How would that be? Probably in E flat — with one of those

dreamy, catchy 40's tunes like, uh, *Stairway to the Stars*. Then the lyrics. I would say how the moment you opened your hotel room door, I felt as though we were fourteen years old again. All the decades in between had never happened.

Your voice, not the mature-lingerie-shop-owning-world-wise artist from the phone, but the demure, tender tone of my teenager. Your voice now two octaves higher. Eyes wide, glancing up at me, lovingly.

I'll write a verse about how easily we melted into each other, like young eager sweethearts. Oh, and if that isn't sappy enough for you, there'll be a verse to mark the supreme pleasure of sleeping through the night into sunrise — our faces 2 inches apart whispering — then watching each other dream--no one to knock on the door and send us home.

How's that? I'll get to work on it tonight. I never wrote a song before. Oh, and just so you know, I won't bring up about how I jumped every time a new text message dinged on my stupid phone. Or write about my unceremonious departure on Saturday morning to cover for Jesse. I should never have let those things intrude.

Sarah, I love you so much. I long to see you again. When? Where?

I'm regretful that neurotic old Adam Wolf ever made us wait to be together.

From: **Sarah Ross** <sarahross64@gmail.com>
To: **Adam Wolf** <adam.wolf1402@gmail.com>
December 28, 2014 7:58 pm
Subject: Re:Thinking back on our time together

My verses? They'll be about all the things that real togetherness, not virtual, provided. Perhaps about my hand shaking at the doorknob, too nervous to open it. And then the height of you next to me — familiar, comfortable — how my head always fit into your shoulder, as if we were formed for just that.

And there, at the door, those hypnotic blue eyes. (Skype turned them magenta. Should I mention that in a love song?) I was lured by your gaze again, weak-kneed again. Just like then.

And I would mention the wonder of hearing my own voice in a register I couldn't reach again if I tried—remarkably young. Remarkably open and giddy with you. I love you so much again, I would say, in the refrain.

---

*From: **Adam Wolf** <adam.wolf1402@gmail.com>*
*To: **Sarah Ross** <sarahross64@gmail.com>*
December 28, 2014 8:32 pm
Subject: Re:Re:Thinking back on our time together

We need to be together for keeps. Let's plan to meet in La Jolla in a few weeks –pick the place. I love you.

---

*From: **Sarah Ross** <sarahross64@gmail.com>*
*To: **Adam Wolf** <adam.wolf1402@gmail.com>*
December 28, 2014 9:28 pm
Subject: a mess

Rough go of it tonight. Gordon wonders if I've had time to "mull over" his proposal. I tried to brush it away as a slip of the tongue, under the influence. He took umbrage. Now what?

---

*From: **Adam Wolf** <adam.wolf1402@gmail.com>*
*To: **Sarah Ross** <sarahross64@gmail.com>*
December 28, 2014 10:45 pm
Subject: Re:a mess

Tell the Captain not to pout too long. Remind him that he, better than anyone else, knows there are plenty more fish in the sea.

ILU

---

*From: **Sarah Ross** <sarahross64@gmail.com>*
*To: **Adam Wolf** <adam.wolf1402@gmail.com>*
December 28, 2014 10:57 pm
Subject: Re:Re:a mess

I should have known better than to ask your advice. ilu2

---

*From: **Sarah Ross** <sarahross64@gmail.com>*
*To: **Adam Wolf** <adam.wolf1402@gmail.com>*
December 29, 2014 8:50 am
Subject: Come visit soon

I suspected when we met, if we really did mesh, I'd need to see you constantly. "For keeps" has taken on this intense imperative for me. It's not volitional. We have no choice in the matter. At least it feels that way. Yes, yes, yes. A few weeks — that's all I can bear to be apart. You name the dates, and I'll book a romantic room, *mit* ocean view, at the Coronado.

---

*From: **Adam Wolf** <adam.wolf1402@gmail.com>*
*To: **Sarah Ross** <sarahross64@gmail.com>*
December 30, 2014 9:11 am
Subject: Update

How would La Jolla on Valentine's Day suit you? The station has a fund-raising drive that week and I'm not really needed.
Lola's back. Unusually cheerful.
I'm still running the gauntlet here at the studio, though — A.S.brusque, especially imperious. Yesterday I had my weekly lunch with her. First icy silence, then banter. She imperceptibly segues to an interrogation about you and me:
"Do you talk all night to her … does she believe she's your wife just because you once went to the prom together … how can you do this to Lola … you've made Sarah your priority, haven't you?"

I halt the interrogation by raising my palms at her.

The moment arrives. Yes, I finally say, yes, Sarah's a priority. I declare my relationship with you makes me happy. I propose I have a right to be happy, at last. Then I tack on my usual apology. I express regret that all this is hurtful, but it is the fact. Sarah and my bond is—I look for a word—unbreakable, I say.

She just stares into me and past me. Small voice, "Why are you doing this to me? Why did you do this me?" Then she stiffens, leans forward, raises her finger at me, and adopts her controlled-anger-intimidation voice. "You've jeopardized not only the station, but our friendship too. By continuing this obsession, you lost us the Milwaukee Symphony sponsorship (*as if it's my fault*). You're not just a misguided and foolish old man, but a destructive and misguided, foolish old man, whose fantasies are destroying everything around him."

I respond by telling her you and I have plans to meet in California soon. She storms out of the restaurant.

At least it's out there now.

---

*From: **Sarah Ross** <sarahross64@gmail.com>*
*To: **Adam Wolf** <adam.wolf1402@gmail.com>*
December 30, 2014 11:54 am
Subject: Re:Update

Adam, maybe now she'll let you have a life. You've asserted your right to it. I'm proud of you.

I talked to Gordon last night and tried to be gentle. Told him I have thought about his proposal, admitted I was taken aback by it at first. That I wasn't even sure it was serious. I asked if we could just stay friends. That I hoped he'd understand that I preferred to stay home alone New Year's Eve.

He asked if I had seen Adam Wolf when I went to Cleveland.

From: **Lola Wolf** *<lola.wolf1402@gmail.com>*
To: **Joan Margolis** *<jmargolis@carswell.net>*
December 30, 2014 1:19 pm
Subject: Thanks for Xmas

I'm back home safely and just missed another one of this year's dramatic snowstorms. Thank you again for including me in your holidays. It helped more than you know, got me out of a very blue funk. I came to you reeling from a life, a marriage, a house that I barely recognized. There have been no conversations at all with Adam. We don't even chat about humdrum things. We certainly don't talk about the future anymore. There's no future to talk about.

It felt so good to be away, and in your safe nest.

You're right, there are a lot of imperfect marriages out there. But somehow all I saw around me were couples, happy couples, even old happy couples, walking close together, animated, holding hands, laughing as they scraped the ice off the windshield of their cars. I was wallowing in self-pity.

It did me good to be introduced to Eugene on Xmas Eve. It made me realize that perhaps I'd be better off without the tension or bickering or neglect. Even if it doesn't work out with Eugene, I like to think there's someone out there who likes to take walks. Who likes to plant shrubs. Who will hold my hand and help me grow old. I realize now I looked to Adam for something I could never find.

Thanks for cheering me up, for being such a perfect big sister. I'll keep trying to hold these more positive thoughts. With your help.

Love!
Lola

*From: **Adam Wolf** <adam.wolf1402@gmail.com>*
*To: **Sarah Ross** <sarahross64@gmail.com>*
January 2, 2015 7:56 pm
Subject:

Sarah, it was difficult, but I took heart, knowing it's what you would want me to do. I told Lola, told her that I would soon be flying out to see you in California. I'm relieved.
"Do whatever you want. I don't care. Just don't bother coming back."

---

*From: **Sarah Ross** <sarahross64@gmail.com>*
*To: **Adam Wolf** <adam.wolf1402@gmail.com>*
January 2, 2015 9:14 pm
Subject:

Adam, I'm relieved it's out there, that we don't need to sneak around anymore. But I know how difficult, dreadful, these moments are. For us, and for them too.
I don't know what more to say. ilu.

---

*From: **Michael Wolf** <Michael.R.Wolf@brookstead.com>*
*To: **Adam Wolf** <adam.wolf1402@gmail.com>*
January 4, 2015 12:26 pm
Subject: What the hell's going on?

Hey Dad,

Mom seems unusually stressed. She tells me you're going out to California to meet this woman. Maybe you should think twice, Dad. Couldn't you wait until you've moved out of the house? Aren't you taking this late-life crisis too far? What are you going to do if Mom relapses?

From: **Adam Wolf** <adam.wolf1402@gmail.com>
To: **Michael Wolf** <Michael.R.Wolf@brookstead.com>
January 4, 2015 2:57 pm
Subject: Re:What the hell's going on?

Michael,

Don't think I'm not scouring real estate ads looking for a place. But it's
not easy to find something suitable AND affordable, in Evanston, or
anywhere in the North Shore area. I'm not about to move into a noisy,
depressing apartment in Logan Square or Lakeview. I can't put my life
on hold until something turns up. I'm looking. I'm looking.
I've been accused of being deceitful, secretive, a liar. It's time now to be
honest. Anyway, life at home is untenable.
Despite all this palaver about senile delusions, my age has actually
brought perspective and clarity. These revelations came on suddenly,
but they are nonetheless persuasive. I've compromised myself out of
existence with Amanda and with your mother. Now I have a chance,
however brief, to reclaim myself.
Do not doubt that I'm concerned about Lola and need to care for her in
some way after I leave.

Love,
Dad

ADAM > SARAH   1/5/15   3:24 pm

Lola, please for right now understand I'm
feeling sad and depressed. Sorry I haven't been
responsive. I have a lot on my mind. Maybe the job,
or worry about what's to come in old age. What if I
come back home early from work and we can stop
for a bite at Koi's and talk about everything.

SARAH 3:36 pm

Adam, can you tell me what this is about? A text meant for Lola, I see. Sad and depressed? I didn't know. Surprised you and I haven't talked about it. Perhaps I've been misled and need to step back.

ADAM 3:44 pm

At work now. Will explain later. My apology for the mistake.

---

*From: **Adam Wolf** <adam.wolf1402@gmail.com>*
*To: **Sarah Ross** <sarahross64@gmail.com>*
January 5, 2015 8:29 pm
Subject: I'm weary

Sarah, dear Sarah, I love you so very much. Always remember that. I'm not trying to reset Lola, just trying to apologize for being gruff with her this morning. Just trying to make that right. I don't like hurting people. That's all. And it's right that I have a lot on my mind.
It's true I'm sad and weary. Sad. Everything I do now seems to upset someone. I don't know how to make everything right for everyone. I feel too old to try. It's all taken its toll.

From: **Sarah Ross** <sarahross64@gmail.com>
To: **Adam Wolf** <adam.wolf1402@gmail.com>
January 5, 2015 9:19 pm
Subject: Cutting the stress

Oh, Adam, I understand how you feel. We've spared each other these moments of regret, sympathy and sadness. But I know one thing. There is no way to make everything right for everyone now. Everyone can't be happy at once.

I don't blame you for wanting to give up. I'll be okay. And never mad at you, if you decide to stay in your present life.

From: **Adam Wolf** <adam.wolf1402@gmail.com>
To: **Sarah Ross** <sarahross64@gmail.com>
January 5, 2015 9:34 pm
Subject: I'll figure it out

I repeat. Lola and I live separate lives in the same house. We hardly communicate. She issues demands, as I've told you, but I ignore most of them. That's all true.

Maybe I haven't been fair in my description of her. Here are the facts about Lola you should also know. She's greatly admired, accomplished, and successful.

At the same time, Lola is dependent, emotionally unpredictable. In the last few years, she's had extended bouts of depression, for which she has not sought treatment. I should have divorced years ago, but now everything is complicated by her emotional state, as well as the expectation by the world around me that I have to be her caretaker. It's my plight. But, whatever else, I'm committed to you and will figure this out.

From: **Sarah Ross** <sarahross64@gmail.com>
To: **Adam Wolf** <adam.wolf1402@gmail.com>
January 5, 2015 9:49 pm
Subject: Is it possible to go backwards?

Guilt is a hard emotion to overcome. I'm so sorry that yours is so deeply felt that it leads you into depression. Even if the others could move on beyond their own sadness, I doubt they want to let you off the hook.

I, of course, love you too, with all my heart. But this kind of stress will surely take its toll on your body, not just your psyche. I need you well and intact. I fear you'll get sick from this pressure. Terrified of it really. Should I back off?

Your text to Lola, no matter how it's meant, sounds to me like a peace offering. Giving her hope. Adam, I do not want to interfere in a workable marriage. Might it be best for us to try to return to just a loving email relationship? I couldn't bear losing you altogether. But I need resolution, for my own sense of well-being, as much as I need to see you healthy and alive.

From: **Adam Wolf** <adam.wolf1402@gmail.com>
To: **Sarah Ross** <sarahross64@gmail.com>
January 5, 2015 9:59 pm
Subject: I can't be without you

Sarah, my feelings of sadness and regret do well up from time to time, but they are transitory. Ambivalence, I suppose, has been everybody's story. Here's something I'm not ambivalent about — wanting to see you and be with you.

---

*From: **Sarah Ross** <sarahross64@gmail.com>*
*To: **Adam Wolf** <adam.wolf1402@gmail.com>*
January 5, 2015 10:10 pm
Subject:

You put me through the wringer, Adam, but I need you too.

---

*From: **Adam Wolf** <adam.wolf1402@gmail.com>*
*To: **Sarah Ross** <sarahross64@gmail.com>*
January 6, 2015 11:11 am
Subject:

Sarah, I need to ask you not to tell me how to relate to and how to speak to other people. However imperfect my interactions with them may be, they've been forged over decades. I don't want them controlled.

---

*From: **Sarah Ross** <sarahross64@gmail.com>*
*To: **Adam Wolf** <adam.wolf1402@gmail.com>*
January 6, 2015 1:45 pm
Subject:

"Where did that come from?" I guess I should stop kidding myself that I know who you are now just because I knew who you were back then.

---

*From: **Adam Wolf** <adam.wolf1402@gmail.com>*
*To: **Sarah Ross** <sarahross64@gmail.com>*
January 6, 2015 1:56 pm
Subject:

Your leaps to judge me are nonsensical. In some ways they remind me of our days together in high school. "I saw you walking down the hall with Cheryl Lieber. If you want to go out with her, be my guest, but just be honest with me about it." Yours is now a familiar ring from infinity ago.

From: **Sarah Ross** *<sarahross64@gmail.com>*
To: **Adam Wolf** *<adam.wolf1402@gmail.com>*
January 6, 2015 2:21 pm
Subject:

And I'm struck by *deja vu* too, remembering how you, right after our breakup, collected female trophies. As many at one time as you could. No serial monogamy for you. Have I jumped into this stewpot again, I ask myself?

From: **Adam Wolf** *<adam.wolf1402@gmail.com>*
To: **Sarah Ross** *<sarahross64@gmail.com>*
January 6, 2015 6:47 pm
Subject:

There goes that irrational leap I was talking about. My gesture of kindness to Lola, with whom I've spent the last 30 years, or Amanda, with whom I have certain traditions, becomes fodder for your backing out. Come on!

From: **Sarah Ross** *<sarahross64@gmail.com>*
To: **Adam Wolf** *<adam.wolf1402@gmail.com>*
January 6, 2015 7:02 pm
Subject:

Frankly, Adam, I'm just sick of the melodrama. Amanda's email to me — to get lost? That's certainly the point of a letter Lola sent me. I never told you about it, our correspondence. Thought I handled it okay by myself and didn't need to bother you about it. But I'm attaching the letters here.

From: **Adam Wolf** <adam.wolf1402@gmail.com>
To: **Sarah Ross** <sarahross64@gmail.com>
January 6, 2015 7:18 pm
Subject:

I've read the letters and recognize Lola's words. They're thrown at me most days. I do like your response and am surprised by the sympathy you express. I'm so sorry you had to deal with this. Sarah, you must realize I'm not responsible for other people's behavior.

From: **Sarah Ross** <sarahross64@gmail.com>
To: **Adam Wolf** <adam.wolf1402@gmail.com>
January 6, 2015 8:04 pm
Subject:

Yes, but you can put an end to their behavior. You certainly could be more firm, but who am I to tell you how to behave? You have no trouble being firm with me from time to time.

From: **Adam Wolf** <adam.wolf1402@gmail.com>
To: **Sarah Ross** <sarahross64@gmail.com>
January 6, 2015 8:17 pm
Subject:

I've lived with a lot of women, not wanting to hurt them. I guess it's inevitable now. But it's not in my nature.
Look, Sarah, how about you in all this? Perhaps with your personality, you can tell Gordon about us more easily. But are you going to admit your plan on leaving him for me?

From: **Sarah Ross** *<sarahross64@gmail.com>*
To: **Adam Wolf** *<adam.wolf1402@gmail.com>*
January 6, 2015 8:34 pm
Subject:

   No, I'll be more gentle than that. Why should I hurt him? He's not like those women. He's cool about you and me. Sort of. Please don't tell me what to say.

From: **Adam Wolf** *<adam.wolf1402@gmail.com>*
To: **Sarah Ross** *<sarahross64@gmail.com>*
January 6, 2015 8:48 pm
Subject:

I see that my Sarah can dish it out, but she can't take it. You don't like being told what to say any more than I do.
I love you. You know that. But trust me. I know how to be clear with "those women".

From: **Sarah Ross** *<sarahross64@gmail.com>*
To: **Adam Wolf** *<adam.wolf1402@gmail.com>*
January 6, 2015 9:04 pm
Subject:

   I can't tell you how to behave, but I can observe, extrapolate, and decide how I will relate to you, given your choices. You're right—to be controlled by others is an impossible way to live. I can only control my own feelings and decide whether I can withstand the protracted pain. Or retreat.

---

*From: **Adam Wolf** <adam.wolf1402@gmail.com>*
*To: **Sarah Ross** <sarahross64@gmail.com>*
January 6, 2015 9:18 pm
Subject:

CONTROL is the operative word for me. In my life, these last many years, I've been passive, rendered CONTROL to others. Did their bidding to avoid conflict. You need to be patient. I'm breaking free. It may be in small increments, but I'll get there. Frankly, I'm afraid of falling into old patterns in our relationship too. I must have the right to conduct my life as I wish, without intervention. That has to be part of our relationship. They've sucked the oxygen out of the air around me. I don't want that again, Sarah.

---

*From: **Sarah Ross** <sarahross64@gmail.com>*
*To: **Adam Wolf** <adam.wolf1402@gmail.com>*
January 6, 2015 9:46 pm
Subject:

But, Adam, aren't you permitting them to control you over and over again, even now — when you beg for Lola's forgiveness? When you obey Amanda's commands? When you take their abusive tongue-lashings? Perhaps I haven't told you emphatically enough how hurtful it is to watch your constant attempt to mollify. And see the hope it reignites in your women.

I wonder what your texts to Amanda sound like. Obedient? Servile? I fear even at age 69, you still like to keep a lot of gals in love with you in the name of "not wanting to hurt them". Look, my presence in your life will hurt them. There's no other way out. Not everyone can love you at the same time. It's mutually exclusive.

---

*From: **Adam Wolf** <adam.wolf1402@gmail.com>*
*To: **Sarah Ross** <sarahross64@gmail.com>*
January 6, 2015 9:56 pm
Subject:

I notice how the sweetness and "lovin' spoonful" seems to have evaporated in this conversation. Whenever you speak of Lola and Amanda your voice becomes bitter. And the bitterness is directed to me as well as them.

---

*From: **Sarah Ross** <sarahross64@gmail.com>*
*To: **Adam Wolf** <adam.wolf1402@gmail.com>*
January 6, 2015 10:00 pm
Subject:

No, Adam. Just to you.

7

ADAM > SARAH   1/7/15   12:12 am

duslm?

*From: **Sarah Ross** <sarahross64@gmail.com>*
*To: **Adam Wolf** <adam.wolf1402@gmail.com>*
January 7, 2015 3:44 am
Subject: sense of urgency

Adam,

Can't sleep. I think about the obstacle course, the time we need to run it, and I feel consumed by a sense of urgency.

We are now 69 years old, my father's age when he died. How much longer can we stay well? Things could happen quickly now — in terms of health — even with yoga and swimming and hockey. Gifted as I am at dissociation, I don't think about my own health going, but what if something happened to yours, when you're legally bound to Lola? Or Lola's health goes? Cause then you'd be stuck. Life happens, and the downward spiral accelerates. If anything serious happened to you, an accident or even a serious diagnosis, anything, I couldn't come to you. I fear that while you're still married, I wouldn't even be allowed near you if you landed in the hospital. NEXT OF KIN ONLY flashing in neon at the nurses' station. And I even picture Amanda Schreiber getting into the act. There she is now, guarding the hospital room with her Uzi poised, just in case I tried anything funny.

Or, how about this for a storyline? No one even tells me something happened to you. The scenarios drive me mad. You, in need of me. Me, unable to get to you.

And then, what if we died before we were legally free to be together? What then? And, here goes my confession, stupid as it may sound. This is what makes me cry. If you were legally tied to Lola when one of us died, then, oh then, we couldn't be buried together. We would be apart for eternity. Stupid, stupid, I told you, but it feels devastating.

Just imagine that no one who ever passed by our graves would know that you and I belonged together, that our hearts and our souls were one, that Adam Wolf and Sarah Ross loved each other once and forever.

Hey, here's an answer. Maybe I should compose my tombstone now, and make sure an executor sees to it:

"Here lies Sarah Ross, 1946- , in love all her life with Adam Wolf, who lies elsewhere. Don't ask."

There, now I feel better.

From: **Sarah Ross** <sarahross64@gmail.com>
To: **Adam Wolf** <adam.wolf1402@gmail.com>
January 11, 2015 11:32 am
Subject: Gordon

Adam — I'm shaken, but I thought it was right. I knew it was necessary to tell Gordon about our plans to meet. You know I needed to end the secrecy about us. It's no longer the same. Yesterday evening when we went out for dinner, his mood was dark from the outset. He seemed preoccupied. I tried to carry on a conversation, but one-word answers at best. Then he straightened his back ceremoniously and folded his arms across his chest, and puffed up at me like Capt. Bligh dressing down Fletcher Christian on the starboard bow. I knew what was coming. You. The topic of Adam Wolf, before I even brought it up.

He insisted on knowing. "What exactly is going on with you and him? Don't equivocate. If you have any plans with him, shouldn't you have the decency to tell me?"

I actually thought of lying to him, telling him there was nothing to worry about. But here's what came out of my mouth. I did not tell him that I had already seen you in person, but confessed we do have plans to meet before long.

He seemed shaken. Too quiet. Pushed away his plate. And then he said "Why? Haven't I been good to you? Haven't I been attentive enough? Am I disappointing you in any way? I take pride in how I treat you. I supported your correspondence with your old boyfriend. I think you're deluding yourself and he's deluding you. You don't know this guy. He's not 15 anymore. Who knows who the hell he really is. Do you love him?"

And, Adam, I said, "Yes I do." And he replied, "You haven't even seen the guy. You really are nuts if you intend to throw away what you and I have built. Ours is a good relationship, Sarah. Don't destroy it."

I asked Gordon if this meant we could no longer be friends. He didn't answer at first. And then he said, "If you see Adam Wolf, we're through." And I said, "No, we're through now."

From: **Adam Wolf** <adam.wolf1402@gmail.com>
To: **Sarah Ross** <sarahross64@gmail.com>
January 11, 2015 2:34 pm
Subject: Re:Gordon

Two regrets. First, that I should be the cause of any unpleasantness with Gordon. Second, that you will have to forego further cruises on the H.M.S. Blowhole.
The most amusing part of Gordon's dinner theatrics was his assertion that you and I are deluded. I have a feeling that every time someone in

Gordon's sphere of influence hasn't behaved according to his own Law of the High Seas, then they are "deluded".

Sarah, here's da facts. We ain't delusional. And even if we are, then I say "Hurrah for delusions".

Gordon is a moron to make your relationship a matter of "HIM or ME". But that's his decision. At least you got to see what Gordon was like without his gentleman's camouflage. You know what? He's too damn old to play the righteous rear admiral.

Enough about Gordon.

Sarah, my love for you just deepened immeasurably because you shoved his ultimatum down his throat.

---

*From: **Sarah Ross** <sarahross64@gmail.com>*
*To: **Adam Wolf** <adam.wolf1402@gmail.com>*
January 11, 2015 4:52 pm
Subject: Re:Re:Gordon

Adam —

I've been thinking. Is Gordon's reaction really that irrational? Wouldn't you say the same thing to me? Wouldn't you be jealous if the shoe were on the other foot?

Or, how about this? In the shouldn't-make-it-him-or-me argument, how would you feel if I decided to continue seeing Gordon even after you and I see each other again? Do you see my point?

I guess I'm starting to feel sad for Gordon. Maybe it would help if you stifled the testosterone-driven impulse to ram anything down anybody's throat.

Amanda Schreiber
211 E. Garfield Street
Hinsdale, Illinois 60521

January 14, 2015

Mom,

I'm glad you're back in Palm Springs Manor. Is Maria still working out well? She seemed so competent. Your Doctor Hirsch certainly is. He called me twice when you were in the hospital to tell me you're good for many years to come.

I'm thinking of moving up my trip to see you, if that's okay. If everything goes according to plan, you'll be seeing me in a couple of days. I hope you're in the mood for some daughter-to-mother talk. Turmoil here. Something even more unsettling than the buffeting after Roger's death. I'll tell you in detail. I didn't want to trouble you while you were recovering, but I need your sage advice.

I'm fighting a low-grade depression and am losing interest in the station. I feel stuck and at loose ends at the same time. I realize I have no real friends here in Chicago. At least no one I can count on anymore. Perhaps I should move away. But I haven't a clue where I'd go. Whatever wisdom you can impart will be welcome.

It'll be wonderful to see you. Get better quickly. I'm still counting on you to take that barge trip in France with me.

Mandy

From: **Sarah Ross** *<sarahross64@gmail.com>*
To: **Gabriella Fratelli** *<gabriella.fratelli@orange.it>*
January 17, 2015 6:08 am
Subject: Belly landing

Cara Gabriella,

My head is splitting open. You've always been able to calm me. I wish we were together again, at that little villa in Palermo. Our relationship was such an easy one, uncomplicated.

That's how it started with Adam. Relaxed. Untroubled. But now that we've been together, now that we wish to always be together, nothing seems easy anymore. We're both besieged—by demands, by complications. Grueling at any age, but particularly at this one.

The excitement has been heady. But I need to be on firm and not shaky ground. The situation reminds me of Tom Hendrick's story. Weren't you with me in Sorrento when he recounted it? He was on Aero Condor flying to Colombia. The plane's landing wheels wouldn't come down. And they had to circle for hours jettisoning fuel to get ready for a belly landing. In that time there was, no surprise, some hysteria among the passengers, and grave fear. But, Tom said, after three hours of circling, he just wanted the goddamn plane on the ground no matter what the consequences.

I'm yearning for resolution too. No matter what.

From: **Sarah Ross** *<sarahross64@gmail.com>*
To: **Adam Wolf** *<adam.wolf1402@gmail.com>*
January 18, 2015 4:29 pm
Subject: It doesn't let up

Amanda came to visit me. She materialized. I recognized her the minute she walked into the shop. Imperious air. First scrutinized the merchandise. Then spoke to me directly.

She charms. "I've heard a lot about you. Nice little place."

She buys something expensive without looking at it. Something seductive. Something not age appropriate.

I'm disarmed by the woman. She introduces herself, "I'm Amanda Schreiber, Sarah." That made me listen. "I came all this way because I thought it was important you hear things I need to tell you."

Amanda asks for just a half hour of my time, at lunch. "No, I don't want go to lunch," I say. "I don't have time for lunch." But I finally agree to half an hour. "I have nothing to say," I tell her. "Don't worry," she answers, "I have plenty."

So she begins:

"I know all the reasons Adam may be in love with you."

"What does he tell you about me?"

"Let me tell you about this guy you've reconnected with, before you go counting on him."

Amanda claims to be a person who "shoots from the hip".

"What has Adam told you about us? I really would love to know."

She goes on. "I suspect he may not have told you the truth. It's often hard for him to tell the truth. He's set in his ways by this age, which includes concealing the truth."

I don't answer. It's a monologue.

"From Day One that he contacted you, he acted weird, as if concealing something. Why? I told myself not to worry about it. My old Adam will be back to normal soon."

"This type of thing has happened before, Sarah."

"Don't believe, even at this age, he doesn't snatch opportunities when they present themselves. I caught him, not that long ago, with one of the Board members in the elevator. When the doors opened they were standing too close. She was blushing and disheveled."

"I guess I can forgive a mindless dalliance, but this thing the two of you have, has gone on too long. The relationship that's primary for him, no matter what fantasies you may harbor, the one healthy relationship in his adult life has been with me. I look after him. I take care of him. I've counted on him to ultimately be with me."

"Times when we've traveled, times I need to stay downtown, we've often shared a room. We've shared a bed. We've been romantically involved for decades."

Then Ms. Amanda Schreiber leaves.

I didn't respond to her, but I can respond to you. Adam. Where do I begin? Let me see. How about with this? In the same goddamn bed? I suspected something like this from the beginning.

Adam Wolf, I'm not ready to be hurt by you again. I won't even ask you to level with me, because leveling doesn't seem to be in your repertoire.

From: **Adam Wolf** <adam.wolf1402@gmail.com>
To: **Sarah Ross** <sarahross64@gmail.com>
January 18, 2015 5:17 pm
Subject:

Yeah there was a big bed. I laid on one side and she on the other. I'm enraged and humiliated that Amanda would have carried out this theatrical gesture.

There's been nothing romantic between us for years. What remains is delusion. Okay, here's the way it is.

Over the years Amanda and I have fallen into some familiar patterns. Dinner. Shopping. And, yes, when she stays in town, she's come to expect me to stay in her room and keep her company.

Let it go.

From: **Sarah Ross** <sarahross64@gmail.com>
To: **Adam Wolf** <adam.wolf1402@gmail.com>
January 18, 2015 6:43 pm
Subject:

I'm the type to let it go?

Adam, am I ever going to learn the whole story with you and Amanda?

I'm not getting it. You told me there was nothing. You complained about the demands she was placing on you. You talked about how you need to push her away. And now both of you tell me of the quaint tradition you have. Bundling!

From: **Adam Wolf** *<adam.wolf1402@gmail.com>*
To: **Sarah Ross** *<sarahross64@gmail.com>*
January 18, 2015 7:15 pm
Subject:

Stop hounding me please. Believe me, that's all there is to tell. And at this age, I can't believe I'm listening to the jealous girlfriend act again. I'm going to invoke my prerogative of old age and declare this conversation over. Yes, in the same bed. Yes, long ago there was more than sleep. That's years now. Can we get past this? I love you. I do not love Amanda. I have never loved Amanda.

From: **Sarah Ross** *<sarahross64@gmail.com>*
To: **Adam Wolf** *<adam.wolf1402@gmail.com>*
January 18, 2015 8:54 pm
Subject:

You may not feel about Amanda the way she feels about you, but your relationship hasn't really changed, has it? Would she travel all the way across the country to tell me something that is merely delusional? Is she crazy? Are you? Am I? All I ask is for complications to cease. Can you make that happen?

I fear that Amanda is in control of your life and intends to keep it that way. And it's clear that there's little you can do, or want to do, about that. That woman travelled 2000 miles to notify me of her prior claim.

From: **Adam Wolf** <adam.wolf1402@gmail.com>
To: **Sarah Ross** <sarahross64@gmail.com>
January 18, 2015 9:30 pm
Subject:

I do not do whatever Amanda bids. Not anymore. I know I need to re-
gain your trust. I need to be with you. Being together will help us wrest
free of Amanda's grip, and all the rest of it.

From: **Adam Wolf** <adam.wolf1402@gmail.com>
To: **Sarah Ross** <sarahross64@gmail.com>
January 19, 2015 8:12 am
Subject:

You're right. I need to protect you. It's too long in coming. I promise
Amanda will not trespass on our relationship again. By the time I'm
done she won't have any more delusions. Even if it means my job.

From: **S.Gordon Wilson** <S.Gordon.Wilson@csulb.edu>
To: **Adam Wolf** <adam.wolf1402@gmail.com>
January 21, 2015 7:08 pm
Subject: Wolf

I trust you know who I am. I damn well know who you are. But here's
something maybe you don't know. I will go to any length to protect her
from a degenerate like you. I can smell your type. A wife isn't enough?
A mistress isn't enough? You need to hoodwink women with your romantic babble, don't you? Does that sustain your ego? You've managed
to fill her head with this manufactured nostalgia of yours. It's either an
act or you really believe you can go back to being a love-struck teenager.
Either way, you're pathetic. Back off.

From: **Adam Wolf** <adam.wolf1402@gmail.com>
To: **S.Gordon Wilson** <S.Gordon.Wilson@csulb.edu>
January 21, 2015 8:12 am
Subject:

In case you didn't notice, Sarah is of sound mind, of age, and competent to make her own decisions.

From: **Adam Wolf** <adam.wolf1402@gmail.com>
To: **Sarah Ross** <sarahross64@gmail.com>
January 21, 2015 11:14 am
Subject:

I'm attaching Gordon's threat here.

From: **Sarah Ross** <sarahross64@gmail.com>
To: **Adam Wolf** <adam.wolf1402@gmail.com>
January 22, 2015 4:13 pm
Subject:

Adam, I'm grateful you sent me this note. I wish I could apologize for Gordon. It's too late for that. I'm mortified. I'm no goddamn damsel in distress. I do not need to be rescued. How dare he talk that way about you. He doesn't know you. He has no business nosing around in your life. Please call me after work.

From: **Sarah Ross** *<sarahross64@gmail.com>*
To: **Gabriella Fratelli** *<gabriella.fratelli@orange.it>*
January 31, 2015 1:43 pm
Subject: A big mess

Cara Gabriella,

I've been on edge most of the time recently. Alternately lonely, longing, resigned. Adam Wolf. Gordon Wilson. They can kiss my ass.

Gordon won't give up. He even hounds Adam directly. I communicate my outrage. And still he won't stop. He's been poking around and claims to know all about Adam. Leaves messages on my phone. His latest "revelation" (believe it or don't): Did I know that one Adam Wolf was arrested, some fight in some gay bar somewhere in Chicago back in 1978? "Could this be your Adam, Sarah? Fair warning."

My dear Gabriella, Gordon doesn't know me very well, I guess.

Enough on this subject. I need to wrap my mind around other topics. You know, the Affordable Care Act. Climate change. The Pluto Mission. I have simply got to shake off this obsession with Adam Wolf and push away the primitive impulses of adolescence. I now realize we don't grow older and wiser, just older.

Adam Wolf. Maybe he's just too much trouble. I don't need to be caught up in this craziness. But just when I get the most fed up and furious, I think back to 1959, our first date and the sweet 13-year-old boy who cried because he had to go home. What's the matter with me?

my love to you,
Sarah

From: **Lola Wolf** *<lola.wolf1402@gmail.com>*
To: **Adam Wolf** *<adam.wolf1402@gmail.com>*
February 5, 2015 1:40 pm
Subject:

Since you decided to ignore me, spend evenings sequestered in your room, maybe email's a better choice for us. I'll keep it simple. If you do go through with your plans to leave me here alone while you go out to visit your Sarah Ross, then you're not welcome to come back here. I suggest if you're going ahead with this plan, you look for a place to move into on your return. Even you might understand how humiliating it would be if you were to stroll back into this house after such a betrayal.

You're not welcome here. I'll change the locks on the door ten minutes after you leave for the airport. I promise you that. I'll throw your belongings into the garage and you can pick them up there.

What you plan to do is a shocking act of betrayal. I'm numb with sadness that you would abandon me like this. I suppose you have plans to be with this woman permanently. Have you made such plans? When you are together will you hold hands? Will you walk with your arm around her? Will you kiss her goodnight?

From: **Adam Wolf** <adam.wolf1402@gmail.com>
To: **Paul Bishop** <Paul.R.Bishop@dewey.com>
February 6, 2015 7:09 pm
Subject: TKO?

I'm in my corner awaiting the bell for the tenth round. One eye closed. Blood dripping from my mouth. Body bruised, but still intact. I've tried rope-a-dope for the last 5 rounds, but I don't know if I'll be able to take the battering for these last three minutes. I peer with my one good eye through the haze and try to focus on Sarah, in the front row. She stares back, a half smile that tries to disguise her trepidation. Bell rings. Amanda comes charging from her corner with renewed fervor. I fend off a few of her left jabs, but then a crushing right upper cut sets me reeling. Turns out the week of my trip to California, my presence at the station is required. And get this, to cover the overnight show. She demands I be there.

Now Amanda tags off and it's Lola in the ring coming for me. Left cross. Right cross. Call the Red Cross. I'm being thrown out of my house. I'll never make it through the three minutes. I go down to the canvas. Lola throws the family album down at me. The crowd is cheering. I try to find Sarah. Her seat is empty.

Okay Paul. Lousy analogy? It's the way I feel. Should I try to get up and finish the match? Or stay down and let the ref call it a TKO?

From: **Sarah Ross** *<sarahross64@gmail.com>*
To: **Adam Wolf** *<adam.wolf1402@gmail.com>*
February 7, 2015 10:22 am
Subject: Postponing

    Adam, sorry I exploded during the phone call. You do what you need to do. We'll postpone. But aren't you suspicious Amanda's up to her old tricks, interfering with us? Please. You promised. Here we go again.
    But I do love you. My plight.

From: **Adam Wolf** *<adam.wolf1402@gmail.com>*
To: **Sarah Ross** *<sarahross64@gmail.com>*
February 7, 2015 11:00 am
Subject: Re:Postponing

I had it out with her. She knows the score. I don't think this is manipulative. I love you for understanding. Let's make it early March. I'll let you know. Can't wait. Believe me, it's torture being away from you.

From: **Adam Wolf** *<adam.wolf1402@gmail.com>*
To: **Sarah Ross** *<sarahross64@gmail.com>*
February 7, 2015 1:23 pm
Subject: Gorgon

Has the Rear Admiral finally settled down? Behaving? Is he gonna come gunning for me?

From: **Sarah Ross** <sarahross64@gmail.com>
To: **Adam Wolf** <adam.wolf1402@gmail.com>
February 7, 2015 4:54 pm
Subject: Gordon misbehaving

If you must know, he's searching Google trying to discover unsavory details about you. Discovered that in 1978 Adam Wolf was arrested for a brawl in a gay bar on Clark Street. As if I cared.

From: **Adam Wolf** <adam.wolf1402@gmail.com
To: **Sarah Ross** <sarahross64@gmail.com>
February 7, 2015 6:19 pm
Subject: Re:Gordon misbehaving

Entangled with a homophobe, eh? Congratulations! But you can inform the asshole that I wasn't even in Chicago in 1978.

ADAM > SARAH   2/8/15 5:10 pm

What do you think I should do? Feeling odd. Not just tired, but nauseated and dizzy. I'm a little scared.

SARAH   5:30 pm

Take an aspirin right away. Always keep a chewable with you. Are you able to take your blood pressure? Are you home? If Lola's there, she needs to take you to the emergency room if you don't feel better. ILU. PLEASE CALL.

ADAM   6:01 pm

Forgive me. Not up to calling. I'm sure it's nothing. But I'll take myself to the emergency room if I need to. No need to upset Lola. ILU2

SARAH   6:21 pm

Take your blood pressure. Better??

SARAH > ADAM   2/9/15   9:04 am

How are you feeling this morning, love? Will I be allowed to attend your funeral?

ADAM   9:31 am

Feeling fine. Back at work. Sorry I set off alarm bells. I'm just glad you and Bayer were there for me.

SARAH   10:14 am

Was Lola upset?

ADAM   10:59 am

I didn't even mention it to her.

From: **Amanda Schreiber** *<Amanda.D.Schreiber@wcmq.com>*
To: **Frieda Reigel** *<Frieda.M.Reigel@therapypartners.com>*
February 16, 2015 9:51 pm
Subject: Cancel appointment

It's a busy time at the station. I won't be able to keep Thursday's appointment, but might we be able to have a phone session this week? My head is splitting in two. I don't even have time for cortisone shots for my knees.

It was good for me to see my mother. It helped me become more self-aware about some things. It doesn't mean I'm cured, but I hope I'm on the way to being less sad.

Perhaps I've been the sentinel of my own concocted world. I've railed against Adam for fabricating feelings for this Sarah Ross. But maybe I'm guilty of harboring the same kind of illusion about Adam. Since Roger passed away, I assumed my routine would always be the same. I needed everything around me to stay put. It's been my security.

For a long time I could control that life. I think I'm discovering, though, that I actually can't control any of it. There are too many things that take place hidden from my line of sight. I try to beat sense into people, but I can't make them listen. It's so hard to change the life I'm used to, especially after all this time. It's as if I've practiced the same piece on the piano for years and years, and then someone comes along and asks me to perform it in a different key. It's not so easy to adjust. Maybe it would have been earlier in my life. But it's a blow to discover at my age that I need to transpose.

Sorry for rambling. My fingers wouldn't stop typing. Clearly I need to talk to you. Let me know.

From: **Sarah Ross** *<sarahross64@gmail.com>*
To: **Adam Wolf** *<adam.wolf1402@gmail.com>*
February 22, 2015 7:15 pm
Subject: Re:Re:Gordon misbehaving

Gordon stopped by the other day to drop off some things I'd left at his place. I'm feeling sorry for him. He looked pale with gray circles under his eyes. His yellow shirt was stained. I've never seen him anything but neat. You know, I'm actually worried about him. Gordon wasn't his usual confident self. He sat hunched on the edge of the sofa, wouldn't look me in the eye. Then he said he meant it when he asked me to marry him, but could understand that I need someone younger. Perhaps, he said, he's too staid for the likes of me. Then he teared up. Adam, I feel like a heel. He asked if I still had plans to meet you. And I let slip that you're coming out this way soon, and that, yes, we'll be together. No, not at the house. Yes, if you must know, the Del Coronado.

Does it really need to cause so much pain for us to be together? Our main mission, I suppose, is to learn to live with the fact that we've upset people. I'm sorry that's so.

From: **Adam Wolf** *<adam.wolf1402@gmail.com>*
To: **Sarah Ross** *<sarahross64@gmail.com>*
February 22, 2015 8:09 pm
Subject:

If you're feeling too guilty about Gordon, maybe you'd like to read this email he just sent me:

In case you're interested, Wolf, San Diego, and especially the del Coronado, are my home turf. By that I mean off limits to you. By that I include Sarah. If you want to remain her playpen pal, go right ahead. You'll be out of the picture soon enough.

From: **Sarah Ross** <sarahross64@gmail.com>
To: **Adam Wolf** <adam.wolf1402@gmail.com>Subject:
February 22, 2015 8:39 pm
Subject: Oh no!

Adam, in a way, I wish you hadn't given this note airtime. It's taking up too much space in my brain. I apologize for Gordon's unforgiveable behavior. Again and again. You're not to be threatened, ever. I've never seen this side of Gordon. Nothing and nobody will disrupt our time together. You and I have vowed to shut off the noise. No Gordon. No Lola. No Amanda. Totally with each other. At last. Alone, as it should be. He won't intrude. You and I have made a promise. I promise again.

8

LOLA > ADAM 3/5/15 7:12 am

I know you're on your way to the airport or there already. Please call as soon as you get this txt. I'm feeling sick and having trouble breathing. I can't believe you're doing this to me. I think you're going to need to postpone. If I don't hear from you in the next few minutes, I guess I'll have to call Carol to take me to the hospital. She might be home.

ADAM 7:34 am

I'm sorry you're feeling poorly. That you were able to write this email is a good sign, I think. If not, you should call 911 right away. I'm checked in and I'm going.

AMANDA > ADAM   3/5/15   7:37 am

Adam, contact me ASAP. Urgent.

MICHAEL > ADAM   3/5/15   7:56 am

Mom msgd. Not well. Mentioned u r
going on a trp and hadn't left yet.
Can u reschedule?

ADAM   8:01 am

I'm at the airport. Checked in. Your mother
doesn't want me to go on this trip. I'm
convinced this is theatrics.

MICHAEL   8:06 am

Maybe. She sounded pretty sick to me.

ADAM   8:11 am

Would you mind checking in on her and
making sure she's okay?

MICHAEL   8:14 am

I guess so.

ADAM > AMANDA   3/5/15 8:15 am

What's up? Going to board soon.

AMANDA   8:23 am

Adam, Karl Sorensen just called, said he can't decipher your scheduling notes. You need to take care of this before you step on the plane. I'm not going to let the station go up in flames just because you insist on going. Please don't believe I'm writing this because I'm angry about your trip to San Diego.

ADAM   8:34 am

OK. Spoke with him. Took care of it. Boarding in 10 mins.

AMANDA   8:37 am

Goodbye. When you come back I want to see my old Adam come through the door, the one who pays attention.

SARAH > ADAM   3/5/15   8:37 am

I can't wait. I'm jumping out of my skin with anticipation. All these decades and I still love you beyond words. Promise me you meant it when you said we would shut out the world this time.

ADAM   8:40 am

It will take a Herculean effort to shut them up, but I will do my very best to keep that promise. If only the world would lay off. ILU.

MICHAEL   8:44 am

Boarding!

AMANDA > ADAM   3/5/15   8:45 am

I'm not trying to disrupt your getaway, but you need to know this: Carl Turner and I have been talking again. Looks like this time Source Media will make me an acceptable offer for the bandwidth. And I'm determined to accept.

ADAM   9:02 am

Plane about to take off. Please don't do anything in haste. We'll talk about this when I get back on Monday.

AMANDA   9:11 am

Not possible to hold off. How soon do you think you can get back? I have to act quickly. I've tried everything I could to keep this station afloat. My accountants say I'm crazy to keep tossing money at it. I've had it, Adam. I don't want to lose this chance.

ADAM   9:14 am

Mandy, surely it can wait until I get back.

AMANDA   9:18 am

I'm feeling sad and depressed about this. I need you to be available to me. Maybe you can talk me out of it.

ADAM   9:22 am

You know I'm always here if you need me.

AMANDA   9:31 am

A year ago you would have postponed your flight. That's something Sarah should know about us. That's the Adam I remember. That's the Adam I need to have back.

---

*From: **Adam Wolf** <adam.wolf1402@gmail.com>*
*To: **Paul Bishop** <Paul.R.Bishop@dewey.com>*
March 5, 2015 10:56 am
Subject: Up in the air

Paul,

En route. 30,000 feet. You once lectured me on the subject of documentary film-making. "Just let the camera roll. Don't plan. Don't anticipate. The great themes of life will naturally emerge. You know. *Titticutt Follies. Salesman. Warrendale, Welfare.*"
Picture this. Twenty minutes to boarding. Three and a half hours to Sarah. What does the camera see? An aged Jewish guy, a quiet fixed smile, torment free—now 15 and 69, both at once.
But the Life Camera lingers too long. The *Scriptus Veritas* shatters Adam Wolf's dream state.

A text from Lola: "panic attack—don't go—take me to Northshore Hospital."

A menacing text from Amanda: "Your trip will destroy the station."

Now it's Sarah. The old man's smile goes to grim. Sarah has demanded a warranty for the weekend: "Promise that nothing will disrupt us."

And the camera tells the rest. A beaten, stoop-shouldered geezer shuffles to the jetway.

But out of camera range, a Hollywood finish.

NBC announcer: *A Jet Bonami airliner en route from Chicago to San Diego has crashed into Scotts Bluff, Nebraska. None of the 245 passengers aboard is believed to have survived ... It has now been confirmed that among passengers in the doomed airliner were longtime crime family patriarch, Federico "The Sous-Chef" Ricci, scientist Burt Lowen, inventor of the electric broom, and Adam Wolf, Chicago classical radio personality. All three men were 69 years old. Ricci and Lowen were in the Business Class section. Wolf in Coach ...*

Tributes to the late Adam Wolf continue to flow in. Amanda Schreiber, the owner of the little classical radio station inside of which Mr. Wolf toiled away his youth: "I'm sure this is all a mistake. He's due here Monday."

Lola Wolf, the grieving spouse: "I wish I had one more chance to tell this man how I felt about him."

Sarah Ross, Wolf's high school sweetheart: "I wish I had one more chance to tell this man how I felt about him."

Gordon Wilson, a sometime acquaintance of Wolf: "His loss cannot be measured."

Paul Bishop, lifelong pal: "Adam was a man who would not accept his old age as a time of quiet contemplation."

No! No! Cut! Burn it, Paul! Here's the scene. I think you'll like this better.

Intense light bathes the RKO Palace Theater near Playhouse Square in the heart of Cleveland, Ohio. Hundreds crowd a rope line along Euclid Avenue. WEWS cameramen at the ready. The caramel-colored marble sparkles like bronze.

A crane shot carries us up to the grand marquee. World premiere: **When Adam Met Sarah et al.** *Under the portico, blinding multicolor strobes. A red carpet leads to the central doors, their great bronze handles pulled open by two ushers in livery, standing at attention.*

A limo pulls up. Adam Wolf waves to the crowd. Sarah Ross scoots across the seat and takes his arm. Five hundred cell phone cameras click in unison. The Plain Dealer arts editor wants an interview. Several figures push forward to the front of the rope line.

First, Gordon Wilson shoves two kids out of the way to be seen. He catches Adam's eye and closes his hands, in prayerful pose, mouths, "Forgive me. Forgive me." Then he issues the two-finger salute, like a true naval officer.

Next, Amanda Schreiber, gripping the rope line, slowly nods in approval.

And then there's Lola. At first she stares coldly. But in a moment, lifts her palms and shrugs in benign resignation.

As Adam and Sarah glide past the trio, they reach out their hands and invite their former significant others to join them. The crowd roars, bursts into cheers and whistles.

Better, Paul? I know, I know. Maybe not. I know what you're gonna say, "Your Fellini is showing."
Whatever. I'm on my way to my Sarah. No longer the victim of the Furies. They can't touch me. I am immune to them now.

ADAM > SARAH   3/5/15   1:47 pm

Landed!!

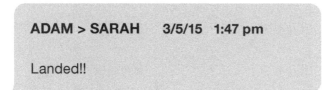

ADAM > LOLA   3/5/15   2:01 pm

Are you feeling better?

ADAM > MICHAEL   3/5/15 2:16 pm

At airport. Your mother's not answering.
Do you know how she's doing?

MICHAEL   2:24 pm

She seems to be ok. Didn't see doctor.
Maybe just stress. She's probably
sleeping. Or just not answering you.

ADAM > SARAH   3/5/15 2:27 pm

On my way to Avis. I'll call from the car. I
love you so much!

SARAH   2:36 pm

Shaking with excitement. The suite's
perfect — walk-in closet larger than my house,
sizeable balcony right off the bedroom. Looking
at the Pacific. The room — shades of soft gray,
and an elegant grasp handle by the tub. That
especially means a lot to me nowadays. Hurry.
The escape we deserve.

*From: **Adam Wolf** <adam.wolf1402@gmail.com>*
*To: **Paul Bishop** <Paul.R.Bishop@dewey.com>*
March 6, 2015 am 3:27 am
Subject: Battle of the Sunset Bar

Junior Ocean View Suite
Hotel del Coronado
Coronado Beach, California
U.S.A.

Paul,

It's now 3 am.

Soft breeze rustling the sandy curtains. Sarah safely abed. Able now to recount for history the momentous events of earlier.

My Sarah and I together! We leave our nest to have a sweet dinner downstairs. My arm around her, we walk to the waves, retreat to their nice restaurant, the *1500 Ocean*. Some background music plays. Latin samba? A corner table. Our faces close, giggling.

Without notice her mood darkens. She curses under her breath. Leaves go of my hand. When I ask, she nods her head toward the *Sunset Bar.* "He's here, Adam. I can't believe it!"

I glance. I don't need to be instructed on who she means. It's Gordon. Seated at the bar, sideways on a stool, glowering in our direction. I could have picked him out anywhere: dark blue blazer, red lobster face, monogrammed white shirt, open. His gray chest hairs bristling. He sports a Nick Nolte sneer and keeps his stare fixed on us.

Sarah pushes herself away from the table. "Please wait here. I'll handle this. " She strides toward his bar stool, like Shane marching into Grafton's Saloon.

For his part, Gordon turns quickly back to the bar. I lean sideways —watch.

She fires the first salvo from 30 feet away. "What the hell are you doing, Gordon?" Everyone at the tables and the bar simultaneously turn.

Gordon remains immobile, eyes now locked onto the bottles behind the bar. Sarah touches his arm. He turns to face her, his white moustache fluttering. He appears to push her away. "I have a perfect right to be here. What the hell are you doing with that fairy?"

Now Paul, I leap out of my seat and launch myself toward him. I'm determined to strangle the SOB. I never reach him. At the entrance to the bar area, across my path, a waitress carrying someone's long-awaited Cortez Halibut with heirloom cherry tomatoes appears from nowhere. Plates, waitress and I crash to the floor.

Now I hear some oohs, aaahs, some light applause as Sarah stands over me.

"Are you OK? I told you I would handle this, Adam."

I sit up, and as the waitress scrambles on her hands and knees to rescue the dinner, Gordon smirks. "What a pansy! How unlady-like!"

Then Paul, I ask forgiveness of the waitress. Lean down. Grab the fish, sauce and all, and catapult it toward Gordon. A three-point shot. My aim is true. The Cortez Halibut strikes his forehead, slithers down the front of his white shirt and drops onto his lap. "Dinner is served, Captain," I crow.

I notice everyone in the bar is now standing at attention. I hear more applause. A woman asks, "What the hell is going on?" A male voice: "Those two geezers are fighting over that old lady. Can you believe it? He threw my dinner at him."

Sarah is in my peripheral sight, pleading: "Adam, Gordon, for crissake! Stop this!"

Gordon extricates himself from his stool. Chest heaving rapidly. Eyes narrowed in fury. "You fuckin' fruitcake!"

(I haven't heard that phrase since 8th grade. Have you, Paul?)

The Gordo lunges with both arms extended and pushes me. I'm not ready.

I sail backwards over a piano bench in the corner, then to the floor. The room goes in and out of focus.

Ooohs from the paying customers.

Sarah grabs Gordon's sleeve. He wrestles free and stands over me, takes a theatrical boxing stance, inviting me back to my feet. "Get up, you goddamn faggot."

Two official-looking types appear at his shoulders. Hotel gendarmes. They each grasp a Gordon arm.

He tries to struggle free. He's yowling. "Let go of me! Let go, goddamn it! I'm Professor Gordon Wilson. This homo threw food at me. Sarah, tell them."

Sarah stands at a distance — mute — her hands across her mouth.

As I return to my feet, I notice Gordon seems to have run out of steam. He looks down at the floor, drained, finite. He drops his struggle, shoulders droop. The security guys turn him toward the door and slowly start his perp-walk to the exit.

I look around. The patrons are all standing — hushed — watching me, waiting.

Paul, I'm inspired! I pull myself onto the piano bench and address the keys. And I'm suddenly transformed into Nancy Faust playing for the Comiskey Park crowd. Gordon, the opposing pitcher is being yanked in the third. I pound out and sing at top volume, "Na Na, Na Na Na Na, Hey Hey-ya, Goodbye." A few onlookers join in as Gordo is marched to the dugout.

He never looks back. But I couldn't stop there. I switch tunes. Pound the keys and yell out in his direction, another oldie but goodie. "Oh, oh, oh, yes, he's the Great Pretender, pretending he still has a dick." My rendition should have been received with thunderous laughter, applause, cheers. But an awestruck silence prevailed.

Soon enough, a humorless manager stands cross-armed in front of me. Sarah remains at a distance, staring. Her hands are now over her eyes. I stand and walk to her. I put her head in my hands and plant a kiss.

The manager intones softly, "Perhaps, Sir, you should retreat to your room." I agree. I swoop Sarah away. I soothe things over. Ply her with drinks. Cover her with kisses.

Paul, I tell you, this battle will appear in Naval Academy textbooks for decades.

From: **Sarah Ross** <sarahross64@gmail.com>
To: **Gabriella Fratelli** <gabriella.fratelli@orange.it>
March 5, 2015 11:45 pm
Subject: Rattled

Carissima,

Adam's passed out.

I am old and growing older by the nanosecond. My life flashed before me tonight. The del Coronado with its Grand Dome and all around grandeur, thousands of people milling around. Like the Lusitania, First Class Ocean View—candlelight, surrounded by waves.

Then the torpedo. And I'm depleted. Sunk.

I thought I could have another sweet weekend with my Adam. Tranquil. Far away from those who wish us ill. But tonight was anything but calm, almost from the start. Turbulence.

The sun was waning over the ocean. We settled in for drinks. Kissed a bit. Felt like silly teenagers again. We had dressed up for each other. I wore a long peachy dress. Adam wore a camel-hair cashmere sweater I brought him as a gift. We looked good for our age. We giggled a lot.

But then the lethal shot. The torpedo landed dead on. Gordon. At the bar. How long he'd been there and how many Jack Daniels he had sloshed down was anyone's guess. I spied him smirking our way. I stormed over. And then the public melodrama began. I asked him to leave and to leave us alone. He macho-ed some ridiculous Tarzan yowl, grabbed my arm and announced I was coming with him. All the while shouting insults about Adam.

I would have hauled him one myself, but Adam charged into the fray. Two geriatric patients, huffing and puffing at each other in mortal combat. Unbelievable. Others must have found it comical. Not I. Certainly not I.

Oh, and there was a food fight, to boot. I thought Gordon, vermilion-faced, was about to have a heart attack. Maybe he did, after he was asked to leave. I give a shit!!! The man stalked me. Tried to ruin the weekend.

I have never been a femme fatale, and it was ludicrous at this stage of my life to have two guys go at it as if I were. Ludicrous? No, humiliating. Mortifying! I must have been a laughingstock. I certainly felt grizzled and old.

Oh, it was such a public spectacle — these septuagenarians exchanging insults. A rumble in the high school parking lot. Not about me, but about one last chance to show the world they "still had it".

I was in tears. Adam triumphant. I was sobbing. He seemed not to notice. He was lost in a daze. Acting imbecilic. And the manager ushered us, not so gently, to the elevator. I still want to crawl into a hole and disappear.

What more can I tell you? I am trying to forget. He's awake again, coming out of the dressing room, heading for the balcony. He's called room service for celebratory watermelon margheritas. A pitcher. I need lots. I hope we can salvage the rest of the night. This nonsense is not for someone my age. I need to restore calm. Not just for the moment, but permanently.

all my love,
Sarah

From: **Sarah Ross** <sarahross64@gmail.com>
To: **Gabriella Fratelli** <gabriella.fratelli@orange.it>
March 6, 2015 9:39 am
Subject:

Lovely surprise this morning. A soft kiss. Room service. Eggs Benedict. Champagne. Flowers. Adam remembered I love yellow roses and came in with them singing "Yellow Rose of Texas". I suppose this attentiveness is meant to undo the slapstick farce of last evening. I'm still trying to shake that off.

Something's not right. Why do I need these days to be perfect? He's distracted. He's not present a good bit of the time. Checks cell phone obsessively. I try not to be annoyed, but it's hard.

LOLA > ADAM   3/6/15   12:02 pm

I need you to take a few minutes away from your lady love to call. Still not feeling well. I'm still your wife. Simply can't believe you walked out like this. If you can fly all the way to California to see her, you can spend 10 mins. on the phone with me.

From: **Sarah Ross** *<sarahross64@gmail.com>*
To: **Gabriella Fratelli** *<gabriella.fratelli@orange.it>*
March 6, 2015 2:21 pm
Subject: When is it too much?

I'm sick of the pings on Adam's cell phone. I don't ask. He doesn't tell me. He's tightly wound. "Ping". He's in the bathroom again with the cell phone in hand. Always checking. I can't stand it. He promised.

From: **Sarah Ross** *<sarahross64@gmail.com>*
To: **Gabriella Fratelli** *<gabriella.fratelli@orange.it>*
March 6, 2015 4:19 pm
Subject: calming down

Sweet ride. Long walk on beach. (My bones, my hip still hurt a little, but getting better. I'll shake it off.)

Took Adam to the shop. We had lunch at The Cottage and again the cell phone is front and center on the table. Calls, not one, but two, and he takes them. During the meal. Ducking out. I've had it. It's not just rude. It's demoralizing.

AMANDA > ADAM   3/6/15 7:00 pm

Adam, what time does your flight get in
Mon.? I'll pick you up.

ADAM > PAUL   3/7/15 6:07 pm

Some incoming flack — deflecting it
well — glad to be far away — and with my
Sarah — holding hands, smooching — will
give you full report next week. We had to
see the zoo — great fun — spoke with a
dolphin, who said to say hello to you.

From: **Sarah Ross** <sarahross64@gmail.com>
To: **Gabriella Fratelli** <gabriella.fratelli@orange.it>
March 8, 2015 8:58 am
Subject: Leaving

This morning his cell phone rang. He reached over in his half sleep
and cooed, "Is this my Mandy?" He's whispering on the phone with her
now. I'm packing.

From: **Adam Wolf** <adam.wolf1402@gmail.com>
To: **Sarah Ross** <sarahross64@gmail.com>
March 8. 2015 11:43 am
Subject: ??????????????

Sarah—Sarah—I admit I am completely flummoxed by the way we
parted this morning.

I'm sitting here in our room at the Coronado, staring out the window
going over what happened, trying to figure it out. I'm a little dizzy trying.
Haven't started packing for the trip back. Can't leave it like this.

There was an awful suddenness to it. You said something came up at
the shop, but that sure seemed fabricated to me.

After all the wonderful hours together—everything we wanted—you
suddenly were unreachable.

This morning—tell me why—that abrupt kiss and brusque goodbye?
What was that about? You said there was no problem when I asked, but
I'm not buying it. Is it Gordon after all? Did I spend too much time
answering calls and texts from the Chicago world? Did I disappoint you?
I need to see you. Can I come to your house? Can we meet at that res-
taurant in La Jolla near the shop?

Don't leave it like this, love. I'll wait here for your reply

---

ADAM > SARAH   3/8/15 12:27 pm

I checked out, sitting down in the lobby,
please pick up. I've called 10x.

You know I love you. Please let me know
where we can meet. Should I drive to your
house?

ADAM   1:40 pm

Sitting here across from your house. If
you are there, come out, if only just to
say goodbye. Please pick up. Was at the
shop — It was closed. I'm feeling a little
panicky, Sarah. I need to know at least
that you are all right. Please love. I'll wait
here another 15 mins.

SARAH   2:12 pm

Right now I need to retreat. Please
understand. IDLU

ADAM   2:37 pm

So I guess you are either at Gordon's or
have hidden yourself elsewhere. Rid of me
and this weekend for whatever reason. I
guess I did disappoint, probably in every
way imaginable. Maybe it was a delusion
of our old age.
I'm off to the airport and YISLU.

ADAM   4:08 am

Landed in Chicago. I'll turn around and
come back if you want.

From: **S.Gordon Wilson** *<S.Gordon.Wilson@csulb.edu>*
To: **Sarah Ross** *<sarahross64@gmail.com>*
March 11, 2015 6:03 pm
Subject: Us

My dearest Sarah,

Please keep reading this no matter how strong the temptation to erase and forget me.

Last week I suppose I returned, in those sorry few moments, to my own teenage days in Memphis, just like you've returned to your long-lost days with him. I put up a pathetic fight. I know I lost.

I guess it was he who undid me. A nothing with nothing to offer. He swooped effortlessly and snatched you away, as if you and I never existed and didn't matter.

In the days since my meltdown, I've tried to measure him calmly against what we had, or, should I say, what we could have had in our remaining years. We've been over it. We talked about the beach house, the boat, trips to wherever the dart landed when we threw it at my map. I will miss the comfortable quiet old-people's strolls.

Sarah, I wanted to grow old with you at my side. Despite what happened, and as improbable as you might think it, I would still want that again, if you did too.

But none of it matters now, I suppose. It's just one more regret to take with me into my senility.

Best,
Gordon

*From: **Adam Wolf** <adam.wolf1402@gmail.com>*
*To: **Paul Bishop** <Paul.R.Bishop@dewey.com>*
March 28, 2015 7:08 am
Subject: All's lost

Paul — I've lost Sarah. Not like the time we stopped talking for two weeks. Not like that. This time it's over. And I'm devastated. After all the tribulations of youth, here I am at 69 and I've never felt more un-nerved. So much for the seasoned veteran. That something like this came along at all — that with Sarah I had one last chance. Paul, you're not supposed to fuck up your last chance for love, for real love. It doesn't happen in movies, doesn't happen in books, plays, but it happened to me. You'll have to rank this at the top of the list of the Adam Wolf His-toric Fuck-ups.

---

*From: **Paul Bishop** <Paul.R.Bishop@dewey.com>*
*To: **Adam Wolf** <adam.wolf1402@gmail.com>*
March 28, 2015 3:15 pm
Subject: All's not necessarily lost

Domage. Adam, there is a script: Several days later, Matt Damon puts in his notice, takes his modest belongings from the house, piles into the back of a 2006 Equinox and starts west. A helicopter shot tracks the green car along Interstate 40 — a red mesa is seen in the distance. Then there's a close-up of the headlights and windshield wipers clacking through the night. Cue: Dean Martin, *If You Were the Only Girl in the World.* Cut to the woman in the bright sunshine, watering the roses along the picket fence in front of her adobe hacienda. Equinox pulls up. Fade to black.

---

*From: **Adam Wolf** <adam.wolf1402@gmail.com>*
*To: **Sarah Ross** <sarahross64@gmail.com>*
March 28, 2015 8:29 pm
Subject: ILU

I'm lying face up, replaying our adventure on the ceiling, wondering if I'll ever talk to you or see you again. Almost 3 weeks now and I still don't understand the reason for your silence, but trying to learn to accept it.

You know one of the things I miss most from our time together? Your laugh— so boisterous, raucous— so unladylike— that loud guffaw that used to earn you detentions in study hall has not changed a bit in five decades. And I rediscovered the delight of making you emit that laugh, have everyone stare, have you lose control. Like that afternoon at the restaurant in La Jolla. I loved how you laughed at my impersonation of a Pete Seeger social protest song:

"(EVERYBODY TOGETHER NOW)
Oh, the rich folks flush their toilets
And it travels to the Hudson
Where the poor kids sip the water
And their stomachs start to swell up
And the mothers take their babies
To the graveyard by the river
Where the rich folks flush their toilets."

I love that I can still make you roar at the drop of a hat.
Nobody else can do that— can they? Tell me. Please answer.
ISLUSM

From: **Adam Wolf** *<adam.wolf1402@gmail.com>*
To: **Sarah Ross** *<sarahross64@gmail.com>*
March 30, 2015 11:17 am
Subject: ILU

I'm blue. Gray day (typical Chicago). Some boring Haydn symphony droning on over the PA.

I've been staring at the same schedule grid for the last 3 hours. No concentration. Jesse has been complaining about some goddamn thing or another. I'm just making motions — don't care to be here anymore — keep conjuring images of us hand in hand, face on face, entwined on that soft bed.

I just want to be back there with you. Could we be? You don't have to write anything extravagant. Just send me a Y or N when you have a chance.

From: **Adam Wolf** *<adam.wolf1402@gmail.com>*
To: **Sarah Ross** *<sarahross64@gmail.com>*
April 2, 2015 1:51 pm
Subject: ILUSVM

I'm in the waiting room at the dentist — lost a filling. My back tooth is very sensitive.

Anyway, thought I would write. I've been trying to figure what happened there that last morning in La Jolla. Rolling it over and over again in my memory. I'm trying to find what Magic Words might prompt you to finally write me back. Or at least tell me — if your silence is punishment, when is my sentence up?

In case it got lost in translation, I still love you, Sarah.

---

*From: **Adam Wolf** <adam.wolf1402@gmail.com>*
*To: **Sarah Ross** <sarahross64@gmail.com>*
April 4, 2015 5:03
Subject: ILU ILU

Michael is in town. He and I went to lunch (Corner Bakery). Then we went over to see *Interstellar*. What a celluloid mishap that was! Although it gave me an idea. What if you and I volunteer to be sent together on that Mars expedition? We wouldn't have to come back. Isn't that a romantic notion? 30 million miles from the Earth — just you and me with nothing to do but hold each other, read to each other, kiss. No cell phones. No texts. No distractions. No one yelling at us. Of course no oxygen or food either, but who needs that when you have love.

I'm ready to give up, Sarah. Tell me not to. ILU

---

*From: **Adam Wolf** <adam.wolf1402@gmail.com>*
*To: **Sarah Ross** <sarahross64@gmail.com>*
April 8, 2015 6:27 pm
Subject: Apartment hunting

I thought I found a place to move — in Chicago, off Clark Street in Andersonville — beautiful one bedroom sublet for 6 months. Furnished! Cable TV!! But alas, the woman renting the place tells me that she has some conditions. Get this: that she be allowed to stay there overnight every other weekend when she's in town. I made it down the three flights of stairs and out the door in 9 seconds
I'll keep looking — I have to — unlivable at the house.
I'll keep writing. I hope you won't erase me.

From: **Adam Wolf** <adam.wolf1402@gmail.com>
To: **Sarah Ross** <sarahross64@gmail.com>
April 11, 2015 1:10 pm
Subject:

Suddenly hot today — 80 degrees. Not ready — air conditioning at the station balked.

Do you remember that time — probably during the summer of 1959 or 1960 — it was 100 degrees or so? We went to the Center-Mayfield to get out of the heat, and cool off for a couple of hours. Only trouble, their air conditioning was kaput. To make matters much worse, the film was about men stranded in the jungle during WW2 — The *Purple Plain* (I think). We made it about an hour in. I whispered we should leave. You didn't want to. You put your hand across your lips to tell me to shush. You told me how realistic the film seemed. So I suffered in silence, sweating from all pores. To this day I think you were turned on by Gregory Peck, who kept taking his shirt off. Am I right? You don't have to answer, sweet. Just a distant memory.

From: **Adam Wolf** <adam.wolf1402@gmail.com>
To: **Sarah Ross** <sarahross64@gmail.com>
April 23, 2015 6:31 pm
Subject: ILU

I got excited before, heard a ping. I thought perhaps it was a text from you. It was Walgreen's.
I spent most of today searching for a new place to live. I looked at four apartments, all on the Northside, all hovels. It stunned me to think that I could be living in any of them. Two furnished, two not.
In one, the landlady told me that male tenants must agree to sit down when they use the toilet, so as not to stain the tiles in the bathroom.
In another, a two-flat off Ashland, the owner informed me that I would not be allowed to use the front entrance because he doesn't want mud in the vestibule. I would have to climb the outdoor backstairs.
They are all clinically insane.
All in all, it was an "out of body" experience, a humbling exercise for an old man. I felt like an ex-con, just sprung after serving 30 years in Stateville, searching for lodging, hiding his past.
But the quest will go on. Somewhere, my Sarah, there is a sweet, quiet (hopefully furnished) joint with our name on it. ILU.

From: **Adam Wolf** <adam.wolf1402@gmail.com>
To: **Sarah Ross** <sarahross64@gmail.com>
May 1, 2015 7:39 am
Subject: ILU

Now almost two months since the Coronado. Memory still fresh. I think I know the reasons I disappointed you.

But am I not entitled to hear a word from you? I called (as you know), again. I guess I don't understand your silence or maybe I do understand.

---

*From: **Adam Wolf** <adam.wolf1402@gmail.com>*
*To: **Sarah Ross** <sarahross64@gmail.com>*
May 2, 2015 5:17 am
Subject: ILU

I started reminiscing about us again—how we reconnected.
I went back almost a year to the beginning of the emails, the ones from the days before the high school reunion.
Look at them again, Sarah. It's astonishing—how easily, naturally, joyfully we fit back together. You will be stunned how soon we declared love, as if we were always there with each other and would always be there. Nothing else seemed to matter. Don't we deserve to be together again?

---

*From: **Adam Wolf** <adam.wolf1402@gmail.com>*
*To: **Sarah Ross** <sarahross64@gmail.com>*
May 3, 2015 11:11 am
Subject: ILU

I thought again about resting my case—letting it go, accepting the situation. I realize that you are now gone (again) from my life. I blame myself, of course, because I let everything and everyone intrude. I didn't protect what we had.

I'll plead to the jury one more time.

Sarah, I've tried, in my erratic, stumbling way to put us back together. When I thought I could untangle myself from decades of others' expectations, I got too easily frightened inside my old man's head. Negative voices told me it's unreal, insane, a delusion to be with you. I'm immune to them now, I promise.

I know I can recover myself and keep going. Give me the chance. I rest my case.

---

*From: **Adam Wolf** <adam.wolf1402@gmail.com>*
*To: **Sarah Ross** <sarahross64@gmail.com>*
May 4, 2015 9:32 am
Subject: ILU

I'm close to my inevitable announcement at the station — close, but not there yet.

Only my old man trepidation restrains me and mundane concerns like "Who pays the Medicare Supplement premium?" "How do I pay the mortgage on the house in Evanston?"

I've rehearsed my "giving notice". It's got to be laconic, firm, unsentimental, unapologetic.

But Sarah you know all that.

From: **Adam Wolf** *<adam.wolf1402@gmail.com>*
To: **Sarah Ross** *<sarahross64@gmail.com>*
May 9, 2015 4:55 pm
Subject: Found a place

I believe, my Sarah, that I have found me (us) a place — modest, clean, partially furnished, a reasonable two-family upstairs in Rogers Park. Quiet. I told them I'd decide by tomorrow.

I walked to a nearby diner on Sacramento to think. I sat at a booth near the back. Alone, staring at the comings and goings. My euphoria in finding the apartment soon dissolved in a wave of self-pity. Here I was, the stranger in a strange land, uprooted and lonesome, among chattering pals, all unfamiliar to me. I noticed the young, vibrant, beautiful ones at other booths, laughing, on display. I noticed them. They not me. Who's to notice or care about some *alter kacker* picking at his BLT?

Then from far across the tables, on the other side of the diner, a man, about our age, caught my gaze. He smiled and shrugged. Then nodded slightly.

For some reason, I became emboldened.

Sarah, I believe I'm ready to reclaim my life. Could we reclaim ours?

ADAM > SARAH   5/11/15 7:12 am

I realized today that you are the only one who ever knew me fully. That feels so reassuring.

From: **Adam Wolf** <adam.wolf1402@gmail.com>
To: **Sarah Ross** <sarahross64@gmail.com>
May 15, 2015 4:49 pm
Subject: I did it!!

The *Venerdì Del Destino* has arrived.
And I did the deeds:

Took the place in Rogers Park.
Gave notice at the station.
Told everyone concerned the news.
Finished my last program guide — packed it with Mahler.
Warded off insults.
Went for a ride on Lake Shore Drive.
Retreated to my new-found diner.
Felt so young and in love.

Hoped you might want to reply.

From: **Sarah Ross** <sarahross64@gmail.com>
To: **Adam Wolf** <adam.wolf1402@gmail.com>
May 15, 2015 8:19 pm
Subject: hi

hi

From: **Adam Wolf** <adam.wolf1402@gmail.com>
To: **Sarah Ross** <sarahross64@gmail.com>
May 15, 2015 8:59 pm
Subject:

Why, it's Sarah Ross. Must you always be so verbose? You got some 'splaining to do. I'm relieved.

From: **Sarah Ross** *<sarahross64@gmail.com>*
To: **Adam Wolf** *<adam.wolf1402@gmail.com>*
May 15, 2015 9:07 pm
Subject: relieved for you

What you've done, Adam, is brave and right, though I imagine it might be frightening. I suppose courage can only exist when it's not in our nature. Please take heart. You've given yourself space to exhale. We both need that. Perhaps all the people in our lives do.

From: **Adam Wolf** *<adam.wolf1402@gmail.com>*
To: **Sarah Ross** *<sarahross64@gmail.com>*
May 15, 2015 9:18 pm
Subject: Together

Yes, I understand that you needed space. Can we be together soon? I've missed you more than you can imagine. Yes, it's frightening to start fresh, especially at this age But in a way exhilarating, especially now that I have you back. I need you right here.

From: **Sarah Ross** *<sarahross64@gmail.com>*
To: **Adam Wolf** *<adam.wolf1402@gmail.com>*
May 15, 2015 9:27 pm
Subject: Re:Together

Adam, dear Adam. You'll be just fine, believe me. My heart always, always wants to be with you, but I can't be there. Not now. Being alone, I've discovered, is not the same as loneliness. And we know from experience, you and I, that we'll never really be apart again just because two thousand miles separate us. I've always needed you in my life and, one way or another, I've always had you in my life.

---

*From: **Adam Wolf** <adam.wolf1402@gmail.com>*
*To: **Sarah Ross** <sarahross64@gmail.com>*
May 15, 2015 9:38 pm
Subject: Huh?

It's you by my side. That's what I need, not aloneness. To share life with me. For real, damn it! What are you saying?
This is about the Gordo, isn't it? Are you back with him and trying to let me down easy? I can take it.

---

*From: **Sarah Ross** <sarahross64@gmail.com>*
*To: **Adam Wolf** <adam.wolf1402@gmail.com>*
May 15, 2015 9:55 pm
Subject: not Gordon

No, Adam. Gordon and I ended the night of "the scene". I haven't seen him since, and have no plans to.

I love you, my Adam, as much as ever. Please know that. But it's true, if you hadn't been able to extricate yourself, no, I wouldn't have been in touch again. Now though, we can stay connected. For real.

"Reclaiming" yourself, your life—that's a great gift to both of us. Long distance is no distance for us. If you're like me, you'll thrive in the calm of your own place. My little hacienda in La Jolla cradles me. Lately I've been sketching all the little objects in the house—the toaster that no longer browns, the rickety lamp on my nightstand, even the broken tiles on my kitchen floor. These are my touchstones to healing.

---

*From: **Adam Wolf** <adam.wolf1402@gmail.com>*
*To: **Sarah Ross** <sarahross64@gmail.com>*
May 15, 2015 10:13 pm
Subject: Stop joking

What are you talking about? That you don't want us to be together?
After all this? Cut the comedy. We belong together. You know that. My
shoulder was made for your head on it. Remember? When can we arrange
a rendezvous? You know you don't mean it.

---

*From: **Sarah Ross** <sarahross64@gmail.com>*
*To: **Adam Wolf** <adam.wolf1402@gmail.com>*
May 15, 2015 10:45 pm
Subject: Re:Stop joking

For now, my Adam, please understand I mean it. Here I've created
a quiet, shaded space in my garden—a bench, a stream that cascades
over polished white rocks, a pool where my fat goldfish thrive. There,
in my hideout, I meditate. There I find serenity. There I don't feel scared
about the future.

Dearest one, we both needed time, but there may not be much of
it left for me. I got news from my doctor. He took a bone scan and now
says I have to see my oncologist to schedule more tests. I'm trying to be
brave. It won't be anything to worry about, I'm sure.

---

*From: **Adam Wolf** <adam.wolf1402@gmail.com>*
*To: **Sarah Ross** <sarahross64@gmail.com>*
May 15, 2015 10:59 pm
Subject:

I'm starting to load my gear into the back of the old Equinox. I'll set off
in a couple of hours. It'll take me about four days, maybe three, to get
to you. But I'll be there before you know it. I'll call you en route. Luckily

I haven't yet signed the lease on the apartment. Fuck 'em. Not such a great place anyway. Don't worry about a thing. You'll be just fine. I'll see to it.

___

From: **Sarah Ross** <sarahross64@gmail.com>
To: **Adam Wolf** <adam.wolf1402@gmail.com>
May 15, 2015 11:14 pm
Subject: no need to come

Adam, dear, you need to stay put. Please. I'm healthy and plan to stay that way.

___

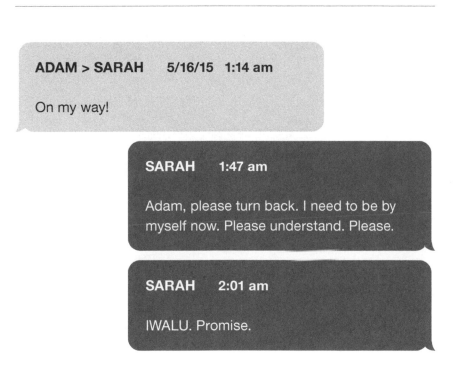

ADAM > SARAH   5/16/15 1:14 am

On my way!

SARAH   1:47 am

Adam, please turn back. I need to be by myself now. Please understand. Please.

SARAH   2:01 am

IWALU. Promise.

Acknowledgements

We're grateful to readers of early drafts of *Save the Last Dance*. Their thoughtful insights helped us shape the final version of the novel. Thank you Sophie Grudin, Chan Lowe, Sandy Weiss Karp, Roselle Chartock, Merrilee Redmond, Audrey Thier, Deborah Rothschild and Paul Miller.

Dean Crawford, Roland Merullo, Peter Sarno and Merle Saferstein generously shared with us their knowledge of the publishing world.

Our sincere thanks to our editor, Meredith Gilbert, not only for her attention to the smallest detail, but also for her understanding that hesitations and recapitulations are vital to a story like this one.

Thanks too to Dr. Randi Gunther and Dr.Nancy Kalish for writing about and understanding the force of first love reignited.

We appreciate the skill and expertise of our designer David Moratto. Special thanks to Maureen Nicoll for creating such an evocative image for the front cover.

We remember fondly Bernice van Sickle, our high school English teacher, who encouraged us to write coherently and creatively.